The Amsterdam Deception

The David Knight Series
Book 1

By Tony Ollivier

pandamoon
publishing

www.pandamoonpublishing.com

Jacket design and illustrations © Pandamoon Publishing
Art Direction by Don Kramer: Pandamoon Publishing
Editing by Zara Kramer, Rachel Schoenbauer, Forrest Driskel, and Ashley Hammond, Pandamoon Publishing

Pandamoon Publishing and the portrayal of a panda and a moon are registered trademarks of Pandamoon Publishing.

Library of Congress Cataloging-in-Publication Data is on file at the Library of Congress, Washington, DC

Edition: 1, version 1.01
ISBN 13: 978-1-950627-26-4

Reviews

"International intrigue at the highest level, and with grave stakes. The Amsterdam Deception is technologically savvy and brilliantly unique. Wildly entertaining." — **Robert Dugoni, Internationally Best-Selling Author of** *The Eighth Sister*

"The Amsterdam Deception is an explosive start to a new thriller series. Olliver's characters, European settings, and twists will keep readers turning pages late into the night." — **Eileen Cook author of** *You Owe Me a Murder*

"Fascinating, fast-paced and wildly inventive, Tony Ollivier's THE AMSTERDAM DECEPTION is a treat for fans of Robert Ludlum and Dan Brown, or anyone who likes high-stakes, action-packed spy games. If Jason Bourne did ballet, he'd be David Knight, the protagonist in this the first book in what's sure to be a spectacular series." — **Owen Laukkanen author of Deception Cove**

"In his debut novel, THE AMSTERDAM DECEPTION, Tony Ollivier takes on a load few writers can carry. Written in a quick, clean style, plotted across three continents and five countries, loaded with a cast of well-armed and pernicious characters, TAD kicks into high gear from the first scene."

"Read this novel. Review it. Pass it on to your friends. They will love you for it." — **Jack Remick author of** *Gabriela* **and** *The Widow*

Dedication

To my father for my love of reading. He once told me that as child, once he'd read all the books in the children's section of the library, the librarians were forced to give him an adult card.

To Jo-Ann, Jacob, and Ruby who give me reason to get up in the morning and keep going.

The Amsterdam Deception

CHAPTER ONE

Amsterdam—February 28

David Knight felt in his bones someone was watching him. Walking along the icy cobblestones and narrow bridges, he couldn't shake the feeling. Maybe it was the jet lag or the grueling rehearsals.

Or it might be the cold.

Canada was cold, but the wind blowing off the North Sea chilled him faster than getting rejected from one of the troupe's female dancers. He wished he'd brought a hat to cover his long blond hair, but his friend Razor said they didn't need one. He'd never listen to him again.

A shiver went up his back and he spun around trying to catch whoever was looking at him. But no luck. Lots of people walked the streets. Some pulled suitcases. Some wore backpacks. A few darker-skinned men stood with their backs to the corners with their hands in their pockets. Maybe drug dealers, but none gave him or Razor a second glance.

He and his friend, Frederic Razour, faced a skinny alleyway, rough brick on both sides. This one looked newish, as in less than a hundred years old. Other alleys appeared plucked from the eighteenth-century and inserted into the streets like Lego blocks.

But the fact remained that he and Razor were lost in a city that was lost in time. Hard to determine what direction they were going, and the crappy tourist map Razor snatched from the hotel didn't help.

"Nice of you to charge your phone before we left," David said. Razor sneered at him and stared at the map.

"You have a phone, too, smart-ass."

"Didn't think I'd be making any calls tonight, bright boy. Look, we've been out here for an hour," David said. He zipped up his leather jacket and tightened the scarf around his neck. "Let's grab a cab and head back to the hotel." He wanted to crawl into bed and drift off. The show opened tomorrow, and every muscle ached from the ballet class in the morning and the grueling rehearsals all afternoon.

"Don't be a pussy. We're virtually there," Razor said. "Do you want me to tweet you were too tired to go out tonight? And besides, what did your Dad say in his final breath?"

David turned and said. "It wasn't his final breath. He told me several weeks before he died."

Razor cupped his hand to his ear. "Okay, what were his words of wisdom?"

David grunted. "Life is here to be lived."

"And what else?"

David regretted confiding to Razor about this Dad. "Don't waste it like I did."

"My point exactly!"

Razor's coat hung open. Cold didn't seem to affect him. Back in Canada, he wore shorts most days. Maybe he was some kind of android or alien.

"All right. But let's get to it. I'm freezing my ass off."

Razor pulled out the tourist map again, checked a street sign, and pointed. "It's this way," he said.

David touched the bump side of his head and grimaced. Before leaving for Europe, he told Sophie he might want to see other people. In a wordless response, she'd thrown the copy of Kahlil Gibran's *The Profit* he gave her at his head and caught him on the temple. Her anger didn't make the process any easier and since the split, he didn't realize how much he missed the scent of the desert rose perfume she dabbed behind her ears. Or how much he missed the clean smell of her auburn hair and her soft and yielding lips.

Tonight, in Amsterdam, all he smelled was incense, weed, and dog shit, and all he felt was cold.

They turned a corner and above a narrow opening in the wall, David saw the word *Trompettersteeg* engraved on a brass plaque above the passage. A skinny guy would fit through the archway, but a fat one might not. As they stood in front, a steady stream of men disappeared through it like a gate into Hades.

"This is the place!" Razor pumped his fist.

"Yeah. Imagine my excitement," David deadpanned and tightened the scarf around his neck to ward off the icy wind the archway pulled off the harbor. Razor, however, had a goofy look on his face as if his brain had left on vacation. David felt like he was taking a puppy to his first dog park.

"You okay?" David asked.

"The tab I dropped is kicking in."

David stared at him and said, "That's just what I needed tonight. I'm a wingman to someone who's high. What did you take?"

"Ecstasy."

David rolled his eyes and said, "Are you nuts? We have ballet class in the morning."

Razor said, "Don't be such a grandma. I have another hit if you want it."

"No."

"No? Just no? Not, thanks Razor for thinking of me?"

"Just no," David said. He was tired of being the only adult in the room. "I said I'd watch your back tonight, but couldn't you hook up with one of the women in the company instead?"

"How did that work out for you, lover boy?" Razor raised an eyebrow said, "Plus, what kind of fun would that be?"

"More fun than I'm having right now."

Razor laughed and entered the doorway. David held back for a second. Alone on the street, a shiver raced up his back.

The narrow portal widened into an alleyway with door-sized windows on both sides. Behind each pane of glass stood a blonde or brunette or redhead. Some looked Dutch, but many looked eastern European or maybe Russian. All were gorgeous.

Inside, the rooms resembled large walk-in closets, with a single bed in the center and mirrors on the ceiling and walls. A small sink, shower stall, and a tiny table with an iPhone and speakers completed the decor.

Mood music with clean-up on aisle three.

Some rooms were plain, but others sported beaded or translucent curtains enclosing the beds. David shivered, but couldn't tell if it was from the cold or the spectacle.

Razor seemed not bothered by either.

A bespectacled girl with long auburn hair and black lingerie cracked her door open. A grinning Asian man talked with her for a minute before waving goodbye and moving to the next window. She smiled at David and said, "It's warm inside. Want to come in and play?"

David was curious but not enough to do more than ask a question. "What does this cost?"

"Seventy-five euros for a suck and fuck. Come in, I give you a good time."

Jeez, David thought, it's like a Starbucks drive-thru, if Starbucks sold blow jobs. "Thanks." But no thanks. He kept walking.

Razor called to him from twenty feet away. His friend was speaking to a bottle blonde in a red bustier. After several minutes, Razor gave David the thumbs up and disappeared behind the door.

Wow. He didn't think Razor would go through with it.

A red curtain slid across the window to signal the start of the most unromantic fifteen minutes of Razor's life. Probably closer to ten.

The alley and the stream of men emptied into another set of streets. As David leaned against a wall near the end, a busty brunette behind a door waved to him. David just smiled and stamped his feet.

The cold had climbed from his toes into his legs. The men streaming through the alley didn't stop. Black, White, Asian. Large, thin, short, tall.

But David noticed two men out of place. They weren't browsing and looked like they were on a mission. Both looked familiar and he realized he noticed them at the hotel when he and Razor left on this adventure. David remembered both men standing across the road from the hotel talking to each other. One sported a shaved head and a spidery black tattoo rising from under his shirt to his face, his body refrigerator-wide. The other man was thin with olive skin and wore a wool skullcap. The thin man stopped at a door covered by a red curtain. Both men glanced at David before the refrigerator yanked the door open and both men entered.

It couldn't be.

The guy opened the same door Razor had. Why would they be going in there? Had he misplaced Razor's choice? David shivered again, and he pulled away from the wall. Two seconds later, the blonde hooker jumped out of the door and ran against the stream of men with her red housecoat wrapped around her. What the hell? David pushed against the flow of men, scrambling to get to his friend. He jerked the door open as a large pair of hands grabbed him and hauled him inside.

The door slammed behind him.

A fist hit him hard in the stomach. He doubled over and gasped for breath. Something cold and metallic jammed against his temple. A gun.

He tried yelling, but nothing came out. Instead, the gun barrel pushed harder against his head and a voice said, "Keep quiet!"

David saw a nearly naked Razor kneeling on the threadbare carpet while skullcap held a knife under his chin. "My mate asked you nicely. Did you take drugs tonight?"

Tears rolled down Razor's cheeks as skullcap pushed the blade into his neck. A spot of bright red blood bloomed. "Stop yer blubbering. We've been following you both all friggin' night. Did you do any drugs?"

"Leave him alone," David yelled out.

The gun barrel pushed hard into his temple and forced his head to the floor. "Shut yer yap."

"Ecstasy!" Razor screamed out. "One tab. That's all. I swear!"

"Shit. That's just great. We were told you dancers were a clean livin' bunch!" Skullcap stood up and pulled the knife away from Razor's neck.

David realized that instant he and Razor were targeted. Watched from the time they'd left the hotel. He hadn't been paranoid, but that didn't matter now.

But why them?

4

"What about this one?" the refrigerator asked. He pulled David's head back. The sharp tug on his hair made David wince.

Skullcap asked, "Did you do drugs like your idiot friend?"

"My partner just asked you a question, you little shit." The refrigerator jabbed the barrel into David's face.

David struggled to fight the fear that coursed through his body. One part of his brain wanted to reason with the attackers and find out what they wanted, but instead his father's voice came through and said, "Fuck you."

The refrigerator pulled his other arm back and balled his fist. "Wait. Slow down." Skullcap gestured with a staying hand. "Let's give these boys a chance."

"He didn't take anything," Razor cried. "I was the only one!"

"Are you sure? No hash, weed, crack, or smack?"

"I didn't take anything," David said.

A smile spread across Skullcap's face, like the Grinch. "Well then. Maybe tonight isn't a total loss after all."

Skullcap flipped the knife in the air. He caught it by the hilt and swung it at Razor's head, catching him hard in the temple with a fleshy *thunk*. Razor collapsed in a heap on the floor.

David gasped. "Razor—"

Something bit him on the back of his neck. The room spun. Just before everything went black, he heard Skullcap say, "Hopefully they can use this one."

CHAPTER TWO

Palo Alto, California—February 25

Twin stretch limos left from a private terminal of the San Jose Airport and traveled north on the 280 freeway. On Sunday morning, the traffic was light; an unusual occurrence in Silicon Valley. The Chairman sat deep in the leather seat and sipped from an icy bottle of San Pellegrino. Today's meeting was just a formality.

From the 280 to the West Valley freeway, the cars swung onto Saratoga Avenue and, after another mile, turned into the complex. The Chairman liked the new signage and name. RRT Corporation instead of Reynolds Technology was his idea. The salesman's arrogance around the company name always troubled the Chairman, but after today it wouldn't matter much.

The complex sat nestled on the edge of Castle Rock State Park, hidden from all but a direct view. After the cars pulled into the front of Building 1, the Chairman rose from the car to the sidewalk with a polished black cane in hand and glanced up at the morning California sun.

The winding walkway to the entrance echoed the rolling landscape. Clumps of California hyacinth and bird-of-paradise dotted the edges of the flagstones while yellow lupines filled out the canvas of the landscaping. Stooping over a lone orchid hiding in the shade of one of the stunted redwoods, he smelled the delicate scent. "I love the flowers here. Pity we don't have more time to visit."

Richard Reynolds stood at the entrance of the building in a dark blue suit, white shirt, and red tie. The salesman, the Chairman thought.

Reynolds extended his hand. "Mr. Chairman, I'm glad you could fit this meeting into your schedule. It's an exciting time around here."

Reynolds ushered him into the lobby. After a short walk, they entered a large boardroom with a deep mahogany table surrounded by leather chairs. Chilled bottles of Perrier sat on a tray on a side credenza along with several glass bowls filled with M&Ms.

The Chairman sat first before the others sat at the table in unison.

A younger woman appeared at the back of the room, sat on a chair, and opened a steno pad. Long dark hair pulled into a bun, she hid her voluptuousness with a demure white top. The Chairman suspected Reynolds dipped his pen in the company ink. No wife to complicate the situation but that habit pointed to the character of the man standing behind that Cheshire smile.

"With your permission, I'd like to start this meeting," Reynolds said. On the front projection screen, the RRT logo appeared.

"In case you want to take notes, your binders contain a copy of the slides I'm using." Some of his entourage opened to the presentation while the Chairman ripped open a bag of M&Ms and ate a few that spilled onto the polished table.

"As you can see, we've had a banner year. Sales from the pharmaceutical division are good, with the Alzheimer drug doing well under the FDA trials," said Reynolds.

"When will the testing be completed?" asked one of the men.

"I'll get to that in a minute," Reynolds smiled, took a breath, and continued. "Our government work has stepped up because of the success with the memory drugs; however, the research is classified." Reynolds sipped from a bottle of water. "But projections show that with the current run rate, the company will return to profitability within eighteen months. Compared to some of our competitors, we are ahead of the curve."

"Let me stop you for a second," the Chairman said. "I may not have a complete view of the situation, but unless you are holding an ace up your sleeve, within nine months you will run out of your reserves and won't be able to stick it through to eighteen months to reach a positive cash flow."

Reynolds paused for a second. "I'm not sure I'd characterize it in the same way."

"But you would admit the company is at a crossroad?" the Chairman asked.

Reynolds' eyes darted around the table looking for support but got none. "That's an accurate statement," Reynolds said with a hint of reluctance in his voice. "Like any tech company, the operative word is growth. As our R&D costs are a large percentage of our income, without significant sales growth in new markets, we would die or be a takeover target." Reynolds pressed the button on the wireless control and the presentation advanced.

"If you turn to the next page, here's our plan to increase our revenue, via new licensing partners and some acquisitions."

Squinting through a tiny pair of reading glasses, the Chairman read the paper in front of him. "I'm curious about the Europe acquisition. Can you tell us more about it?"

"We're negotiating with an Eastern European company that has proprietary technology we believe we can leverage."

"But as I understand it, gaining the technology has been problematic," the Chairman said.

Reynolds broke out into a large smile. "Like any acquisition, due diligence is required. As this company was not on the block so to speak, we made them a deal they could not refuse. There are risks but I have my best people on it."

The Chairman stared at the salesman. "Let me get this straight, your current cash flow position is weak, your product lines are mature, and your competitors are catching up. Your plan to boost revenues is hinging on a deal with a company fresh out of an old communist regime?"

"It's just a minor acquisition, with some assets that will round out our product line."

"Yet, without this, there's nothing on the near horizon to bring the company back to profitability." the Chairman said.

"There is always a risk, but I have done this before and provided sizable returns to your investment. I believe I deserve leeway in getting the company back on the road to profitability," said Reynolds.

The Chairman laughed and chewed a few more M&Ms. "We have already bent the rules close to the breaking point. You need to realize for us to continue our involvement, your company has to be wildly profitable."

"It has been," said Reynolds.

"Yes, 'has.'"

None of the other men said a word. The Chairman swore he could hear Reynolds' heart beating.

"Richard. We've known each other for a long time but let me be clear. Unless you can return to profitability within three months, we will change our investment position." The Chairman pushed back from the table and stood up. "I regret I have another meeting I need to attend."

The other men stood up in unison. The younger man grabbed the two briefcases and held the door open for the Chairman.

"One last thing. Don't take this as a failure of faith. I have confidence you can execute your strategy, but confidence and results are two different things." The younger man handed the Chairman his cane. "I don't confuse them," the Chairman said.

Once the group had re-assembled into the limos and pulled out onto the 280, the younger man did a quick electronic bug check. "All clear."

"That went well, don't you think?" the Chairman asked of the other men in the car.

One man piped in, "Do you think he can pull it off?"

"He's a resourceful son of a bitch, I will give him that," the Chairman said. "But he's up against a wall that he can't climb over. But you know how you tell when a salesman is lying?" The other men smiled but didn't offer an answer.

"His lips are moving." The group laughed as the limos mounted the first hill up the 280 and away from the lovely California flowers.

* * *

Reynolds watched the old man and his little stable of sycophants swarm into the limos and drive off.

Good riddance.

In another couple of days, he wouldn't need to kiss his geriatric ass ever again. He couldn't wait for the day when that self-righteous asshole would come and ask *him* for money. But now he needed to focus on getting the deal done.

He'd asked his assistant, Hannah, to take notes in the meeting but she had disappeared with her steno pad. She probably didn't write anything in the damn thing worth keeping, anyway. However, she had other qualities he valued.

His secure cell phone buzzed and James Wyatt, his security chief, was on the other end. The encryption light glowed green. "Was the operation a success?"

"Yes, sir. The professor met with an unfortunate accident."

Reynolds sighed both with a touch of remorse and relief. "Thank you. Any problems?"

"No. Just like clockwork."

"The jet is waiting for you at Mirabel," Reynolds said. "Now get your ass to Amsterdam for the delivery and I'll meet you in New York."

"Roger that," Wyatt ended the call.

Reynolds sat back in his chair. Everything was going according to plan. This last meeting didn't mean anything, contrary to what that asshole said. Once Wyatt took delivery of the device, they could move up manufacturing and the all-important launch date. The first version might fail, but he didn't care. Just announcing the prototype would be enough to triple or quadruple the stock price. After launch, he'd tweak and release new versions in rapid succession. No upgrades. That's the way Apple did it. Why not here as well?

Once he had the device back here, he'd usher in the dawn of a new era personally.

And the Chairman could go fuck himself.

CHAPTER THREE

Amsterdam—Three Days Earlier

Jonathan Brooks hid in the shadow of the doorway, his breath billowing against the light of the streetlamp. He overlooked the Torensluis; a wide bridge over Amsterdam's famed Singel canal. Although the snow and darkness did their best to obscure the fine details, he still noticed everything.

Without turning his head, he watched a woman bent with age, hobble with a cane up the side of the canal, over the bridge, and disappear into a narrow street. A teenaged couple followed, the boy draping his arm over the girl as if he was protecting her from some unseen enemy. Minutes later, a dread-locked Rastafarian, in a rainbow hat, ambled across the bridge puffing on a large spliff. *He probably doesn't even notice the snow,* Brooks thought.

After almost sixty minutes, a fireplug of a man with a dirty ponytail shuffled from the west side of the canal to the bridge deck and stopped. It had to be Vogler. Few could fake his troll-like physique.

When he last saw Dr. Miles Vogler, a high and ugly concrete wall separated East and West Berlin. He had no animosity against the man but seeing him again brought back memories he didn't want.

Twenty years ago, Vogler was a leading East German researcher in computer anti-viruses and grid computing. The United States saw technology as potential weapons of the new cold war and needed specialists to ready their arsenal. During the operation to bring Vogler to the West, an agent and friend of Brooks' had died, and died badly. Vogler wasn't to blame and, in fact, had accidentally saved Brooks' life. Seeing him now just poked at memories he thought he had buried long ago.

Vogler leaned against a large bronze statue at the end of the bridge and looked left and right. Crystals of snow had gathered on his scruffy beard. Over the phone, Vogler promised a simple pickup and delivery. Acquire in Amsterdam. Drop in Paris. But nothing was ever straightforward with this man.

If it was so easy, Vogler should have called Fed-Ex.

Brooks scanned the area again but saw nothing out of the ordinary. Satisfied, he emerged from the shadows. "Hello, Miles."

Vogler spun but then broke out into a smile. "Jonathan! It has been a long time. You're looking well." Vogler sounded happy but strained.

Brooks kept scanning the bridge and the buildings behind him and refused to make eye contact. Old habits. "Do you have the package?"

"No time for small talk. Just like always. Twenty years it has been?"

Brooks said nothing.

"Yes, twenty years. I keep track." Vogler pulled his backpack off and withdrew a shiny aluminum case out of it and handed it to Brooks. "This is it."

"You told me fifteen pounds. This is closer to five."

Vogler said, "I was nervous, so I hid the package. Inside is a key that unlocks the hiding place. You will need to recover the package first before you deliver it."

"That wasn't our agreement."

"Things have changed. Some people are dead. That's why I need your help."

People died? Brooks felt a sudden flush. "You should have told me this before." He sat the case on the bridge deck and turned to walk away.

"Jonathan! Wait! I can't be sure they died because of the device. Please help me! I will double your fee!"

Brooks stopped. Double the cash. Shit. He's stashed away almost enough to retire from this kind of work. The double the money would put him over the top. He looked at Vogler for a second and said, "Where is it?"

"Come closer and I will tell you. It isn't something I wish to be yelling."

He kept scanning the area, but nothing caught his eye. He also owed the man from a long time ago. Vogler's pungent odor stunk even through this cold night. *Jesus, he still hasn't learned to wash.* "Tell me from there."

"Fine. One moment."

When Vogler reached into his pocket, Brooks grabbed for his Glock. Vogler edged out a weak smile. "Don't worry. Don't worry. This is something I built to stop unwelcome listeners." He withdrew a small black box and pressed a switch. "It's an ultra-high frequency scrambler. It interferes with any listening device, like a parabolic microphone. Plus, it drives both dogs and teenagers insane."

Brooks didn't like the situation one bit.

Vogler beckoned to him. "Come close. I need to give you the password. Once you can remember that, I will give you the location."

"The password?"

"The password will help you remember where I hid the device."

"Write it down."

"No. You need to commit it to memory."

Brooks glared at him but stepped closer. Miles Vogler was a paranoid little shit, but there was no profit by getting into an argument.

"Okay. Tell me the password."

"It's not just one word. It's a phrase." Vogler smiled for the first time, withdrew a thick envelope from his coat pocket and handed it to Brooks. "This is something extra for your trouble."

Brooks took the envelope and peered inside. A wad of new fifty and hundred euros stared back.

"Five thousand extra. Think of it as a bonus."

Brooks looked at the money. A bonus plus the negotiated rate was a big win for him. Maybe he'd been too hard on the old man. He stuffed the envelope into the pocket of his suit jacket.

"Come closer and I will tell you the password," Vogler said.

Brooks bent forward and Vogler whispered into his ear. He made Brooks repeat the words twice to make sure he had heard it right. Brooks didn't understand the reference but once Vogler disclosed the location, it made sense.

Out of the corner of his eye, his hind brain saw something out of place. Something unusual at this time of night. Something no one would see except for him. Twenty years ago, his reflexes would have kicked in, but he was older now. And older meant slower.

* * *

From across the canal, and hidden inside one of the many Singel houseboats, Nikko Palokangas pulled back his long hair and tied it with a rubber band. He had removed his coat and shivered in the cold air. Moving to a prone position on the old sofa, he braced the rifle stock to his shoulder. The Hessman 10X optical scope gave him pinpoint accuracy at two hundred meters. He scanned the target, filled his lungs with a long slow breath and then as he held it, squeezed the trigger twice. Through the scope, he saw two slugs from his silenced rifle rip into Brooks' throat spraying the East German with a burst of hot red blood.

Nikko switched aim and fired a second set into Vogler's head, turning the target's brain into three pounds of pink sludge.

Vogler collapsed first, face down into the cobblestones. Brooks remained upright for several seconds, his hand still gripping the metal briefcase until the body collapsed in a heap beside the other dead man.

On the wide cobblestone bridge deck, a large pool of red seeped out of Vogler's shattered brain while Brooks' still-beating heart squirted blood through the ripped artery. After several minutes, the red bloom from both men slowed. The snow continued to fall, heavier now, trying hard to cover their deaths with a cold blanket.

CHAPTER FOUR

New York—The Ritz-Carlton

The sun peeked over the top of the Empire State building and pushed the winter chill out of the city.

Richard Reynolds stood on the warm marble floor of the Ritz's penthouse bathroom, his tanned body wrapped in a cotton bathrobe. An Armani jacket hung on a wooden hanger with a fresh white shirt and muted red tie. His meeting with the Chinese went late and they insisted on touring two high-end strip clubs.

Although he considered that activity pedestrian, he'd do almost anything to seal the deal. His Plan B, just in case the board closed on their threat. However, this morning, the veins on his forehead pulsed as he spoke into his cell phone.

"We've got a problem," Wyatt said.

"The problem better be that the jet ran out of caviar and champagne," Reynolds said.

"We don't have the device. Both Vogler and the courier were killed just before the transfer," Wyatt said.

Reynolds stood quiet for a second trying to grasp the enormity of the situation. "Who's responsible?" Reynolds said.

"Don't know yet. A sniper got them and escaped. We had surveillance but not for the perimeter. But before the police got there, we snatched the bodies."

Reynolds slid the teak bathroom door closed. "Did the shooter get the device?"

"No. Vogler had a metal case with him, but the only thing inside was a key," Wyatt said.

"Nothing else?"

"No."

"Is it possible one of your shithead contractors did it?"

"Everyone was accounted for. The courier's partner, Fitzsimmons, contacted me earlier to verify the delivery requirements. Vogler paid the courier directly."

"Let me get this straight. I paid this German ass-wipe ten million euros for a working prototype and all we have is a stupid key and no idea what it opens?" Reynolds asked.

"Correct," Wyatt said.

Reynolds pressed mute and kicked the teak bathroom cabinet door until the hardwood splintered and broke into pieces. He jerked his foot to the top of the counter and yanked a long sliver of wood from his big toe. Blood dripped onto the marble counter.

"We had a microphone trained on them, but Vogler activated a device that scrambled the feed. It's logical to assume Vogler told the courier the location."

Grabbing a white towel from the counter, Reynolds wrapped his toe and un-muted his phone. "Vogler must have set some kind of password on the device."

"That's a logical conclusion."

A wave of dizziness hit Reynolds. "Just a minute." He pressed the hold button and dropped the cell phone on the counter. Bad news always spiked his blood pressure and he had to bring it down. After closing his eyes and taking several long slow breaths he un-muted his phone. "Any idea where Vogler has been for the last few days?"

"Several places. We tracked him from Berlin to Paris, and then Amsterdam. All by train. He didn't like to fly."

Reynolds squatted down and examined the pieces of wood on the floor. The cabinet door was destroyed.

"Where are the bodies?"

"On ice in our clinic here."

Reynolds squeezed his toe and a large drop of blood welled up from the wound and spattered on to the white tile. "Wake the doctor in California and tell him to get his pet project together for a road test. The jet will be waiting for him in San Jose. They can pick me up on the way. We have a slim chance of recovering from this screw up. I've got too much riding on this demonstration to give up now. Bring Fitzsimmons in to assist." Reynolds thought for a moment and said, "Here's what else I need you to do." Reynolds dictated a set of instructions to Wyatt. "There's a time clock on this. It needs to happen tomorrow if it will work at all."

"I understand," Wyatt said.

"It's more difficult, but not impossible. The doctor's tests show great promise." Reynolds took another deep breath and straightened up. The dizziness passed, and he felt his blood pressure dropping.

A gentle knock came at the door to the bathroom. The door slid back, and his assistant, Hannah stood in the doorway wearing a white bathrobe and holding two steaming lattes on an ornate bone china tray. A crucifix on a golden chain peeked out from between her breasts.

"I'll call you back in two hours, but I expect to be picked up at 1:00 p.m. New York time." Reynolds closed the cell phone and dropped it into the pocket of his bathrobe.

"I'm your 7:00 a.m. wake-up call." She kissed him and set both mugs on the countertop. She didn't glance at the damage to the cabinet door.

Reynolds undid her cotton belt, and the bathrobe parted. Hannah touched a button on the wall and started the steam in the shower. As fog rose above the glass, Reynolds stepped into her, kissing her hard and pushed her voluptuous body up against the glass. His hands grabbed her heavy breasts then he pulled her leg up, moving close in. She held on to his shoulders as he entered her. Her robe dropped to the marble floor covering the splinters of teak and drops of blood. The crucifix offered her little protection as he slammed into her.

CHAPTER FIVE

Amsterdam

Asher Fitzsimmons stared at the intricate roof line of the row house as snow dusted the shoulders of his coat. Before street addresses were common, the only way a drunk Dutchman could find his own house was by the gable.

Years before, he stood in front of a similar house, in a similar temperature, waiting to kill the occupant. Today, he was visiting someone already dead.

The front door cracked open and a wide man with short red hair and a bushy goatee squinted at him.

"G'day, you the English bloke?"

"Fitz," he said.

"Charlie. Pleased to meet you."

Fitz nodded but didn't return the greeting.

Charlie waved Fitz inside to a modern front office with a large flat screen embedded into a wall. Pinpoint ceiling halogens reflected off the polished floor and several leather chairs sat empty against the other wall. After a minute, a tall man with a trimmed beard appeared. He wore a white shirt and jeans.

Fitz extended his hand, "I'm Fitz."

"Richard." Reynolds said. "I see you've already met Charlie." And nodded towards the red-haired doorman.

As Fitz looked at Reynolds, he saw no smile, just tight lips and bags under his eyes that signaled exhaustion. Not a good way to begin a cleanup operation.

Before the meeting, Fitz's research found only vague information about Richard Reynolds. Silicon Valley *Wunderkind*. Made a fortune in Biotech and software. RRT Corporation—Richard Reynolds Technology. Privately owned. Rumors about Reynolds' shady business practices. Lots of litigation. Reynolds' lawyers spent a great deal of time in court. A couple of his competitors died before critical product launches. Nothing linked the deaths to Reynolds, but Fitz liked to understand his employers.

As Fitz followed him down a narrow hallway, he estimated Reynolds to be forty-seven to fifty by the look of the grey hair. Tailored expensive shirt. Expensive jeans. Geek formal. Fitz's automatic assessment said Reynolds was a narcissist and an egoist, not uncommon in the CEO trade.

"This is James Wyatt. My head of security." Reynolds nodded towards a big man at the end of the hallway. Wyatt wore a tailored suit, covering a larger frame, hundred kilos at least. He had broad shoulders and walked with no wasted movements. A thin scar trailed from the man's left ear to his jaw. Ex-military probably. Maybe first Gulf War or military security.

"Sorry about your man," Wyatt said.

Fitz felt a brief wave of sorrow. He'd received a text that Brooks had been killed but not the circumstances. Brooks had been on a delivery run. Simple. Pickup and drop off. He took a breath and pushed the sadness back down. He'd deal with it later. Scotch would be involved. "What happened?" Fitz said.

"The transfer went bad. Someone didn't want the delivery to occur," Reynolds said.

"A sniper took out your man and Vogler during the exchange," Wyatt said. "We were close and managed to grab both bodies before the police showed up."

Fitz digested that nugget of information. "Any idea who the shooter was?"

"Not yet," Wyatt said.

Fitz glanced around the room. "Can I see him?"

"You can, but he's not pretty," Wyatt said. He pushed a door open at the end of the hall and the three men entered. The sharp smell of antiseptic mixed with the coppery odor of blood filled the room. A sheet lay over a body on a stainless-steel table.

Jonathan Brooks.

"The procedure is invasive, but then so was the bullet," Reynolds said.

Wyatt pulled the sheet back and exposed the chalky white skin of a dead body. Brooks' throat bore a large hole and one side of his skull was removed exposing what looked like a grey cauliflower. Even in death, Brooks' sixty-three-year-old body looked fit—the result of years of obsessive physical training. Too bad, it didn't matter anymore.

"Why didn't you try this on the German instead?"

"Too much damage. The bullet fragmented on impact through the areas we needed. But we think Vogler passed Brooks the package's location just before his death."

"Why do you need me then?" Fitz said.

"Vogler gave your man a case with a key inside. We are hoping he told your man what the key opened and where it was."

Fitz smirked. "A little hard to ask him now, don't you think?"

"I'd be the first to agree. However, we can extract the last few minutes of your man's memory."

Fitz frowned but stood silent for a moment, taking the information in.

Wyatt said, "We'd been tracking Vogler the moment he arrived in Amsterdam but gave him space so he could deliver the package."

"He lives in Berlin. Why didn't we arrange for Brooks to meet him there?"

"He specified Amsterdam for some reason. He was a paranoid sort."

"Apparently for good reason," Fitz said.

Wyatt looked for the first time into Fitz's eyes. "We screwed up. We didn't realize there was a conflicting interest."

Fitz remained quiet but accepted the apology.

"Any idea of who the other party is?"

"We are following up on several leads," Wyatt said.

"What's in the package? Anything dangerous that I should know about?" Fitz asked.

"Just some technology I was buying. No viruses or plutonium or anything restricted if that's what you're thinking," Reynolds said.

"The case should have contained tech the size of a large laptop. It's important I get it back," Reynolds said.

Fitz glared. He wanted to know who killed his friend, but Reynolds seemed more concerned about some stupid computer. "I'm still a little unclear why you wanted to employ me?"

"As I was saying, we can implant the last thirty seconds of his memory into a suitable volunteer."

"What does suitable look like?" Fitz asked.

"Young and drug-free. We found a few possibilities that met the criteria, and my men invited them to volunteer," Wyatt said.

"Why didn't you use one of your own people?" Fitz asked.

"The procedure is risky," Reynolds said.

Perhaps the rumors about Reynolds weren't just rumors. Fitz heard a crash at the end of the hallway. A door to the outside opened and a wide Indian man walked in carrying a man over his shoulder and laid the body on an empty gurney. A thin man with a long nose followed behind him.

Reynolds ignored the men. "As Vogler had a prior relationship with your man, maybe they both knew the location. A place they once met, perhaps. However, Brooks' memories will be fragmented. We might need your help to make sense of them. Plus, I'm sure you'd like to get a crack at whoever pulled the trigger."

Fitz stood stone-faced. He didn't like the situation very much, but he wanted to see where this rabbit hole would take him.

A dark-skinned man in a white coat appeared. He swiveled the gurney containing the volunteer. Fitz noticed the subject was less a man and more of a kid; good looking and muscular with long blond hair.

"This is Dr. Pirani," Reynolds said. The doctor didn't look up.

"Is the kid going to hold the memories?" Fitz asked.

"Yes," Wyatt said.

"He doesn't look like a volunteer," Fitz said.

"He will be paid well for his inconvenience," Wyatt said and turned to the men. "Is he the dancer we initially found?"

The thin man said, "No. There were two, but we disqualified the first one."

"Dancer? Is there some kind of performance later?" Fitz asked.

Reynolds chuckled for the first time. "No. When we first realized we needed someone healthy and drug-free, the team on the ground discovered a dance troupe had checked in to a local hotel. We found a couple of the men and convinced one to sign up."

Fitz looked down at the kid. Couldn't have been more than twenty-one but looked in good shape. But he hated getting civilians involved in operations. Too much additional risk.

The doctor glanced at Fitz, but then gestured to the two men that brought him in. "Was he clean?"

"He said he was."

"We'll find out soon enough," the doctor said.

"He was convincing in his denial," the thin man said.

A cold cigarette dangled from the lips of the shorter man. "No smoking please," the doctor said. The man snorted and put the cigarette behind his ear.

"What dose did you give him?" the doctor asked.

"Everything in the syringe," the thin man said.

Dr. Pirani nodded as if they did something correct but said nothing else. From the other end of the hallway, a white woman in a white coat entered with her dark hair pulled back in a bun.

"We need to get him into pre-op and do another toxicity screen fast," the doctor said.

The woman grabbed the end of the gurney and swiveled it through a wide door into a larger room, sharp with the smell of lemon cleaner. Stainless steel panels rose from the hard tile and stopped midway up the walls. She kicked the bottom of the gurney and locked the wheels into place.

"We need to strip him," the doctor said.

She pulled the kid's boots and socks off along with his jeans before dropping them into a plastic bin. The doctor struggled with the shirt buttons and instead tore the shirt open.

"Our good doctor isn't used to working on patients that are still alive," Reynolds said.

Dr. Pirani said out of breath, "Sorry. It's a big day for the project." The nurse produced a pair of trauma shears and cut the sleeves and shirt open, lifted the kid's body up and pulled the fabric from underneath him. Everything went into the third bin. She unfolded a green hospital gown over his semi-nude body.

"Who is he?" Fitz asked.

The doctor pulled open one of the kid's eyelids and flashed a small penlight in it. The nurse produced a wallet and flipped it open.

"His driver's license says his name is David Andrew Knight. Born in Canada. His birth date makes him twenty-one."

"Weight?"

"He's muscular. His license says eighty kilos."

The doctor scratched a calculation on a piece of paper. "Can you administer a hundred mils of Fentanyl? I want to make sure he doesn't wake up during the procedure."

She wrapped a rubber hose above the kid's elbow and after swabbing the skin, she drove an IV needle into a bulging vein. After filling two glass tubes with his blood, she attached the IV to a saline drip and emptied the sedative into the IV port. The kid didn't move during either procedure.

The doctor stared at a laptop perched on the counter and said, "We're doing a standard toxicity screen. There's a higher chance for success if the subject is alcohol and drug-free." The nurse inserted the first blood vial into a machine on the counter.

"A tall order for someone in Amsterdam," Fitz said.

"Agreed. That's why we pre-choose the test subjects," Wyatt said.

Fitz only saw one guinea pig. He wondered how many more there were. "What happens if he fails the test, will you continue the procedure?"

The doctor looked at Reynolds and then at Fitz.

"We don't have much choice."

The nurse attached a sensor to the kid's index finger and checked his temperature. "Temperature and oxygen saturation normal." She glanced at the readout from the machine testing his blood. "Type A. No alcohol and no THC, opium, or heroin. His cortisol and blood sugar are a little high but within normal ranges."

"Let's get started," Reynolds said.

The nurse and doctor together wheeled the gurney into a room next to pre-op. In the center, an operating table sat embedded into the floor, with twin LED screens suspended from the ceiling on either side. The room smelled like the last one; clean and sharp with a hint of lemon. They slid the kid's body on to the table and the nurse strapped his arms to movable rests. She reconnected the EKG, blood pressure, and EEG sensors to the room's monitors. Near the head of the table, a crash cart sat ready with defibrillator paddles in case of an emergency.

Fitz felt Reynolds' hand on his shoulder. "We watch in here." Beside the operating room was a small antechamber with large glass windows. "We can hear and see everything that's happening."

The nurse reconnected the IV's to a blood bag hanging from an IV stand and pulled the arm boards out until they were 90 degrees from the table. Fitz wondered if the nurse planned to hammer a few nails into his palms.

"How long will the procedure take?"

"We should know within an hour if the procedure is successful."

"How long if it's not?"

"Immediately," Reynolds said.

Fitz noticed a yellow warning symbol attached to the blood bag that dripped into the kid's veins. The nurse hoisted a heavy cover over top of the doctor's gown and then pulled on one herself.

"Why the protective gear?"

"We use a radioactive tag to monitor the progress of the induction to the host."

The doctor peered at his laptop screen. "The concentration is the best we can get it. It's now or never."

"Go ahead," Reynolds said.

The doctor opened the box. With tongs, the nurse grabbed a vial filled with a brown liquid. The vial had a smaller yellow radiation sticker on it.

"Please administer the solution," the doctor said.

The nurse filled a large syringe from the vial and injected the mixture into the port in the IV line. "50 ccs injected."

"Thank you," the doctor said.

The kid's body jerked underneath the hospital linen. The nurse called out, "Pulse rate rising; body temp one hundred degrees. I'm seeing bursts of electrical activity in his brain."

Inside the observation room, a smaller LCD screen showed the kid's heart rate spiking. The kid's body jerked again; she pulled back the linen. Every strap strained against his muscles.

"He's seizing!" the nurse yelled.

"This shouldn't be happening. He has enough anesthetic to keep him under for hours," the doctor said.

All his muscles struggled against the nylon straps. His face twisted in agony. His thick legs pulled up like a kicking horse. Fitz heard the Velcro straps tearing open.

"100 ml of Dilantin! Quick!" The doctor leaned on the kid's legs and pulled the straps tight. The nurse pulled a vial from the tray, filled a syringe, and drove the needle into the IV port.

The kid strained and thrashed like a wounded shark against his bonds. The nurse yanked the straps tighter on both legs and the doctor tugged the webbing tight on his arms and hands. Within ten seconds, the thrashing eased and then ceased. Fitz watched the kid's face soften; his heavy leg muscles relaxed, and his breathing slowed.

"His brain activity is back to normal," the nurse said. "His pulse and blood pressure have dropped too."

Thick beads of sweat dropped from the doctor's temples. "I have a trace. Twenty percent of the solution has reached his brain. We've hit phase one. Within twenty minutes we will be at phase three."

Fitz swallowed and wished he had a scotch in his hand. Watching the kid struggle was like watching a boxing match. He didn't know how torturing this poor boy would help find Brooks' killer. And he didn't trust Reynolds.

"Explain again how this will help find the package?"

Reynolds said, "Transplanting memory is like chasing a rat in a maze. The good doctor extracted tissue from probable areas of where your man's short-term memory resides. The tissue was mixed with a special compound that allows the memories to be implanted."

From the operating room, the doctor said, "But there's a time limit. The memories will degrade if we don't implant in the right spot. And we need to remove the same memories within seven days or there may be consequences."

Fitz said, "What consequences?"

"Well, the memories could be rejected."

"Rejected?"

"All the tests we've run show the body eventually rejects the implantation. Like the first transplant operations without all the anti-rejection drugs."

"If I remember right, all those patients died."

"Yes."

"Have you had any success at all?"

"Some promising results, but in all cases, the memories were rejected immediately. We've never hit the seven-day mark or had them conscious enough to see if the memories took."

Reynolds said, "The other test subjects died. The doctor's research showed that because the enzymes that encode the memories degrade fast from the donor brain, we are out of time. This is our last try."

CHAPTER SIX

Amsterdam

David couldn't move. Couldn't hear. Couldn't see. He tried to open his eyes, but at first, nothing happened. In the distance, he saw something. A white light; small at first but growing. Larger and larger into a hot white, scalding light.

He tried to squeeze his eyes shut, but the light blasted through his eyelids. He wanted the cool darkness again. His arms and legs felt like they'd been cast in concrete. A beat pounded in his ears; was he alive? Disinfectant and the metallic odor of spilled blood assaulted his nose. He pushed, this time feeling the thin edge of something holding him in place. Where was he? Why couldn't he move? He tried to grab at anything in his head but couldn't remember his own name.

A blast of memories hit him. Random disconnected images of shapes, people, and objects. The color red, sounds of a helicopter, smell of burnt flesh, the strumming of a blues guitar. Then the memories vanished like smoke.

He heard whispers. Calm quiet voices. A woman and a man. English.

"How is our patient doing, Nurse?"

Patient? He must be in a hospital. What happened?

A strong odor moved close; sweat and perfume mixed with curry. A rough finger yanked his eyelids open, blinding him with a sharp light. He tried to close them, but something held his eyelids open. He tried twist to away from the light, but his neck was locked in steel.

He tried to yell, but nothing came out. Sand filled his mouth. Was he going to be tortured again? The question bounced inside his head and didn't make any sense.

"His pupils look fine. There's good brain activity," the man's voice said.

"Water," he whispered.

A straw appeared at his lips and he sucked a small bit of cold water down his throat.

A female voice said. "Just a sip, David."

David? Was that his name? No. It was something else. David sounded right, at the same time it didn't.

"You've had a rough time of it," she said. "How are you feeling?"

He grappled inside his head for the answer. It was at his fingertips, but each time he went to grasp the answer, it faded into vapor. But then an answer surfaced.

"A…truck."

"What?"

"Like a truck ran over me."

Laughter. The voice changed from caring to concern. The man's voice. "Based on his vitals, he should be feeling better, but if pain is an issue, we can prescribe an analgesic. Nothing with opiates however; that could cause problems with the extraction."

Extraction? He kept his eyes closed, but inside, a wall of fear built; enormous and paranoid. Emotions crashed like heavy waves onto a shore. Every few seconds a different feeling. Sadness, happiness, fear, guilt, and rage cycling back and forth. Different sensations. Hundreds of needles poking at his feet and stopping. A fever washed over his body from his head to his toes and disappeared.

What did he know? Two people in the room plus him. Male and female. The male was the dominant position. A doctor perhaps.

"David, do you remember what happened to you?" the man asked.

"No." He still couldn't move his head. A wide strap across his forehead. Similar straps on his arms and legs cut into his skin.

"Please relax. We have restrained you for your protection. Struggling won't help your recovery."

He unclenched his hands and relaxed his legs even though the fear grabbed him tight. *Illness?* He didn't remember being sick, but when he searched for a coherent memory, he remembered nothing.

"Doctor, his blood pressure and heart rate are still elevated," the nurse said.

He fought for long and slow breaths, trying to push the fear away, but the anxiety remained, causing his body to shiver and shake. Something formed in his mind and screamed to take notice. A disembodied something. He understood the message.

He had to escape.

* * *

In the operating room, the kid's vitals glowed in green numbers from the LED screens. His pulse rate and breathing had slowed, and it appeared he'd fallen back asleep.

"Should we contact Mr. Reynolds?" the nurse asked.

"I will, right after I have completed my examination."

"He won't be happy if we don't notify him immediately."

"Be concerned about your patient. I'll handle Reynolds," Dr. Pirani said.

The nurse looked at the kid's thick sculpted thighs and melon calves and wondered what kind of dance he did. She hadn't realized how athletic a dancer needed to be.

She examined his body and noticed the straps had cut into the kid's skin. Probably when he struggled.

Dr. Pirani pointed to the same scrapes that she noticed. "Can you clean up his forearm? He's bleeding all over the sheet," the doctor said. Without waiting for confirmation, he turned and exited the room.

The nurse sighed and pulled scissors, gauze, and medical tape from a side cabinet along with a padded strap that she attached under the arm tray. "I'm going to clean up that cut."

She pulled the padded strap around his arm, fastening it loose before removing the other strap. To make cleaning the wound easier, she released the Velcro that held his wrist tight to the bed.

"I'm so glad you are feeling better," she said.

Dr. Pirani re-appeared at the door just as his vital signs monitor started beeping. The kid's pulse rate and breathing had spiked. Dr. Pirani came close, pushed her out of the way and barked, "Never remove the strap!" The kid's eyes snapped opened and his free right arm exploded with an uppercut to Dr. Pirani's chin and knocked him to the floor. The kid reached over and ripped the straps apart on his other side.

Dr. Pirani yelled from the floor. "Get him sedated now!"

The nurse grabbed a syringe from the tray and tried to jab it into his leg, but the kid grabbed her wrist and took the syringe before shoving her back on to the floor.

The kid yanked the Velcro from around his waist and his legs and jerked out the IV from his arm. As he jumped off the gurney, Charlie appeared from the other room and grabbed him from behind. "Relax, mate. I don't want to hurt you."

Whipping his head back, the kid smashed hard into Charlie's nose, twisted free and spun on his toe driving his elbow into the man's bloody face. Charlie collapsed into a heap, his broken nose smearing blood into the polished floor.

Dr. Pirani stood up; blood dripping from his mouth and holding the syringe in front of him like a knife. "Get back on that table right now!" He lunged at the kid, trying to stab the needle anywhere into his body. Instead, the kid grabbed his wrist and flipped him to the floor. In one smooth motion, the kid scooped up the syringe and plunged it into the doctor's side. After a few seconds of struggle, the doctor lapsed into unconsciousness.

* * *

As David stumbled and shook from the adrenaline rush, a hot steel band of pain tightened around his forehead. He screamed. But the formless thing inside his head pushed him to escape, pain or not. He climbed over the three bodies and barged down a hallway. The first door opened into a large, cold room with a body on a metal table, covered with a white sheet. He pulled it back and exposed a dead man. A mound of clothes sat in a nearby basket.

A massive wound decorated the neck and a chunk of his skull was missing. A blast of nausea and revulsion hit him, along with a brief feeling of recognition. But his body kept moving. He dug through the pile of clothes, sticky with blood. He wrinkled his nose, but his hand pulled out a thick envelope from a jacket. He didn't look inside, but his hand held the envelope with a death grip.

The last door opened into a cleaning closet filled with a janitor's sink and supplies. A stack of blue hospital pants and shirts sat neatly folded on a shelf and a long blue janitor's coat hung on the wall with rubber boots below. More pain rose as the metal band tightened, but he pulled on a pair of the scrub pants and the janitor's coat over his naked chest and arms. He jammed his bare feet into the boots and his hand stuffed the envelope into the long pocket of the coat on its own accord.

Get out! The words came from nowhere and everywhere. He pushed open the fire door, stumbling into the cold Amsterdam night. Feathery light snow fell and covered the cobblestones. He didn't know where he was, or who he was, but was sure of one thing. He had to keep moving or he would die.

* * *

Across the canal, standing in the shadows, a man with a wonky eye put the tiny telescope into his coat pocket. Only one eye worked, so binoculars seemed a waste. A telescope worked better and was easier to hide. He lit a cigarette, withdrew a phone, and selected a number. "There's a new development." He took a drag on the cigarette. "Yes, I'll keep you apprised of the events."

CHAPTER SEVEN

Silicon Valley—March 1st

William Morgan felt the wind on the top of his head as he zoomed down the 280 with his silver Porsche Boxster convertible. He shot past a slower Jap car and touched the small gold crucifix hung from the rear-view mirror. A gift from the Reverend; God's radar detector.

He balanced his cuff links and adjusted the sleeves of his dress shirt to the top of his wrists, making sure they were even. The calluses on his right hand reminded him to double his training sessions next week. Church work made him soft and fat. God needed warriors and warriors needed to be prepared. Regardless if he was in the army or the church, to him, the missions were the same.

Dry and lifeless scrub dominated the rolling hills on his left, and lush green grass and shrubs covered the estates on his right. A good place for a billboard, maybe. Showing the difference between the God-fearing and the godless. Alive or dead. But those idiots wouldn't get it. They would think the billboard was about saving the environment and not their eternal souls.

Heathens.

Morgan shifted gears and ramped off the 280 to Menlo Park making his way into the Stanford Industrial Park and its many two-story buildings filled with wannabe millionaires, working on the next big thing.

The Church's target demographic.

When the Reverend hit his stride on television, Morgan convinced him to move the entire campus from Hicksville, Texas to south of San Francisco. To, as the Reverend called it, "Sodom Valley." A good location to boost the church's status. If money is the root of all evil, this place was the center of it. As Morgan did his part, he knew that God wanted him to get a cut of the action.

At the end of a cul-de-sac, tall steel gates wedged between clogged holly trees opened as he approached. Employees only. A winding driveway cut a wide swath through a thick California forest of white fir, pine, cedar, and arbutus. The surveillance was invisible, but he'd ordered so many sensors installed, security called this section the DMZ. Morgan mirrored design used by the CIA in Langley.

Around the last curve, the tall spires of the glass cathedral appeared. The keystone to the Church's image. Shiny satellite up-link dishes sat juxtaposed with the old time preaching. A sign near the parking read. "The Worldwide Church of the Holy Spirit—Bringing the Word to the Planet 24 hours a day, 7 days a week."

Marketing is everything, Morgan thought, but the product must be quality. But even with his less than stellar reputation of bending or breaking the Lord's own rules, the old man still delivered.

He climbed out of the car and filled his lungs with the warm California air. He lived in the city because it had what the valley lacked. Culture, restaurants, and pretty women that weren't only coders. And having some distance between him and the Reverend gave him much needed perspective.

The grounds were whisper quiet. Heavy rammed-earth walls circling the compound blocked any traffic sounds from the surrounding roads. Money has its privileges.

Morgan entered the building, past a black man in a sharp suit and continued through a series of controlled access doors that led to the Reverend's office complex.

He walked by the Public Relations department that kept the church's humanitarian efforts on track. Streaming video servers rotated emotional stories of the third world starving and the bankrupt morality of western civilization. A holy media conglomerate.

Morgan knocked once and entered the Reverend's semicircular office. A large desk controlled the top of the curve with high bookshelves on either side. Several religious sculptures dotted around the room like chess pieces. The biggest one showed an archangel trampling Lucifer. Morgan knew the Reverend patterned his life after this piece of marble.

Maybe it was.

The Reverend stood bent over a large Bible. "No matter how many times I read the word of God, I never fail to learn something new." He looked up at Morgan and asked, "How are you, William? Can I have my assistant bring you a soda?"

Morgan walked over to a small statue perched on a stand and traced his index finger along the smooth lines of Michelangelo's David. "Fine, thank you."

"How are our latest projects doing?"

"That's why I'm here." Morgan pulled a sheath of papers from his bag and spread them over the corner of the desk. "Here are potential locations that need divine intervention."

"All business, I see." The old man sighed and laid a red silk bookmark on a page in the big Bible and closed the book.

Morgan unfolded a child's map of Africa. Large colorful areas with artificial boundaries. Cheery compared to the reality of what was happening on the ground.

"The last campaign took place here." He pointed his finger at Liberia, "But we think there's good potential over here." He touched a few inches over. "The Ivory Coast is worth reviewing again."

"How much this time?"

"Ten million to influence the warlords. Another five for weapons and incidentals. Twenty in total. Plus, my administration fee."

The Reverend shook his head. "The costs rise with each mission. How do you justify it?"

"Using heathens to bring the Word to the people is expensive. We can't use any of our followers; too much at stake. Muscle, plus bribery, drugs, extortion. Everything has a cost and all parties want more each time."

The Reverend waved the map away. "Fine."

"You can thank me later, once the new marketing campaign takes hold."

Morgan looked out the window at the Reverend's vibrant and colorful garden. The view was crystal clear considering it was bulletproof glass.

"Is there anything else?"

"There's one more thing," Morgan said. He produced a grainy telephoto picture. "That potential problem I identified?" He dropped a glossy picture on top of the map. "It's been solved."

In the photo, two bodies lay sprawled on the deck of a bridge. Both heads hidden in a dark shadow.

The Reverend drew back and winced. "Take it away! Why do you insist on showing me this vulgarity? I've warned you before!"

"Reverend. Everything I do has a specific purpose." Morgan grabbed the photograph and held it between his fingertips. "I learned a long time ago to validate before we pay out any of the church's money. Unless you wanted an ear, this was the next best thing." He pressed a hidden button on a side table and dropped the photo into a shredder that connected to the office incinerators. The Reverend still looked like he'd just swallowed a bug.

"The contractor we hired specializes in this work. I tried recruiting from our membership, but his skill was unsurpassed." Morgan said.

"There were two bodies. Which one was the blasphemer?"

"This one." Morgan's dropped another picture on the desk. "Here's a German Stasi photograph from before the wall came down." A bearded man with a ponytail and rheumy eyes looked back. "The bodies were removed by the buyer before the police came."

"No evidence of any wrongdoing then. That's good news. What about the device?"

"The case was empty. The whole thing might have been an elaborate con," Morgan said.

The Reverend took a deep breath and slumped back into the chair. He reached for the glass on the coaster and sipped from the glass of soda.

"The greed of some people. Who was the other man?"

"A courier but he deserved the same judgment as the blasphemer."

"I'm confused." The Reverend peered over the top of his reading glasses.

"About what?"

"You told me you heard a rumor that the device might exist."

"Yes."

"You verified the rumor and believed it was a potential threat to the ministry and everything I've worked for. But I forced you to wait because I didn't want to act on hearsay."

"Yes. We waited until the blasphemer had produced a prototype to sell."

"You convinced me to pass judgment on the blasphemer as it was in the Lord's best interest."

"You did."

"But now you tell me, we acted on false information and there was no device." The Reverend's eyes narrowed at Morgan. "I'm very disappointed in this development. I don't like to pass holy judgment indiscriminately. That's why I wanted you to wait."

"I still believe there was a threat. I verified he was engaged in some limited research in the area, but we now think he wasn't able to produce a working prototype."

The Reverend closed his eyes and touched his fingertips together for two seconds as if he was praying. "There's always casualties in God's war, William. Was there anything else we needed to talk about?"

"No."

"Very well."

The Reverend patted Morgan on the back. "Good to see you. I'm glad we're doing God's work together."

Morgan's cell phone chimed. He read the display and frowned before putting it to his ear.

"Yes?" Morgan listened for several seconds and his face flushed crimson. "Yes. Wait for further instructions."

"Who was that?" the Reverend asked.

"My source in Amsterdam. There's a problem," Morgan said.

"What do you mean problem? I thought you took care of the problem," the Reverend said.

Morgan cleared his throat. "I did. But there's a complication. There's a chance the device might exist after all." The Reverend frowned, but Morgan continued. "A key was found inside the case. A key that might unlock where the device may be stashed."

The Reverend looked at Morgan. "Good Lord! Do they know where?"

"The courier did."

"The dead courier," the Reverend said.

Morgan cleared his throat and said, "The buyer wants to implant the courier's memories into someone else to find the device."

"Memories from a dead man? Is that even possible?"

"The buyer thinks it's possible. But this shows we were on the right track to destroy it. This whole thing smacks of the devil."

The Reverend stared at Morgan and said nothing. After a few seconds, he nodded his head. "I agree. You need to clean this up."

Morgan took a breath, calmed his heart rate and said "I apologize. This is now my top priority. But there may be more collateral damage."

"I don't care. I just want this mess cleaned up."

Morgan said nothing and grabbed his satchel.

"William, this is an unfortunate turn of events. You or I could not have foreseen what would transpire. Only God can do that." The Reverend walked around his desk and squeezed Morgan's heavy shoulders.

"Make me proud, son."

Morgan remained silent as he nodded. *Son*, Morgan thought, there's a first time for everything.

The Reverend reached up, hugged him for a split second and let him go. Morgan realized with cold memory that this might be only the third time his father had hugged him.

Morgan left the building, walked up to his car, and took the Lord's name in vain. Several times. A black and shiny California beetle sat in the shade of his Porsche. He opened the door, and crushed the bug with his heel, grinding it into a black mess. Scrapping the guts off his shoe against the asphalt first, he got in and started the engine.

He hated bugs. Although he believed most insects were God's creatures, he imagined the devil sent this black demon to torment him.

Why hadn't he dealt with the inventor when he first heard about the device? If he'd been there in person to supervise the operation, none of this would have happened. But what upset him more than anything was that he still wanted his father's approval. When would that end?

When the old man dies, a voice said.

The sharp pain of shame overcame him, and his face flushed. To wish his father was dead was a sin. He'd sworn, too. Taken his holy father's name in vain. He'd need to take the discipline to clear his thoughts and atone for that sin, along with the others he'd committed for the last few days.

He pressed a button inside the Porsche and caused the hidden roof to slide out from the edge of the trunk and lock to the windshield.

He didn't wish his father dead, but the church needed a succession plan. The Reverend had grown obese and drank too much. But when he died, Morgan planned to take control and install a good-looking mouthpiece that could whip the crowd into a frenzy like his father. However, he needed the new face of the church to only answer to him.

But unless he took care of this infernal device and the buyer, all his careful plans might be dashed by some technology designed by the devil.

He pressed a second button on the dash and peered into the rearview mirror, looking at his red-tinged irises flecked with blue and yellow. Distinctive, his mother said. A gift from God, his mother said. But he didn't like them. He was too recognizable. Sunglasses helped. Outdoors and indoors.

He pulled out the cufflink from his left arm and rolled up the sleeve of his sharp cotton dress shirt. Old and white scars along with new angry red ones dotted close to his elbow and bicep. As the button finally clicked, he clenched his fist and pushed the red tip of the cigarette lighter into his skin. As the skin burned, he said a silent prayer and counted, gritting his teeth. One, two, three, and pulled the tip away. The sweet sharp pain of the discipline caught up to the branding and his eyes watered in the agony of atonement.

For some reason, he liked the smell of his flesh burning as it circulated inside the vehicle. A new round and red brand bubbled on his skin. He replaced the lighter with a shaking hand and put the car into drive.

If he hurried, he could catch the 6:00 p.m. flight to London. Then on to Amsterdam by morning. Already he felt better. The discipline was taking hold. Starting this spiritual practice was the best decision he'd ever made.

* * *

The Reverend sat down at his desk and leaned back in his chair. He pulled open a drawer and withdrew a crystal tumbler and a fifth of Jack Daniels. After pouring himself a few fingers, he called a number on his cell phone.

"William's on his way to Amsterdam. I need to know everything he's doing, when he's doing it, and who he's doing it to. You have full discretion to use who and what you need to get me that information."

He ended the call and sipped from the glass. As a boy, William lied about getting in trouble at school and that unfortunate situation with that young girl. Both incidents cost him a lot of money to keep quiet. He'd hoped William's time in the army had forced him to outgrow his adolescence, but perhaps not. Parents want to trust their children and put their faith in them, but with William, he wasn't sure if he could.

CHAPTER EIGHT

Amsterdam Red Light District—3:00 a.m.

The refrigerator-sized Lenny pulled a wool cap over his shaved head and used a tiny awning to shield his wide body from the falling snow. He scratched at the spidery tattoo that rose from under his shirt up the side of his face and swore at the cold. They hadn't made a decent score in several days. Snatching that kid from that hooker didn't pay much either.

Time to move to Ibiza or Nice. Better weather. More money.

His skinny olive-skinned friend, Hassan, stomped his heavy army boots behind him.

Without turning around Lenny asked, "Anything?"

"Tonight is for shit." Hassan said, "Nobody's round. No tourists. No drug heads. No gypsies."

"It's too God-damned cold." Lenny zipped up his coat. "Do you think you are in Hawaii?"

The Arab smiled and zipped his jacket closer to the top, but his white T-shirt still showed.

"Happy now?"

Lenny said nothing. He was looking elsewhere. "Check that out."

Across the canal on Bloedstraat, a man wearing rubber boots and what looked like a cleaner's coat staggered down the snowy street. Every few steps he doubled over and screamed.

"Looks like the loony truck missed one tonight," Hassan said.

"Nah…he looks like a derelict."

"My friend," Hassan grabbed Lenny's shoulder, "Let's see if a derelict has any money for our retirement fund."

Grunting, Lenny pushed off the wall and followed behind the Arab. The derelict turned and disappeared into another street.

* * *

David staggered down the cobblestones as large patches of color burst like fireworks in front of him. Buildings and landmarks appeared blurred and out of focus.

A translucent woman blocked his path then evaporated. He shook his head trying to rid himself of the visions, but it didn't help. He trusted nothing and kept going.

To an unknown destination.

He stepped into a stench of rotting blood and the buzz of swarms of flies. Daggers of pain sliced into him. He doubled over, his skull exploding.

And then. Silence. Nothing. No sounds. No smells. No pain.

Standing now, his image reflected from a shop window. He didn't recognize his face.

What the hell was going on?

A large and ancient building stood guard over the street he navigated. A church or maybe a sanctuary. A sign said *Oude Kerk*. Old Church. How did he know that? The church stood dark and empty. No sanctuary for him tonight.

A block away, it started. Again. The rancid smell of a dead body. A whiff of C4. The tang of cordite. His arms and legs started shaking as a wave of tremors coursed through his body. Vertigo hit him and he lost his balance and landed hard on the cobblestones.

He didn't move. He needed time. Time to close his eyes. Time to go to sleep. Sleeping forever would stop the visions and stop the pain.

Open your eyes.

The voice was back.

He blinked, and a giant shiver kicked him awake. Above him, a lone star in a patch of clear darkness caught his attention. Something else too. Something bright. Another light. Red this time. From a window high above. Red light filtering down from a window.

All the buildings above him glowed red. Red meant warmth. Red meant love. Red meant salvation. He willed his eyes closed. If he kept still, he'd drift back into the delicious sleep.

Get up, the voice said.

No. He wanted to sleep.

Get up! the voice ordered.

He stood and steadied himself against a wall. Behind him, the sounds of heavy boots scraped on the pavement.

Fear licked at his gut and he staggered into a narrow-bricked alley. The boots followed him, the scrapes echoing off the walls growing louder. He had to keep going. He had to keep moving.

A voice in front of him talked. A voice stinking of cigarettes. He recoiled. The voice was familiar, but he couldn't place it.

The image in front sharpened. Two men. One brown with shiny hair and skinny like a spider. A wide one like a truck behind the spider. Both in leather. The skinny spider had a white chest. Peppery long legs of a bigger spider climbed up the wider one's neck. The skinny spider reached out and grabbed him.

He was a spectator, watching everything play out of sync. The camera was not center. The camera focused on the red light at the end of the alley. He wanted to return to the red. The reek of tobacco got worse, but he only saw the red.

* * *

Lenny watched Hassan grab the derelict and say, "Look at me, asshole. I said, *look* at me!" Hassan tried to turn him, but the derelict resisted moving.

"Let's go. He's a nobody," Lenny said.

Hassan stared at the man. "He looks familiar. Doesn't he?"

Lenny leaned against the cold wall. "I don't remember."

"Shit! I've got it. It's that kid we picked up for that American asshole. Remember his hair?"

Lenny said, "Lots of people have long hair. He looks different. Check his pockets."

Hassan dug into the left derelict's coat and pulled out a dirty putty knife. "What were you going to do with this, shit for brains?"

The derelict ignored him and kept looking off into the distance.

"What's this?" Hassan grabbed for a white envelope in the other pocket. Instead, the derelict deflected Hassan's hand, grabbed his wrist and, in a quick motion, twisted backwards, dropping Hassan on his ass.

"Son of a bitch!" Hassan yelled.

Lenny unfolded his arms, but Hassan said, "Back off, this is my show." The Arab pushed himself up, snapped open a switchblade and faced the derelict.

"Hand over the envelope, asshole!" Hassan scythed the knife back and forth, but the derelict didn't flinch.

"Okay. Enough playing around." He switched hands and sliced the blade across the derelict's torso, but the man shifted right, grabbed Hassan's wrist, and twisted him to the ground again. Lenny heard something snap as the knife clinked to the ground and Hassan screamed.

"He broke my arm! Kill him! Kill him!"

The derelict kicked the knife down the alley but turned to look back toward the red light.

Lenny pushed off from the wall and came at him full speed. The derelict twisted, grabbed Lenny by his leather jacket and drove him face first into the bricks.

Hassan scrambled after the knife and charged with the blade in his left hand. The derelict parried the weapon, slamming an elbow into Hassan's nose. Grabbing the knife, he spun and rammed the blade deep into Hassan's chest. The Arab fell to the ground in a heap.

"Asshole!" Lenny stood up, blood pouring from his smashed nose. He pulled a long thin knife from under his coat and said, "Try that stuff on me again!"

The derelict stood statue still. Then as Lenny swept the knife in a wide arc, he leapt close and grabbed Lenny's arm. Lenny pulled the knife back and sliced into the derelict's neck. Growling, Lenny lunged with the knife, but the man pivoted, grabbed Lenny's wrist, and pulled the knife across his side, gutting him. Lenny screamed and fell to the ground, blood and guts leaking out on the cobblestones.

* * *

Blood dripped from David's hands and neck, rapid fire images and changing emotions now gone. Two bodies lay splayed on the ground in front of him, both dead. It wasn't real. It couldn't be real. Nothing was real.

But he knew everything was. He looked for help but saw only darkness and a light glimmering from a streetlamp. He stood immobile. Stuck in the moment. He didn't know what to do.

Then he did.

After wiping his hands across the skinny man's white T-shirt, leaving thick strokes of red, he yanked off the man's leather jacket and slipped his arms in it. A steel band tightened around his head again as he walked out of the alley towards the red light. He staggered forward as the pain spiked. Then he saw her. Above him, a shape bathed in red looking down from heaven. An outline of an angel.

Her golden hair and alabaster skin shining in the night sky. He prayed to the angel for help. Take the pain away. He watched her in silence as she stared at him, not frowning, or smiling. Just looking.

As he relaxed in her presence, the pain spiked and, with a scream, he collapsed to the ground.

CHAPTER NINE

Amsterdam—6:30 a.m.

Fitz entered the back door of Reynolds' building and surveyed the scene. The clinic was a mess.

He stepped around the broken glass and streaks of blood on the recovery room floor. Dr. Pirani held a bag of ice to his chin as the nurse applied a bandage to his forehead. Reynolds stood to the side with a cell phone to his ear. Wyatt, the head of security, was gone.

This situation keeps on getting better and better.

"I don't give a shit for your conditions. I need the loop closed today." Reynolds snapped the phone shut. The veins on his forehead bulged.

"It looks like the procedure worked," Fitz said.

"You got that right," Reynolds said.

Fitz walked over to the counter and stood up an overturned tray of vials.

"Don't touch anything," Dr. Pirani said.

"As you wish." Fitz turned to Reynolds. "What happened?"

"He escaped. That's what happened," Reynolds said.

"But we don't know why he became violent," Dr. Pirani said. He removed the ice from his face displaying a swollen and red contusion.

"Maybe you made a mistake, and the kid was high on PCP when he snatched him," Fitz said.

"We tested for that and it came back negative."

"Maybe the witch's brew you injected into him induced psychosis," Fitz said.

"No. He was lucid and in control. I saw it in his eyes."

Reynolds said. "If it wasn't drugs or a drug reaction, what else could it be?"

"Brooks could have done this easily if he was still alive," Fitz mused. "If the kid gained his memories, maybe he received his skills as a bonus."

Reynolds jammed his finger at the doctor. "Asshole! You told me this was foolproof!"

"All my simulations showed…"

"Screw you and your simulations. We only wanted the last thirty seconds of his memory, not his whole fucking life!"

The doctor grimaced and put the ice back to his chin.

"It seems we have a difference of opinion," Fitz said. "The doctor says it worked and that's why this happened. But I can see there's an argument for the other point of view."

Reynolds said "Okay, doctor. Let us imagine that your genius is untarnished and that all the money I've been paying you has been worth it. How much time do we have?"

Dr. Pirani grabbed a handful of paper from the floor and dug out a sheet covered in handwritten notes.

"After seven days, the chemical we used becomes inert."

Fitz asked, "What happens on the eighth day?"

The doctor looked down at his feet and then back to the broken equipment.

"What could happen, asshole?" Reynolds said.

"He might forget everything, or remember everything, or he could die."

"So, you don't know a damn thing," Reynolds said. He turned to Fitz. "Let's say the boy has your man's memory. Where would he go?"

"It's not so much where he would go; it's what he would do," Fitz said.

"Excuse me?"

"You have information on me, but I suspect you don't know much about Brooks. He's former CIA and was resourceful." Fitz looked at Reynolds in the eyes. "But if he's being hunted, he's not very forgiving."

"What's his likely course of action?"

"First he'll try and gain control over the situation and look for a safe place to hide out for a while."

"And second?"

"He'll seek as you Americans call it, 'payback.'"

"What do we do now?" Dr. Pirani asked.

"I need him found," Reynolds said. "He's nearly naked, and it's cold out. He's huddled under a rock somewhere and there's a chance he will remember what the East German shit told your man." Reynolds got up and walked around the room. "We need the package I bought from Vogler."

"He expected Brooks to deliver it to Paris, then it has to be somewhere between here and Paris," Fitz said.

Reynolds shook his head. "We need to focus and find the boy."

"A hospital check would be the first order," Fitz said.

"Already on it," Reynolds said. "I sent Wyatt for some reinforcements, but I'd like you to help."

"...and what if the other party finds him first?"

"The other party thinks their problem was solved," Reynolds said.

"What if they discover the operation is still active?"

Reynolds looked at Fitz for a long moment and said. "We need to find him before that happens."

CHAPTER TEN

Amsterdam City Hospital—3rd floor

He heard breathing. Rhythmic. Machine-like. A Darth Vader sound. Like someone scuba diving.

Where was he?

Lying on a bed. Rough sheets covered him. His blond hair hung in front of his face. He tried to rub his eyes, but handcuffs attached to the hospital bed stopped him. He tried moving his legs. Wide leather straps held his legs in place. A hog trussed up for slaughter.

Where was he?

Single memories burst like fireworks into his consciousness. Young people sweating and laughing. Music, but he couldn't tell what kind. The cold walls of a jail cell. But the memories were out of focus and disconnected.

The sheets were sandpaper rough. Was he in jail? Would a jail have sheets? The memory swam past him again. He only saw the ripples after.

A large bandage pulled the skin on his neck. He'd been hurt. Another fragment swam by. This time he saw two dead bodies and a knife. Nothing else.

Normal memories were links in a chain. A toy links to a child that links to a mother. His memories weren't linked. Each one stopped cold.

"*Goeiemorgen*, how you are feeling?" A blonde woman in a white outfit appeared beside his bed. A nurse.

"Where am I?" he said. The words sounded odd. His head hurt.

She smiled. "You're in the hospital."

That made sense. Hospital.

"What city?"

She smiled again, "Amsterdam."

He remembered Amsterdam, but not why he was there.

"Why am I restrained?"

"You can ask the doctor," she said.

Across the room, a winter morning sun streamed through a streaky window. In the bed beside him the source of the Darth Vader breathing. An old man connected to a machine. With all the tubes and wires connected to him, he looked like a broken string puppet.

"Do you remember anything from last night?" the nurse asked.

A voice in his head said, *say nothing*.

He hesitated for a second. "No."

A man in a white coat and grey hair appeared from the door. The doctor. "You were admitted bleeding and suffering from hypothermia." He grabbed a clipboard from the foot of the bed and flipped the pages.

"I don't remember anything. The last thing I…" David looked back towards the window as if seeing outside would help.

"Were you in a fight or did someone try and rob you?"

An image of blood flashed in front of him. Along with the sight of a knife. A hunting knife.

"I don't know."

The doctor traced the chart with his finger. "You weren't carrying any ID. What's your name?"

The voice inside whispered, *Quiet.*

"Well, I…"

Quiet! the voice said.

"I don't remember. Everything is still fuzzy," David said.

"The type of wound indicates you were sliced with a knife or a razor. It wasn't deep, but you lost blood. Another inch to the left and we wouldn't be having this conversation."

David rubbed his temples. Sliced with a razor. Razor. The word echoed in his head like it meant something.

The doctor asked, "What's the matter?"

"I've got a headache."

"We didn't check for a concussion, but that might explain the amnesia."

"Do you remember hitting your head?" the doctor asked.

"No."

"Did you use drugs last night?"

His heart spiked with the question. The anger shocked him, and he took a couple of seconds to calm down. He didn't know why.

"I don't use drugs."

"Are you a dealer?"

"No. I don't sell drugs either."

Frustration built inside him. Both at being questioned and having no real answers.

The doctor stared at him, looked at the clipboard, but said nothing.

"Why am I restrained?" David asked.

"Based on your condition last night, it is standard protocol. We test for drugs that could make you violent. Like PCB or crystal meth perhaps?" The doctor squinted at the paper.

David saw a smear of dried blood on the sheet and wondered. "Did I have any drugs in my system?"

"No," the doctor said. "That's the funny part. You were clean. Sparkling clean in fact. Not even THC, which is surprising, considering how you were dressed and your condition."

David closed his eyes and tried to will the pain away. Names and places skirted on the edge of his memory. But like fireflies, they evaporated. "What was I wearing?"

"A leather jacket that didn't fit you and a janitor's coat and some kind of scrubs like from a hospital. You had rubber boots on your feet. Does that help?"

"No. I can't remember anything." David raised his chained hands. "Can you let me off the leash?" The doctor looked over his glasses with a smile.

"Well…without further tests, it's hard to tell if you are telling the truth about your use of drugs. Your arms are clean, so you aren't injecting at least." He pointed to a wound inside of David's arm. "However, that looks to be a recent IV puncture. Have you given blood in the last few days?"

"Not that I know of." Everything seemed out of focus. Fuzzy. Like he'd misplaced his car keys. His name was here somewhere. He had to remember where he put it.

"I don't think you are a danger to yourself. Nurse, please unlock him."

David asked, "What happens now?"

"Because your injury seemed the result of a weapon, the police have been notified. With all the cutbacks, they should be here in a few hours. Maybe they can find out if someone is looking for you."

David thought for a second. He was in a hospital recovering from a mugging the night before by an attacker he couldn't remember. He didn't even know why he was in Amsterdam. Did he live there? Or did he live anywhere? What happened last night?

He had to find out.

"Doctor?"

"Yes?"

"Where did you find me?"

The doctor turned and hung the chart back on the bed.

"That's the interesting part. A working girl called the ambulance. She said you collapsed outside her brothel." The doctor smiled. "Perhaps you just were looking for love in the wrong place."

David said nothing.

"As we've been talking, I've been trying to place your accent. American perhaps?"

David looked towards the window again. American seemed close but not quite.

"No, I don't think I'm American."

"But your Dutch is excellent, just like a native. Do you have any idea where you learned it?"

"I don't speak Dutch."

The nurse and doctor both laughed.

"What do you think we've been speaking all this time?"

David frowned.

"Well then. As you ponder trying to understand how you could speak Dutch without knowing the language." The doctor moved a tray over to David's bed. "Please. Enjoy your breakfast."

* * *

David wolfed down the orange juice, scrambled eggs, and toast off the small tray. His neck and body still hurt, but at least the handcuffs were off. The doctor told him that his neck injury wasn't serious; they'd used glue to stop the bleeding. The nurse had pulled a curtain around the other patient.

"Mr. Heysel, we need to keep the respirator on for another day before we can let you breathe on your own. We've given you something to make you sleepy. You need lots of rest."

The nurse emerged from the curtain and handed pills and a glass of water to David. "Here are tablets for your headache. They should help. Try to get some sleep. I'll check on you later." She left the room, and the door closed behind her.

David swallowed the pills and laid back on the bed thinking about the conversation. The doctor said he'd been cut by a razor. That word meant something. Razor. More than for shaving, something else. Again, a memory floated past. This one was important.

Get out. The voice again.

David ignored it. He probably hit his head last night.

Get out!

His heart rate spiked, and his mouth dried up. After a long breath, he took stock. He was warm and safe in a hospital in Amsterdam. What could happen?

Get out now!

He yanked back the sheets and swung his legs over the bed, bare feet hitting the icy floor. His hand pulled the IV out of his arm before he could stop himself. His muscles were moving on their own, without his conscious thought. He gritted his teeth and tried to force himself back into bed, but instead, the effort shook him like he was having a seizure.

Okay, this is weird. I must have hit my head. His body jerked towards the door. This would not work. Time to try something else. As his leg moved, he willed it to move. When his arm moved, he went with it. The more he gave into the movements, the smoother they became. At the door, he peered through the window. A nurse's station guarded the end of the hallway. The EXIT door was across from him.

He searched the room and found a stash of clothes from Darth neighbor. A pair of dirty jeans. An old T-shirt. A heavy wool sweater stinking of cigarettes. As he pulled on everything, he seemed like he was forced to learn a new dance, but backwards.

Dance.

An alarm rang in his head. Dance. Something to do with dance. But the thought evaporated like steam from a kettle. He tried taking other steps, but as he moved, everything felt rough and unnatural. He found a pair of dirty running shoes in the closet and jammed his feet into them. The shoes were too big, but he didn't care.

One last thing. He reached into the closet and found a bag with a leather jacket. The jacket didn't look familiar. But his hand reached into the inside pocket and withdrew an envelope that he stuffed into the back of the baggy jeans. He didn't know why he did that.

He cracked the door open to the hallway and stopped. Down near the nurse's station, two men in suits talked to the nurse sitting in front of a computer screen. Police or work. He didn't need a voice to tell him to get out anymore.

CHAPTER ELEVEN

Amsterdam Music Theater—10:00 a.m.

A thin sun poured into the high windows of the rehearsal studio. A mirror along the long wall reflected the sixty National Ballet of Canada dancers readying themselves for the morning's class. The pianist sat at a grand piano and Margo, the ballet mistress, smiled at everyone.

Portable ballet bars stood perpendicular from the mirrors. Eight lines of dancers faced Margo with their left hands on the barre. The principal dancers stood together, then the soloists, the second soloists, then the corps du ballet. The pecking order was absolute.

Sophie had two minutes before the class started. She dropped her bag near the pile of others by the door and pulled up her wool leggings. March in Amsterdam was as cold as in Toronto. Chilly with a hope of an early spring, but not today. She and Celeste wanted to explore the city, but with class in the morning, rehearsal after lunch and a performance in the evening, they were exhausted by the end of each day. Maybe on Saturday before the train to Paris, they could squeeze in a bus tour. She couldn't wait to visit Paris, but she'd heard the Parisians looked down at the Québécois, because of their "pedestrian" accents and pronunciations. But the first one to try would see what happens when you piss off a girl from Montreal.

David found that out. The hard way. He gave her the talk. The end-of-the-relationship-let's-just-be-friends talk and it hurt. So much she'd flung that damn book at him and caught him in the head.

Good. No one could say she wasn't passionate. But her heart and body still ached for that little anglophone shit. But she hated to admit, he might be right. A serious relationship between dancers meant trouble for one or both. So instead of pining for him, she'd use the resolve that got her through ballet school and put her anger into her dance.

As she and Celeste took their position and prepared for the class, she didn't see David or Razor.

Strange. Where were they?

Margo said good morning and started the warmup. Not complex, but just enough varied movement to get the dancer's blood flowing. The ballet mistress nodded her head at the pianist and the music started.

Throughout the class as they did their pliés, tendus, and glissés, she expected the door to fly open and the boys rush in, apologize, and join the class.

They never showed.

"Where are they? They can't miss class!" Celeste whispered behind her.

"Maybe they went out drinking last night," Sophie said.

"David doesn't drink," Celeste said. "He's allergic to alcohol."

The class continued with the ballet mistress giving more challenging exercises as the dancer's muscles warmed up. The room warmed too, but Sophie couldn't tell if it was the air or her body.

As the class stopped for a five-minute water break, the main door swung open. The artistic director, Robert Lester, appeared with his trademark white sweater, white T-shirt, and white pants. A talented dancer in his younger years, Lester's body aged, and he moved into choreography. Now he ran the show.

And was a huge asshole.

"Good morning, everyone, I hope you all slept well as we have a tough rehearsal planned."

The company stayed silent, not wanting to encourage him. A few months ago, one of the principal dancers talked back to him in jest and he tore a strip off her in front of the entire company.

No one wanted to be the second one.

"Everyone accounted for I trust?" he smiled and nodded at the ballet mistress.

"We're missing two," she said.

"Who?"

"Razor and Knight aren't here," she said.

"Where the hell are they? Does anyone know?" No one said anything. "They better be at rehearsal or I will send them both back to Canada."

Lester looked down the rows as if the men were hiding somewhere. "Please carry on, Margo. I'll be here in the afternoon." He grabbed a water bottle and swept out of the room.

"The white tornado has left the building," Celeste whispered. She put her hand to her mouth to stifle a laugh, just as the pianist started the next exercise.

Sophie turned to the door. She didn't want to laugh. Where were David and Razor?

CHAPTER TWELVE

Amsterdam Hospital

Asher Fitzsimmons and a contractor Reynolds supplied named Marcus stood in front of the nurse's desk. Fitz estimated his new partner was half his age, but twice his weight. Coupled with a lack of a neck and flattop haircut he looked like an American football player in a tailored suit. No last name. It didn't matter. Marcus would work.

"Can I help you?" the nurse asked. She didn't look up from the computer screen.

"We're looking for a friend. We think he might have been admitted to the hospital. He drank too much at a party last night and we are trying to find him," Fitz said.

"What's his name?" The nurse's English was perfect.

"David Knight. But he lost his wallet, so he might be listed as a John Doe." Fitz leaned over the desk. "He's blond, young, and good-looking. Very fit."

The nurse paused for a second and looked up to the ceiling as if she recognized the description. "It was busy last night. We've had a few John Doe's in the last twenty-four hours."

The nurse scanned her computer screen then looked up to the left as if she was about to say something but didn't. Fitz thought without Marcus hulking beside him, he'd have more luck getting the information. As it was, Marcus hovered over the nurse's desk like a small moon.

"If you'll take a seat, I'll notify the attending physician to come and talk to you."

"Don't worry. We will just have a little walk through the ward and not bother the overworked doctor."

"You have to wait…"

Both men dashed down the hallway, glancing into each room. The younger man was in front. Fitz turned and saw the nurse pick up the phone.

"We only have a few minutes," Fitz said.

The first room held a kid the right age but with dark hair. A bandage wrapped around his head and he was unconscious.

"Not him," Fitz said.

They cleared the other rooms in ten seconds. At the last room, an older man lay on a bed hooked to a machine. The other bed was empty. An unhooked IV-line dripped liquid on the floor near the bed. He also noticed a fresh smear of blood on the floor.

"He was here and he's bleeding," Fitz said. "We don't have a lot of time."

* * *

David slipped across the hallway to the stairs. He saw a man at the nurse's desk that seemed familiar, but he didn't get a clear look at his face. The other was a gorilla in a new suit. David turned and as he was about to take the first step down, his body spun and leaped upwards instead.

He struggled for several seconds then gave in to the jerky movements. Someone or something was pulling his strings. As he climbed the stairs, a spark of an idea to escape formed in his mind. He shook it off as crazy, but the more he fought it, like the stairs, the louder the idea became. With no effort, he bounded upwards and realized his legs were Olympian strong. But as he made it to the first landing, the pain hit him again. After a second, he pushed himself upwards again reaching the fourth-floor hallway. Looking down he noticed drops of red following him.

He was bleeding.

* * *

The man known as Marcus stood beside Fitz and took up most of the doorway. As hired muscle, he was to follow Fitz's orders to the letter. However, the man seemed young and not engaged with the mission.

In his career, Fitz had come across agents and contactors that he didn't trust when he first met them. A feeling perhaps. Some people would call it intuition. Most cases, Fitz had been correct in his assessment.

He'd made the same assessment with Marcus.

He didn't trust him. Not for a minute.

"You search a floor above and I will search below. We have maybe five minutes before hospital security shows up with questions, Fitz said. "If you find him, call me. I might be able to get him out of here with a minimum of fuss."

"Roger that." Marcus turned and vaulted up the stairs.

"And don't engage. Your job is just to locate."

As Fitz descended to the 2nd floor, he heard in his earpiece, "Affirmative. Entering the fourth floor."

Fitz said, "I'm on two."

He found the second floor was laid out the same as the floor above. Patient rooms dotted each side and a nurse's station at the end. A supply closet and a small kitchen half way down. If the dancer came down to this floor, he'd be hiding. Possibly under a bed or in a closet. If he tried escaping, the surveillance Wyatt had deployed outside would see him.

An outside grab would be more public, but faster. Grabbing the dancer inside would be problematic unless Fitz could talk sense into him. He hoped that Marcus the Ox wouldn't try anything stupid.

* * *

David skirted the edge of the wall and looked for a room to enter. He wiped the blood from hands on to his shirt. He had a plan coming on to this floor but stopped and shook his head. The plan that was so clear a minute ago evaporated. People were after him. Police or someone worse. He needed an exit. Why didn't his body take the stairs down? It made little sense.

Some images flashed in his memory. Frames from a movie. He fought a man. No, two men. He stuck the man with a knife into the soft parts. Liver, intestines, stomach. He remembered the up-close stink. Cigarettes, bad breath, and the coppery smell of death.

Memories of a bad dream? Based on what the doctor said, he wasn't remembering a dream. He'd killed two men last night. The doctor also said the police would be coming to see him, but the men downstairs weren't the police. He could tell at one glance. He didn't know why he knew that.

Who were they?

And why did he go up the damn stairs?

Morning in a hospital. He heard blaring televisions. Radios. People talking. Some crying. He wanted no sound. An empty room. The third room from the end sat quiet, but not empty. Inside, a man the size of a whale slept on an oversize hospital bed. Tubes and wires radiated out of his body, connected to machines. An IV bag hung on a stainless-steel stand. Red flowers in vases dotted the room. A thick Bible with a magnifying glass lay open on a table. A peaceful setting if you were waiting to die.

David felt anything but peaceful. He shivered as if he was cold. Fear mixed with shock perhaps. Someone was trying to kill him. He knew it. He felt it. But didn't know how he knew that.

He shouldn't be in this stupid hospital to begin with. While he searched the drawers and the closet for something useful, he noticed the Bible was open to a page and talked about King David. Slayer of Goliath.

David.

Something clicked like a key in a lock. David. Clouds pulled back and he remembered his name was David. He was certain of that. He remembered someone else saying his name. When was that? Last night?

Another name pushed upwards like an echo. He had a thread of the name, but it flew away like a lost bird. He pushed it out of his mind. Nothing else mattered other than to stay alive.

The window only opened a crack. If he broke it, he couldn't make it to the ground.

No way to escape and no place to hide.

What a stupid plan.

The pain rose and jammed a point into his brain. As he breathed through it, a glimmer of an idea formed. Just flashes at first and then a more complete thought. He shrugged it off, but image focused sharply like a camera lens. He took the whale's IV bag from the rolling stand and hooked the bag to the top of the bed. The whale didn't stir.

He only had two minutes.

* * *

Marcus moved his large bulk from room to room in rapid succession following the spatters of blood. All the doors were closed, but he heard ambient noise. Some television. A few conversations.

"Security will be up soon. You need to hurry," Fitz said in his ear.

"Roger. Clearing the floor now," Marcus said.

Fitz did the same, perhaps a little slower than his partner. "No sign on the second floor," Fitz said.

The next room's door was open a crack and Marcus smelled a faint stink of cigarettes. The same as the room downstairs where they found the blood.

Through the opening, he watched an enormous man on a bed stuck with tubes breath with a rattled cadence. The dancer was inside or had escaped altogether. He pulled his CZ from his coat, screwed a silencer on the barrel, and chambered a bullet.

"Have you found him yet?" the old man's voice boomed in his ear.

"No." Marcus unplugged his earpiece. He didn't have much time.

It wouldn't take too long.

Pushing the door open wide with his left hand, he held the pistol low and at his side with his right. "Hello, dancer," he said.

From the side of the door, Marcus caught a flash of silver slice down and felt the searing pain as a steel pole snapped his wrist. The Czech pistol fell to the ground with a clatter. The metal tube jabbed upwards and glanced off the side of his head. He shook it off and twisted to use his left hand as a battering ram at his attacker.

Instead, the steel pole stabbed deep into the soft part of his neck skewering him through his throat.

* * *

David jammed the rod deeper as the gorilla clawed at the tube jutting into his neck.

A hot jet of blood sprayed out and hit the floor. David kept pushing as the gorilla fought, but the metal rod took its toll. The gorilla sagged down to the floor as David levered the tube up and smashed the big man's face into the tile floor.

The whale stirred and coughed. David grabbed the gun, stuffed it into his shirt and walked out of the room. The bandage on his neck was slick with blood. He needed to fix that, but he had to escape first.

He slipped into a supply closet across the hall and closed the door. Ten seconds later, he heard the faint squeaks of rubber soles on a tile floor. Short. Quick. A nurse maybe. A man made longer steps, bigger sounds, rubber soles or not. She'd find the dead man soon. The gorilla wasn't a police officer. He was something else.

Linen and sheets sat stacked up like cordwood on the shelves next to him. Paper towels lined up like soldiers. He secured a towel around his neck as an impromptu tourniquet and wrapped heavier linens around his hands and forearms. More images dripped into his consciousness. His name was David, but a ghost name whispered behind it. David, he said under his breath. In his mind, he heard another.

Jonathan.

Jonathan? Who is the hell is Jonathan? David felt right. Jonathan felt wrong. A death mask, an image. "Who am I?" he asked. *I'm a killer,* came back.

A torrent of emotion welled up inside him of what he did. Ignoring the pain and pushing the sadness away, he wiped his eyes, opened the laundry chute, and climbed in feet first. As he pushed his wrapped arms out to the sides and let himself drop, darkness closed all around him. He hoped the cleaning staff hadn't emptied the laundry hampers yet.

* * *

The nurse had just started her rounds when a cacophony of patient alarms rang at her station. By room 404, she stopped. A slick of red spilled from under the door. Inside, a large man lay face down skewered with IV pole in his neck. The room's other occupant was awake, his eyes wide and pushing the alarm button with fat fingers. She drew a breath, stepped around the dead man, and grabbed the room's phone.

* * *

David jammed his arms and feet against the sides of the metal chute and descended. He figured most laundry chutes were smooth inside as to not catch any of the dirty linen on the way down. Great for the laundry. Bad for him. He slipped and lurched along, trying to slow his descent as he fell to the basement.

* * *

Fitz stood outside the second-floor stairway. Marcus had gone silent which wasn't good. Through his earpiece, he heard Wyatt's voice.

"There's been an incident. The police have been called."

"What happened?"

"A nurse found a dead man on the 4th floor and they are looking for the murderer. You need to abort."

"Any description?"

"The man was wearing a suit," Wyatt said.

Marcus. Based on his size, he should have been able to handle himself. Brooks wouldn't kill someone without provocation. He was supposed to find the dancer, not kill him.

Stupid bastard.

The operation was spinning out of control, but the screw up did confirm one thing. Based on the altercation at the clinic and now at the hospital, the memory implant was successful.

Not a good scenario to have Brooks as an enemy.

Fitz adjusted his collar, took the elevator to the first floor, and walked out through the revolving front doors of the hospital. As he walked out, he spoke into the hidden microphone. "The situation has changed. Please re-deploy along the perimeter of the hospital."

* * *

Close to the bottom of the chute, David held his breath as the odor of disinfectant and body wastes filled the metal chimney. Crashing into the laundry cart feet first, the force tipped the basket and slammed his knee onto the hard floor. His neck was slick with blood. He tried standing, but his leg buckled in pain.

He hoisted himself on the fallen basket and stood up. The room felt humid and his body felt raw and exposed. He couldn't endure this much longer.

Industrial washers and dryers filled one wall. Heavy steam pipes hung from the ceiling and out the hallway. He must be deep in the bowels of the hospital. Subbasement even. Every cop show on television had the hospital's laundry and the morgue at the same level. Dirty sheets and dead bodies. He'd seen the laundry. He didn't want to visit the morgue.

Grabbing a clean-looking sheet, he ripped a piece off and held it to his neck. Everything hurt, but at least the headache had diminished. Two men attacked him last night and a big ape just tried to kill him ten minutes ago. How did he defend himself? He didn't know how to fight.

Moreover, what about the voice? The voice protected him or seemed like it.

He stuck the gun he took from the gorilla into the back of his pants, the metal barrel cool against his skin. He thought carrying a gun would feel strange, but it was the most natural thing he had done all day.

He limped towards the door. The room was at the dead end of a long hallway with overhead pipes radiating moist heat. Reaching into his pants pocket, he found a cheap LCD watch without a strap.

8:15 a.m.

Time to go.

Beside the laundry room, a door sat ajar. He glanced inside. After two seconds, he walked in and closed the door.

CHAPTER THIRTEEN

The teaching hospital Onze Lieve Vrouwe Gasthuis or OLVG stood a few miles from the Amsterdam Centraal Station. A police station sat across the road from the ambulance entrance.

Asher Fitzsimmons exited the double doors and pulled the collar up on his coat. "Are you in position?" he said into his microphone.

Wyatt's voice came through his earpiece. "Yes."

Fitz wanted three men deployed on the streets around the hospital plus two in a car. Standard surveillance detail. One man sat inside a Middle Eastern café behind the hospital, the second and third stood on two opposite street corners. All men had a picture of the kid. They waited for a young man with long blond hair.

Two police officers exited the police station and ran across the road. They passed Fitz on the sidewalk and didn't give him a second glance. More police followed. Fitz crossed the tram rails embedded in the road and entered an idling black Peugeot. Wyatt drove, and Reynolds sat up front.

"Your contractor is dead, and the boy killed him. If he's still alive, he'll be looking for an exit," Fitz said.

Reynolds looked through a small set of binoculars and held a cell phone up to his ear.

"This has been royally fucked up," Reynolds said.

"Yes," Fitz said. "There's one of two outcomes. One, the police find and detain him. Or two, he escapes, and we find him. Both outcomes have consequences. Are you ready for either?"

Reynolds nodded but kept the binoculars focused on the front entrance.

* * *

Half-filled cardboard boxes and stacked paper forms filled the shelves. David dug through some boxes then stopped. What was he doing? He should just head to the lobby with his arms above his head and give himself up to the first Dutch police officer he saw. He just killed a man. Police should be swarming the place.

A nice sensible course of action.

No, the voice said.

He shook off the voice and thought about his next steps. Leave the room, find the stairs, and head to the lobby. He grabbed the doorknob, but his hand pulled back as if the handle was red-hot.

No!

Fear ripped through him as his muscles froze. He took a few breaths and his body relaxed.

Stalemate.

He couldn't go forward. He couldn't go backward. He twisted the black ring on his finger and stopped. The ring. The ring meant something or someone. Something for him to remember. Who gave him the ring? A gossamer-like memory appeared. Not formed, but he felt it. Trust. He needed to trust the voice. It wasn't implanted radio; it was more like intuition with a bad attitude.

And the voice made the choices. He had no real vote either way.

Taking a deep breath, he pawed through the boxes. After the first one, the pain ramped up and the two steel bands clamped hard around his head.

Driving his thumbs into his temples, he massaged and pushed as hard as he could. The ice picks backed off enough for him to continue.

From the boxes, he scrounged a pair of battle grey trousers with suspenders and a stained white shirt smelling moldy or worse.

He remembered something the gorilla said. *Hello, dancer.*

Dancer. A memory. Not made up or dreamed. A wave of recognition came over him. He remembered listening to a slow adagio and dancing with fluid and enfolding movements. The music in his head changed to allegro and his remembered dancing brisk and quick and lively. Then the perfumed smell of hairspray hit him. The dancers spray it on their hair like varnish. He knew that.

He was a dancer. A ballet dancer. The memories of dance class connected with rehearsals and auditions. Sweat. Muscle and joint pain. All of it. All at once.

His heart rose. It was just a matter of time before all his memories came back. But for right now, he had to focus on staying alive.

* * *

Muhammad Hakim straightened his back and leaned against his mop for a second. Known to others as Mr. Hakim: managers, doctors, nurses, security guards, even when the police stopped by, he was always Mr. Hakim. He liked that. The label gave him a dignity he'd never experienced in his homeland. Amsterdam was different. Open. Liberal. Fresh thoughts and fresh air. Unlike his place of birth.

As usual, he focused on the floor in front of him. Last night's snow dragged dirty footprints and scuff marks into the ER faster than he could clean them.

Since the start of his 6:00 a.m. shift, he had washed, mopped, and cleaned the floors and hallways of the first floor. He prided himself on keeping everything clean and dry. Clean from the dirt, the blood, and the fluids the patients would drag in. This morning, the only thing on the floor was water.

While mopping, he played a game to keep his mind sharp. He noticed everything. A few times he repeated the Arabic proverb *Ki nchouf ham el nass nansa hami*; when I think of other's misfortunes, I forget mine.

He was old, happy, and healthy except for his bad back.

His mop sloshed in the white bucket before he swung it to the tile. An old man, even older than him, appeared from a door to the basement and walked out to the clean side of the floor. Cloaked in a shabby black winter coat, he wore a wrinkled fedora over top a shock of dirty grey hair. A battered metal cane steadied his walk and his left hand hung limp against his body as if he'd had a stroke. He hobbled down the narrow hallway to the Emergency entrance as if oblivious to anyone else, past benches and chairs jammed full of women, children, and other aging patients.

Mr. Hakim wondered where he'd come from. A man with a cane takes the elevator. But he came up the stairs. Lost perhaps?

Ten meters from the large double exit doors, the old man stopped and bent over. Hakim recognized that stance; he was in pain. Pain from years of working hard at the same job day after day. Pain from a bad back or stomach trouble or gallstones or a gallbladder. Old age meant pain was always a companion.

The man straightened, tapped his cane to the tile, aiming towards the large exit doors.

Mr. Hakim rubbed his own back in solidarity, before swinging the mop into the bucket, swishing it through the murky water and taking another swipe at the dirty floor.

CHAPTER FOURTEEN

Shards of glass pushed again into David's temples. This time, all pain and no voice. He caught his breath and let the knives stop. A pattern was emerging. Intense burning for several seconds and then with some breathing, the needles would pull back. Maybe a schedule he could endure. But for how long?

He adjusted the brown wig he'd found in the boxes and touched the wad of gauze and cotton wrapped around half his face. He discovered bandages in the storeroom that he applied to the wound on his neck and came up with going with a full-on homeless look. Through one eye he watched as two Dutch constables talked to a tall man in a suit and long, dark overcoat near the exit doors. A detective or hospital security maybe?

His feet wanted to run to the door, but he stopped the movement and bought a little time.

What were his options? Raise his hands. Walk to the police and turn himself in. No heroics. He could do it. Explain everything or what he remembered of it. Throw himself on the mercy of the court.

He stood at the end of the corridor from the constables.

As he leaned on the single crutch, he hoped he looked like a charity case. As he moved in halting steps towards the door, sweat trickled down from under the old cancer wig he'd found in the storage room. Visitors entering the hospital with bouquets of flowers and baskets passed him on the way to loved ones. But at the exit, a line had formed as the two police subjected people leaving to a brief conversation before letting them leave.

He took another breath. His scalp itched like crazy.

An elevator near him chimed. Steel doors opened and an elderly woman in a wheelchair rolled out in front of him. A younger man in jeans and a down parka pushed the wheelchair. Grandson perhaps.

David let them pass and fell in behind tapping his crutch on the floor as he limped along towards the thinning line at the exit. The constable smiled and waved the woman and the man through. As he tried to follow, the police officer put out his hand.

"Sir, do you have any identification?"

Dutch again. He winced as the pain hit hard. The emergency doors opened and a third officer with a police dog entered the building.

The dog breezed past after first delivering a wet sniff to David's pant leg.

David looked up, his shoulders hunched to look beaten and a little crazy.

"Sir, did you understand the question?"

This was it. The end of the road. He took half a step back. No voice interrupted him this time. He prepared to put his hands against the wall. His head itched underneath the grimy wig. Maybe he should just pull it off and lie flat on the floor.

A voice behind said, "Johan, here let me help you."

David turned. The tall man who had talked to the police earlier was talking to him. Thin and lanky with sunken cheeks and a wonky eye. The eye looked real, but it didn't track like the other one. He draped his arm around David's shoulder, leaned towards the officer and flashed something David couldn't see.

The constable nodded and stood aside as the emergency doors parted, and the winter chill whipped the inside of the hospital. Fresh air. David steadied himself with the cane and tapped ahead on the sidewalk as he and the man walked out. The man still had his arm around David's shoulder.

"What do you want?" David asked. No warning of danger, but no great feeling of trust either. Was he going to jam a knife in his ribs? But as they walked to the street without urgency, his alarm evaporated. His encounter with the gorilla upstairs broadcast danger like a siren, but now the only feeling he had was mild irritation at not being able to give himself up.

The man helped him maneuver across the street and stayed silent until they reached the tram stop. A train approached from the next block.

The man said, "The tram will take you away from here. I understand you've had headaches. These may help." He pressed a bottle of pills and a transit card into David's hand.

The tram stopped, and the doors opened. David squeezed into one of the first seats and watched him disappear around a corner, as if he'd never existed.

As the tram pulled away from the stop, he swallowed two tablets from the bottle of pills dry. If the man intended to kill him, he wouldn't have just put him on a streetcar. As he relaxed enough for the pain to lessen, the last few minutes circled through his mind like an old film strip. He woke up, men came for him, he killed one, and escaped. A miraculous escape.

But why was anyone trying to kill him and why were others trying to help him? And what happened in the first place?

* * *

Arthur Westlake watched with his good eye as the streetcar pulled away from the curb. He dialed a number on his cell phone. Three beeps played into the earpiece.

"It's progressing. The test subject has done well. Better than I expected. We will see how far he goes," he said and ended the call.

CHAPTER FIFTEEN

Palo Alto, California

He sat in the big chair, leaned back with a glass of Jack in his hand. He clicked on the screen and HD images flickered in the darkness like firelight. The first shot was the Reverend standing on the Rock Star stage with his hands raised to the sky. The camera cut to a teary-eyed man and woman in the 4th row. The camera cut back to the Reverend.

Back in the chair alone in the room, he swallowed some Jack and felt the liquid burn all the way down.

On the screen, the Reverend lowered his hands. Rivers of men, women, and children dropped to their knees. From the chair, he pressed a button on the remote and through hidden speakers, his voice boomed. "Dear lord, before you today are drinkers, addicts, adulterers, thieves, and even murderers."

The report sat across in his lap. Revenues dropped last month. Even with the Liberian crisis, donations were down across the board. He dropped the page and pushed himself up on the arms of his chair, wincing as his gout burned like hellfire.

"Like all sinners, O Lord, they struggle with the devil's temptations." The Reverend raised his hands skyward. "But they are here today to enter into the kingdom of God as your humble servants." The camera zoomed to his crystal blue eyes looking out over the crowd.

"Make no mistake, we are here to commit ourselves in the war against the devil!"

The side camera close-up to the woman on the 4th aisle with swollen and red knees. Her crutches lay on the ground. She struggled to kneel and the helper on either side lowered her, touching her knees to the ground while her face contorted in agony.

The Reverend returned and used a fresh white handkerchief to wipe the sweat from his forehead. The cloth for sale after the show. "We are *ready*, O Lord. We are *ready!*"

"…and as we raise our hands in prayer to you." He raises his hands. "We commit to you, O Lord."

The crowd followed. "We commit to you, O Lord."

"Bless us, O Lord in our sacred…"

He clicked off the screen. He liked critiquing his performance, making small adjusts with his hands or eyes, but today he felt empty and he couldn't stand looking at these people anymore. These so-called followers of his. Wanting someone else to do the heavy lifting. Wanting someone else do the work that needed to be done. Wanting someone else to tell them what to believe.

He was sick of it.

He swallowed more of the Jack and felt the fire. His doctor said the alcohol wasn't good for him. *Doctor be damned*, he thought. His big toes, ankles, and knees burned with the pain radiating up to his hips. His drugs sat in a drawer out of reach.

His cell phone rang.

Gripping the edge of the chair, he didn't want to stand up. He didn't want to answer it. The phone kept ringing. He pulled himself forward past the pain, feeling around on the big desk until he found it and put it to his ear.

"Reverend? You asked for a report on your son as soon as possible," the voice scratched over the cell phone.

He sat back in the chair and took a deep breath. His feet were burning. "Yes. What is he doing? Is he taking care of the situation?" He looked out the window and saw the outline of the frame, but the pain clouded the center of his vision. He turned and focused on the statue of Jesus by the bookshelf. The Savior's features came back into focus.

"No, Reverend. He…he…"

"What is happening?" the Reverend asked.

"Your son engaged in debauchery through the night and a demon has gotten loose."

His jaw tightened, and he ground his teeth before slamming the glass down on the desk. "I don't understand. Morgan told me he had the buyer under surveillance."

"He did. However, he left it up to someone else. We saw the demon break out of the hospital and escape."

"Demon? What do you mean?"

"The demon carries the memories of the courier and the location of the device," the voice said.

The Reverend remembered what Morgan had said about memories. He didn't care about the specifics. He just wanted the thing cleaned up. Looking down at his glass he saw a single ice cube floated in what was left of the Jack Daniels.

"We've sent the information to you." The voice on the cell phone said.

"Thank you. You will be rewarded."

The Reverend ended the call and shifted his bulk over to the side of his desk. The gout flared to volcano level heat. Gritting his teeth, he managed to open his desk drawer and grabbed some antacids and a couple of Oxycontin. He swallowed them all with a chaser of Jack Daniels and burned a trail down his throat. He hated more than anything else incompetence. Especially his own. He pushed himself again and landed back into his chair. Closing his eyes, he pushed his hands together in prayer.

"Oh God, I've failed you. Please show me the way!"

Something made him open his eyes and turn to the window. The glop of clouds over the Valley pulled back revealing crisp stars of a California winter night. He squinted and saw it. A group of shooting stars. Bits of rock from the heavens catching fire and blazing into nothingness. For several seconds the display continued. This was the sign he looked for. He prayed to God and he had answered. Hallelujah! The meteor shower ended, and he turned back to his desk and grabbed his cell phone. He knew what he had to do.

He had been shown the way.

CHAPTER SIXTEEN

Amsterdam—Sofitel Hotel, Room 202

The city woke to a flat and grey Dutch sky, but not all its visitors had bothered to get up. The cell phone vibrated on the mahogany table beside the bed. The vibration switched to a loud ring. From underneath the white duvet, Morgan's hand felt around for his cell phone. He rubbed his eyes and squinted at the number on the tiny LCD screen.

He touched screen and said, "One minute." He pressed mute and yanked back the duvet. A young woman with hard tits and messy blonde hair pulled her head up from the pillow.

"You need to leave now," Morgan said.

"What time is it, lover? Is it too early for another one?"

"You need to go." He pulled some euros from his wallet and handed them to her. "Here's your money."

The girl sat up. Her breasts and her body moved as one. She smiled then noticed the self-inflicted scars on his arm from taking the discipline. "I didn't notice those last night. Were you in an accident?" she traced her finger on the scars on his arms.

"You need to go now," he said.

"Sure, lover, I'm just going to grab a quick shower. I'm all *dirty* from last night." Her eyes twinkled.

"I think not."

He grabbed a red dress and shoes from the floor and pulled her out of the bed to a standing position. He dragged her to the door and pushed the clothes into her arms. "I'd get dressed if I were you. The hotel frowns on naked whores roaming the hallways." He opened the door and pushed her out.

"Asshole!" Her blonde hair hung limp over her face. She spat at him as he slammed the door in her face. He heard her scream and then nothing.

He pulled on a white bathrobe and unmuted his phone.

"Yes?"

"Incompetent fool! The mission is in jeopardy," the Reverend said.

Morgan rubbed his eyes. "Everything is going according to plan." He turned on the small espresso machine on the desk. "I've got a loyal asset looking for him. He will be dead before the day is out and the device will be found."

Morgan heard the Reverend taking big gulps of air before he talked.

"Idiot! The asset is dead. The demon has escaped, and it's your fault he's gone."

Morgan stood near the window and peered out.

"How do you know this? Anyone with a pulse would have been a match for the little faggot."

"It's not your place to ask where the information comes from. The Holy Spirit guides my actions. *You* should have been doing the job. *You* should have been there, not sleeping with a hundred-dollar hooker," the Reverend said.

Morgan pulled the blinds on the window. The whore stood outside and was trying to hail a taxi. She looked like hell. He looked through a monocular at the people standing on the street. Tourists mostly, but he caught an older man snapping pictures of the hooker as she got into a cab. "Shit," he said under his breath.

"Why are you checking up on me? I told you I would handle it," Morgan said.

The Reverend sighed and said, "William, if you can't clean this up, I will be forced to find someone else to help me conduct the church's business."

Blood rushed to his face. His father was serious and wouldn't take the fall for this. Morgan would. A father would turn on his son. Morgan counted to five in silence and then said, "I will handle the problem myself," Morgan said.

The Reverend spoke again. "I will call you in an hour for an update." The connection died.

Morgan typed out a terse message on his tablet and sent it to an email address. He expected an update within minutes.

Morgan made an espresso from the tiny machine in the room and replayed his conversation with his fat father to put himself into the right frame of mind. He felt the heat, the anger, and the rage build until he let go. He punched a jagged hole in the bathroom door and threw a roundhouse kick into the wall three times until the drywall fell apart. Finally, he smashed the side table with the chair until both were in pieces.

As his chest heaved up and sweat dripped from his forehead, he picked up the telephone and dialed the front desk. "I need a new room; this one hasn't been satisfactory."

CHAPTER SEVENTEEN

David pressed his forehead against the icy glass of the tram window. Flashing lights screamed by in the opposite direction. Police or ambulance. Going to the hospital. Maybe looking for him.

Pain radiated from his knee and he stunk from the sharp chemical smell of the antiseptic on his neck bandage. No more bleeding, but the wound burned and itched. Falling four floors into a heap of laundry didn't help either.

The tram slowed and stopped on Oosterparkstraate. Doors opened. People got on and off. All the other street names piled on like a car wreck. Wibautstraat came next. Then Prinsengracht. Each name hit his awareness and almost brought up his breakfast. He closed his eyes and dropped his head to his knees. After a few seconds, the nausea lifted.

He pulled the white envelope out of his pocket and slit the flap with his fingernail. It had weight to it. A wad of crisp bills stared back. Hundreds and fifties. He figured four or five thousand euros at least. No note. No letter. No get-out-of-jail card. *I've got all the money and a ticket to nowhere*, he thought. The tram turned north towards central Amsterdam and after a few minutes pulled to a stop. Doors opened.

Another wave of nausea broke. He had to get off the tram before he threw up.

Without thinking, David launched himself out the front of the tram, pushing past people climbing on. He found a bench and collapsed, dropping his head to his knees again.

The nausea lasted longer this time.

He walked without raising his head. He followed a group of people that laughed and pointed at things. A few pointed cameras at buildings. He heard German this time with tiny blades of glass translating into English. Comments on the weather. Dinner last night and where to explore next. After a few blocks, he raised his head and realized he'd walked to Dam Square. The center of Amsterdam. Facts cluttered his mind. Seven hundred meters north was the train station. The Royal Palace to the west. Beside the palace, the 15th century, Nieuwe Kerk or "New Church." More facts flew by until he yelled, "Enough!"

The noise in his head complied.

None of the passersby paid him any attention. He looked like a crazy person. And smelled like one, he was sure. If he kept the act up, he might go unnoticed.

This time of the morning, the square filled with people. Two old men tossed crusts of bread to groups of pigeons. Over-caffeinated tourists with cameras. Backpackers looking for weed.

No threats so far.

He thought about that for a moment. How was he sensing danger? Was he bit by a radioactive spider?

Straight ahead, Damrak curved to the right. In the distance, the Amsterdam Centraal station. The way out of town.

His first instinct was to get as far away from the people trying to kill him. Get away from the crime he didn't remember committing. Wait for his memories to surface and regroup. Easy. Cash wasn't a problem.

But before he could run, he needed to clean up. Wait here until the shops open and purchase jeans, a T-shirt, a sweater, and a coat. Wash up at the train station. Hop a train somewhere and get the hell out of Dodge. He frowned at the reference. He knew what is was, but he'd never used it before.

He settled back on the bench. The square looked familiar, but not enough for pain. A wave of exhaustion set in and he closed his eyes. A scene appeared in his mind's eye. Late at night. Lights shining and people strolling around. He shivered in the cold as light snow fell. But he looked over as the blonde girl that hung on his arm smiled back at him.

Then the memory disappeared. He opened his eyes. Same vantage point as his vision. He'd been here before but hadn't. How could that be? And who was the girl?

Some cyclists crossed the square in front of the palace and their movement triggered something. He shivered, and his sight dimmed. Standing up, his legs pulled him straight towards the palace.

A white Citroen honked and swerved, just missing him by inches. Other cyclists rang bells and muttered at him in Dutch, but he didn't stop. He pushed past the palace, past Spuistratt to Singel until he reached a bridge. In front of a large statue, a dark circle stained the cobblestones. A bloodstain.

He teetered and lost his balance, falling hard to the ground and skinning his hands. His vision was a dense fog. An image appeared. Two men arguing. One short and fat; the other tall and dapper. The fat man's bad breath made him gag. Words came through, distorted. The words repeated. This time clear, like a radio locking on to the station. The fat man said, "It's poetry." Behind the men, a reflection. A houseboat. A swish of long black hair through the window. Four flashes of light.

Bullets.

David screamed as in the vision, lead slugs sliced into the tall man's throat and his hospital breakfast erupted on to the cobblestones. He heaved again. The image of the long black hair in the window returned along with the flashes of light. He heaved until there was nothing left.

After a few minutes, the images receded, and he pulled himself to a standing position. The dark stain on the ground was the only thing left. What did he just witness?

By holding on to the railing, he staggered to the houseboat. Cardboard covered one window. Lights off. No movement. The place was empty. What was he supposed to do now?

All at once, a stream of characters floated across his vision like a ticker tape. Single numbers in sequence. An address? Lottery ticket? A phone number? He looked for a phone booth and a block away, he found a lone handset and cradle under a small roof. No phone book of course. With some loose change from the pocket of the coat, he dialed what floated across his vision.

"Yes?" A woman's voice. Unfamiliar. No pain. "Hello?" the voice asked. He waited; something held him back from saying hello. "First word?"

"I don't know it."

"You have a wrong number."

"No. Don't hang up. People are trying to kill me."

"First word?

A name appeared. "Kafka," he said.

"Thank you. Please stand by."

A wave of relief rose in him like he'd just found a lost cell phone.

Seconds went by. Clicks of the call transferred to another line. A man answered. Gravel in his voice. "Name?"

"David."

"How did you get this number?"

"I need help. Someone is after me." Silence. "I…I…I killed a man trying to kill me."

Silence. "Second word."

Another word bubbled up inside his mind, "Conrad."

"Who gave you this number?"

He caught a whiff of burning weed as two teenagers passed within twenty feet of the phone.

"I…I don't know."

"You don't know the person?"

"No. No one gave me the number."

"Where are you now?

"In Amsterdam."

"That's already clear. Where?

"Near the Torensluis bridge." The location jumped out of his mouth.

More gravel. Then a wheeze. "Do you know the Abraxas Café near Dam Square?"

"No." An image appeared. A pinprick of pain. "Yes."

"In fifteen minutes, go to the back of the bar. Wait by the pay phone by the lavatory for a call."

David hung up. Across the bridge, a group of young women rode past the statue on bikes. Down Spuistratt, two kids with backpacks exited a building into the street, followed by an older woman.

No threats. At least none he could see.

His feet moved south back towards Dam Square. Instead of resisting, he rode it, feeling his legs move and his feet flex in an almost mechanical motion. All at once, the movement became natural, like learning the new steps in a difficult dance. He didn't know what he was walking into but the sense of relief from the call gave him hope. Hope the person could help him with what he didn't know.

* * *

Inside the Abraxas Café, pinpoint lights dotted the hobbit-like ceiling and elaborate frescos built with tiny mosaic tiles decorated the walls.

Near the door, two men and two women passed a hookah pipe back and forth sucking in sweet hemp smoke. An old man with a pure white ponytail read a newspaper, smoked a joint, and drank coffee. Jim Morrison sang about a girl he loved madly.

David cleared his throat. The smoke didn't mix well with the bile from his breakfast. The only other customer was a Dutchman staring at a soccer match on a flat screen.

He reached into the envelope in his pocket and pulled off a fifty euro note and handed it to the bartender.

"Water, please."

The bartender scowled at him but took the cash and handed him a bottle of water and a pile of bills before going back to his newspaper.

The wig itched, but he didn't want to go back to his appearance just yet. Looking crazy was an advantage. He took the bottle to the back, down a half stair and set it beside the lone pay phone. Two doors; one to the toilet and one outside.

He leaned against the wall and yawned. He felt safer than he had all morning. A blonde girl with horn rims and a dumpy sweatshirt came down the stairs and disappeared into the bathroom. She didn't even look at him. Jim Morrison changed his tune and sang about a woman in Los Angeles.

The telephone rang. David grabbed the phone.

"Second word," the man with the gravel voice again.

"Conrad."

"Good. Would you still like to go through with this?"

"Yes."

"Okay, please face the bulletin board beside the phone."

David looked from side to side.

"Why?"

The bulletin board was covered in Dutch advertisements. He chose not to read any.

"Do you want a way out or not? You're in a lot of trouble at the moment."

David heard the toilet flush.

"I need your help."

"That's a good boy. Please face the wall and try to relax."

The blonde walked out of the toilet. This time the needles hit. The sweatshirt and the glasses were gone. Her blonde hair hung down on the side. Low-cut T-shirt. Full lips held a trace of color. Stunning blue eyes. He'd seen those eyes before.

"I'm your contact," she said.

David turned to look at her but still held the phone to his ear.

"Please don't cause any problems," the man with the gravel voice said.

Something hard pushed into his back. A man leaned into him and said, "Hands behind your back and no tricks."

David complied. He didn't get a danger vibe from the woman or the man behind. He did feel annoyed however and wondered where that came from. The girl reached around and snapped on handcuffs before David was led out the back door and into a waiting van.

"Sit down. Face the back." David felt a chain attached to his handcuffs that didn't give him much room to move.

As the van started, the woman said, "We normally don't do this. Don't give me a reason to shoot you."

CHAPTER EIGHTEEN

Amsterdam

"The contractor had his own agenda. He had a weapon," Fitz said.

"Do you think he was just protecting himself?" Wyatt asked.

"No."

Wyatt's white Mercedes sped down the Nassaukade, running parallel to the Singelgrach canal. One of Wyatt's men drove. Wyatt and Fitz sat in the back.

"He pulled a gun before he made contact. I heard him snap in the first round. That points to an agenda." Fitz removed his glasses and polished them with a small cloth.

"He came recommended. We are checking the source," Wyatt said.

"Who's the broker?" Fitz asked.

The car passed a series of rusty boats tied up against the sides of the canal. Most looked ready for the scrap heap.

"He calls himself Mr. Dominic, but his first name is Arthur."

Fitz thought for a second. He knew many of the so-called brokers in and around Europe, but Arthur wasn't familiar.

"I'm still wondering why my man and the East German were killed. Doesn't this device have a value?" Fitz asked.

Wyatt stared straight ahead. "It does. But sometimes there is more money in destruction rather than ownership." He pulled a 9mm blue steel Berretta out of a briefcase and slipped it inside his jacket.

Fitz checked the magazine in his Glock as well. Full. Ten rounds. Hollow points. He pushed the web of skin between his thumb and forefinger against the rough molded plastic handle. Guaranteed grip in all kinds of weather.

It was Jonathan Brooks' gun.

The driver stopped in front of a two-story building. Wyatt entered with Fitz trudging up creaking wooden stairs to the second floor. Mold dotted the scarred walls. The lone door at the top stood ajar.

Wyatt pushed the door open.

"Good afternoon. What do I owe this visit?" A fat man with shiny, jet-black hair sat behind a narrow desk. Black jacket, crisp white shirt, and blue tie. His hands were open and placed on top of the table. His fingernails gleamed. An old-style telephone, a writing pad, and a single red rose in a tiny vase sat on the desk. Behind the desk were two open doors. Fitz checked both with his gun drawn.

Empty.

"Arty, the contractor you sold us had a different agenda. I need an explanation," Wyatt said.

"I prefer Mr. Dominic if you don't mind." He stared at his computer. "A white Mercedes no less. I expected one of those overgrown phallic trucks you Americans like to flaunt around the world."

Wyatt scowled at him but said nothing. Dominic looked everywhere except at Wyatt. He glanced at Fitz for a second and his eyes grew wide. The fat man looked like he hadn't expected to see someone.

A corner screen rotated video feeds of the building's entrances and exits. No one else entered the building. Fitz stared at him. His face shone like his fingernails.

Fitz had seen him before.

"Regarding your inquiry Mr. Wyatt. This is a cash business—but in the interest of customer satisfaction, I'll see what I can do. What was the nature of the problem?"

The phone rang on the desk. "Will you excuse me?" When Arty moved to pick up the phone, Wyatt grabbed the handset and slammed it back to the desk.

"I don't think you understand how pissed off we are," Wyatt said.

Arty sat back in his chair and let his hands drop to the desk.

Fitz went back into one of the rooms. A laptop sat open on a table with a closed Bible. No bed.

"That room is for employees only." Arty rose, but Wyatt clamped a big hand on his shoulder and pushed him back into the chair.

"My colleague is just browsing. You should be worried about me," Wyatt said. The man stopped smiling.

In the bedroom, Fitz touched a key on the computer. The screen brightened, and a list of emails appeared. Fitz looked through his bifocals and read from the screen.

Fitz called out "Who is Eprivate482?"

"A spammer probably."

"You have quite a relationship with this person," Fitz said.

Fitz clicked on an email. A dialog box appeared and asked for a password.

"The emails are encrypted," Fitz said.

"Can't be too careful," Arty said.

He opened the Bible beside the computer and flipped through the thin pages. The Old Testament.

Wyatt leveled his gun at the man at the man's head. "I've had enough of this bullshit. The contractor you sold us was dirty. He had his own agenda. I want to find out why."

Fitz returned from the bedroom and sniffed the air. After two seconds, Fitz said, "We've met before."

Arty kept eye contact on Wyatt's gun and didn't glance up at Fitz.

"You are mistaken."

"I don't make mistakes, and when we met, you were a different person. A much different person."

Arty pulled the writing paper towards him, uncapped the pen, and moved his hand across the pad.

"West Berlin near Checkpoint Charlie. Your name then was Larry," Fitz said.

Arty's hand scrawled on the page strokes of blue ink. "I've never been to Berlin. I'm from England."

Fitz watched as tiny beads of sweat formed on his brow. "You have hair now. More weight, glasses, different accent, but I remember your apartment smelled of tobacco and semen. You had a large pornography collection you liked to show off."

Arty's hand wrote fast on the paper.

"But here you are now; clean cut, organized, an international man of mystery. With even a Bible on your desk. You are a changed man. But there's one thing that's the same."

"I don't know what you're talking about."

Fitz stood behind him and sniffed the air. "You still smell like semen."

The man bolted up and stabbed at Fitz with the pen. The tip had retracted, and Fitz stared at the point of a razor. Wyatt reached across the desk and grabbed at Arty, but he slipped from his grasp.

"I will kill you sons of bitches!" Arty spat at him. He grabbed Fitz's coat and spun him around holding him like a shield in front of him. Arty reached in his coat and pulled out a Berretta.

Wyatt leaped to the side of the desk and leveled the gun at Arty's head.

The man bent Fitz's arm back behind him. "The Pervert. That's what we called you," Fitz said.

"Shut up or die."

"Drop the gun," Wyatt said, "We want answers on the contractor. Who pulled his strings?"

Arty dug the metal barrel deep into Fitz's neck. "You don't get it, do you? God pulls the strings just as the devil pulls yours."

Wyatt yelled, "Who are you working for?"

"As I walk through the valley of death, I will fear no evil. For thine is the spirit, the power, and the glory."

Arty shoved Fitz into Wyatt and put the Berretta to his own temple. "Amen."

The sound of the 9mm firing deafened the room. The mushroom-shaped charge blew a large hole in Arty's head. His dead body dropped to the floor.

Wyatt said, "We've just been screwed. Grab the computer."

Fitz staggered to the bedroom and closed the black laptop. He grabbed the Bible and stuffed it into his coat pocket. His ears rang from the gunshot.

"A refund would have been easier," Fitz said, as he stepped over the dead body and out to the hallway. The red rose sat untouched on the desk.

CHAPTER NINETEEN

Two women in black veils hung over David like vultures. Giant tears fell down their cheeks. Beside them, a man with a white collar read from a black book. David opened his mouth to scream, but it was filled with dirt.

The woman had pulled a black hood over his head in the van and he'd been brought into a building, tied to a chair, and left. He'd been so tired, he'd fallen asleep until a hand shook him. "Time to wake up," a man's voice said. The bag was pulled off his head and he blinked as light hit his eyes.

The handcuffs cut into his wrists and his ankles had been tied to the chair as well.

He sat in the middle of a narrow and sparse room with a polished hardwood floor. A role of carpet leaned up against one wall. A metal table with a laptop faced him.

A raspy voice spoke through the laptop. "Would you like water?"

"Yes…please." Words crawled out of his dry and scratchy throat. A tall man in a suit jacket tilted a paper cup with water to David's lips.

"I'm sorry for all this, I really am, but in my business, I can't afford to take chances with someone who knows me, but I don't know him." The voice stopped and took in a long wheezy breath.

"Now then, where did you get the number to contact me?"

A flash bomb of thunder exploded in his temples. David cried out and bent over in the chair.

"He seems to be in pain," the tall man said.

"I can see that," the voice said. "Was he injured while bringing him here?"

"No, sir. We followed your orders and he was compliant."

Phone numbers, faces, maps crashed into David's brain. Visions snapped by like high-speed film. Gunfire. Explosions. Acrid smell of cordite. The metal taste of blood. David's heart pounded hard as if it was looking for an exit from his chest.

"Can you tell me the source of your discomfort?"

"No," he took a big breath, and the needles subsided. "I mean I don't know."

"What just happened? Are you prone to seizures?" the raspy voice asked.

"No. Or I don't think so."

"How long has this been happening?"

"All day."

A keyboard clicked through the laptop speakers.

"You are a popular young man. Very popular indeed. Several people want you." Silence. "And they would either reward me or kill me if they discovered I had you right now."

More typing through the speaker.

"The people looking for you aren't very nice, but I can't ascertain who they work for."

"Why is someone trying to kill me?"

The voice ignored his question. "The local police are looking for you. They suspect you killed someone this morning in a hospital if my Dutch is correct.

"It was self-defense."

"Oh yes, of course, self-defense. The man died when a large metal rod entered his neck. He outweighed you by, I'm guessing, fifty kilos. Not an easy trick."

"Someone else is controlling my body, I couldn't stop myself."

"Yes, yes. Ted Bundy said the same thing. We knew the man you killed in the hospital. He was a free agent."

"He tried to kill me."

"Your name is David. Correct?"

"Yes. This is my first tour." The last sentence was automatic like he'd said it many times.

"Your first tour, as a tourist?"

David frowned. Memories clicked together like puzzle pieces. "I'm a dancer. My last name is Knight."

"Knight? A Knight-errant perhaps?"

David said nothing as he tried to move the memories around in his head so they would make sense.

"Turn the lights up a little, will you, Samuel?"

The room brightened. The man called Samuel was tall with jet black hair, jelled upwards. He looked like someone who would park your car at a hotel. The voice didn't speak for a few seconds, "Ah here we are. David Knight, from the National Ballet of Canada. No missing person report yet. A ballet dancer would explain your obvious state of fitness."

Ballet. Dance. Moving. Leaping. No fighting. More images. Sweat. The glare of lights against hardwood floors. Music. But this time no pain.

"I'm in the corps."

"The marine corps?"

"No, the ballet corps."

"Oh yes, you are right. The corps de ballet. The hospital admitted two John Does last night. One was you. The other…one second." More typing through the speaker. "The other had dark hair, he's the same age and has the same physicality as you. Another dancer perhaps?"

A memory zipped by. A friend. Dark hair. Then nothing. He grasped at the fragment but couldn't make it stay.

"The police found two bodies last night near were you rescued. Drug dealers, it appears. I'm not a betting man, but I'd wager those men tried to mug you and you bested them. Not an easy task for an amateur."

Samuel stood by the table like a waiter ready to take an order.

"Where's the woman?" David asked.

"The woman? Who do you mean?" the voice asked.

"The woman from the pub that distracted me. I recognize her from somewhere."

"You do? Interesting. Very interesting indeed. Where do you know her from?"

"I'm not sure." He frowned and tried to grab a passing memory. "Alicia, isn't it?"

The voice said nothing, but David heard an asthmatic wheeze.

"You have been on a real adventure tour here, David-the-dancer. I was unaware that dance included both weapons and martial arts training."

"It's doesn't. I've never even been out of Canada before. Why is this is happening?"

Another wave of pain hit and he gritted his teeth.

"What's the problem, young dancer? You seem in distress."

"My head is pounding. I see and hear images and sounds. Some are mine and some aren't. The ones that aren't, hurt."

"Samuel, can you get our guest some analgesics?" The man left the room but reappeared within a minute and pushed pills in David's mouth before holding a cup of water to his lips.

"You're Max, aren't you?" David asked.

"Now, how do you know that?"

"The names just appear. And you drink Dubonnet on the rocks," he paused for a second. "but I don't know what that is."

"Well, David, you appear to be much more than I expected. Samuel, can you please release him? I don't think he will cause us any harm. Will you?"

Samuel produced a key and unlocked David's hands and legs. The man didn't smile or scowl. David wondered if he was some kind of Dutch android.

David rubbed his wrists. "Can you help me find out why these people are chasing me?"

"First we need to get you cleaned up. I will instruct Samuel to incinerate your stinky clothes and I suspect you could use a bath."

The voice stopped for a second. "On second thought, I think you are the only one that can find out why, but I can at least help you find out who."

* * *

In a tiny bathroom, David peeled the dirty bandage off his neck and rinsed off the dried blood. He expected to see a Frankenstein style scar but found the wound healed. No pain or infection. All in less than 12 hours. Maybe he was just dreaming and this wasn't real.

He slid his aching body deep into the hot water of the old claw tub. Submerging his head, he scrubbed his scalp and his scruffy beard. He didn't shave as Samuel had only produced a toothbrush and toothpaste. After soaking in the heat as long as he could, he got out of the water, dried himself and looked again in the mirror.

David Knight, ballet dancer or David Knight, killer?

How did he feel about killing? The ape with the gun wanted him dead and fragments of two others floated around in his head. He remembered jabbing the pole into the ape's neck but he still felt disconnected from it. Like recalling a passage in a book instead of living through it.

The memory of taking another man's life should bother him but it didn't. Were all killers this disassociated from their brutal acts?

But the deaths brought him no satisfaction. No thrill of the hunt. Like stepping on a bug or swatting a mosquito. No remorse.

In the mirror, everything looked familiar and unfamiliar. Like he was seeing his body for the first time or expecting to see something else. After wedging a chair under the door handle of the room Samuel prepared for him, he slid into the single bed under a white duvet. Almost as soon as he closed his eyes, he began dreaming another man's dreams.

CHAPTER TWENTY

Alicia stopped at the top of the curved stairs that led her up to the attic, her long blonde hair pulled back with a simple red elastic. Balancing a tray of food in one hand, she pushed the door open with the other.

"You need air in here. It smells like a mausoleum." She set the tray on a table and raised the single ancient window up halfway. The attic held two desktop computers, several screens, a few oxygen bottles, and a man in a wheelchair.

Max Shueck. Her father.

"Most of our clients wished it was," Max said. He'd moved his wheelchair in front of a bank of flat screens and a keyboard. She leaned over and kissed the old man on the head. "Your mother once told me I couldn't die because there were more people to irritate."

Alicia smiled at her father. His skin and bony frame barely made a dent in the wheelchair. An oxygen mask hung open around his neck, like an old-time fighter pilot.

The screens streamed video from every room inside the house and all outside entry points. One window showed the dancer sleeping on the cot.

"How's our guest?" she asked.

"You should have been here a few minutes ago. It was quite the show." Max tilted his head up towards his daughter and winked. "What do you think of him?"

"I don't know. He's still a kid and seems like a lost soul."

"Like most of our associates," Max moved a joystick hooked to the arm of the wheelchair and rotated the images. "I can play back the video of a few minutes ago so you can base your intuition on something more tangible."

She smiled again. Some things never change. "What do you think happened to him? Was he brainwashed?"

"No. Early brainwashing techniques made men into automatons, but that took months. It appears he arrived in Amsterdam just the other day.

She stacked up the plates of untouched and stale sandwiches. A protein drink sat half full. "You need to eat. You can't survive on oxygen alone."

Max ignored her and turned to the other screen.

"Perhaps he's an elaborate ruse for a yet undiscovered reason." A burst of text appeared. "He has information he shouldn't have and doesn't know how it got there. Or at least so he says."

"What else could it be?"

"Unless this was planned and executed in Canada, it doesn't make a lot of sense to give him information about our little operation. I'm past my expiry date and most of our high value work ended years ago."

Alicia frowned. "I've read there is some research around removing traumatic memories for PSTD victims. Do you think they've found a way to implant memories as well?"

Max typed on his computer for a couple of minutes. "There is research that suggests they can. Flatworms that learned to navigate a maze were ground up and fed to other worms that found their way through the maze faster than other worms." His spiny fingers lighted over the keyboard at the speed of a secretary, "But even if this was possible, I don't know the purpose."

Alicia checked the oxygen level on the bottle behind the chair. Two other bottles lay on the floor near the window.

"Based on our interaction and the information I've been able to gather, he's killed three people without weapons, but hasn't got a clue what's going on." Max continued to type. "I'm intrigued by those looking for him. Fitzsimmons, for instance. This isn't usually a place for him. Our old nemesis, Morgan seems part of this as well."

"I thought he went back into the family business," Alicia said.

"After a long hiatus. More money and better hairstyles."

The old man coughed and wheezed until he grabbed for the oxygen mask. Alicia placed her hand on his back until his coughing settled.

"Too much humor will kill me."

"I'm concerned," she said.

The old man coughed again and spit into a tissue.

"About?"

"Our ability to hide our guest from prying eyes."

The old man took a deep breath and spoke, "We don't owe him anything."

Alicia straightened a stack of newspaper her father had flopped over a desk and grabbed one of the dirty plates. "He did call and ask for our help."

"Yes…but with an old code," he said.

"When was the last time it was used?"

Max clicked his mouse and de-encrypted a document. He typed a few more keys and stared. "Brooks was the last agent to use that code."

Alicia gasped, and the plate slipped from her hand and bounced on the wood floor.

"Just one second." Max typed a few keys into the computer.

"The police have evidence of a foul play on a bridge over the Singel canal a few days ago. No bodies. Just lots of blood."

Pictures appeared on the screen. On a bridge. A dark area. Blood.

"And Fitzsimmons arrived the next day. He doesn't do field work anymore. Let me see if I can get a security camera scan."

A set of images appeared.

"A local pensioner saw two men talking on a bridge before collapsing. He called police, but when walked over, the bodies had disappeared. Living in a surveillance state has some advantages."

A series of black and white videos filled the screen. Alicia saw men and women. A few teenagers. Finally, a well-dressed man in a long coat appeared. His hand shielded his face. Max shifted to another camera. Two men on the bridge. One man turned. Then both collapsed. The picture as grainy and rough, but the blood spatter was clear. Max reversed the video a few frames. The man's face was uncovered. A little older. More wear lines. But recognizable.

"Jonathan."

Alicia stood back from the screen and gasped. Her father looked up and said, "Alicia, I'm sorry." She grabbed the tray full of dishes and walked downstairs until she reached the galley kitchen. In the silence of the room, she sat on an old wooden chair, put her face in her hands and cried.

CHAPTER TWENTY-ONE

The morning sunlight filtered through the blinds into the main room. David rubbed his eyes and sipped strong coffee from a large mug Samuel provided. A large ginger cat took up a position around his legs. Max still spoke through the laptop sitting on ornate wooden table. David wondered if he wasn't just a computer program with a bad attitude.

"I have questions," David said.

"I'm sure you do," Max said.

"Why are you helping me?"

There was silence for a few seconds before Max spoke through the speakers. "Part of our services is sanctuary when someone is in dire need."

"Sanctuary? Why?"

"David, I operate on the knife edge of most laws here in the European Union and sometimes the laws are bent or broken for a particular operation. I discovered early in my career, that live customers are better than dead ones. Please view this as an advanced form of customer service."

"And I used a code,"

"Yes. A correct code."

David remembered the words and the phone number, but something else tugged at him. An itch. "Do you have a cigarette?" David asked.

"My young dancer, I didn't realize you smoke," Max said.

"I don't but it's been bugging me all night."

"Interesting. Samuel, please offer young David here one of yours." Samuel stood still for a second, but Max spoke again. "Go ahead, Samuel. I've known you smoke for some time. I abhor people that smoke in my presence, but as you are there and I'm here, you may do whatever you would like, with certain restrictions, of course. Make sure the windows are open."

David looked around the room. Where was Max? He assumed he was in a different location, but why would he be worried about smoke if he wasn't in the house? Samuel pulled a cigarette out of a thin gunmetal case and gave it to David.

"All the other dancers smoke. I was the exception." David said. "The public assumes we are the poster children for healthy living, but the truth is a bit different." David lit the cigarette and inhaled the smoke deep into his lungs but after a second, he coughed as if he'd just inhaled a bug.

"It's so curious. I suspect you play a part in an elaborate experiment."

"What do you mean?" David coughed more and stubbed the cigarette out.

"I see you are as naïve as you are young. All evidence thus far points to the memories bouncing around in your head aren't just yours."

David sipped more coffee to wash the taste out of his mouth. Yesterday, he thought he was having a mental breakdown, but someone else's memories seemed more plausible, however crazy that sounded.

"False memories can be implanted with hypnosis in a Manchurian Candidate sort of way. But hypnosis can't teach you how to kill someone in close combat."

David remembered the hell he'd gone through and all the weirdness. Information appearing as needed, the headaches, losing control of his body and killing those men.

"But they can't just transfer memories. Can they?"

"Thank goodness for Google. We've found research from England that never went past animal testing. But unless you are the most elaborate ruse I've seen for a while, you may be the first human test subject."

Through the laptop speakers, Max erupted into a violent coughing fit. The sound cut for several seconds and then he heard Max's voice again. "Excuse me, I can't talk for long stretches. My doctors recommend I rest every few sentences."

David swallowed more coffee trying in vain to wash out the lingering taste in his mouth. How could people do this every day?

"One theory hypothesizes that memory is stored in the brain holographically, instead of memories stored in specific places."

"So, what has that got to do with me?"

"A hologram is a three-dimensional image that can be only viewed by shining coherent light through a special photograph. However, if you split the photograph, the full image appears in both halves. This might explain why you've gained new abilities."

"Then why is someone trying to kill me?"

"Not everyone wants you dead. There is another group that wants you alive. In fact, there's a handsome reward for either scenario."

A wave of anger started to build as Max talked. "Why in the hell is anyone after me at all? I'm just a dancer"

"I can only theorize. During the cold war, the Americans spirited people out of East Germany on a regular basis. Not for some altruistic reason of course; the person leaving had something to trade for their freedom. Most of the time, the person had information valuable to the Americans. In this case, I suspect you are right; a dancer from Toronto has nothing of value. So that leaves me with one conclusion. The memories must contain something of value. So much value that some people want to kill you to stop it from being released."

"You said there's a group that wants me alive," David said.

"Correct. They would want access to that information. But based on the resumes of either group, I suspect you wouldn't survive either scenario."

"What do you mean?"

"You'd be disposed of, unfortunately."

David thought about what Max said. He was in the middle of a spy movie and on the wrong side of the screen.

"What if I just turned myself into the police? Would I be protected?"

"Perhaps. But police can be bought as well." Max said.

David's frustration at the whole thing was rising. *Damned if you do and damned if you don't.* "Can't we bargain somehow? If I found what they wanted, couldn't I trade it somehow for my safety?" David asked. His head ached but not as much as before; the sleep and food helped. He popped another pill from a bottle Samuel supplied and swallowed more coffee.

"Very good, David. You're thinking like a spy already. Yes, if we have the information, it's a poker chip we can use. And based on a variety of things, including the phone number and the code words you used, we know whose memories you have and he's unfortunately dead."

A memory fragment surfaced. A man with part of the skull missing. "I saw a dead body I recognized," David said.

"Where?"

"Near the red-light district, I think. I remember a clinic of some sort. But that's all."

Max coughed again. "If it's who we think it is, we considered him a friend. I can think of worse people's memories to have bouncing around inside you."

"I'd like just my own, thank you."

"If you can clear up a loose end. You had several thousand euros in your pocket when we found you. Did you liberate it from one of the people you killed?"

David winced and looked up at the ceiling. An ornate glass chandelier hung from the center. He remembered his hand reaching into a coat. "No. I found it with the dead man. I only realized I had it after a man at the hospital escorted me outside and put me on a tram."

"Someone helped you escape?" Max asked.

"An older man. Well-dressed. One eye didn't track right. These weird-ass memories didn't register him."

"What a lucky man you've become. A ménage à trois of puzzles and a fairy Godfather as well! Oh, my word, this is so interesting! I haven't had this much fun since we brought the wall down."

David squinted at that reference, but then stood up and yelled, "I'm tired of someone screwing with my life!"

"Yes. I'd imagine you are. In this business, screwing with other people's lives is a condition of employment. But we won't focus on that for now."

David realized he raged at a speaker attached to a laptop. Samuel stood with his back to the wall and his arms crossed. His outburst didn't elicit any response. "What business other than saving dumb Canadians?" he asked.

Max snorted. "Information, David. It's the only business, really. Information to make money, buy countries, or defeat governments. Information defeated Germany in World War II and brought the wall down in Berlin. But unlike pork bellies or orange juice, this commodity can be life-threatening."

David stood up again and paced around the room like a cat. At the front window, he peaked behind the curtain and saw an Amsterdam canal with a row of parked cars in front of the house. "How do I get out of here?"

"What is so urgent that you will put your life at risk? By your own admission, you killed a man yesterday. The Dutch have a somewhat relaxed legal system, but they treat homicide the same as their North American cousins."

David's stomach dropped with the realization he was a wanted man. "But I was defending myself."

"Let me continue. We will get to the options in a minute." Max stopped talking and David heard him struggle through several asthmatic breaths. "Based on an operation being mounted, the information is high value. But getting his covert skills was a bonus they didn't plan for. Even though they wanted a specific memory, like a hologram, you downloaded everything. And lucky for you, the memories take over at the appropriate time. For instance, when those thugs accosted you in the alley."

An image of two spiders formed in his brain. Big ones, walking on two legs. He thought he just imagined them, "How do you know about that?"

"I know everything. I find the relevancy of everyday events. Two dead bodies found in the red-light district. The police report suggested one attacker. These thugs were known to the police and one of them was big and ugly. You also demonstrated skill by killing your hospital attacker and escaping the hospital unscathed. The phone number you called and the code words you recited. Your neck wound has already healed—much faster than normal—possibly another byproduct of the experiment. I don't know yet."

David felt queasy and dropped his head down between his knees.

"Is this all too much for you?" Max said.

David lifted his head and stared straight at the webcam. "I'm fine. Then what are my options?"

Max's tone changed, "The choices are limited. Whatever information you carry, several people are willing to risk quite a lot for it."

"I could try to go back to Canada on my own. The euros should get me there."

"That might work if the information is perishable. If they can't find you after several months, they might stop looking for you. However, we might be wrong, and the contract would be indefinite. Ultimately, it's your choice. But if you leave, I can't protect you."

"But don't I need to tell someone I'm fine or that at least I'm not dead? Maybe contact the ballet company?"

"In your current situation, being dead is an advantage."

"What if I just leave here and take my chances?"

Max's voice spiked up. "Then you will be on your own. Samuel or I won't be there to help you if you run into trouble."

"I understand."

"Somewhere inside of you are memories of a person that would not be recommending this course of action to you. However, you're a big boy and can make big boy decisions. But I say this for the last time. If you leave, your decision is irrevocable."

CHAPTER TWENTY-TWO

David bent forward, arms extended, as Mozart played from an ancient CD player. Samuel had found him a T-shirt and a pair of ill-fitting shorts, but they did the trick. He needed the familiar and thought dance might help reduce his anxiety. Using a chair as an impromptu ballet barre, he warmed up his legs with simple exercises. He progressed the movements; building up a sweat and warming his muscles. He winced; his hip ached. Jabbing a knuckle below the joint, he massaged the muscle before continuing. As he worked his legs back and forth, beads of moisture formed on his chest.

He let go of the chair and tried a few turns, but his balance was off.

"Shit."

Hands clapped. Alicia sat in a chair by the door. He hadn't seen her enter the room. "Sorry about handcuffing you at the cafe yesterday. We needed to be careful."

David restarted and practiced an attitude turn using the chair for balance. "I'm sorry about the whole damn thing."

"How long have you been a dancer?"

He turned with ease on one leg, finishing with a sustained balance. He repeated it with his other leg, "Since I was six."

"What's Canada like? I've never been."

"Beautiful. Cold in the winter and hot in the summer."

Moving back to the center, he tried the attitude turn again and lost his balance, "Damn!"

"What's the matter?"

"My timing and balance are off. This thing, whatever this thing is, has screwed with my dancing."

She walked over to him. Her long blonde hair pulled into a ponytail and her blue eyes staring at him. "Maybe you're trying too hard."

David looked at her as if he'd seen her before but didn't remember it. "Have you danced before?" He raised his arms and spun once again, this time without falling.

"When I was a teenager. Then I rebelled and stopped."

He pressed stop on the player. "I haven't used a CD for years," he said. "You are in the memories." A headache started as he brought a memory forward. "You and that guy were in love."

"His name was Jonathan."

"Paris, I think…" David closed his eyes and drifted into his mind's eye. "Most of his memories are painful. This one isn't. I can hear the tapping of your shoes against the cobblestones besides a river. You are ahead of him. You've been crying."

"Stop. Those aren't yours." He saw a well of emotion appear on her face as he spoke.

"I don't want them. They're tampering with my life."

He looked at her. Same face as in his mind. A few years younger. Little girl pretty. Sad blue eyes. Dark streaks on her cheeks from falling tears.

"You cried that night. What happened?"

"You said…he said he loved me, but we couldn't be together."

David followed her to the side of the room and moved near her. His heart pounded in his chest.

"This is stupid. I'm feeling things I shouldn't."

"So am I." He kissed her. Soft at first, her lips gentle, but harder as he pulled her in close.

* * *

Three floors above, Max stirred. He stared at the computer screen and zoomed into the image. The camera caught the lovers locked in an embrace.

Max turned to another screen and typed SEARCH then DAUGHTER. He once told Alicia that searching for important information on his collection of hard drives sounded different. Auditory hallucinations, Alicia said.

Maybe.

His search retrieved over a thousand items. Pictures, sound clips, videos. Taken by Alicia's American mother when she was young. Refining for more recent images. Ten years ago. Another image. Another kiss. Jonathan and Max's little girl. She was twenty-something. He was over 50. No salt and pepper yet. Dreamy eyes. Lover's eyes. Emotional, non-thinking, lover's eyes.

He watched again the feed from inside the house. His little girl wasn't anymore. With David. A younger man. Same age as Alicia was ten years ago. Dreamy eyes. Lover's eyes. Emotional, non-thinking, lover's eyes.

He frowned. He didn't want to see his daughter hurt again. Some things shouldn't be relived.

CHAPTER TWENTY-THREE

Silicon Valley

"Where is he? You promised this abomination would be dealt with yesterday," the Reverend said into his speaker phone. He peeked behind the window coverings into the California night. All he saw was the darkness surrounding the moon.

"He can't hide forever. Your followers are combing the streets for him as we speak," Morgan said, his voice coming through clear like FM radio.

"Hiding? The devil never hides. He's waiting. Waiting for the right time to once again do battle."

"We will find him. Be patient," Morgan said.

The Reverend sat back at his desk. "What about these other sinners? The ones that want him alive."

"It's under control," Morgan said.

The Reverend leaned forward on the chair and yelled at the phone. "You have nothing under control. The operation is in shambles. The person you seek, you can't find, and your ineptitude has jeopardized the entire ministry!"

"Have you looked at the pictures I sent you?"

The Reverend opened the high-resolution image from his email. A man in a dark suit lay dead on a floor in a pool of blood with a large hole in the side of his head. "Why do you insist on sending these horrible things?" He swallowed more Jack from a tumbler. The melting iced diluted the bourbon, but still the liquid burned down his throat.

"His name was Arthur Dominic. One of your more devote followers. He helped manage an operation to find the boy. The other party discovered his identity, but he decided to prevent any information from being revealed," Morgan said.

The Reverend dropped the glass on the desk and bowed his head for a second. "He made the right sacrifice. May God have mercy on his soul."

"We've doubled our efforts to locate him," Morgan said.

"Remember, the beast is working through him," The Reverend said.

"But he is still only a boy. He can't elude us forever."

"No more excuses!" the Reverend pushed his bulk up from the chair, limped over to a bookshelf and pressed a button to open the drapes. He needed to breathe real air. The room's window sank into the wall and California night and the full moon entered the room.

"We will find him. He will surface. I've organized surveillance and we are checking—"

"Enough! I don't want the specifics. That's why you are over there. I want to know when it's done. Until then, I will pray for the boy's soul as it will to go straight to hell without my intervention."

The Reverend pressed a button and ended the call. He drained the Jack Daniels from the glass and looked up at the moon, the light glaring at him like an angry angel.

CHAPTER TWENTY-FOUR

Amsterdam

The ringing jerked Razor out of his troubled slumber. He was safe in his hotel room but his head was already pounding. The doctor told him he had a mild concussion from an injury he couldn't remember. He recalled walking the streets with David but then nothing until he woke in a hospital bed with a police detective staring at him.

The detective told him his friend David was a "person of interest" in a murder, hours before in the same hospital. He said the person killed wasn't a patient or an employee but nothing more. Later that day, Razor wobbled out of the hospital with the help of one of the ballet's administrators.

David as a killer? Razor couldn't bring himself to believe that. He wanted to search for his friend himself, but the doctor wouldn't hear of it. The phone rang again and this time he answered it.

"Razor, it's me," David said.

"David? Are you all right?" Razor rubbed the sleep from out of his eyes and felt the room spinning. He laid his head back on to the pillow. The bedside clock said 2:00 a.m.

"I'm okay at least for now. But it's not safe," David said.

"What happened the other night? Lester is having kittens and the police said you killed someone."

"People are after me."

"What people?"

"No idea. Has anyone else come looking for me?"

"The police talked to Lester and several other dancers. They asked me if you were violent or used drugs."

"Anyone else show up without an invitation? Men in suits?"

"Anyone else? Isn't that enough? What's going on?" Razor reached over and turned the light on.

"Listen. People are trying to kill me."

"Kill you? Why would they try and kill you? Look, the police want you for a murder."

"I know."

"Did you?"

"Razor, look I need you to do something."

"Did you kill someone?"

"Yes, but it was self-defense."

Razor rubbed his head. The headache moved into a full drum solo.

"Jesus, David. I don't know what to say."

"Razor. Look, I need you to do something for me."

"What?"

"Grab my passport and meet me in an hour."

"Why don't you just come to the hotel? I can wake up Lester and—"

"Just stop. I just need my passport. It's locked in the closet safe. Someone is trying to kill me, and I don't even know why. Except I've fallen into a serious bucket of shit and I need to get away from here."

Razor threw his legs over the side of the bed. The carpet was cold to the touch. The vertigo subsided somewhat, but his head still ached.

"When and where do you want to meet?"

* * *

The man blew out a smoke ring and removed his headphones. Surveillance had come along way. No tapes to stop, no wheels to rewind. The young ones wouldn't even know what a tape looked like. Everything was digital now. He didn't need to be in the same building or even the same city.

He balanced the cigarette on the edge of the ashtray and picked up his cell phone. Still a nasty habit no matter the decade. "Your hunch was correct," the man said.

"They usually are," Morgan said.

"I've got you a time and location. Is there anything else you need?"

"No, close up shop and go home."

"I'm at your service."

"You will be the first one I'll call." Morgan said.

* * *

William Morgan downed a tiny cup of his hotel room espresso, dialed a number, and spoke for less than a minute. Professionals were so much easier to deal with. A request would be completed without inane questions or quoting scripture. The word of God was fine. He just chose to handle things his own way. Much easier. He transferred the money with his phone. There is an app for everything. No muss or fuss. Click and shoot.

He glanced at the picture he sent the Reverend. Even in death, whiny little Dominic wore the same shit-eating grin as when he'd first accepted the church and the teachings. The Reverend mirrored the grin during his television and Internet appearances.

He tipped the tiny cup to get the last couple of drops. Dear old dad. He'd secretly wished he'd just die from a heart attack and felt guilty for thinking those thoughts. But away from California and back in the real work he loved, he realized he wanted to squeeze the air from the old man's pudgy body personally. His father wasn't a real man of God. He faked it. And faked it for a hand full of silver. He wanted to feel the pile of shit struggle and wheeze and realize at the moment of death, his son killed him.

The mythic irony of wanting to kill his own father wasn't lost on him, but he didn't want to rule in his place. He just wanted the money. Plus, many years had passed since he'd last thought of the fat man as his dad. But he started thinking through scenarios. If the old man died of natural consequences after a long illness, he'd have time to put someone in place that he could control. A quick heart attack would seriously screw things up and cause a power vacuum that might be challenging to overcome.

He'd never had a chance to ask his mother. She died before he'd managed to put together the implication. He didn't look like his father. His father still had his hair and he didn't. His father had fair skin and hair. Morgan didn't. His father was angry at him much of his childhood and he never knew why. Until he finally realized, the Reverend, his "father" probably wasn't. He didn't blame his mother for sharing the bed of another. But he was torn between shame and guilt and didn't like either.

He'd kill the old man once all this was done. He was sure of it. But he shook the image from his head. No thoughts like that until the mission was completed and make sure the old man had done the proper estate planning.

Some pleasures are best delayed.

CHAPTER TWENTY-FIVE

Amsterdam

Dressed in black jeans and sweater Samuel supplied, David felt his way down the banister in the dark. As he reached the bottom, the hall light clicked on. Alicia stood beside Samuel with the ginger cat purring in her arms. "You don't have to go."

"I need to," David said.

"If something happens, don't come back here. Max has forbidden it." Samuel said and dropped a key into David's hand. "This opens a locker at the train station. The contents are there as a courtesy until the end of tomorrow."

He handed David a small black backpack. "You may need this."

"What's in it?"

"I hope you don't need to find out," Samuel said.

Alicia dropped the cat to the floor and it wove through David's legs before disappearing into the kitchen. He opened the door and listened. No cars. No people. Any traffic this late would be around the red-light district anyway. He heard Alicia's soft steps behind him.

"You forgot something."

He turned. Alicia held a black baseball cap in her hand. "Every spy needs a hat." She placed it on his head and straightened it. Tears streamed down her cheeks.

"What's wrong?"

"You are leaving. Just like the last time," she looked away.

"This is my first. I need to get my life back. What's left of it."

She wiped her eyes with the back of her hands. "Where are you going to go?"

"I don't know yet except every instinct of his and mine are telling me to leave."

Her blue eyes were still wet. She reached up and kissed him hard before walking into the house without a word.

* * *

Samuel held the door for her as she realized she felt both maternal and at the same time strangely attracted to this man. More than she thought possible.

Her father emerged from the tiny elevator sandwiched near the back of the house and the kitchen. The long thin oxygen bottle hung on from the wheelchair like a parasite.

"Why aren't you in bed?" she asked.

"I'd hoped to speak to him in person before he left. But alas, I was too late."

She laughed. Her father was never late for anything. "I didn't think you cared."

"Interested and caring are two different things. His situation is interesting. But I don't care about him. He's just a boy."

She looked away. "Do you care about anything?"

The old man took a big breath of oxygen. "I care for you deeply. And occasionally for Samuel."

"Anyone else?"

"The baker that makes the lovely croissants you keep bringing me every morning."

She laughed. "For a second, I thought my grumpy old father had been replaced by a machine. I see that's not the case."

"The night is still young," the old man said and took another breath from the mask. "I need you to run an errand for me."

"Pick up another stray in the back of a pub again?"

"No. Reconnaissance this time."

She raised her eyebrows. She loved anything that took her away from a computer screen. "Where and who?"

"San Francisco."

She looked at him and frowned.

"Not everything is on the Internet you know. Nothing replaces firsthand reports."

She dumped the half-eaten food stacked from his attic hideaway into the trash. "I can't be gone for very long otherwise you'd die of starvation."

He pushed the joystick forward and his wheelchair followed. "Nonsense. Samuel does an adequate job at keeping me alive."

"Why can't you send Samuel to the U.S. instead of me?"

"You have an American passport thanks to your mother's insistence on your birth location. Samuel's current citizenship might cause a problem."

"Isn't there anyone else you can use?"

"I only trust you to do this. I suspect there's more to the dancer's story than I've been able to find."

She sighed and said, "I'll make the arrangements and leave at the end of the week."

Max pulled out an envelope from the side of his wheelchair. "You have a seat on the next flight out of Schiphol. Three hours from now."

She looked at the tickets. First class. Direct to San Francisco.

"I've prepared a packet for you to peruse while you drink champagne and eat caviar on your flight." He produced a thick file folder and handed it to her.

She looked at the gnarled old man with the oxygen mask. She could never say no to him even when she wanted to.

"I will be back as soon as I can," she said.

"I'm counting on it," Max said.

CHAPTER TWENTY-SIX

Amsterdam

South of the city's core and in the shadows, David watched the Dutch National Ballet and Opera theater for any activity. A mouthful for sure. The side steps resembled a long twirl of icing on a layer cake. Hours ago, the National Ballet of Canada delivered its final performance on the first leg of their tour.

Even this late at night, traffic zoomed up and down the Amstel to places unknown. A group of backpackers passed by sharing a joint between them and took no notice of the man dressed in the baseball cap.

Crossing the bridge on Blauwbrug, he looked for anyone that might watch for him. No parked cars with a lone driver. No men or women hidden in the many alleyways. He chuckled that his surveillance knowledge came from watching too many spy movies with his Dad growing up.

As he looped around the building, he found the stage door. He now needed help. Closing his eyes, he pictured entering the theater and being grabbed by men hidden in the shadows. All at once, he felt the other presence.

Jonathan.

He willed himself to let go. He willed himself to relax and to breathe. Needles of pain hovered at the surface but manageable. Ducking into a notch in the building exterior, he slid the backpack off and reached inside.

A few minutes later, a ribbon of fear went through him as he pushed open the stage door. Razor must be inside.

Wooden crates marked "National Ballet of Canada" sat stacked and ready for transport to Paris. The dancers would follow by train. He felt a pang in the pit of his stomach. He should be with them instead of running for his life.

He closed his eyes and listened for every squeak and thump from the heating and ventilation system. All theaters seemed to use the same lemon cleaner on the stage with the pungent odor of dancer's hair spray following a close second. But he caught something else. Cigarette smoke. Body odor. Acidic and metallic. Different from a dance company. The smell of fear.

A low moan came from the curtains on stage right. David pulled back the curtain and found Razor in a heap on the floor blindfolded but breathing, his hands tied behind his back to his feet.

"Don't turn around." a man's spoke behind David. "Raise your arms above your head."

Pain hit David's temples. The memories recognized the voice. An assassin. A good one at that. The voice was eight or ten feet behind him. Too far for a direct attack.

"Turn towards me and we will walk down the back stairs."

"What happens if I don't?" David asked

"I will shoot your friend," the man said. "That would be unfortunate. I saw him dance in Toronto. He shows lots of promise."

Great. A dance critic with a gun.

"Let's go. I haven't got all night."

David turned and saw the man. The Professor, the voice said. Older now. Less hair. Same crystal blue eyes. Black pants and turtleneck shirt. Dark rubber-soled shoes. The Professor held a gun. Glock 26. A "baby" Glock, small and light and easy to conceal. A custom silencer screwed to the barrel. Hollow point rounds to generate maximum damage at close range."

He wasn't going to acknowledge his name. Not yet.

"Downstairs," the Professor motioned with the gun. "You should know the way."

David walked with his hands above his head. The man kept behind him. Eight feet at most. Too close for David to run and too far to turn and attack.

"We're coming down," the Professor said.

David frowned. Who was downstairs? If it was just a contract, the Professor should have shot him backstage.

"The ballet tonight was magnificent. You missed a good show."

Extra people. Chaos. Advantage. David listened to the voice. Take advantage of what? The man has a gun aimed at my heart.

"Why didn't you shoot me on the stage?"

"Be quiet or I will shoot you in the hallway."

David didn't say anything more and walked past the whitewashed walls and doors. "The first door on the right," The tip of the silencer pressed into David's back. Heart level.

"Why are you doing this?" David asked

"If you are what they say you are, you should understand."

They entered a long windowless room with mirrors along the back wall. The main rehearsal space. A well-dressed man with a receding hairline and sunglasses stood by the lone piano. The memories registered a distant awareness, but not enough to cause pain. Bono wore sunglasses indoors but had more hair. Who was this guy?

"This is him? This is the little shit causing us all this trouble?" The man tipped a thin flask towards his lips, swallowed, and walked up close to him.

"Where's the device stashed?"

"Who are you?" David asked.

The man slipped the flask back into his front suit pocket, smiled, and punched David in the stomach. "I'm the guy that's kicking your ass." He leaned in close and whispered, "Ask those locked up memories of yours who I am." The man pulled David upward and punched him again. "Where is the device stashed?"

"I don't know anything," David said, but a flash of memory and an image of an empty briefcase welled up within him. Was he looking for something in the briefcase?

The man threw a right cross into David's chin dropping him to the ground. "Where are your precious memories now? Why aren't they kicking into gear?"

The man squatted close, and the smell of his hair gel came closer. "Look. You're mixed up in something that doesn't concern you. Just tell me where the device is, and we will make this quick."

David grunted and clutched his stomach "I don't know anything."

The man straightened up and said to the Professor. "Go get his buddy from upstairs. Maybe some additional entertainment will help."

The Professor looked at him in the eyes. "No."

"No? Go upstairs and bring him down here!"

The Professor pointed the pistol at David. "The contract was for him only."

"I don't give a shit about the contract. Go upstairs and drag the little bastard by the hair if you have to."

"I suggest you continue this interrogation. I'm a contractor, not an inquisitor."

The man's face flushed red and stared at the Professor, but after a few seconds, he threw his hands up and said "Whatever. This whole thing has been a fool's errand."

David's chin ached, and a fire burned in his stomach. But then the memories needled their way into his body, their sharp points drilling new pathways.

"Waste of my time." The man kicked again and connected with David's gut.

"I know who you are," David grunted out.

"Now we are getting somewhere. What else do those memories of yours tell you?"

David turned his head and looked him in the eye.

"That you're a dickhead."

The man's face turned red and the veins on his forehead formed a big V until he took a long slow breath and laughed.

"Nice try asshole. I hope that felt good." he nodded to the Professor. "Go through with the contract. I transferred the money earlier."

"As you wish," the Professor said.

"Wait until I leave the building. I hate the smell of gun powder," the man said.

He straightened his suit and slicked his hair back into place. "Memory transfer? Bullshit. An excuse to cover incompetence. Anyway, you won't be a threat to the church for much longer." Before he walked out the door he said, "Two bullets. One in the head and one in the heart."

The door slammed shut behind him.

David lay bent in the fetal position, his hands near his feet but grunted out, "What…what was his name?"

The Professor stood with the gun extended and a poker face. "Doesn't really matter now, does it? William Morgan and yes, he is a dickhead." He raised the gun and said, "But to the matter at hand."

"You are the Professor," David said.

The man frowned and stuttered out, "How did you know that?" In one swift motion, David reached to his calf, withdrew the stiletto knife Samuel gave him, lunged up and sliced into the man's hand. The gun dropped to the floor.

The Professor yelled, "My hand! You little bastard!"

David rolled up and swung the knife in a wide circle, but the Professor jumped out of the way.

"Poor little ballet dancer. I actually felt sorry for you." The Professor pulled a knife out of his front pocket with his other hand and snapped it open. "You almost had me. I should have listened to my inner voice."

"I did," David said.

David reached under his jacket to the small of his back, pulling out a Czech CZ pistol and firing twice. The two slugs slammed the Professor back as it tore a ¾ inch hole into his forehead and the same sized hole through his chest. One in the heart and one in the head.

David retrieved the fallen Glock. Easier to take it with him and easier to hide. He raced upstairs, untied Razor's hands and removed his blindfold.

"Razor? Are you okay?"

He helped Razor sit up. "What happened?"

"Sorry, Razor, this is all my fault."

"Your passport… It's in my back pocket."

David extracted a slim blue Canadian passport from Razor's pants.

"David…David. You are in serious shit. Get out of here!"

He pulled Razor up and onto an old wooden chair near the wall. A bandage covered one temple, and he looked like he might pass out.

"I can't leave you."

Razor grabbed David's arm and smiled. "I'm fine. Just call the cops and disappear, will you? I will tell them what happened."

Then Razor bent over and retched.

Leave, the voice said. *Leave now.*

Razor wiped his mouth with his sleeve and waved a hand at David before leaning his head back against the wall. As he exited the building, David pulled a red handle on the wall starting the building fire alarm.

Help should be a few minutes away.

CHAPTER TWENTY-SEVEN

David stood under an awning across the canal until firetrucks, police, and an ambulance appeared. Satisfied that Razor was safe, he walked north until he saw Amsterdam's Centraal Station.

Shielding his eyes from the fluorescent lights inside the main lobby, only a few students with their backpacks sat on the floor waiting for an early train to somewhere.

The bank of lockers was one floor down and he found the right number, but his hand shook as he tried to insert the key Samuel had given him. The episode left him in a state of shock. Every spy movie was bullshit. No way could a spy play a game of poker after just killing a person. Too much adrenaline.

He waited and slowed his breathing. After a minute of thinking happy thoughts he tried again. This time he inserted the key, unlocked the door, and withdrew a large black nylon duffel bag. A minute later, locked inside a stall in the men's washroom, he read a letter, hand printed on shiny paper. There was no signature.

"If you are reading this, you've gotten farther than we expected. You may need to change your identity. Change clothes and drop the old ones in a locker. Your name is now Thomas Jamison. Supporting ID in the envelope. You have black hair in your passport picture. Take the first train to Frankfurt. Train tickets enclosed. Fly from Frankfurt to anywhere else. Set fire to this paper with enclosed matches. Good luck."

David examined the other contents. Black cargo pants, dark blue rugby shirt, black combat boots and dark sunglasses. He also withdrew a padded leather coat plus a first aid kit and smartphone. In a sleeve was a UK driver's license, Barclay's Visa and passport. A small plastic bag held a tube of hair dye, plastic gloves and a pair of hair clippers.

Everything a spy needed to change his identity.

He wanted to look around for the large camera as he told himself he must be starring in a movie. But he wasn't. His experiences of the last couple of days told him otherwise.

He put the CZ pistol in the bag and pushed the Professor's Glock into the back of his pants.

He lit the paper with a match and it flashed in his fingers like a magic trick. He felt like Tom Cruise in *Mission Impossible.*

Sitting on the covered toilet seat, he dropped his head as big shivers hit his body. *I can't do this anymore*, he thought. A memory said he was going into shock, but he didn't care. Dying might be an easier choice.

He closed his eyes to let the shivers run their course, but the stink of urine and something else caused him to stand up in disgust. He looked at his hands. Big patches of blood covered the top of his gun hand. The Professor's blood. He'd killed again. No. The memories of this goddamned spy killed. He wasn't a killer.

Him or me, the voice said. An image rolled passed his memory like a film strip. His father appeared—large, loud. Coffee and cigarette fueled by day and lite beer by night, but the big man was a big teddy bear that fell asleep in front of the TV every night. After his mother died, his father tried as hard as he could and raised him. Or at least raised him long enough for David to audition and get accepted into the National Ballet School. "Dance? Don't you want to go to a regular school?" his father had said. David shook his head and his father had arranged everything. School, dance classes, and tutoring to keep his grades up.

When David was shy of his 20th birthday, he watched cancer ravage his father's body. From his hospital bed, his father looked up at him. "I'm proud to call you my son." A lump formed in David's throat and he nodded. "I never said much, but I've always been proud of you," he said. "After I'm gone, remember no one will give you a free ride. Look out for yourself. Nobody else will." He coughed again, his lungs filling up with fluid.

That's what I did tonight. I took care of myself because no one else would. After a couple more minutes, the shivers stopped.

New memories from tonight bounced back and forth. Surprise on the Professor's face as the gun fired twice. The smell of cordite and the Professor dropping in slow motion, falling face first with a wet splat.

No remorse.

He looked out for himself.

He replaced his clothes with the ones in the bag and slipped his arms into the leather coat, before exiting the stall. He stuffed the old clothes in the trash bin.

As he washed the blood from his hands at the single sink, the person looking back from the mirror looked like a drug addict. Splotches of blood on his right cheek. A purple mark on his chin where the other man punched him. What was his name again? Morgan? He bent over the sink, scrubbed the blood on his wrist and threw a handful of water on his face.

A hand tapped him on his shoulder. He whirled around, grabbed the man's throat and threw him to the ground. A grizzled old duffer with a thick and dirty beard lay under him, pressed into the dirty tile floor. The man's eyes bulged and his mouth hung open. A crumpled and unlit cigarette lay on the floor beside him.

David backed off and the man sputtered with a look of terror in his eyes. "I… just wanted some change."

David peeled off a ten-euro bill from his money and placed it into his hands before muttering a halfhearted apology. He quick walked out of the toilet before anyone else appeared.

He needed Max. He couldn't do this by himself.

After crossing the train tracks towards Dam Square, he found his way to Max's tall thin row house. The blinds were open and a lone light from the kitchen shone into the living room. The table and computer had disappeared. All furniture had shifted, and the big carpet had been unrolled.

He knocked and waited. Nothing.

Using the cell phone Samuel had provided, he dialed the same number he used to contact Max a few days ago.

Out of Service.

David swore and threw the duffel bag from the train station to the floor. "I should have stayed here."

He found a lone key in the post box and searched the entire place. Tables, carpets, cups, and saucers placed back into the right spots. Was this the right house? As he stood in the kitchen, a ginger cat pranced in and wove itself through David's legs.

Right house with no people. But he could still smell the lingering odor of Samuel's cigarettes. Where have they gone?

He searched once more and found a small book of matches stuck behind the entrance door.

Moulin Rouge—Paris. A burst of neon and music filled his eyes like a projection screen just for a second. He'd never been to Paris. But Jonathan had. A memory told him Max had as well.

He checked the train schedule on his smartphone. He had a couple of hours before the train left. He locked the front door and dyed his hair and eyebrows in the tiny bathroom on the first floor. After he was done, a different man looked back from the mirror. One he didn't recognize. But once he closed the door and replaced the key, he headed back to the train station. He wasn't going to Frankfurt; he was going to Paris.

CHAPTER TWENTY-EIGHT

Amsterdam Centraal Station

An hour after leaving the house, he climbed the stairs to the south platform of the train station. Rent-a-cops stood by the doorway and near the currency exchange booth.

The platform was full of early business travelers, disheveled students, and some elderly men and women. A few with wheeled suitcases but more with backpacks. At the far end, he noticed a woman with long dark hair wearing an unbuttoned caramel coat that revealed a black skirt and knee-high stiletto black boots. Wide sunglasses covered her eyes. A model? Maybe she was rich or wanted to be.

She glanced in his direction but turned away as the bullet shaped TGV train entered the station. Once it stopped, and the doors opened, David jumped aboard the last car.

Inside, airplane style seats alternated backward and forward instead of the usual continental trappings. He grabbed the window seat in the end row closest to an exit. An asshole named Morgan wanted him dead, and the memories provided nothing more. Now he was on a train bound for Paris to find the only person he knew with answers.

He wasn't sure why he left Max in the first place. Did the memories force him or was his own twenty-one-year-old arrogance his downfall? *Arrogance* flashed in this mind. Great. A conscience with an attitude. What every dancer-turned-assassin needs.

But if he couldn't find Max, he didn't know what else to do.

He leaned his head back as a wave of exhaustion hit him but shouting from outside snapped his eyes open. Groups of uniformed police swarmed the platform and stopped any backpacker with blond hair. Other officers fanned out to the trains on the other side.

They were looking for him. That was clear.

Breathe. Slow, the voice repeated.

He'd made it this far. No mean feat for a twenty-something dancer who had been abducted, chased, and attacked. But his luck might be ending.

A constable entered the train and walked down the aisle, glancing at each passenger. David pulled a magazine from the seat pocket and stared at the second page as he stopped at David's seat.

"Sir, may I look at your passport?" he said in English.

Still staring at the magazine, David reached into his coat pocket, pulled out the thin leather folder and hung it in the air with two fingers. He hoped Samuel did a good job. The constable leaned forward and grabbed it from his hand.

"Your destination please?"

"Paris." David's heart pounded. He had limited options to escape. He squirmed as the baby Glock he acquired from the Professor dug into the small of his back. The constable looked at the picture, and at David, then back to the picture again.

"Have a nice trip." The man handed the passport back.

David swallowed another pill as his neck tightened. He watched the constable talk to other single men in the car, but after a few minutes, he left the train. Through the window, he watched another officer talk to a man in a suit. But as the man turned his face towards the train, David saw the wonky eye. Why was the man that helped him escape the hospital now talking to the police?

Examine the details, the voice said.

What details? David thought.

He didn't get an answer.

A few minutes later, the train started, and the police grouped back together like drops of spilled mercury. The man with the wonky eye had disappeared. Did he get on the train without David seeing?

Out of the cavernous station, the silver cars strung together emerged into the sunlight as a butterfly would from a chrysalis. David pulled the sunglasses from the top of his forehead to his nose, closed his eyes, and fell asleep.

* * *

Fitz rested on a formed plastic bench on the east side of the station with a newspaper open on his lap. He wore a French beret, a long leather jacket, and dark glasses. His brown Italian loafers replaced by walking shoes with jeans instead of gabardine. He hated disguises, even though as a covert operator, a change of look saved his life many times.

"Possible target approaching, through the south door." One of Wyatt's contractors spoke through his earpiece. Several Japanese tourists pushed through the door, hauling over-sized suitcases. Behind them, a man with short black hair and a leather jacket moved past them and walked up the stairs to the station platform.

Fitz sized up the man in the leather jacket and thought back to the muscular boy strapped on to the operating table at the clinic a few days ago. Long blond hair, strong face, wide shoulders. He looked the man's shoulders through the leather jacket. Same width.

The chin and cheekbones were the same as the boy. Fitz adjusted the sunglasses and smiled. Good disguise. Perhaps the boy wasn't helpless after all. Or he had a benefactor. The train schedule said two trains were leaving in the next thirty minutes. Frankfurt and Paris. Frankfurt made the most sense if he's trying to leave Europe. Central and flights to anywhere. But Paris might also make sense.

"Did the old East German go to Frankfurt from Berlin or just direct to here?"

"One minute," Wyatt's voice spoke over the earpiece. "We think he stopped in Paris before arriving here."

"I've got a positive ID."

Wyatt said, "Do we grab him on route?"

"No, we've been unsuccessful with that tactic. He's going somewhere with a purpose. If Brooks' memories are helping, he wants a bargaining chip. The device would be it," Fitz said.

"I thought the device was in Amsterdam," Wyatt said.

"Vogler was smart and liked to complicate things. It's conceivable the device is in Paris," Fitz said.

"Shit." The line went silent for a few seconds. "We will take your lead. He's the only key we have. Once you confirm his destination, we switch operations to Paris," Wyatt said.

The phone call ended.

Fitz stood up and dropped the newspaper on the bench. Goddamned device. People are dying. He thought of Brooks' bloodied body on the wet cobblestones and again on the operating table for the removal of the brain tissue. Bastards. Brooks was murdered for a bloody video game. Non-nuclear, non-lethal. No secret death dealer. Just a corporate investment. He will get the bastards. Save the boy's life if he could. Brooks would have insisted.

The device can go to hell.

* * *

David woke with a start. The TGV hit cruising speed, but the ride was smooth as glass. No "clickity-clack" of a regular train. He'd read somewhere, the high-speed rails were welded together to form an unbroken line. The silver cars flew through fields of patchy snow and past banks of high-tech windmills.

"Did you have a nice sleep?" A well-dressed older black man sat across from him. He had grey hair, flat face, heavy nose, a wide smile, and spoke with a Caribbean accent. An Indian man in a puffy parka slept with his head tilted to one side in the seat beside him.

"No." David looked out the window. A barbed wire fence stood between the track and the fields, but at this speed, the fence disappeared.

The Indian man woke with a massive jerk. He stretched his hands up, unzipped his overstuffed jacked and pulled out a cell phone. Within seconds, he talked rapid fire in another language. A bead of saliva hung from the corner of his mouth.

The black man said, "I'm amazed at how fast we travel in this metal tube. In my day, we'd be on this train for eight or nine hours." He patted the seat. "And not in as much comfort." He frowned as he looked at David. "How did you get that bruise?"

David touched a sore spot on his chin where Morgan had landed a shot. He looked back at the man. No voice. No pain. No danger. Just an old geezer that talks too much.

"I tripped," David said.

The man broke out into a broad smile. Large white teeth. He looked like a shark. "Where are you headed, son?"

"Away."

The man laughed, "We all travel away from something and to something else. Responsibilities, family, loved ones, commitments. What are you traveling away from?"

David shifted in his seat. "Everything."

"Even from God?"

Something snapped in David's brain. God, religion. Something that Morgan the dickhead said. "Subvert the word of God." A religious nutcase. David narrowed his gaze at the man. The top of his head prickled like before lightning was to strike. Was he somehow connected to whoever is trying to kill him?

"You look like a lost soul. I felt compelled to sit down across from you."

Danger. Leave. The voice kicked in with a suddenness that surprised David. Pain erupted in his temples. He stood up, turned, and left the old man without saying a word. As he raced toward the next car, he still heard the Indian man spouting into his cell phone.

* * *

The first stop was Rotterdam. *Thirty minutes*, the voice said. David rolled his eyes. He should ask for the local temperature or what stocks to buy.

The door to the snack car opened with smells of strong coffee and warm croissants. He ordered the continental breakfast. A few minutes later, he swallowed a bite of croissant with a dollop of strawberry jam and washed it down with a cappuccino and watched the landscape slide by.

Near the rear of the car, a man hunched over a newspaper with a pencil in hand. A crossword puzzle. He glanced up at David and then back to the paper. David's stomach soured, but it wasn't from the food.

Examine the details, the voice said. What did that mean? He remembered the Professor pushing the gun into his shoulders and the beating he took from Morgan. The pain started at the top of his head, pushing down. As he took a deep breath, he climbed into the backseat of his mind, watching the ride, but not driving the car.

The devil is in the details. The man wore rubber-soled shoes. Dark suit. Body builder's neck. A tie. Something under his white shirt. Thicker. Heavier than a T-shirt. A Kevlar vest? David read the newspaper's masthead. The New York Times.

A buff American wearing a bulletproof vest on a train to Paris. Coincidence? The latest European fashion statement? Maybe not. He figured the man was waiting for something or someone.

Need to verify.

Before he could fight it, he downed the rest of the coffee, dropped the cup back to the counter and walked towards the man. As he passed, he swung his duffel bag wide over his shoulder and hit the man's coffee cup, sending the last swallow of coffee over the labored crossword before the cup hit the floor with a smash.

"Idiot!" David said. He turned to the man who had grabbed a handful of serviettes to soak up the spilled coffee. "What do you think you are doing?"

Inside, his gut wrenched at the idea of fighting a man twice the size of him with no weapons and other police on the train. Even if he could get outside, jumping off at this speed would be a messy suicide.

The man looked at him for a second. "Your bag hit my cup."

"It did not. You knocked it with your arm as I walked by." Alarm bells rang in David's head. Couldn't these damn memories be turned off somehow?

The man stood up and looked at David in the eyes. The man had a small scar across his nose and outweighed David by about fifty pounds. He had two inches on him in height. He smiled. "You're right. It was my mistake." The man reached down, grabbed the cup from the floor, and sat back in the chair.

David saw the vest bunch up under his shirt and a bulge on the side of his jack. Holster and gun.

"You're bloody right!" David swung the duffel bag over the other shoulder and walked out of the car towards the front. *Surveillance,* the voice said. Where there's one, there's more.

He walked two cars farther and found an empty seat. His hands and arms trembled as the adrenalin from the encounter with the man in the restaurant car pumped through his blood. He closed his eyes, counted to ten and took long slow breaths. All these extra skills felt bolted on. He had the strength and endurance, but not the mental toughness for this spy stuff and he wasn't sure if he could build up to it either. But one thing was clear, he needed to gain some control.

With that thought, he felt the train starting deceleration into Rotterdam. He hadn't been to the city before, but as he watched the city building up from the outskirts of houses and farms to buildings and roads, maybe he had. Soon, a plan formed that might help.

* * *

As the train doors slid open, David jumped from his seat and out to the platform, racing to the arrivals level. He crossed the road, entered a small café, and walked to the back before exiting the back door to the alley. A block away, he caught a cab to the center of the city. The war had destroyed much of Rotterdam, but from the ashes rose a jungle of modern steel and mirrored buildings.

He navigated the glass jungle, entering and exiting stores and office buildings. In one store, he bought a hat, a coat, and a knapsack and left his leather jacket in a change room. As he left the last building, he caught sight of his trackers: a man with a baseball cap and headphones and a woman with mousy brown hair, flat shoes, and a dark coat. He hailed a cab and a few minutes later he bolted back into the railway station.

A slower Benelux train was pulling out the station heading south. He raced to the platform and jumped through the doors just as they were closing. His trackers ran to the platform and scanned the windows of the train, but they didn't see him. They couldn't be sure if he made it on the train or not, but they wouldn't take the chance. More surveillance would be waiting at the next stop.

But they weren't police. No one tried to arrest him. Just watched. Morgan, the man from the ballet theater wanted him dead. Why? Morgan asked where the device was stashed. What the fuck was he talking about. Device? Some kind of bomb? Money? The Ark of the Covenant? Stashed meant hidden for later recovery. Did the spy inside him know the location? He prodded the memories for a clue but earned nothing except silence. At least the pain in his head had stopped.

The train picked up speed, albeit slower than the previous train and he grabbed an open window seat. Slow is good. He needed time to think and to plan. Something he sucked at in his regular life. However, this time, his planning ability hadn't gotten any better. His plan only had one word. Paris and maybe stay alive while getting there. These damn memories didn't seem to help much either.

The door at the front of the car slid open and a large police constable entered. Stone-faced, he began a slow walk down the aisle, looking at all passengers. He stopped several times and interrogated only single young men with blond hair. David watched as the men handed over their passports and the officer ran them through a machine in his hand.

As the constable came closer, more sweat trickled down David's neck. The passport Samuel procured him would stand up to casual viewing, but David didn't know what happened if the validity was checked.

The officer didn't smile. Didn't engage in any small talk. Each time, he handed the passport back without a word and continued the inspection.

David could hide in the bathroom for a short time, but Officer bitch-face might just wait for him. In a cramped space, on the last car on a train to Paris, David had limited options.

He sat back and closed his eyes. Looking not guilty was the first option. But a few minutes later, he felt someone sit down beside him. He turned and saw the woman on the Amsterdam train platform pushing a brown satchel underneath the seat in front of her.

The constable stopped in front of David and said "Passport?"

The woman looked up, smiled at the officer, and turned to David. "Are the passports in my bag or yours?" She spoke English with a French lilt. "Never mind, I'll check." She leaned over and dug into her bag, her breasts peeking out from beneath her silk camisole. The constable stared at her chest, but his face never changed. She looked up and flashed a bit of a smile. "The passports are in my other bag. Do you really need to see them?"

The officer said, "No, Mademoiselle, don't bother about the passports. Have a nice trip." She smiled, adjusted her bag and shirt, and leaned back in the seat. David noticed a small smile on his face as he turned around and headed out of the train car.

Who is this woman? he thought. Why she would help him and how had she made it onto this train? He caught her perfume. Light, subtle, intoxicating. "Excuse me," he said, "Do I know you?"

She put her hand up and whispered, "Wait until he's gone."

CHAPTER TWENTY-NINE

Brussels

The train slipped into Belgium from the Netherlands farmland without a shudder. David looked at the woman beside him. She hadn't said a word since they left the Rotterdam station.

She stirred and pushed her sunglasses to the top of her head. After looking out the window, she pulled a thick copy of French *Vogue* from her bag and flipped through the pages. "Men are so easy to fool. Look at this." She pointed to a model in the magazine, wearing not much more than a smile. "A woman's breast turns them into salivating idiots." She closed the book with a slap and looked at him.

"Why did you help me back there?" David asked.

"Men," she said. "Always wanting explanations for things. Your seat was open, I sat down. The police were bothering every man on the train, so I had a little fun." She lowered her head and looked up at him. "You own a passport, don't you?"

David smiled, "Yes. Want to see it?"

"No. You can't go anywhere without proper identification. But I'm tired of the government always checking everything." She turned towards him and raised an eyebrow.

"American?" she asked.

"Canadian," he said.

"Land of the free and the brave. No, that's not it." She frowned for a second and then smiled. "Our home and native land?"

"Correct." The thought of Canada pulled at his heart. He wasn't sure if he'd ever get back.

Her smile showed a delicate schoolgirl mouth. Soft and small. Her green eyes twinkled as she talked. "But what illegal things were you doing in Amsterdam such that the police wanted to bother you?"

His face flushed at her question. "Nothing."

She stared at him and smiled. "You might fool the police, but not me. You look as guilty as a man just caught with his mistress. I rode your train from Amsterdam and watched you jump off in Rotterdam. A man and woman chased you, but I suspect you outran them."

David leaned back in the seat and frowned. "Why did you get off the train then?"

"These high-speed trains make me nauseous. I waited for the next one and noticed you jumping on just after we started moving."

He sat silent. Was this woman part of the group chasing him? Would she pull a knife out of her polished brown bag and jam it between his ribs? He waited for the voice to say something. But all he got was silence.

"I'm sorry, it's none of my business. I'm Jenna—short for Genevieve." She held out her hand. He grasped it, feeling the warmth of her touch and the softness of her fingers.

He stopped for a second and recalled the name his ID was under. "Thomas," he said.

She opened her magazine again and flipped to the middle page. "See this?" She pointed to a glossy photograph of several men and women lounging by a pool. "This is mine."

"Yours?" he said. Her perfume snuggled up to him again. Light and feminine.

"I'm a photographer, but I'm sick of it. Advertising is selling things to people they don't want or can't afford." Out the window, dark storm clouds hung on the horizon blotting out the sun. She closed the magazine and slipped it back into her bag. "Where are you going?"

"Paris."

"Paris is beautiful any time of the year. Living there is a different matter and all French men are assholes."

In David's mind, images of streets and buildings appeared. Dark rooms and darker alleys. Everything was fuzzy, like a dream.

"Have you been before?"

"I'm not sure," he said.

She laughed. "If you have ever been to Paris, you would know."

"I...I had an accident." David looked out the window. "I can't tell if my memories of Paris are from a movie or if I've been there."

He thought she was about to say something but didn't. After a few seconds, she said "I'm sorry. I didn't know."

"Neither did I." He changed the subject. "I noticed you on the train platform too."

"When I noticed you, I wondered if you had done any modeling," she said.

A memory bubbled up of him standing in costume while a photographer snapped pictures for the latest promotion. "A little."

"I liked the way you stood. Most men hunch over, their neck jutting forward like a bird. Models and dancers have good posture."

"Which one am I?"

She leaned back into the seat and adjusted a scarf around her neck. "I don't know, except I sense you are carrying the weight of the world on your shoulders."

"You're psychic and a photographer. My lucky day."

She scowled at him. "You aren't French. You don't have to act like an asshole to me."

"I'm sorry. That was uncalled for."

She frowned and turned away. "You must be a dancer then. Every dancer I've shot was a flake."

"That's been my experience, too."

She laughed. "As I've saved you from the police, I'd appreciate if you let me sleep and stop anyone from bothering me." Without waiting for an answer, she pulled her sunglasses back down on her face, leaned her head back and closed her eyes. The conversation was over.

CHAPTER THIRTY

The train stopped in Brussels and then once more before the long last leg to Paris. Dusk settled as they sailed over the landscape, the rhythmic clanking of the steel wheels on the rails, lulling David to sleep.

He dreamed of pudgy black women with painted fingernails smoking long cigarettes. The thick stink of rose water mixed with cigarettes filled the air. A black woman smiled at him. Her teeth were chalk white.

He woke with a start as a heavyset white woman in a blue smock stood beside their seats with a food cart in front of her. David bought two wrapped baguettes stuffed with cheese and meat and bottles of Evian. He devoured the sandwiches and washed them down with gulps of the water.

Max was in Paris somewhere. All he had to do was find him.

No problem. Other than he had no idea where to look. He'd hoped the voice would help but for the last couple of hours, he felt no other presence than the beautiful woman beside him.

He remembered the matchbox. Moulin Rouge. Can-can girls. He opened his smartphone Samuel bought for him and launched maps. A few minutes later, he virtually walked into Place Pigalle and examined the streets and buildings for a long time, but nothing seemed familiar. Had the memories evaporated?

The open farmland gave way to low rise office buildings, roads, and apartments. They were on the outskirts of Paris. Jenna stirred again and sat up.

"Where are we?" she said.

"We should be at Gare du Nord in the next 10 minutes."

She grabbed her bag and left the compartment without saying a word. When she returned, her face was bright, and her makeup had been re-applied.

"Where are you staying?" she asked.

"Not sure yet." David closed his eyes. A fountain, a statue, and a river formed in his mind. Latin Quarter.

He frowned at the realization he had his answer. The memories of another man still sat on the edge of his consciousness.

"Near the Latin Quarter."

She tilted her head like she was about to say something but didn't. After a few more seconds, she stared straight ahead and said, "Enjoy your time in Paris. Maybe you will remember your visit this time."

The train pulled into the cavernous Gare du Nord in the north of Paris. The terminus for the northern railways, the station sat at the intersection of Rue De Dunkerque and Boulevard De Magenta.

Jenna looked out the window and her eyes went wide. She ducked her head, grabbed her bag, and said, "Good luck with finding what you are looking for." She ran down the length of the car and jumped off. He watched as she disappeared into the crowd.

What spooked her? She seemed to panic at whatever she saw. Or whatever saw her.

The dull ache started again. The spy had been here. He popped a painkiller, swallowed it with the last of the water, and left the car. As he watched the crowds of people coming and going, it was hard to tell if there was surveillance.

Around one corner, several French police had cornered a blond backpacker. No guns but the backpacker looked scared. David pulled his baseball cap down on his head and left the train walking the same direction as Jenna. He knew something wasn't right.

Once outside the station, his first Paris evening started with light rain and cold air. He followed his intuition and walked to Rue De Compiegne, past an alleyway and heard a scream. Down the alley, a black BMW sat with the lights and doors open. A heavyset man had a beefy hand across the mouth of a woman. David saw the woman's black bag. The heavy copy of a *Vogue* magazine fell to the ground.

Jenna.

The man opened the back door and threw Jenna into the car. David ran up to the car and dropped his bag. The man was getting in the driver's door, but instead turned and faced David.

"Go away! This isn't your concern."

David grabbed the passenger door and pulled it open. Inside, another man had Jenna's arms pinned to the side and tape over her mouth.

The man's large hand gripped his shoulder like a vise. "You should have left well enough alone."

An icy calm slid into his body like a tight-fitting suit. He grabbed the man's wrist, twisted in reverse, dropping the man to the ground before kicking him in the head.

Behind him, a switchblade snapped open. The other man had circled around the car and leaped at him swinging the knife in a wide arc.

As David's heart pounded, his mind detached from the action. The man swung the knife again, pushing him back into the wall. David pivoted, grabbed the man's knife hand, and twisted. The man dropped to his knees and David brought his knee up high and sharp into the man's jaw, dropping him to the pavement.

The first man stirred and rose from the ground, blood streaming from his eye where David kicked him. He pulled out a pistol and as he brought it up to fire, David threw the knife into the man's neck. The gun dropped, and the man fell face first into the ground.

David opened the back door, pulled the tape from Jenna's mouth, and undid the rope. "Let's go." Her face was white as a sheet. She sat in the car not moving. "We have to go now," he said.

She climbed out, bent over, and vomited on the sidewalk. She heaved twice more and then straightened up. "I'm all right," she said. He pulled his coat off and wrapped it around her shoulders.

Before leaving, David reached inside the car and pocketed a smartphone sitting on the dash. They left the alley and walked to Boulevard de Magenta and hailed a blue Citron taxi.

"Place Saint-Michel," David said. The driver never looked back; a half-smoked cigarette hung from his lips and the ashtray overflowed with ashes.

"*L'Villa s'il vous plait,*" Jenna called out.

"Can you put out that cigarette? My friend isn't feeling well," David said.

The driver grunted, rolled down the window and tossed the lit butt into the rainy street. David cracked the back window and fresh air streamed against the smoke. The inside windows were fogged, except for a tiny porthole in front of the driver. David hoped the driver had X-ray vision.

Jenna shook beside him. Her long hair was wet and messy; her blouse ripped. As they drove in the dark cab, the reality of his situation came clear. Amsterdam felt like a different world, but here in Paris, minutes after arriving, he had killed another man. Killed him with no remorse. Killed him like he'd kill a bug.

Would this ever stop?

Jenna gripped David's hand and wouldn't let go. She stared straight ahead and said nothing. The cab threaded its way from Gare du Nord, crossing the Seine at Pont Neuf to the left bank and drove until they greeted a large statue of Saint Michel fighting the dragon.

Years ago, a terrorist bomb exploded a hundred feet below in the subway station. Mass terror reigned in the streets for several weeks after, but not much could unseat the balance of Paris life. Tonight, the wet sidewalks stood empty, except for the odd Parisian with an umbrella over his head and a baguette under his arm.

The cab stopped at a hotel called La Villa on Rue Jacob. As he helped Jenna to the entrance, the door buzzed open.

"Good evening, *monsieur*," the clerk said.

"We'd like to check in," David said.

"Certainly, *monsieur, madame*. Name please?"

Jenna spoke. "Jenna…Jenna Samson."

The clerk squinted at the computer terminal. "We have you in a nice big room. Room 302. Can we help you with your bags?"

"No. The airline lost them. We will need to purchase some things tomorrow."

The clerk looked at them both. "Your wife, *monsieur*, doesn't look very well. Would you like me to call a doctor?"

"No. She slipped on the wet ground. But she will be fine in the morning." Jenna managed a smile. The clerk shrugged and handed David a large metal key. "If there's anything you need, don't hesitate to call me."

Once in the room, she let go of his hand and walked into the bathroom. The door locked behind her and he heard water running.

David slid his wet coat off and sat down. He took deep breaths to relax before the pain came. Like clockwork, his vision darkened and a band of metal tightened around his neck. Nausea welled up inside him. He dropped his head between his knees and continued to breathe. He reached into his pocket for painkillers and choked down four.

Hot needles dug into each temple. After several minutes of nausea and pain, the vise loosened, and his vision came back. Colors of objects seemed dull. Lifeless. But the needles had abated, and he didn't want to throw up anymore.

The night's events replayed across his memory again and again. He remembered the knife in his hands. The weight. The balance. Overcompensating for length. Throwing the blade as the man's gun came up from his hip.

Slice.

He had to get rid of this thing, this possession that both cursed him and saved his life. He took a breath and wiped his eyes. They were slick with tears, but the colors in the room began to reappear.

"Thank you." Jenna stood at the door to the bathroom, covered head to toe in a bathrobe. Her face was clean. Her hair was wet and pulled back. A bruise glowed purple on the side of her neck. She looked like a scared little girl.

"Those men work for a French asshole."

"I gathered as much."

She sat beside him "He said I owed him money or sex and I told him to fuck off. He tried to rape me but instead, I kicked him in the balls and escaped."

She began to cry. Big tears streaked down her face. David stood up and hugged her tight.

"He told me he would kill me. I'd be dead right now if it wasn't for you." She nestled her head against his shoulder. She smelled of lavender.

David relaxed his grip. "Get some sleep. We can talk in the morning."

He left the bedroom and slid the French doors together behind him. He lay on the couch and closed his eyes. More images of the day swam through his head. The car. The alley. The copy of *Vogue*.

The last thing he remembered was an image in the magazine. A black girl tarted up, sitting by an open door. Something looked familiar. The woman or the pose. Maybe it was the door.

He couldn't put his finger on it.

CHAPTER THIRTY-ONE

A black woman in a tight pink top waved him inside the room. Cheap perfume and cigarette smoke overpowered him. Inside the room, girls on stools by the bar; breasts and asses squeezed into overstretched material. Thick blue eye shadow. Blood red lipstick. The scene shifted. He stood inside a wooden shack surrounded by sweltering heat and rotting meat. Disembodied hands and forearms hung from the ceiling like ornaments. A hand grabbed his shoulder. Two more pulled his arms and yanked him towards the other bodies.

He screamed and opened his eyes. He was drenched in sweat. Light from twinkling streetlights filtered through the window shade.

"You were talking in your sleep, and then you yelled," Jenna said.

She had knelt beside him on the couch. He smelled the lavender from her bath. She still wore the white bathrobe.

Paris. He was still in Paris. But the dream was vivid. Maybe another memory and not a dream.

She leaned her head against his shoulder. "What were you dreaming about?"

"A War. In Africa. Rebels terrorized the population by chopping off limbs. I found myself in a hut where arms were suspended by wires like ornaments. The stink was overpowering."

She wrinkled her nose. "Bad dreams."

"No. Bad memories."

"How could they be? You said you were a dancer," her voice raised an octave.

"I am." David turned and looked out the window. "My accident…" His voice trailed off.

"What happened?"

He shook his head. She wouldn't believe him.

"You can tell me."

"I have memories that aren't mine."

"What do you mean? Like false memories?"

"No. Real memories from another man. Someone dangerous. I remember places, street names, and people. I have skills that aren't mine." David looked at a painting on the far wall of the room. "But mostly I remember death."

She looked into his eyes before looking away. "You sound crazy, but you shouldn't have been able to stop those men. A dancer shouldn't be able to fight like that."

"I was a dancer and still am. The memories killed those men. They take over me like I'm possessed. I'm a backseat driver."

David remembered the fight at the car. He acted without thought, but somehow, he felt more in control. As if the memories and the experiences were somehow merging with his own. There was still pain. But it ended faster than before.

"I think I'm going crazy." He rubbed his eyes. They were wet. "I don't want these fucking memories. I shouldn't even be here right now—I should be performing at the Paris Opera!"

"Without you, I'd probably be dead."

"It wasn't me who saved you. It was the memories of someone else."

She leaned into him and kissed him on the cheek. "There was no him. Just you. You were the one that saved my life. I'm grateful."

He nodded but realized she was right. He didn't want to admit it but without his ordeal, he would have not been on the train. He would have not met her and probably this beautiful woman sitting with him would be dead right now. Somehow, all this trouble had a positive outcome. But it didn't reduce him wanting to get rid of the memories.

"I dreamt about something else too. A black woman in a brothel. The dreams are clues."

"Clues for what?"

"To help me find a man that can help me get my life back."

"I need your help right now." She leaned over his supine body and kissed him this time on the lips. Gentle. Soft. He kissed back and opened his mouth. His hands stroked her long hair. Her hands slid down his chest. She climbed on to the couch and straddled his legs. She opened her robe and her breasts pushed into his chest. His hands slid down her back to her ass. He cupped the cheeks and pulled her farther up his body.

The love they made started quick as if there was a ticking clock. She rode him up and down, pushing into him and engulfing him with her body.

For the first time, he relaxed. The need to discharge as fast as possible was gone. In its place was a fire, moving from the hot flame of excitement to the burning coals of passion. He pushed into her with long periods of silence and holding tight with no movement. Jenna moaned with each touch and caress of her body until they both reached a point of communion. Their two souls joined in their embrace.

She collapsed on top of him. Tears slid down her face.

"That's never happened to me before."

David looked at her. Her long hair draped over one side of her head. "Me as well." He kissed her neck and then her mouth.

She smiled, and her eyes twinkled. "Who drove that time? Him or you?"

He looked up towards the ceiling and smiled, "A bit of both I think."

CHAPTER THIRTY-TWO

Paris—Latin Quarter

Wake up! The voice startled him out of his sleep. Sunlight filtered through the double pane glass along with the faint sounds of cars and the occasional horn. Jenna had gone.

The clock said 10:00 a.m. A note on hotel paper beside it.

"I won't be back, but the hotel is paid up for two nights. I loved last night. Can we dance again soon? J."

David focused on the words and frowned. He felt a little sheepish about last night. She'd been attacked, abducted, and almost catatonic. He hadn't planned to take advantage of her, but she started it. Sophie crossed his mind for a second, but that seemed like a million years ago.

He peeled off the bandage covering the knife wound from a week ago and rubbed his finger across the faded pink scar. A side benefit from the procedure maybe.

The fucking procedure. Jam another man's memories into an unwilling patient and then try to kill him when he escapes. His heart rate spiked as rage filled him at the injustice of what happened. He'd been stabbed because of the procedure. If he hadn't been abducted, he'd be at ballet class right now sweating with the rest of the company.

After a hot shower loosened the knots in his shoulders, he checked for more cuts or bruises from the fight last night. Nothing. The two men didn't get as much as a scratch on him. He shook his head. David, the international man of mystery. If Razor could see him now.

The memory of his friend flooded back to him. He hoped Razor was okay, but he wouldn't try to call him. Not until all this was over. Morgan must have tapped the hotel's phones or maybe even Razor's own cell phone. Contacting anyone else would be too great a risk.

He dressed, pulled on a hoodie for warmth, and removed the Glock from his bag, squeezing the release and letting the magazine fall into his hands. Nine bullets. Nine soldiers in a line. He broke the gun into pieces and laid them on the small table, realizing after he broke down the pistol without thinking. He was the same guy that couldn't assemble an IKEA desk at his apartment in Toronto without help. He left the CZ pistol Samuel had provided in the bag as backup.

He reassembled the gun. His hands knew where to go. How much pressure to use. He removed the magazine, pulled back the slide, and checked for a bullet. Like breathing or in his case, like dancing.

He stood and used the chair for balance and ran through a few quick warmups. Stretching, raises, knee bends. Just enough to get the blood flowing. He did the movements also without thinking.

Whoever did this to him failed. Somehow the muscle memory hitched a ride with the facts and saved his life. He filed that information away for later use but didn't know why.

He focused back on the gun. It looked clean, and since gun oil wasn't normally available in the mini bar, he snapped the clip into the grip and chambered a round.

Downstairs, a blonde waitress made him coffee while he reviewed a tourist map. Outside, the street was alive with activity. Some cars honked and swerved passed the hotel, followed by a flat panel van and several scooters. Across the street, a man in a beret carried two baguettes under his arm as the March sun had peaked through the grey sky.

"I've found you fresh croissants," the server said in accented English. She placed a heaping plate of pastries on the table. David devoured them with large sips of coffee and swallowed another pill to blunt the pain he knew he'd feel today. Only a matter of time.

He opened the map and found his location in central Paris. Familiar as an old novel he'd read many times. The book of matches from Max's house said Moulin Rouge, 32 Rue Richer, 9th *arrondissement*. He remembered Max's voice and then relaxed. Just like a Ouija board, his finger moved around lines on the paper, starting at the 1st *arrondissement* and pushing through the districts until he stopped at Place Pigalle. His search for Max would start there, but after that, the plan got a lot fuzzier. He had no Plan B.

* * *

Fitz and Wyatt sat at a small wooden table in a cafe near the Champs-Élysées. They had flown into Paris from Amsterdam.

"Your men lost him in Rotterdam, but we still think he made it to Paris. Near the train station last night, police found two dead bodies in an alleyway across the road."

Fitz scanned the copied police report. "Who were they?"

"Thugs, low-level enforcers as far as we can tell, but we aren't sure who they were employed by. Witnesses said a young man and woman left the alley and got into a cab.

"A woman? Another dancer perhaps?" Fitz said.

"We don't know. On the first train, he sat alone." Wyatt sipped an espresso. "Any idea where Brooks would go when he came to Paris?"

Fitz nodded. "I know of a few possibilities."

"Look. We don't have time. If we don't find him and the device in the next couple of days, it will all be over," Wyatt said.

Fitz didn't know what that meant but he wasn't going to press it. "I don't think we will wait much longer," Fitz said. "Based on the events in the last couple of days, he's searching for someone or something. And if Brooks is driving, I have an idea that might shorten our search."

* * *

David bought a ticket and pushed through the turnstile of the Place Saint-Michel metro station. As he descended the old stairs, he remembered learning about the 1995 Terrorist attack when he'd been in school. Images on the giant television on a wheeled stand. Twisted metal. Bodies in stretchers. No bombers were ever caught. The French media whispered Algerian terrorists. But they were just stories.

Stories have a life of their own. His story did. Last night, he killed two men and made love to a beautiful woman. His life in Toronto felt like ancient history. He remembered Sophie, the beautiful dancer that threw a book at him when he broke up with her. She felt five years ago, her face distant in his memory. He tried to bring her closer to his awareness but failed. Were the implanted memories overwriting his own?

Alicia seemed nearer in time, but still weeks or months from today. She said goodbye to him two nights ago. He shook off the memory strangeness and focused on a man that could save his life. A good story for sure. A newsworthy story. Spy movie of the week. If he ever lived long enough to tell it.

The smell of stale piss wafted from tile steps leading to the old subway platform, now filled with people.

His steps echoed off the ancient walls as he passed people reading books or necks bent over their smartphones. A few wore earbuds. As he waited, he noticed a man in an ill-fitting suit snapping cell phone pictures of younger white men, ignoring everyone else. He'd walk up to a younger man, snap a picture, and move on without a word.

David went cold. Something about the way the guy moved. A few of the targets yelled "fuck off" as the man flashed the smartphone in their faces. He ignored the cursing and just continued to the next man.

A wind pushed from the subway tunnel as twin headlights appeared. As the train pulled to a stop, and the doors slid open, the man reached David and pushed the phone into his face. Without conscious thought, he swatted the device out of the photographer's hand and sent it skipping across the tile floor until it smashed against the back wall.

David jumped into the train as the doors slid shut. The man pounded on the door. David smiled and sat down on the hard seat and giving him the finger as the train moved. Screw you, Jimmy Olsen.

He pulled his hood over his head. His stomach knotted as it appeared a geek army might be looking for him in the city. He had to hurry and find Max and hoped he could make this whole thing stop.

Max. He didn't know what he looked like. He imagined an old man with a bottle of oxygen. Wheelchair perhaps. The voice didn't help in this case. That was the problem. No way to cheat the dealer. An ace would appear only when needed. The rest of the time, the memories were opaque.

David rode the #4 until Barbes Rochechouart and transferred to #2 Porte Dauphine. As the Metro stopped at Gare D'est, a large crowd exited. David switched to a corner seat in the back of the car. Two men in dark suits entered and scanned the car. Clean cut. White shirts. One was balding, heavy set. Expanding middle. The other was muscular with dark hair, high and tight. He looked at their hands. Both had cell phones open in their palms. Baldy walked towards David and Short hair went the other direction.

"Pardon, *monsieur?*"

David didn't look up.

"Excuse me, sir, may I ask you a question?"

David looked down. "No."

Baldy stood back across from David's seat. Out of the corner of his eye, he saw Baldy pointing a cell phone at David's face.

"No matter. This won't hurt," Baldy said.

David swept his foot across the man's legs and knocked him off balance. The cell phone fell to the ground with a crack and bounced under a seat.

"Excuse me," David said.

Baldy reached for the cell phone and swung it upwards trying for another picture. David jumped up from the seat, grabbed the man's wrist and twisted back. The camera flashed but snapped a picture of Baldy as he yelled. The cell phone dropped from his grip and David stomped his heel on the naked phone, smashing the metal body and screen into bits.

"I like my privacy," David said. The other subway passengers shrunk back into their seats. He couldn't tell if the terror in their eyes was for him or them.

Short hair came running and threw a wild swing. Ducking first, David hit him with a right hook followed with an uppercut dropping Short hair to the floor in a heap. Baldy had gotten up and swung a black nightstick at David's head, but overshot. David threw his elbow into the man's nose with a crack followed with a right cross into his chin, dropping him to the floor.

The train slowed into Anvers Station and doors opened. Most of the passengers pushed their way out and, in the chaos, David leaped over the two bodies to the platform, and pulled the hood over his head. The doors hissed closed and the train rumbled away.

He defended himself and any witnesses would report that. His hood might help a little if any cameras caught his escape, but he hadn't seen an overabundance of security in any of the stations so far. *Keep moving*, the voice said. He agreed. Moving was safer.

Anvers, 9th *arrondissement*. A short run to Pigalle. Close to the Paris Opera House. Adrenaline pumped through his body after the brief fight and pain danced around the edge of his consciousness.

He needed more pills.

To the south, the ballet company would be unloading at the Paris Opera House. East was Pigalle. Would he find Max there tucked against the strip joints and whorehouses?

Going south would be a mistake. For him and anyone in the company. Razor got hurt helping him and he couldn't take the chance for anyone else. What would they do? Offer seasons tickets to the people trying to kill him?

Sophie's face surfaced again. Clearer this time. In focus. His heart pulled at the thought of pulling her close, but the deep longing he'd felt before all this started had all but evaporated. Was that a good thing? At least in his present predicament it was. He couldn't afford anything that distracted him away from finding the answers and the truth. One more time, he took a deep breath and felt the tingle of the other. The other memory. The other presence.

Ballet company or Max?

Max. The word beamed to his consciousness like a light. Not shouting, but definite. Max was more important. The company could wait. His body turned around and started towards Pigalle.

CHAPTER THIRTY-THREE

London, England

Nikko Palokangas' phone rang early in the morning. He kept odd hours, but he preferred to talk business when most of the civilized world was asleep. In Chelsea, his flat was small but luxurious, a benefit of his chosen career. His snooty English neighbors thought him an eccentric art collector but no one in the apartment building knew what he really did.

A Picasso hung over the hallway table. From his Blue period. Nikko purchased it last year with the proceeds from killing that idiot Spanish politician. Picasso painted a woman's body sitting huddled, her back to the artist and always took his breath away. Genius didn't have an age limit. He painted her when he was only a teenager. Picasso's genius and Nikko's genius. Two peas in a pod.

He pressed a button on his cell phone. "Yes?" He sipped his first espresso of the day. He'd used a full teaspoon of cane sugar.

"We have an urgent need of your services." He knew the voice.

Morgan.

"Again?" He marveled at how Picasso pulled the light in from the room to put his subject into silhouette. He painted her a hundred years ago. "That won't be possible. You've used up my quota for the month." Nikko sipped from the glass. "I should be able to work for you again perhaps in June." Nikko limited his work to once a month. Twice if the contracts were in different hemispheres.

"Well...I'd like to extend your earlier contract," Morgan said.

"What do you mean?" He finished the sweet and bitter coffee and sat the tiny cup back on the matching saucer.

"One second," Morgan disappeared on the phone for five seconds, not one. "Your last work was completed to our satisfaction."

"But?" Nikko said.

"But the work didn't prevent the delivery."

Nikko replayed the bullets slicing into the scientist and then into Brooks. He missed Brook's head preferring to sever the carotid artery and watch him bleed to death. A bullet through his heart would have been useless. Nikko imagined the bullet would just pierce an empty cavity. But the blood pouring out over the cobblestones was satisfaction enough.

"Not my problem. My contract was specific as to the terms and conditions."

"I understand, but we need your skills. The new target is a protégé of the courier, and we will double the payment."

Nikko thought for a long second. A Henry Miller caught his eye a month ago and the job would more than pay for it. Still, two contracts in the same country, the same city in the same month seemed ludicrous. "Again in Amsterdam?"

"Paris."

"Paris, the city of light. The city of love." A different country and city. He might be able to double up this once. "How will I find him?"

"I'm emailing you the logistics, but it could be tomorrow or the next day." Morgan's voice muffled as if he covered the phone but then cleared up again. "As flexibility is your strong point, I expect you to be in Paris in the morning."

Nikko stood up and switched off the tiny halogen that illuminated the girl in the painting. It's time all good girls went to bed.

"Understood." He closed the call. One change of clothes would be needed, but he might be forced to shop in Paris if the time extended. The horror.

Nikko unlocked a drawer in his Queen Anne desk and reached for a brown envelope. He shook the contents on to the table and found the picture he had taken at the last job. Staring back through the lens was a dead Jonathan Brooks. "Still trying to reach me, eh? Death wasn't final enough?" Nikko touched the picture with the tip of his finger. "Don't worry, Jonathan. I will take care of everything."

CHAPTER THIRTY-FOUR

David walked two blocks and noticed three suits across the street kept pace. Behind him, another suit stood by the bus stop and stared at him, not even trying to be inconspicuous. How the hell did they find him so damn fast? He turned into the first street and ran. Two suits appeared halfway down and converged with the three from the street and forced him into a dead end. The others ran ahead and blocked him getting to the end of the block.

Jeez, I must have pissed off an entire menswear store.

Two held hunting knives. One had a cell phone to his ear. All three gripped a red card. They looked at him and then the card. Did assassins have their own trading cards now?

Five men. Shit.

A few metal balconies hung above him out of reach. A drainpipe ran from the roof to the ground. He could attempt to climb up, but he wouldn't be fast enough. The suit with the cell phone said, "We have a signal and positive ID."

Signal? Signal from what? The clothes he bought? Something from Max? How are they tracking him?

Glock, the voice said.

The Glock. The damn gun he took from the Professor in Amsterdam. *How could I be so careless?*

The men stood side by side, like riot police. Not advancing, not retreating. Guarding, corralling. The suit with the cell phone yelled. "We aren't to touch him. He will be in here in a few minutes."

Who will be here? Morgan again or some other asshole? David thought. "You guys get a group discount at Men's Warehouse?"

No smile. No sound. Just red cards and cutlery. David's heart pounded as the presence slipped back into his skin. Tight but workable. Smart ass David is leaving the building. The pain vanished as the memories took over and David took a back seat. His mouth went dry, but not from fear. From anticipation. Just before a show. Just before on stage.

What was on the cards?

It didn't matter now.

Forward or back. He wouldn't wait for door number three. Forward meant alleys. More protection, but more danger. The open street gave him more escape routes but could expose him to unseen assailants.

Great choices.

He felt the Glock wedged into his waistband. With it, he might take out two or three, but not five.

Straight ahead. Two men versus three. The weaker point.

In front of him, the men weren't brandishing guns. What modern hit team faces an enemy without a gun? They might as well be all wearing red shirts. One of the men in front wore a flattop haircut over a thick neck and shoulders. A rusty hunting knife gripped in his hand. A gun was loud. A knife wasn't. The other looked old but slim and brandished a shiny switchblade with the price sticker still attached. Brand new or very old. Why? Who were these men? The old guy with the switchblade vibrated like he'd been snorting crack.

Flattop said to the other men, "Put the damn cards away. It's him."

"I don't have any money," David said.

"Let me see your hands," Flattop said.

"Please just let me go, whatever you think I did, I didn't."

"Don't talk. Keep your hands up," Flattop pointed with his hunting knife. The man spoke in a faint English accent.

"We don't want your money; we want you dead!" a suit from behind yelled as they pushed David to the wall. The pusher waved a black handled dagger and his whole body shook as if he had palsy. With a skiff of wiry hair on the sides and deep pockmarks on his face, the man swam in the oversized suit jacket. The knife looked like a serpent's tooth and could strike at any second. The man still had a tight grip on the red card.

The suit with the cell phone yelled. "Back off and give him some space. It's forbidden to interact with him."

Wiry hair pointed at David with his knife. "You just wait. He's coming soon."

Another yelled, "Your death will come soon enough."

Five men. Four with knives.

"I'm not a killer," David said

"What did you say?" Flattop pointed at him with the tip of the rusty knife.

The man with the cell phone yelled, "I said, don't engage him! Keep your distance."

Flattop looked over at the man. "He doesn't look so tough. We can handle anything he can deliver."

"I'm not a killer," David said.

"You are going to die like a dog, devil. God will be triumphant."

"I'm not a killer."

Wiry hair behind David spat, "You will beg for mercy, devil!"

David's breathing slowed, like before the rise of the curtain. He felt the presence envelop him, but he felt more control and less like a puppet. Blood pounded in his ears. He focused on the man's knife. The handle had been polished bone, now worn away. It wasn't a combat knife. It was a knife used for hunting, maybe long ago.

"Have a look what I have in the bag," David said.

David dropped the black satchel on the ground and the big man stooped over to pick it up.

"Don't do it!" yelled the man with the cell phone.

Wiry hair rushed towards David, the dagger in one hand. David pivoted on his left leg, grabbed the man's knife wrist, and twisted up and then towards the ground. Wiry hair screamed as his wrist snapped with a crack. Flattop dropped the satchel and leaped with the hunting knife extended, but David parried the knife and jammed the dagger into Flattop's throat. Blood gushed from a sliced artery and the man dropped to the ground.

Three men.

Two rushed at David with their knives high. David parried the first blow and twisted the man into the oncoming knife of the second. Grabbing the handle of the second knife, he sliced deep into the other man's neck before the body dropped to the cement. The guy with the cell phone turned and ran.

Those men found him because of the Glock. Or was there something else? He thought back to the clothes he wore. He'd changed the coat a couple of times. He didn't want to believe it, but he had to start somewhere. He felt around Flattop's dead body and extracted a pistol from inside the jacket. Full clip. Escaping from the dead end, he turned away from the main street away from the crazies. As a garbage truck lumbered by, he tossed his Glock into the back but kept the pistol from Flattop. He needed a weapon and a pistol made more sense than a Swiss army knife.

The truck disappeared around the block, the driver oblivious. That should keep the suits off my back for a little while. Who were they waiting for? At the next corner, he waved down a cab.

Inside, the cab driver turned to him and smiled. "*Anglais?*"

"English is great."

"Where to, *monsieur?*"

"Pigalle, please."

"*Oui, monsieur.*"

As the cab pulled into the street, David mentally checked his body.

A little pain, but not much. Why did they call me the devil? What did I do? He remembered the guy from the theater in Amsterdam talking about religion. What the hell kind of thing had he been thrown into? He looked at his hands. Flecks of red dotted his fingers and palms. He hadn't thought of himself as a killer but he'd just defended himself again.

Maybe he was.

CHAPTER THIRTY-FIVE

The taxi screeched to a stop at the corner of Place de Clichy and Rue Caulaincourt, the outside edge of Pigalle. After paying the driver and waiting for the light to change, his feet wouldn't move. Something stopped him. The voice said, *clothes*.

What are you, my mother? He looked at himself. Spots of blood dusted his hoodie. His right knee was dark from one of the men's blood. Yeah. He needed new clothes. After a few minutes rummaging through a French thrift shop, he walked out to the street wearing torn black cargo pants, a long-sleeved shirt, and baseball cap. A long wool jacket hung down close to the ground. Horn-rimmed sunglasses changed his look and spared his eyes from the sun piercing through the clouds. He dumped his old clothes in a hamper in the back of the store.

The voice had gone, but the sight of side-by-side porn shops and strip clubs triggered a set of rapid-fire memories. Dark rooms filled with smoke and slow jazz. Body odor mixed with heady perfume. The smell of sex. Skin. Lingerie. Blood rushed to his groin. He shut his eyes to stop the images, but naked women rolled through his head like cards from a Rolodex.

Then the memories stopped and were replaced by the image of a dead woman on a floor. A wide smile sliced under her chin. Farther down her body, the killer gutted her as well. Bile erupted from David's stomach as he collapsed to the sidewalk and puked. Two older men and an elderly madam walked past him giving him a wide berth.

He heaved a few more times, and the nausea passed. What remained was a memory of a memory. He took another breath and stood up on shaky legs.

Leaning against a wall, he got his bearings. Groups of Asian men walking clumped together. Just like Amsterdam. A porn shop wedged beside a tiny gas station with a single pump on the curb. Jerk off and an oil change. The French are masters of multitasking.

As he made his way down the street, a half-formed memory arrived. A vague notion of something or someone he should pay attention to. He bought a bottle of water from a street vendor and rinsed his mouth, but the taste of bile remained. He wished he had a toothbrush.

Across the street, a large red neon sign blasted "Moulin Rouge." Bare-breasted Cancan girls sprang to mind. Ballet with fewer clothes. He watched and listened as groups of men passed him as he stared at the neon red windmill. Chinese was still indecipherable. However, anything from Europe he understood: Spanish, Italian, French. Some Russian.

The pain kicked in, but he leaned against a brick wall and closed his eyes, trying to tease out the vague feeling into something he could get his arms around. The matchbook from Max's house was from the cabaret. What was he supposed to do now?

More passing conversations. On or off. He either understood the conversation or not at all. All or nothing. David turned and crossed the alley on to the next block of sex and walked across a worn red carpet leading to a strip club.

A skinny man with slicked black hair sporting a checkered jacket jumped in front of him and smiled rows of white teeth.

"*Bonjour, monsieur*," he said.

David said nothing. He moved to the side and kept walking, but the man moved with him. No internal alarms except for some irritation, like a fly buzzing around his head.

"Good day, do you speak English? *Parlez-vous français? Sprechen sie Deutsch?*" The man seemed almost battery operated. "Would you like to see a live sex show?"

David tilted his head and looked up at the sign above his head. Twice normal-sized, half-clad women danced on the billboard. "No," David said in English. No sense trying to help the headache along.

"Where are you from? Come on, you wouldn't be here if you weren't interested. Look here at some of the girls."

The man raised his arm and tried to corral David towards some glossy pictures of beautiful nude women locked into gymnastic poses. He pointed to a long red curtain covering a doorway.

"It's fifty euros, but if you go in now, I can give it to you for thirty."

David shook his head and walked around him again. But the vague feeling reappeared. As he stopped to focus his thoughts, the man's hand grabbed his shoulder. Without thinking, he grabbed the man's wrist and twisted down throwing the man to the carpet with a thud. "Sorry about that. I'm not interested," David said.

He let him go. Another clump of Asians skirted in front of him. The man yelled for help, but after a few more steps David disappeared into the crowd.

* * *

Still technically morning, buses and tourists with cameras clogged the streets of Pigalle. No one pointed anything at him. At least, not that he saw.

After the fight with the suits and dropping the hawker to the ground, David realized he didn't experience the fear like after the other attacks. Instead, he felt invigorated and confident. The pain hung in the background, but with each access, the memories were more real. As a dancer, his confidence depended on the mood of the artistic director. Funny enough, staying alive didn't need anyone's approval. Continuing to breathe was the win.

As he passed a newspaper stand, a French headline called out, "Canadian wanted for murder in Amsterdam."

He flipped the seller a euro and grabbed the top copy. The article detailed how a murdered pensioner found in a theater was linked to a missing Canadian dancer. His picture from a performance ran underneath the headline along with quotes from several dancers how they couldn't believe he'd be involved in anything like that. Some quotes said David was well-liked and quiet. Nothing from Sophie or Razor.

The ballet. Why did it feel like a million years ago?

He'd been separated from the ballet world in a way he had never imagined. Since the age of six, he'd danced almost every day. A slight child and too timid for most team sports, dance welcomed him. At twelve, his ballet teacher convinced his father to let him audition for the National Ballet School in Toronto. After some work, the old man relented. But reading the article made him miss the anticipation of this first time out of Canada and his first performance on the Paris stage. He'd dreamt of the trip for months, but the article jolted him back to reality. People were hunting him. The police wanted him for murder, and he wasn't sure he wasn't to blame. But he needed to find Max, and he needed to find him now.

He wanted his old life back.

A subtle déjà vu crept over him as he walked the streets. He reached for it and tried to grab hold, but it evaporated. He learned that he couldn't just force a memory to reveal itself. They had their own agenda.

His feet turned and carried him down Villa des Platanes. Bars and small boutiques replaced the porn shops and heavy perfume and the cigarette smoke filled the air. He stopped. The perfume was the same as in his dream last night.

Two tall women sat at stools by a tiny bar. One black and one blonde. Identical uniforms. Long stockings, low cut tops, and stiletto heels. The black woman smiled at him and called out, "*Bonjour, monsieur*, would you like to come inside for a drink?"

The perfume was unmistakable and overpowering. He was in the right place.

"No, madam, thank you." He wanted to find Max and instead the memories took him to a brothel.

"*Monsieur*, you are very handsome, but you are so sad. Come inside, we can help you be happy," the blonde spoke this time.

Something else in this bar seemed familiar. He twisted his head back and forth and realized Jonathan Brooks had been here before, and it wasn't for the inventory.

The blonde said to the bartender, "Sammy, can you pour me another Coke, *s'il vous plaît?*"

David's eyes adjusted to the dingy interior. The bartender withdrew a silver case from his back pocket, liberated a cigarette, and pushed it to his lips.

Samuel.

Max's Samuel. His hair was now blond and gelled back. He wore a tight-fitting white T-shirt instead of a suit and tie. A fresh Coke in a tall glass appeared by magic on the bar and Samuel pushed it with a smile to the hooker. He hadn't noticed David yet.

* * *

Mirrors and red textured wallpaper covered the walls of the tiny bar. Black paint covered everything else. Under bright lights, the place would look hideous. He walked up to the red acrylic and in a hushed voice he said, "Samuel."

Samuel was squatting down filling a tiny refrigerator with tall bottles of beer, but his whole body stiffened. He stood up, closed the refrigerator, and turned towards David.

"How did you find this place?" Samuel glanced outside the window "Were you followed?"

"No, I don't think so. I don't think they know where I am."

"Fool. They always will know where you are. Don't you realize that?"

David locked eyes with him. "I need Max."

"That would be difficult and foolish," he grabbed a white rag and wiped it across the bar.

"Where is Alicia? Is she here, too?" David looked him up and down unable to grasp the change from the person who saved his life a few days ago.

"No. Max sent her on an errand."

"Where?"

Samuel didn't answer. He had said everything he wanted to say. David looked at him. A silver ring pierced his eyebrow, and a nostril boasted a polished metal stud. A small diamond went through his ear lobe. He looked for sale as well as the women.

He leaned over and said. "You were given a chance in Amsterdam, plus the means to escape in any way you chose." He looked into David's eyes. "That chance is no longer available."

"I need to speak with Max. I understand more than I did before and more people are after me."

"What is it do you think Max can do for you?"

David was silent for a few moments. "I'm hoping he can help me find a way out. Maybe negotiate on my behalf or find a way to stop whoever is chasing me."

"That's quite an ask," Samuel said.

"Can I have another Coke, honey?" the black hooker called over to the bar. She hitched up the hem of her dress and smiled as David glanced over at her. Samuel took a tall frosted glass, filled it with ice and soda, and placed it on the bar for the girl.

"Jonathan's memories are more frequent and more painful. I need to find out what information is locked up inside me," David almost whispered, not wanting anyone else in the bar to hear what he had to say.

"You know his name?"

"Alicia told me."

Samuel grabbed two glasses from the back shelf and stacked them beside the counter. "He was an associate of Max's many years ago."

"You knew him?"

"More, he knew of me. Most of what happened between Max and him was before my time."

"I'm not looking for protection, just more information on who is chasing me."

Samuel pulled out a large cutting board along with whole lemons and limes and placed them on the top of the bar. He grabbed the largest lemon and, using a chef's knife, sliced it first in half then into thin slices.

"Can you arrange a meeting?"

"Come back at 8:00 p.m. Now leave unless you plan to become a paying customer."

Samuel's eyes looked towards where two girls sat in the shadows, both chain-smoking.

David said, "I will be back tonight." As he left the bar, he paused outside for a moment until he could clear his lungs of all the dank air.

It was now 2:00 p.m. He had six hours to kill.

CHAPTER THIRTY-SIX

The company's first Paris rehearsal was in full swing. Lester had messed with more of the pieces and the dancers struggled with his frantic changes.

In the middle of a pas de deux run through, Sophie collapsed onto the beige floor and grabbed the top of her foot. The pianist stopped in mid-phrase. Her partner, Evan Bailey, blocked the light and covered her tiny body in shadow. He rolled his eyes. "What happened?"

"Nothing. I hurt my instep." She undid the satin straps, pulled off her pink toe shoe, and massaged her foot. Her dark hair squeezed tight in a bun.

"You stumbled when I lowered you from the second lift after the turn."

Sophie tried to stay calm, but it wasn't working.

"You stepped on me," she said.

"No. You tripped," Bailey said.

Sophie glared at him. "I didn't trip. As you were moving away from me, you stomped on my foot with those big clogs of yours."

Robert Lester, the company's artistic director burst into the room, with an unopened bottle of Evian in his hand. A white towel hung around his neck. "What is it this time?"

Bailey said, "She tripped and she's blaming me."

"This big ape"—she nodded her head at Bailey—"stepped on me."

Lester looked at Bailey and smiled like a crocodile. "I'm sure it was an accident; nothing more. Now let's get up and try it again, shall we?"

Sophie rubbed at her instep again. "I need a few minutes." Bailey reached over to help her, but she brushed him aside. "No thanks, you've helped enough."

From the side, Celeste approached and grabbed her hand and helped her up. "Let's find the doctor and have him take to look at it."

"I'm fine. I need a few minutes." Under her breath she said to Celeste, "I'm worried."

"About David?" Celeste said. Sophie nodded her head.

"I'm worried, too," Lester said.

Sophie stared straight at Lester. "You are?"

"I'm worried that I won't be able to wring his neck for messing up things before I send him back to Canada." Lester's entire face burned red.

Celeste leaned into Sophie, "Don't do it." She put her bruised foot on the floor and winced. "Just what has he done? Razor said they were both attacked."

Lester pulled at the towel off his shoulders. "The police say Knight was mixed up in a drug deal. When Razor showed up without the money, he tried to kill him."

"Then why is Razor defending him? And David doesn't do drugs."

Lester ignored the first question. "I think Razor is lying to save his ass," Lester smirked. "Knight was an addict waiting to happen."

Sophie's heart pounded through the layers of spandex and cotton of her leotard. But she would not let it go.

"You think Razor made up what happened to him? He's got a concussion!"

"Then where is the little shit? Why isn't he here if he's not guilty? And I don't understand why you are protecting him after he dumped you."

Sophie's eyes bulged and her nostrils flared. "You're an asshole. I'm glad the whole company can see your trust and support." She turned and hobbled towards the door.

"After tonight, you better just keep on going. You won't be dancing with us anymore."

She glared at him and walked out the door. The other dancers in the room were stone silent. No dancer dared ever call the artistic director an asshole even if he was.

Celeste followed her. Sophie slammed the studio door shut, and the sound reverberated in the ancient hallway. "That egotistical prick. David could be hurt or even dead we aren't doing anything about it." She pulled the pins out of her hair and unwound her long red strands from the bun.

"But you two broke up," Celeste said.

Sophie stopped. "That doesn't mean I'm not worried."

Celeste said, "The police are combing the streets of Amsterdam. They will find him."

Sophie changed into street clothes and pushed her leotard, leggings, and dance shoes into her shoulder bag. Celeste helped her navigate the stairs and held her arm as she hobbled out to a cobblestone sidewalk. At the end of the road, the noon sun glinted off the steeples of the nearby Paris Opera House. Sophie sighed and said, "I'm just upset I have to dance with that big ape upstairs."

"What about what Lester said?"

"Screw him. My father is a lawyer and will bring up a wrongful dismissal suit against him so large that he will be cleaning toilets."

* * *

137

This time of day, a few Parisians strolled on the street near the rehearsal studio. A large man in a long dark trench coat and a fedora walked towards both girls. He seemed distracted, but at the last second stopped. "Sophie Dumont?" the man asked.

Sophie frowned. "Yes?"

"I have information about your friend David."

A white van screeched to a stop and two men jumped out. Before she knew it, one man clamped a cloth over her face and the struggle stopped. As things went black, she heard the big man say, "We only want this one. Be gentle with the other please. He won't like it if either gets hurt."

* * *

Little Bill lowered the other girl gently to the ground as Big Bill lifted the target into the truck. Wyatt jumped in and the van screamed down the tiny street before merging into the Paris traffic. Twenty seconds had elapsed. Ten more than he wanted. But he got the girl. The right girl, too. Wyatt scanned a ballet program from tonight's performance. Sophie Dumont. Soloist. Twenty-two. Pas du Deux. Whatever the hell that was.

He opened his cell phone and called Reynolds, "We have her. Get Fitz to send the email."

CHAPTER THIRTY-SEVEN

David planned a drive-by of the Paris Opera House. But he wasn't sure what he expected, or what trouble he might be causing doing it, but the pull to reconnect to a sense of normalcy was overwhelming.

"The roads are blocked, *monsieur*." the cabby said. "But the Opera is only a few blocks ahead."

"Just let me out here," David said. After throwing a ten euro note into the front seat, he tilted the brim of his hat farther down his forehead and exited the cab.

He noticed several blocks ahead, police lights flashing. An accident more than likely. After experiencing the typical Parisian taxi thrill ride several times already, he wasn't surprised. Didn't Lady Diana die as the result of a high-speed chase in Paris? The theater sat big and imposing five blocks away.

The company would be rehearsing at a studio nearby, but he'd walk by the theater first. But after a few blocks, the hair on the back of his neck rose and his heart raced. Someone followed him. He felt it. He almost tasted it. Like a tiny stone in your shoe you couldn't remove. However, it wasn't suit-wearing idiots with pocketknives. Someone else.

Who the hell were they?

Highly trained. Unclear objective, the voice said.

Jonathan's voice, but he imagined an older brother whispering in his ear. The pain always followed, but not as debilitating as before.

He watched as the last few bits of sunlight retreated behind a blanket of grey. Did Paris always look this forlorn? Where was Paris in the springtime? Almost on cue, a bus drove by belching thick diesel smoke.

Not at this time.

Two old men speaking Arabic to each other passed him on the sidewalk, and he caught a few of the words with only a touch of pain. Women, wife, money, sex. The same conversation that men talk about in any language.

He reached the corner of Rue Joubert and Rue du Mikado and stepped from the curb to the street.

No.

Pain shot up his neck and he stopped short, stepped back, and leaned against a building. He took deep breaths and rolled his shoulders. Keeping to this side of the street kept the pain away.

At the next corner, he passed a large woman with a green apron selling flowers out of water-filled buckets. She reached into the middle fold of her apron for something and David spun around just before she said, *"Des fleurs pour ta copine?"*

He relaxed and said in English, "No, thank you." He was on edge. That was for sure.

I'm still being watched, aren't I?

Yes, the voice said. The neck pain dropped to a slight tingle.

Two blocks short of the Galleries Lafayette and the gilded roof of the Palais Garnier, a yellow-vested gendarme detoured traffic to Boulevard Haussmann. As he moved closer, he saw police cars pulsing blue lights and enclosing an intersection. Several other constables milled around the area. Behind a group of gendarmes, a group of young people huddled together like waterfowl in the winter in front of a studio used for rehearsals.

Dancers. All of them. He recognized some. His friends and colleagues. Others were unfamiliar. From the Paris company. The ballet company he should be dancing with alongside with his own.

He stepped back behind one of the other onlookers. Beside him, an old woman sat her bags of groceries to the ground and craned her neck for a better look.

A bulbous man dressed in white exited the building and stood near the group. Robert Lester, the artistic director.

"Excusez-moi, madam?" David switched to English. He didn't need any extra pain right now. "What happened?"

"A girl kidnapped. In daylight." She shook her head. "A dancer, one of the gendarme say."

David's stomach flopped. First Razor and now this. Who did this? Was he responsible? A stretcher emerged from the cloud of police and he caught a glimpse of red curls. The smoky voice of Celeste yelled. "I don't want to go to the damn hospital. I want to find Sophie."

Sophie? He tasted bile. *It is my fault,* he thought. As the ambulance pulled away, the dancers dispersed, all unsure where to go. One of the male dancers looked his way.

Bailey.

Not a good time to be recognized. Time to go. David pivoted, ran across the road, and disappeared down a side street. A few minutes later, he hailed a cab and disappeared into the Paris traffic.

"*Monsieur*? Where to?" The man's English wasn't bad. At least David thought he heard English.

"Montmartre." David leaned his head back on the seat. What did they want with Sophie?

* * *

The cab dropped him off near the Basilica of the Sacré-Coeur. He found a café and slipped into the tiny men's toilet at the back. After rinsing his face with a trickle of water from the sink, he stared into the mirror.

He looked like shit.

Big bags hung under his eyes and his skin was sallow and sunken. Would the implant make him fade away completely?

Someone grabbed Sophie. But why? What did they stand to gain from her abduction?

You, the voice said.

The familiar presence hovered around his head. The subtle pain disappeared, but he felt hot like he was too close to a fire. Not a fever, just the heat.

They. The voice began.

Want. The words arrived slow. Like Morse code.

You.

What was he supposed to do now?

Up to now, his only plan was to find Max. He'd believed that Max, the Mighty Max would save him. Max, an asthmatic and geriatric spymaster that could magically save a 21-year-old ballet dancer from almost certain death.

How could he be so stupid? He felt like Dorothy looking for the Wizard of Oz. Even if saw the great and powerful Max, what could he do? His anger flared up at himself and his own arrogance and naivety. He wished those five men idiots were standing in front of him again with those stupid hunting knives. He wouldn't need any voice or super spy to help. His anger would be enough.

A knock interrupted his self-pity. "*Monsieur? S'il vous plaît?*"

He opened the door and a sunken old Parisian man with a wide mustache smiled and slipped inside as David left. Must be an emergency, David thought.

At a table near the back, he ordered food and coffee. Regardless of what would happen, he needed his strength. As he devoured a baguette stuffed with cheese and tomatoes, he formed a plan of his own. He wasn't sure if Max would have a better idea, but he had to start somewhere.

CHAPTER THIRTY-EIGHT

David forced himself to finish his food as he thought about Sophie. Could that sick bastard Morgan have taken her? But if Morgan grabbed her to flush him out, there was no way to contact him. What kind of a plan was that?

He scratched Morgan off the list who might have grabbed Sophie but kept him on top of the who's the biggest asshole pyramid.

The bigger question was why. Morgan wanted some device and ordered his death when he couldn't produce it. The knife guys called him a devil and were waiting for someone. Waiting for Morgan? Seemed like the most likely scenario. Morgan spouted religious bullshit before he left the Amsterdam theater. But none of that explained why this whole thing went religious crazy.

As a child, his mother dragged him to Sunday school. He'd sit in his best clothes and listen to the songs and the stories, but nothing stuck. Easter meant chocolate bunnies. Christmas meant presents and Santa Claus. It wasn't that he didn't believe, it was that he just didn't care. But something about the device threatened this brand of religious crazies.

But if Morgan wanted the device, others would too. He tapped his forehead and realized the secret to everything was stuck inside his cranium with no way to find it.

The memory of an empty briefcase but nothing else. No words. No GPS coordinates. No Google Map location. He swallowed the last of the coffee and thought again about Sophie.

If it wasn't Morgan that took her, then who?

The man with the wonky eye? Or the people that implanted these damn memories to begin with? That made more sense. The Memory men wanted the device and used him as a guinea pig to get it. They were neck and neck for the top of the asshole pyramid.

Three groups. Morgan, Wonky eye guy, and the Memory men.

He felt like an NHL draft pick that was screwed no matter which team he went with.

And he had no plan.

As a dancer, he planned nothing, because everything was planned for him. He went to class, learned the pieces, and rehearsed the roles. Now circumstances were different. He couldn't do this by feel alone, he needed a plan. For a few minutes, he tried to summon the voice, but he was awarded with silence. He opened his eyes and stared down at the half-eaten bun.

Nothing.

A sign inside the cafe said they rented rooms. After a quick conversation with the proprietor, and fifty euros later, he laid he head back on a tiny bed on the second floor. He needed to rest and regroup before he started making bad decisions again.

* * *

As dusk fell in the City of Lights, he returned to Pigalle. An 80's disco beat sung by a twenty-first century rap star boomed inside Samuel's bar. Two made-up girls sat in the low chairs; a skinny bleached blonde and an olive-skinned girl with a bob. Three identical Asian businessmen sat with them. Triplets maybe. Three boys in a family—very auspicious in Chinese folklore. Both girls smiled like Cheshire cats.

Behind the bar, a short black man with thick forearms poured drinks. From the back, the Rubenesque ebony hooker from the morning appeared and pushed a folded piece of paper across the counter.

"Sammy asked me to give you this." She batted her fake eyelashes.

David pressed ten euros into her hands and thanked her. Outside, he read the perfumed note before tearing it into pieces and dropping them into the sewer. The address felt familiar once he read it. Ten minutes later, he popped another pill in front of a three-story walkup just off Rue Clauzel. The brass doorknob gave no resistance as he entered in silence. Two steps up from the bottom, he saw dark drips on the ripped plastic stair tread.

Blood.

He pulled out the pistol he grabbed from the suit in the alley and took a slow breath. With each step upward, a tiny shard of metal drove into his skull. Red splotches continued to the top of the stairs. The body of Samuel sat upright in a heavy wooden chair at the top landing, his hands pulled back and tied behind him. Blood dripped down the chair leg and ran in rivulets, down the steps. His mouth and nose covered with grey duct tape. A large swath of red fell from his head down his face. David touched his neck. No pulse but his skin felt still warm and clammy. Dead eyes stared down towards the bottom of the stairs, seeing things after his world ended.

The wooden handle of a kitchen knife stuck out from under his heart. The blade would have sliced into Samuel's lung, filling it with blood and drowning him in his own fluids.

He closed the blond man's eyes and then moved into the next room. The pain was close to nausea level. Inside, the apartment was a mixture of spartan and chaos. Most rooms filled with books, computer equipment, and DVDs. David didn't have to look very far until he saw Max.

An old body sat leaning forward in a wheelchair, both hands holding his stomach as blood dripped from the metal frame and formed a puddle underneath the wheels. A torrent of disconnected and jumbled memories of Max and Samuel flooded into David. Seeing him unlocked another level somehow. But the nausea and pain hit new levels as David gritted his teeth.

"David…" Max's dirty head moved, and a choked off voice struggled to speak. "How nice…of you to come…and visit us." Max coughed and battled with each breath. "Too bad you couldn't have been to see us a little earlier. Maybe you could have provided assistance."

"Max… I'm sorry…"

Max's head moved upwards with great effort, stopping until he could see David's eyes. Memories of a younger Max appeared.

"Who did this to you?"

"My young David…" Max retched. "Jonathan trained him much to his chagrin." His words slowed. Max looked into David's eyes. "If you'd be so kind as to get the bastard, I'd be grateful."

"Who, Max? Who did this to you?"

"He was always a bad apple. Careful…careful. All roads…are mined. No roads lead to safety."

"Max, I don't know who did this!"

Max took a breath and didn't exhale. He was dead. David's emotions were off. No more pain. No emotions at all. Compartmentalize. The voice spoke one word. Only once. One feeling remained. Not grief, or sadness. Just revenge.

An image formed in front of him, as an apparition might. A face just to the side of his field of vision. Just at the edge of his ability to see. A face. Long thin nose. High cheekbones. Long strands of black shiny hair. A name sounded in his ears. Like it was the first time it had been spoken.

Nikko.

David's vision faded to grey then to green then thick bushes and trees. Africa. Nikko emerged from a dense forest. Khaki bush pants, shirt stained deep red. A steel machete in his right hand. A human head in his left, two dreadlocks tied together for a handle. Smiling black militiamen walking behind Nikko, guns at the ready.

David closed his eyes to stop the images but couldn't.

The mosquitoes and flies swarmed the head. Jonathan recognized the man. An informant. Their informant. Nikko dropped the head to the ground and it rolled, finding a resting place against a large rock. David felt a Kalashnikov 74 in Jonathan's hands. David felt the anger, wanting to shoot Nikko and the men behind him.

David gasped at the regret he didn't.

"The prisoner told me what we needed to know, sir," Nikko laughed, "but then died soon after."

Jonathan stood there, sick to his stomach. Finger on the trigger. Wanting to pull it. Wanting to swing it up and kill all three of them.

"You are a sick bastard," Jonathan said. The mission was to get intel and by any means possible. Nikko did just that.

Jonathan still wanted to kill him.

"Yes, sir."

The dream faded and a wave of regret and remorse smacked David in the head. Jonathan's remorse that he didn't kill Nikko and his own shame he wasn't here to save Max and Samuel.

If he ever got the chance to kill Nikko, he'd take it. The anger washed over him from his head to his toes. Using his breath, he tried to calm himself in this pit of chaos.

He needed to focus. He didn't have much time.

The room was a mess. Slashed couch cushions and books and files spilled to the floor. Nikko had been looking for something. But what? In the back of his mind, he remembered a hiding place of sorts. Good for small things. Microfilm.

Maybe, when dinosaurs roamed the earth.

A gentle memory surfaced, more of a nudge. He put his hand underneath Max's wheelchair and snapped open a hidden compartment. He withdrew a thin stainless USB drive and stuffed it in his pocket.

Outside, police sirens blared. Nikko would have tipped them off. David opened the rear window and climbed up a stairway to the roof. At ground level, a Gendarme vehicle screeched to a halt in front of Max's apartment.

He clambered over the connecting buildings and found a fire escape to the street. A few minutes later, he sat in the back of a cab and heading away from Max and Samuel. The cabbie asked in French *"Où veux-tu aller?"*

"Saint-Michel, s'il vous plaît," he said.

CHAPTER THIRTY-NINE

Arthur Westlake listened to the team's chatter through his earpiece as he sipped a cappuccino in the safety of a Paris cafe. The second team lost the dancer, but the first didn't.

The operation called for a large net; four teams total. If the boy had stayed in one place, he might have noticed the surveillance. However, this was Paris; the city of light and infinite distractions. If the dancer knew he was being tailed, he didn't seem to care.

The game had changed over the years. Bugs the size of a speck of dust broadcast his location to the network of cell towers crossing the city. Not quite GPS, but close. A slight jostle by an old woman on the street placed the bug. A little extra help to keep the subject in sight.

The first team watched the dancer jump across two rooftops to escape from the old cripple's house. Westlake winced as he heard about the carnage in the apartment. The old man had been a minor annoyance for the last few years, but karma catches up. Still, Westlake wasn't a fan of torture.

The second team caught the dancer's scent when he reached the street. One of their cabs picked him up and relayed his location to everyone's smartphones. All the tech purchased off the shelf. If they had this surveillance thirty years ago, the cold war would have ended years before.

"He's on the move. Sending the cab's ID to your attention."

"Thank you," Westlake said.

He waved to the waiter for more coffee and rubbed his damaged eye. A childhood accident; another student rubber-banded a pencil at him and hit a soft spot. Doctors told him he'd need a prosthetic soon, but he wanted to keep his own eye as long as possible. Sentimental reasons maybe. His failed eye was part of him. His enemies underestimated him, and singular vision forced him to work at least twice as hard.

He recruited for the agency like a baseball scout. Find, test, and finally hire new talent. He never toppled governments or engaged in any wet work. Those were other organizations. He had an eye for aptitude, he joked, but if this procedure worked, his job would change for the best.

He watched Pigalle through the bar window and started on the fresh cup. Arthur Westlake was his real name. He didn't use aliases. Never left a trail or did any dirty work. He hired people for that.

But still, the success of Reynolds' experiment surprised him. Take a boy with no skills other than extreme physicality and implant a trained agent. That wasn't Reynolds' intent, of course, but the law of unintended consequence sometimes can with positive results.

Science Fiction. Science Reality.

The boy showed tremendous potential from the implantation. With each test, the boy came out on top. His reflexes and reactions were even better than the original.

Amazing.

Even though this was just one isolated test, the results promised great things yet to come. It helped the other parties set up a nice rat maze for him to traverse. And they weren't done yet. Depending on the outcome, he might approach the boy with a generous offer. But there was still work to do before that.

"Subject heading towards Latin Quarter," came through his earpiece.

The third team was already on the ground at Saint Germain and would sight him in a manner of minutes.

But how much longer could he last? With the cripple dead, the boy was on his own. The implant helped but the ongoing pain might be troublesome. He wondered if the scientist could remove the pain, unless it was a necessary side effect.

He paid for the coffee and left the cafe. In that area of Paris, whores patrolled the streets like sexual gendarmes. As a government agent, he was more of a sex worker than a bureaucrat. In his business, he always made sure someone got screwed.

CHAPTER FORTY

Prepare. Prepare. Prepare. Listen to the music. Take a breath. Don't choke up. Don't hold your breath. Compartmentalize. Remember your part. Remember the mission. You are part of a bigger machine. Feel the music with your body. Exhale as you pull the trigger. Watch for your partner. Use your breath. Don't forget to breathe.

The memories wouldn't stop.

Multiple voices. Multiple instructions. Multiple points of pain. Ballet and tradecraft. Maybe military. The images, sounds, and voices fused into each other so much he couldn't tell which ones were his own.

A wave of nausea hit him as he exited the taxi. The images of Samuel and Max's bloody corpses and Jonathan's African vision took its toll. He grabbed for a lamppost and held on to it until wanting to vomit passed.

He needed to get off the street.

A few blocks away from Place Saint-Michel, he entered a cafe he saw the day before. Dark walls, florescent lights, and stale cigarette smoke. A fat teenager behind the counter nodded to him as he walked to the back. French and English signs said credit card accepted at each computer.

He sat at an empty terminal and used the Barclay's Visa Samuel supplied to buy internet time. Prepare, the memory said. Or was it be prepared? David wondered if he was a dancer, a spy, or a boy scout.

Hard to tell.

He searched Canadian news and found an article about the National Ballet of Canada's cursed European tour. An unnamed dancer's hospitalization and subsequent travel back to Canada. Another dancer missing and linked to several homicides. Look, Dad, I'm a celebrity! But not the good kind.

But Razor had made it home. Safe. That news lifted a bit of the guilt he'd been feeling.

The story also quoted Robert Lester, the company's artistic director. "The show must go on. We are here to perform and will continue in their absence." He knew Lester would be throwing a fit behind the scenes because of the situation overshadowing his own imagined brilliance.

He plugged the stainless USB stick from Max's apartment into the computer and read the contents. Max had come through. Memory implantation was possible. *Tell me something I don't know,* he thought. The words on the second document seemed oddly spaced as if the information had been sucked out through a straw. But the meaning was clear. The Memory Men wanted him because his head contained a password to unlock a machine. The device Morgan wanted.

No mention of why Morgan or the suits with knives wanted him dead.

Last document. He read it through it and stared at the screen. If the information was true, locked in his head was the location of some new video game.

Not a terrorist weapon. Not plans for a biotech virus. Not a secret map to where the celebrities live. He reread the document line-by-line, right to the end.

A fucking video game. A video game that Morgan and the suits with knives wanted to stop and the Memory Men wanted to find.

If he wasn't pissed off enough already. As the revelation spiked his heart rate, a cloud of pain descended as his fingers typed a cryptic web address he'd never seen before. A password box appeared. His fingers typed as if he was possessed. He couldn't follow the keystrokes in his conscious mind. A blank screen appeared once more with an error message. His fingers moved and clicked the mouse on the second to last word. A screen appeared. An email inbox.

One message. In the draft folder. Unsent. Dated today.

"If you are reading this, then you have the memories of an associate of mine. We require them back. By now, you should know we've acquired a friend of yours to trade. Here's what you need to do to guarantee her safety."

David read the rest of the email and the blood drained from his face. The note was signed "Fitz."

Fitz? David gripped the side of the chair. Twin bolts of pain stabbed in each eye and through his head. He almost cried out but squashed the emotion and instead gritted his teeth taking shallow breaths.

A vision of a tall salt and pepper haired Englishman ran through his head like a film strip.

Asher Fitzsimmons.

The film continued with Jonathan and Fitz standing side by side pointing pistols at a fat Russian captain. Next. Fitz bleeding from a knife wound in his side. Jonathan carrying him to safety. Sticky warmth as Fitz's blood soaked into his shirt. Next. Toasting glasses. Fitz drinking wine. Jonathan drinking scotch. Fitz smiling. Grey hair now. Older. Reading glasses. Time had passed since the knife wound.

They snatched Sophie. No, Fitz snatched Sophie. The spy had saved Fitz's life. Could David trust him?

No, the voice said. *Compromised.*

David caught the fat kid from the front staring back at him. The fat kid's eyes went wide then returned to the computer on the counter. But every few seconds he glanced back at David.

Time to go. After unplugging the memory stick and stuffing it into his pocket, he deleted the browser's cache and logged off the computer. The kid at the front might try to recover the deleted documents, but David didn't care. The information looked like science fiction, plus the kid thought he was crazy, anyway.

He left the cafe and turned right. A plan percolated in his mind. He'd need help to first get Sophie back. But there was only one place he could go.

CHAPTER FORTY-ONE

Paris Opera House

The famous Palais Garnier sat in the middle of a triangle bordered by Boulevard Haussmann and Boulevard des Capucines. Home to the Opera and Ballet Company, the building's fame emanated from the 1910 novel, *The Phantom of the Opera*. However, in the City of Lights, the building and the institution was just known as the Opera.

Ballet rehearsals took place a few blocks from the actual theater. Several blocks away, on Rue Rossini, like the actress, down Rue Haussmann, the second building in.

Climbing the stairs to the second floor, he read a note scrawled in blue ink stuck to a door leading to a studio. "Men 16:00–18:00." From the hallway, he heard the men swearing. Not uncommon in rehearsals as dancers worked out spacing and timing issues, but as he listened, he realized he was the cause of the problem. No need to be subtle anymore. He had grabbed the handle and pushed his way in.

* * *

Part of the tour's program was an all-male piece called "Troy Game." Every male dancer was in the piece.

Without Razor and him, and no other men as backups, Lester would be forced to restage the piece to make up for the two missing dancers. Changing the piece from thirteen men down to eleven wasn't easy. But changing it because one dancer had been beaten and the other accused of murder would have made it doubly hard and make Lester double the asshole.

However, from the banter in the room, it appeared Lester was nowhere around.

David stood in a small hallway that opened into the main space. He wasn't sure what he would say. However, one of the men noticed him standing in the hallway.

"David! Oh my God! Are you all right? We have been so worried about you." A dancer grabbed him and gave him a hug. David didn't return it. After the last few days, ballet felt alien to him. The constant rehearsal, cold sweat on his skin, and daily muscle aches seemed a distant memory. Each dancer looked clear, bright, and fresh. David expected he looked at least a hundred years old.

He walked into the studio with all the men crowded around, smiling, and reaching out to touch him, as if he was an apparition. Andrew pushed his tall body through to the front. Friends since ballet school, he and David were close, but Andrew's promotion to soloist last month never sat well with David. All that seemed meaningless at this point.

He was here to see Andrew.

"Are you okay?" Andrew asked.

"I'm better now," David said.

The studio door flew open. "There you are, you little shit!" Lester said, his feet clomping like a horse as he stormed into the center of the space. He pointed his finger at David. "Where the hell have you been?"

The other dancers stepped back and seemed to cower at Lester's tirade. David didn't. Lester frowned as if he wasn't getting the response he expected. He jabbed his nicotine stained finger again at David's chest. "Do you know the problems you have caused? The tour is in jeopardy, Sophie's been abducted, and I've had to reset this whole piece all because of *you!*"

Spit flew out of Lester's mouth and hit David's coat. The pudgy artistic director ranted like a rabid dog. David couldn't believe this man used to strike fear in his heart.

Not anymore.

David ignored him and turned back to Andrew.

"Can we talk for a minute, outside?"

Andrew squinted at David and looked a little amused that Lester's barking didn't seem to affect him.

"How dare you ignore me, you ignorant little prick!" Lester reached out, grabbed David by the arm and squeezed until his knuckles were white. David turned and said, "I would let go of me if I were you."

"Just what will you do, you little asshole? I'm not finished."

With that last comment, David grabbed Lester's wrist and twisted towards his thumb. David pivoted on his right foot and somersaulted Lester to the floor with a crack. The dancers in the room stood in shock. A few laughed. Lester got up from the floor, his eyes burning and rushed him, hands extended. David blocked Lester's attack and hit him with a left jab to the head following with a right uppercut. The once terrifying artistic director collapsed on the floor in an unconscious heap.

All the men stood back speechless. This choreography wasn't part of the rehearsal. Some dancers clapped.

David motioned to Andrew. "I need to talk to you in private." He walked into the hallway and Andrew followed behind. As the door shut, David said,

"Andrew...I..."

"David, it's good to see you again. When Razor got hurt, we thought the worst had happened. Most people thought you were dead."

"I'm in trouble, but it's not what you think."

"Somebody grabbed Sophie after rehearsal this morning."

"I know. Because of me. That's why I'm here. I need your help."

"Me?" Andrew looked around like he got picked to run with the bulls. "We have to go to the police!"

"Look, it's a long story, but I'm the one they want. They grabbed Sophie to get to me."

David looked into the face of his friend. The man that stood beside him during countless dance classes, held his head while he threw up after too much drinking on graduation night from the ballet school.

Andrew frowned "What? That sounds crazy. Come back into the studio and we can talk," Andrew said.

"No, I have to go. But I need your help. I can get Sophie back, but I need you to be here tomorrow morning." David handed him a piece of paper. "They will trade Sophie for me. I have something they want, but this is the only way I can guarantee her safety."

"We need to call the police and tell them," Andrew said.

"No!" David's mood changed. "No police. Just you."

"David, you can't just do that. This isn't like a movie. You can't just go up against some kidnapper and win. Razor almost died in Amsterdam..." Andrew's voice trailed off. "It's the same people, right?"

"No, but it's all connected. It's a long story and I will tell you, but not right now. I just need your promise to be there tomorrow."

Andrew shifted his gaze and stared at the ground between them.

"Look at me." He grabbed his friend by the shoulders. "Do not, under ANY circumstances, bring the police into this. I need you to be there for Sophie when the trade is done. She will be scared, but I don't think they will hurt her."

Andrew nodded and said. "I'll be there."

As David started down the stairs he said, "Be there on time."

David descended to the street. He didn't have much time as Lester would sound the alarm once he came to.

If he was lucky, he'd have the reinforcement he needed, and Sophie would be safe. That was the plan for now. He couldn't see anything past saving her. He'd tell anyone who would like the location of this damn video game, if he knew how to. But first things first. Save Sophie and he'd make up the rest.

CHAPTER FORTY-TWO

Paris—Pont Neuf—5:50 a.m.

David shivered as he looked across the Seine at Notre Dame waiting for the throngs of Sunday visitors yet to awaken. He had no idea what was about to happen, but his stomach was in knots. Twisting his father's ring on his finger back and forth gave him some comfort.

Towards Pont Neuf, two women wearing matching black hats and veils, each pulled matching black terriers. David couldn't decide if they were hurrying to an early Mass or a morning funeral.

Was he walking to his own?

At the top of a stone staircase leading to the water, his feet stopped. He pushed himself to move but remained rooted to the stone. Dragging up an implanted memory of Fitz released some anxiety, at least enough to descend the steps.

At the bottom of the walkway and to the left, two large dinner boats sat closed. To the right, a narrow concrete path snaked under the bridge. He wanted the struggle to be over, but something told him he wasn't at the end yet. The cold barrel of Samuel's CZ pistol jammed into the back of his pants didn't bolster his confidence and his sour stomach didn't help either.

Beneath the ancient stone of Petit Pont Bridge stood three men and one woman.

Sophie.

He expected more of a reaction to seeing her, but only felt more anxious. She wasn't safe until the next stage was complete.

She wore an oversized black wool peacoat and a woolen hat hiding her long burgundy hair. Her eyes looked distant. Drugged perhaps. He thought about it and realized to the other party, this was a business transaction. A placid prisoner always made things better.

An older man stood beside her with his right hand on her shoulder.

Asher Fitzsimmons. Fitz to his friends.

Tall with short grey hair, almost white. A blue suit peaked out from underneath a dark trench coat. Warmth flooded David, but he shook it off. Other memories of Fitz bubbled up and pain rose in his temples.

The other two men looked like opposite sides of a funhouse mirror. One was big and the other stubby. They seemed familiar, but David couldn't place them.

"I'm so glad you made it, David," Fitz said. "It's a lovely morning, don't you think?"

David said nothing. Instead, he tightened his stomach to stop the shaking. Stubby moved towards David and said, "Raise your arms."

American. By his accent, probably New York. A short version of Tony Soprano. David looked down at him and said, "You didn't say the magic word."

The man looked confused then said with no smile, "Please."

David raised his arms, and the man frisked him, finding the pistol, and taking it. Stubby stunk of cigarettes. David thought he must wash with nicotine soap.

"Pretty boy is clean. If you don't count the gun," Stubby said

"Sorry about all this. Little Bill is thorough."

A memory rushed forward. The two Bills. Beefy was Big Bill. Stubby is Little Bill.

David stared at Sophie. "Did you drug her?"

"We gave her a pill to reduce her stress."

"Did you hurt her?"

"My dear David, I'm surprised you would even mention something like that. Perhaps those memories you have inside aren't that reliable." Fitz smiled a poker smile. White, Shiny. A winning hand.

"I assure you, we mean no harm to you or your friend." He gestured with his head towards Sophie. "But you left us no choice. The skills you picked up during the procedure have complicated things a great deal."

David stepped closer to Fitz.

"That's close enough," Little Bill said. He flanked David's side. Fitz and Sophie stood in front, twelve feet away.

Big Bill moved to the other side of Sophie causing her to flinch as he got close. No way for an easy takedown.

"Then who's been trying to kill me?" David stared into Fitz's eyes. "Wait. Don't answer that. Let's do this instead. Let her go and you will never see me again." He didn't expect this to work but can't hurt to ask.

Little Bill pulled out a cigarette and lit it with an old Zippo. The smoke swirled around his head like a snake.

Fitz said, "We have spent considerable resources to capture you. If I wanted you dead, you would be. Your memories will confirm that. Now we need something stuck inside your head. Once we get that, we can remove those pesky memories and give you your life back."

As Fitz talked, fragments formed complete images. Fitz's background. The two Bills. Big Bill was the muscle and good in tight spots. Little Bill was a cagey pit bull. Tenacious and pragmatic. Only worked as a team. Never alone.

David's headache moved to the back of his neck as he weighed the offer. Quick and easy. And he wanted to get rid of these damn memories.

"But you are correct. Someone else is trying to kill you," Fitz said.

David stared up towards the bridge and heard the drone of the morning garbage trucks cleaning the streets above.

"David? Are you paying attention? If you come with us, we will let her go." Fitz said.

Fitz's subtle cologne mixed with the stench of Little Bill's cigarette smoke. The smells indexed to deeper memories.

"That's my fear. It will be over for me. I don't trust you and I don't trust Curly and Moe here."

Little Bill snorted like a Spanish bull. Big Bill ignored the comment and squeezed closer to Sophie. David ignored them and refocused on Fitz.

"David, you have my word you won't be harmed."

The headache gripped the top of David's head and squeezed like a vise. Fitz's voice became thick and hard to understand. The voice urged him to trust Fitz, but also said to get the hell out of there.

He didn't know what to do.

But the fog in his ears lifted suddenly and he said, "Did you pay Nikko to kill Max and Samuel last night or was it the other side?"

"Max and Samuel?"

"I found them dead last night in Pigalle."

Fitz stood silent for several seconds before saying, "My word, do you mean Maxwell Shueck?"

"Yes. Nikko killed him and his assistant." The name Shueck had hit a cord in David's memory. It felt like a true name, however he hadn't remembered it until now. The pain continued.

Fitz's features changed. He glanced from side to side and nodded to both Bills. They withdrew their pistols and looked towards the cathedral and the other building across the river. The mention of Max's murder must have worried them.

"Did you order their death?"

"No. Of course not. Max contacted me several days ago about some of the events in Amsterdam, but I thought he was just trolling for information to sell. Are you sure it was Nikko?" Fitz said.

"Yes"

Fitz glanced at David and said, "We need to finish. I don't want any new guests spoiling our little meeting." He pulled Sophie in closer. She didn't resist.

"I have one question," David said. "Why me?"

Fitz grimaced like he'd had some bad food. "I was told the procedure you underwent needed someone drug and alcohol free. Your ballet troupe had just arrived and the men that grabbed you, waited for a suitable candidate to appear and opportunity to invite to participate."

David said nothing but continued to listen. Fitz looked like he tried to smile but it wasn't happening.

"Just your bad luck I'm afraid. Your friend was the first choice, but he'd disqualified himself which left you."

"For what reason?"

"We need to locate some lost property."

"The device, you mean," David said. Asher frowned but nodded. "Yes. The device. The operation was a simple pickup and delivery. But the contact was too scared to bring the device with him."

"Who wants the device and why?"

"I can't tell you. Jonathan didn't know at the time, but I do. His employer is now my employer." David wanted to ask more questions until Fitz raised his hand. "Let me continue, we only have a little time."

David let him talk, but the fear and anxiety trickled in again. He controlled his breathing to offset what felt like the worst stage fright he'd ever experienced.

"Jonathan was told the location just before he died."

"Who killed him?" David said.

"I'm guessing Nikko. It's his style."

A vision of the Amsterdam bridge appeared. A short and bearded man handing an empty briefcase.

Miles Vogler.

David felt Jonathan's face flush with anger. No package. Just a key. "Vogler didn't bring the device with him."

Fitz's eyes went wide. "Can you remember what happened?"

David's mouth tightened. "Yes. Everything. And Vogler didn't trust anyone."

Fitz looked in David's eyes. "Look, I'm sorry about what happened to you. We only wanted to implant his short-term memories to extract the location, nothing else."

David laughed. "Who did the procedure, Mr. Wizard? I got a whole lot more than the last thirty seconds."

"That is abundantly clear."

"Wouldn't it have been easier to have your superspy wear a wire instead? Do you have any idea what it did to me?" Pain gripped his temples with hot tongs as the bridge appeared again. Vogler's sour breath whispering the location into Jonathan's ear. Poetry. Or lines from a play.

The vision from the bridge returned. Stronger this time. Like he was watching a movie and acting in it at the same time. He watched up close as the bullet tore into Vogler's head spraying blood on Jonathan's face and feeling the second bullet stinging like a wasp, severing the major artery and vertebrae. Jonathan fell, cracking his head on the snow-covered cobblestones. His vision black, but the warmth of his blood, the warmth from his soul seeped out of his body.

David tilted to one side from a sudden case of vertigo. He forced himself to steady and said, "No one should ever have to remember their own death."

As he relived the murder, something happened. A dam burst and Jonathan's memories flooded David's psyche. No longer where they tiny threads to be pulled. Jonathan's memories were his now. His memories were Jonathan's. In the space of a second, he knew everything. Vogler's words. The references. The lines of poetry. He knew where the device was. But he wasn't ready to tell them that.

But the flooded memories came with a cost. A wave of nausea hit him again as each memory connected with the last one. One by one and all at once. He absorbed more of Jonathan than he ever wanted. He wasn't sure if he could take much more of this. He took a deep breath, looked at Fitz, and realized he had no choice. He had to give up to Fitz on the chance he was telling the truth.

Fitz's eyes went wide as he heard something whispered in his ear. Big Bill heard something as well. Who was talking to them? Little Bill stepped closer, but the pistol wasn't aimed at him. Little Bill held it out towards the river as if he was protecting David.

"We have a problem," Little Bill said.

Fitz frowned and touched his earpiece. "Bad form, David, very bad form." He pulled Sophie closer toward him. She flinched this time.

Behind him streamed a line of men. All young. All wearing dark pants and dark shirts. Some wore leather coats and some heavy sweaters. All were lean. Fluid. Many had powerful builds. All walked straight up, and light on their feet.

Dancers from the company. Men he'd danced and rehearsed with for many years. The dancers surrounded Fitz, Sophie, and the two Bills.

This wasn't the plan. Andrew was to arrive alone to take Sophie and whisk her to safety.

But he liked this plan better.

David stopped shaking, his heart rate dropped, and the flood of Jonathan's memories slowed to a trickle. He wanted the memories removed, but maybe there was another way. The other group wanted him dead, but he wasn't convinced his safety with Fitz was much better.

Andrew stepped forward and said. "David. It's your show. No police. Just us."

Both Bills swung their pistols back and forth in a wide arc forcing the men to step back. The Bills' semi-automatic pistols could do real damage, but David counted on Fitz wanting to not escalate the situation.

"Restraint, gentlemen, please. Put your guns away." Fitz said. Both Bills glanced from side to side and then slid their pistols back in their coats.

Fitz's face flushed red. "I underestimated you, David. That won't happen again. But perhaps, you didn't hear what I said before the village people showed up. If Nikko was hired to kill you, the situation has changed."

David blanked as something prevented an image from surfacing once Fitz spoke Nikko's name. Sharp pain again, but still David couldn't see what was being hidden from him.

"Search your memories. You will understand."

Fitz let Sophie go and she walked towards David with her mouth open and her eyes flooding with tears. David caught her as she sobbed into his shoulder, but he only felt concern for her, nothing else. No heartache. No longing. All the feelings he had felt for her a few days ago had evaporated like smoke. Andrew took her and led her away from David. Three other men spirited her up the stone stairs into Saint-Michel.

"Gentlemen," Fitz said to the Bills. "It appears we have worn out our welcome. This operation is over." Fitz looked grim as he motioned to the Bills to go.

"What about Reynolds?" Little Bill asked.

"Reynolds can go to hell as far as I'm concerned. I have gone past where I should have gone. Jonathan Brooks is dead and the information he had is gone with him."

Reynolds? David thought. "Who is Reynolds?"

"He's the one that wants the device and can remove the memories. I was told that if we don't remove the memories, bad things can happen."

"Bad things have already happened."

Out of the corner of his eye, David saw a glimmer of light from across the water and heard a *thunk*. Big Bill staggered and collapsed to the cobblestones face down. David dove at Fitz and knocked him to the ground. Just as a second bullet caught Fitz in the shoulder. If David hadn't reacted, the bullet would have penetrated Fitz's chest.

"Stay under the bridge!" David yelled. More bullets smacked into the stone walls and pillars. The dancers huddled under the bridge. Little Bill lay dead on the cobblestones; a red bloom spilling out on to the concrete below him.

"This is what I was talking about," Fitz coughed. Blood dripped from Fitz's shoulder, but it didn't look life-threatening. Fitz pulled a handkerchief from inside his coat and pushed it into the wound.

The bullets stopped. All the dancers lay flat on the ground, protected by the massive concrete pillars of the Petit Pont Bridge above them. All looked terrified.

"It's Nikko. It has to be. This may be your only chance. Go. If you don't, you won't be so lucky the next time," Fitz said.

David remembered Samuel's tortured body in a pool of his own blood.

"My coat. Inside," Fitz said.

David pulled out a Sig Hauser, checked the clip, and clicked off the safety.

As he leaped up the stairway, no shots rang out. Across the river, he glimpsed long dark locks of hair climbing a similar set of stairs up to the street.

Nikko.

CHAPTER FORTY-THREE

Some of the dancers yelled at David to stop as he vaulted up the concrete stairs, but he kept going. He wouldn't expect them to follow. They wouldn't be of any use as they lacked any training or weapons.

He didn't have the training either, but he had the memories.

He glimpsed long black hair as he raced across the bridge linking Notre Dame to the 2nd *arrondissement*. David wondered how Nikko missed in the first place. Possibly a bad vantage point, but that didn't make sense. He tried to recall more memories, but they seemed blocked by a wall. High and wide like a concrete dam. Hard and immovable.

Why was the wall there?

Notre Dame stood to the right. Across the square more ancient buildings stood, rebuilt, fortified, and rebuilt again. Nikko disappeared to the left. David followed, fueled by the anger from finding Max and Samuel dead.

A few people had ventured outside in the early morning. Some towed tiny dogs. Parisians. Some carried cameras or backpacks. Tourists. All ignored him. Unless he pulled the gun out of his coat and started firing, then things would get interesting.

The angle of Nikko's bullets. Fired from the river. Why did he shoot the Bills first, then Fitz? Wasn't he the target? Think David, think. Why wouldn't Nikko kill him first?

The memory wall stopped him. He tried pulling at the thread, but only a few things slipped out. Nikko needed a cane. He had an injury. The limp was important. How did he get the injury? The wall came down again. But he remembered the *tap tap tap* of metal on concrete. The metal point of the cane.

Nikko had multiple ways to escape Île de la Cité. Ten bridges. A car would work but a cab was too dangerous.

He veered left across Quai de la Corse, a razor-thin road that ran parallel to the river.

Nikko would cross from Île de la Cité into the 1st or 4th *arrondissement* and disappear. A solid plan, but the dancers or the sun disrupted everything. Nikko was on the run, limping with a cane. Not ideal. He'd be slow and off-balance. From behind the wall came an image. Long black hair. Feminine nose. Delicate skin. A woman in a man's body. An artiste.

A killer.

Tourists would soon notice what happened under the bridge and alert the police. Nikko might hide on the island and disappear into the mid-day throng of visitors.

No, David thought. He'd head north, cross at Pont au Change and escape into central Paris. Held hostage on the island wasn't his style. He'd want the anonymity of the city. A thousand roads all leading somewhere else.

A glimpse of black hair disappeared around a corner far up the block. David chambered a bullet into the Sig and ran flat out until he reached another large Paris landmark.

Musée de la Conciergerie. Marie Antoinette's prison before she lost her head. Lovely.

The visitor's entrance was ajar. Inside, a uniformed man with grey hair lay face down in a pool of blood. David touched the man's neck. No pulse and cold as if dead for several hours.

Why? The building had nothing to steal. No crown jewels. No famous paintings. The old guy would have punched in yesterday for the night shift until morning.

Nikko killed him hours before firing upon Fitz. Why would he set such an elaborate trap when there were easier ways to kill him? Like shooting first.

An image of a switchblade strapped to Nikko's gimp leg popped into David's head.

Some contractors liked the emotional distance of shooting a man from 1000 yards. But not Nikko. He worked up close when he could. To know the target. What they sounded like. What they smelled like. Johnny Cash sang "I killed a man in Reno, just to watch him die."

Nikko wanted to watch David die, apparently in a big old French prison.

Inside the building, dull morning light filtered in through windows near the ceiling. The cold damp air held a whiff of some ancient mold. Couldn't the revolution also have been in central heating? David shook off a shiver.

He found a map placard on a wall. To his left, an expansive dining hall. To the right, a massive kitchen. The former guests weren't invited to either.

Jonathan had been here before. A long time ago. David didn't know why.

Silence filled the building but then he heard it. Tapping. Metal on stone. Nikko's cane. Hard to tell his location as the sound echoed off the stone surfaces. But he caught his scent. Overpowering. Like the perfume the whores wore in Pigalle. A wolf in sheep's clothing. Another memory started to surface but stopped.

He checked every corner in the dining hall. The empty kitchen was next. Two massive fireplaces stood clean as he cleared the room. Nothing.

Nikko planned this. Planned to lure David here. That's why he hadn't shot him by the bridge. Even though the memories drove him, he heard his heart pounding in his ears before the voice spoke to him. *Your options are...*

David tried to pick out sounds layered on top of the silence. A low guttural sound, rising in pitch and volume, then reducing on the same angle of decline. A truck passing outside on the street. But he only heard only his own footfalls echoing off the hard stone.

Get with the program, the voice said. He focused on his breath and counted from one to ten to drop his heart rate. He felt clear and ready. Preparing to dance or to kill used the same technique. Anxiety melted away in big chunks. Just like before a performance.

And dancers complain they don't have a good career path.

* * *

Another room brought up another vision. Stronger this time. A younger Jonathan pushing into a room filled with tables with men in tuxedos and women in long dresses. He was after someone. No gun or other weapons. The French women all had dark hair, olive skin, and painted lips. Rivers of pain engulfed David and threatened to drown him. Someone else danced around the edge of the memories. David tried to dredge it up, but the pain ramped up.

Then it was over, and he was drenched in sweat. How long was the vision? He looked at his watch 6:16 a.m. Scarcely any time at all.

The main section of the prison had a set of stone and wooden steps that led to the upper level. An information plaque said the prisoners with money had lived upstairs. No money meant living on the first floor. All lost their heads.

A voice called from higher up. High pitched like Michael Jackson with an Italian accent. *"Buongiorno!* How nice of you to come." The sound came from everywhere. "You may wonder why I led you here."

David squinted in the shadows, pointed the gun in front of him, and searched the area. He found the first voice in a corner. A small wireless speaker that looked like a black apple. He smashed it on the floor.

"One down, many more to go. As you search in vain for my corporeal body, I was asked to test a theory." Nikko's voice spoke from all places at once.

David checked the gun again. All soldiers accounted for. One in the chamber. He snapped the magazine back into the handle. *I will only get one shot at this,* he thought.

"Pain, my young dancer. I'm always interested in pain. The application, the response, the long-term effects. Always have and always will. As a dancer, I expect you know pain. But not the kind I'm intending."

David walked up the stairs and stood on the top landing. The dim light exposed several prison cells. Some open and some closed. A few had furniture and books. Recreations of the final days of prison life before losing your head.

"As I understand, Jonathan's memory might be itself, a trifle incomplete. Allow me to help clear things up."

The next speaker was hidden behind a small statue.

"Jonathan was married at one time. Do you remember that? She was a lovely woman. Simply beautiful. Elizabeth was her name. Does that mean anything to you?"

David's left eye watered like a piece of sand had slipped under the lid.

"She was about five feet six. Long blonde hair. Blue eyes and the most exquisite deportment you'd ever seen."

David staggered as it felt like a layer of skin was being flayed off his entire body. The wall was melting. From impenetrable to transparent. Through the ice block, he saw Elizabeth. Jonathan's Elizabeth. His Elizabeth. David gritted his teeth and tried to breathe, but an elephant sat on his chest.

Nikko is a dead man. The shards of glass stabbed him again and again.

"This is working better than I thought. I'm so glad you remember her. She'd be disappointed if she disappeared forever. Do you remember the way she laughed? The way her eyes sparkled when she looked at you?"

A red-hot needle plunged deep into David's temples. He can see me. How? I can't see him. Ice cracked and melted. The full onslaught of Elizabeth's memory hit him. Words, pictures, sounds. Her smell. The touch of her hand. The feel of her skin. The sweetness of her lips. He clutched the top of an ancient wooden handrail. His whole body shaking as if he had palsy.

"Alas, as you may remember, she died. In much the same way you will."

An invisible blade of memory plunged deep into his gut, twisting, and turning as it went in. David screamed and doubled over.

"Elizabeth! A voice called out. Jonathan's voice. It was lower. Older. More guttural. Nikko talked about how he lured Elizabeth into a clandestine meeting. How he drugged her and tortured her.

Every word stabbed him until he collapsed in a heap on the floor, the gun falling from his grasp and bouncing on the stone blocks.

He couldn't see anything. His vision disappeared, but he still smelled that awful cologne. He heard the clop of the steps and the tap of the cane. He sensed a presence standing over top of him. The voice was now in front of him. His legs and hands were pulled together and bound. He wanted to resist but his body didn't respond.

"Please step into my office."

Something grabbed his collar and dragged him along the floor. David fought to breathe but said, "You are going..." He coughed. "To die."

"Of course, I'm going to die. Everyone dies. But for you, it's different. You will die right now."

David grunted, worked up some saliva, and spat at Nikko. But most of the spit dribbled down his chin.

"I…remember. I…remember." Jonathan's memories hammered on David's mind, each fragment like a sharp grenade. "Jonathan shot you. In the back…" He still couldn't breathe. The pressure on his chest was immense.

"I did take a bullet from Mr. Brooks. It was very unsporting of him. But now, it's payback. Double payback since I've already killed you."

David struggled against the bonds. But his strength had gone. A shape stood over him. His vision returned, but the pain ramped up. His skin screamed like it was being peeled back layer by layer as his bones burned like he was being roasted. He let out a long scream.

"Yes… Let it out. It won't be much longer now. I wanted to ensure the contract is completed. A pity I can't make you suffer the same way as your wife did, but *c'est la vie*. That's the cross I must bear, so to speak."

Nikko screwed a silencer on to the end of his pistol. "I'd prefer to gut you. But I'm going to use the gun first to blow holes in the same spots Jonathan shot me many years ago. An eye for an eye, as the good book said." Nikko rolled David's body over and exposed his back. David didn't respond. He felt like a puppet with the strings cut.

"I'm so glad we had this time together. Just like old times. And I want to let you and Jonathan both know—that this isn't business, it's personal." The safety on Nikko's gun snapped off.

"Goodbye, sweet prince."

A shot rang out. Then another. Then another. A body dropped to the floor. The pain eased, and David's vision cleared. Was he dead? He moved his hands and feet. He twisted and saw Nikko's lifeless beside him. Behind him, Fitz stood with a gun in hand. He coughed twice before kneeling and slicing open David's bonds.

"Come on, son, we have to escape before the police arrive."

CHAPTER FORTY-FOUR

David woke drenched in sweat. He was in a bed and in an attic. A high window provided a view into a Paris suburb, with morning sun streaming in. A small crucifix hung on the yellow wall.

He fought to remember what happened. His arms and legs worked but his body ached like he ran with the bulls and lost.

A pitcher of water and washing bowl stood perched on top of an antique table across from him along with a coffee carafe and croissants on a tray.

Did Heaven provide a continental breakfast? Memories flooded in; Nikko, the prison, Elizabeth, and the pain.

Why wasn't he dead?

Fitz.

Fitz killed Nikko. The rest was a blank.

"And how are we feeling, *monsieur*?" A cheery voice attached to a short and plump woman interrupted his thoughts. "The coffee is still hot." She smiled and poured steaming liquid into a heavy white mug.

"Where am I?" David asked.

"Paris, of course. But no one knows you are here in my place, however." She spooned sugar and a dollop of milk into the cup. "Monsieur Fitz will be back within the hour. He can answer your questions for you."

David struggled to sit up but felt weak as a kitten.

"Here, let me help you sit up." The old woman swung his legs around onto the floor and helped him to the edge of the bed.

"French coffee is always the best thing to have in the morning." She handed him the mug. Her eyes were a piercing green: the color of emeralds. She looked at him like a doctor would. "You look tired and need a long rest. How do you feel?"

"Beaten up." David sipped the coffee. The sugar hit his tongue and made his stomach rumble. He realized he was starving.

"Put your mug here, if your strength is not yet back." She pulled a small table to the bed and placed a tray of pastries. "Take your time and have a little to eat if you can. It will help get you on your feet." She smiled as a mother would smile to her son.

"You must be hungry. You have been here for twenty-four hours and you haven't yet eaten any of my cooking."

He sipped from the mug, but his hands shook. He set the cup back down on the table.

"I've been out for a whole day?"

"Yes. Monsieur Fitz brought you here yesterday. You had a fever and moaned like a banshee. We had to shut all the windows. I thought we might have to get a doctor. But after an hour of that, you fell into a deep sleep. I don't think you moved once during the night."

David believed it. His back was knotted up like a sailor's rope. His sipped more coffee this time with both hands to keep from shaking and finished the pastry in two bites.

"I will let Monsieur Fitz know you are awake when he returns."

"Thank you," David said.

She closed the door and didn't lock it. He was a guest, not a prisoner. He laid back in bed to rest. Gain his strength back.

A noise startled him, and he opened his eyes. "Nice of you to join us," Fitz said.

Sunlight lit up the room. He must have fallen back asleep. Fitz sat on a wood chair. Dark circles hung under his eyes and the old woman was in the middle of changing a large white bandage covering his top left shoulder. She sang a song in French under her breath. Blue suture thread decorated the bullet wound.

"No infection. The antibiotics are working. You are healing fine, Monsieur Fitz. Please, no big movements for the next month."

She squirted salve on to a square piece of white gauze and covered the angry entrance and exit. She followed with more gauze and strips of wide medical adhesive tape.

Fitz said, "We don't have much time."

"No good morning?"

Fitz didn't smile. "Good afternoon, actually."

Fitz's face was lined and rough. "We are in trouble," Fitz said.

"What do you mean we?"

"My former employer is upset, and our options are limited."

"What kind of trouble?"

"Getting killed kind of trouble. However, I am searching out more of the pieces. It's complicated and a little unbelievable. But your life, and now mine are in danger." Fitz grunted as the woman applied the last of the bandage straps. "*Merci, madame.*" She gathered up the supplies on a silver tray and left the room. Fitz said, "Do you remember our host?"

David thought about it. "No."

"Interesting. Jonathan knew about her, but they had never met."

"There's a familiarity, almost like déjà vu, but no direct memories."

"Either the recollections are incomplete or there's something else. What do you remember of the bridge in Amsterdam?"

"I remember getting shot."

"Jonathan was shot."

"I know that, but the memories have merged somewhat. I felt like I was on the bridge and that I died."

Fitz nodded. "What else can you remember? Do you remember who Vogler is?"

David nodded. "Some but not all. Fragments really. Some things are like I'm watching a video. But most are more fractured. However, every time I access a new memory, it hurts like hell. A migraine or worse. At the prison, the pain was so intense I collapsed."

"What memory did you access?"

"I didn't. Nikko forced one. About Elizabeth."

"Oh…I see." Fitz looked away. "Jonathan worked hard to block that from his consciousness, but I always suspected it was still there."

"I can remember her now, with no headache, but my heart aches because the memories feel like my own. I mean, I know she was Jonathan's wife. But I'm the one feeling the grief of her death."

A vision bubbled up. No pain this time. Just a tug on his heart. "Elizabeth was Vogler's daughter, wasn't she?"

"Yes. Jonathan didn't know until the end, but that's why he agreed to deliver the package. It was a responsibility to Elizabeth's memory."

"I have one question."

Fitz turned and winced with the movement. "Go ahead."

"Why am I not strapped down in a clinic right now?"

"Would you like to be?"

"That's not what I mean. Why did you have a change of heart?"

"Before I answer that, you may want to reconsider not being strapped down."

David gave him a puzzled look.

"Can you tell if the memory intensity is increasing or diminishing?" Fitz asked.

"Why?"

"Back at the clinic, I was told that if the implanted the memories weren't removed within a certain number of days, your body might reject them."

"And?"

"And you could die."

"Well, that's a nice piece of information that would have been handy to have a couple of days ago." David grabbed a pastry and took a bite. "The memories are getting clearer, less fragmented, but the pain is ramping up with a big memory. Like what happened with Nikko." David winced at the memory of the pain.

"Part of our negotiation then has to include removing the memories," Fitz said.

David was silent for a minute. He felt warm feelings for the man in front of him, but the feelings weren't his. Fitz had been chasing him since Amsterdam and had been part of the procedure but wasn't sure how much. He was more pissed at him than he realized. "But I'm still unclear. Why did you help me?"

Fitz sipped from the coffee and added a lump of sugar to the mug. "I've been uncomfortable about the whole situation even before Jonathan died. After, Reynolds contacted me for assistance. I was there when they delivered you to the clinic. I didn't know what the procedure entailed, but they told me it was quick and painless. I found out later that you were the third test subject. The other two died."

David's eyes went wide but said nothing.

Fitz looked down at the floor. "I wanted revenge. Revenge for Jonathan's murder and I hoped the information we'd extract would lead me to the killer."

"But instead it led the killer to me."

"Yes. Someone in Reynolds' organization fed the opposite side information of your whereabouts. But throughout the cat-and-mouse game we were playing with you, I grew more uncomfortable."

"Who is Reynolds? I have no memory of him."

"An American. Richard Reynolds. A Silicon Valley entrepreneur. A successful one I gather. Mostly I dealt with his security chief. A man called Wyatt."

Fitz poured coffee into a cup and took a sip. "When Wyatt kidnapped Sophie, I realized I'd had enough."

"Because you felt uncomfortable?"

"You saved my life by pushing me out of the way of the bullet. I only wish you were a microsecond faster." He moved his shoulder and winced. "I owed Jonathan a dozen times over for my life and here a young pup with his memories did it again. Honor is the reason. You saved me, so I saved you."

"Do you still have the key Vogler gave Jonathan?" David said.

Fitz dug into his pocket and pulled out a brass key with a brown plastic cover on the shank. The fifty-three was imprinted on it.

"I took the original, but Wyatt has a copy."

"Did Reynolds tell you what the device is?"

"I'm assuming some kind of a computer. Extra fast or a code-breaking thing. Reynolds never talked about it, other than assuring me it wasn't a bomb or a terrorist device. Throughout the process, there was another event looming that forced a deadline. But I don't know what that was."

"From what Max found, it looks like some kind of new video game," David said.

"Really? That makes no sense," Fitz said.

"What kind of work did Miles do? A memory tells me he was a professor of sorts."

"He was a tenured computer science professor at a university in Germany. But any reference to his research was ambiguous. But the strange thing is when I looked him up the other day, I couldn't find mention of him anywhere. Like he'd been erased."

"Here's the information Max dug up. We can use that as a start." David pushed the USB key into Fitz's old and wrinkled hands. David frowned and felt a momentary feeling of confusion as if the idea of Fitz being an old man wasn't right.

"The document describes the device like a game, but it has to be much more. People can't be trying to kill me because of a new version of Call of Duty?" David said.

"Strange. The people hunting you are religious extremists. Why would a video game cause the faithful to rise up and try to send us to Hell?"

David looked at him. "Did you have a run-in with them?"

"Yes. The man who attacked you at the hospital was contracted through a broker of sorts. Contracted to find you, not to kill you."

"I didn't have a choice."

"I figured that out. We confronted the broker about it."

"What happened?"

"The broker committed suicide, but only after he subjected us to a bunch of religious tripe." Fitz grasped the key by the base. "At the bridge you said you know where the device is and how to unlock it. Do you still remember? Reynolds thought Miles put it somewhere in Berlin, but as of yesterday they hadn't found anything."

"I did, but it evaporated again like remembering a dream." He held out his hand. "Can I hold it?" David asked.

Fitz dropped the key into David's outstretched palm. "Is this something new? Are you going to try to bend a spoon after?"

David laughed. "There is no spoon." Fitz gave him a blank stare. He continued "I can never tell how a memory will be triggered. Usually, it's something I hear, but sometimes it's a smell. I touched a wall inside the Conciergerie and saw Jonathan there a long time ago."

David rubbed the key between his thumb and forefinger. The plastic cover was worn and well used. A thread of something appeared. Something that Vogler said before his death. But these memories were sometimes like a story of a friend of a friend. Lost in the translation. He concentrated, grabbed the thread, and tugged on it. A word formed in his mind, followed by another and another. The code phrase. Miles had made Jonathan learn it and repeat it back to him. Almost the last words Jonathan heard on this earth.

He remembered.

"I know where the device is."

"Where?"

David pulled himself up on the chair and leaned on the edge to steady himself. He walked from the table to the end of the bed then to the tall bureau underneath the window. Two pigeons dozed in the warmth of the sunshine.

He looked out east toward the center of Paris. The top of the Eiffel Tower was in view, the rest blocked by the thousands of old buildings. "If I remember my Paris geography, we're about twenty minutes away from it."

CHAPTER FORTY-FIVE

One floor down in the safehouse bed-and-breakfast, David and Fitz sat at a wooden table. A large yellow pad covered with a mixture of writing, printing, and diagrams. A Mont Blanc fountain pen lay beside the paper.

Fitz wore a white undershirt, blue dress slacks, and black socks. A lump of bandages beneath broke the smooth line of his body. A silver cell phone sat on the table in front of them.

Fitz spoke into the phone. "We are prepared to find the device and deliver it as per our original agreement. But I need to know its purpose and a way to verify its use."

A price tag was still stuck to the side of the phone. Fitz bought it that morning for cash.

"Impossible," Wyatt's voice cracked through the tiny speaker.

"People are dead because of it. If you want the device, I need a reason," Fitz said.

"How about I won't hunt you down and kill you if you deliver it," Wyatt said.

"Unlikely," Fitz said. "Your group has all the subtleties of a rampaging elephant and I've been doing this a lot longer than you have. Besides, you have a deadline and Reynolds needs this device. If I'm dead, you've got nothing."

Wyatt exhaled sharply through the phone like he was about to say something but didn't.

"I'm prepared to make a deal, but it has to be on our terms," Fitz said.

The phone went on mute. David figured he was talking to someone else. After a delay, Wyatt said, "Agreed. But the dancer is part of the package."

"No need. He's remembered the code phrase without the help of the doctor you stole from the Spanish inquisition." Fitz looked over at him and smiled. "However, after delivery, we want the memories removed. He's played guinea pig long enough."

More silence on the phone. "Agreed. But I have one question," Wyatt said. "When did you turn into such a good Samaritan?"

"I would expect someone with your background would understand it in a minute."

"Pardon me?" Wyatt said.

"Honor and loyalty. You above all else should respect that." Fitz let the words hang in the air. "I'll be in contact soon."

Fitz pressed END on the cell phone and slipped it back into his pocket.

David said, "The other side will find out about the deal."

"Very perceptive, young man. Did you figure that out all on your own?" A smile dropped on Fitz's lips.

"Yes, kind sir, it was all me."

Fitz walked to the window and looked towards the dusty sky. "Unless Reynolds changed out all his staff, the opposition will complicate things."

"But who are they? We aren't any closer to figuring that out."

"We are. I've engaged the services of someone who can help us understand what's really at stake. I suggest you get ready. We meet him in an hour."

Madam entered the room carrying a pressed white shirt on a hanger and helped Fitz put it on.

"I feel like a toddler," Fitz said.

"That's just fine, Monsieur Fitz. You've helped enough people to deserve some help now and then."

David raised an eyebrow.

"I'm surprised at what memories have surfaced. He knew about my deep, dark history, so her comment shouldn't surprise you."

"It seems for me to remember something, Jonathan physically needed to experience it, not just hear about it," David said.

"Well, let me implant some of my own memories then. I was a compassionate person until I fell into the clutches of Sir Jonathan. He forced me to remove most of it at gunpoint."

Madam laughed and helped him slip on a jacket. Fitz winced as he brought his arm to his side. "Are you ready to go?"

David nodded. He stood and faced Fitz. His legs were a little shaky, but his strength was returning.

He'd make it.

CHAPTER FORTY-SIX

The cab headed west and south towards the fifteenth. The traffic was stop-and-go, but the cabby pulled a U-turn and weaved his way through some shorter streets until he continued south again. After thirty minutes of high-speed travel, darting in and out of crawling cars, the cab pulled up to a small apartment building on a tree-lined boulevard.

David helped Fitz out of the cab and stood with his back against the door to check both sides of the street. A pedestrian, a block away, walked the other direction.

Fitz dialed a number on the entry system and the door clicked open.

The door glass seemed thicker than usual. He noticed the ancient door frame had been reinforced with steel. Was this an apartment or a bank?

A series of dusty mailboxes and one large plastic plant sat inside the entryway. David wrinkled his nose. The hallway had a dry musty smell to it as if they were the first visitors in years. A double-wide stairway stood at the end of the corridor and light streamed in from a thin window at the top. The building looked and sounded empty except for the person who buzzed them in.

Fitz used David as a crutch to climb the stairs. At the top three identical doors faced them, Fitz knocked on the farthest one from the landing.

The door swung open automatically. David noticed the inside of the door was also re-enforced with metal. "Nice decorator," David said.

Fitz ignored him and walked into the suite.

"In here," a voice called out. The door closed behind them. A short squat man with wild black hair appeared. "Come in, gentlemen. Welcome to my humble abode."

The apartment took up the entire floor. All the walls separating the apartments had been removed. The other doors in the hallway were facades.

"Asher, my old friend. How nice to see you after such a long time." The man grasped Fitz's hand, but held it softly. "Got to be careful of the shoulder, eh?"

The man turned and walked around David like he was a prize horse. "And you must be David. Yes, of course you are. Who else would Fitz have brought with him?" the man laughed. "I'm so sorry. My manners are atrocious. I've just in awe of your little story."

"David, meet Leonard. He is the preemptive scholar on all things strange and religious. However, as he himself will say, he's not a religious man." He turned to Leonard and asked, "Have you picked a favorite yet?"

"I've found a new one. Very New Age. Based in Bali. Lots of sex with agreeable young women seeking the same sense of self-realization as I am. However, the group requires a sizeable cash commitment before joining in any of the religious ceremonies." Leonard squinted. "Let's say, I'm weighing all the options." He laughed again.

The three men entered the main room. Bookshelves covered all available wall space. A stone Buddha in a corner wore a witch's hat. An Indian totem pole hung from the ceiling like an airplane. Other sculptures and artwork dotted the rest of the space. A marble piece of two women in an erotic embrace and a dark painting of what looked like the Virgin Mary. In a semi-circle sat a red couch and several chairs.

"Please forgive the mess, I keep trying to clean up and organize, but soon after more pieces show up and then I'm in the same mess again. But such is life."

"Is the whole floor yours?" David asked.

"The whole building. I'm the sole occupant. My other interests fill the rest of the rooms, but I spend the bulk of my time here. But now, you aren't here to talk about my real estate quirks, now are you? How can I help? Tea?"

A steaming black teapot sat on a tray in the middle of a round table. Three matching mugs stood empty.

Fitz sat down, wincing until his back leaned against the soft upholstery. David took a seat and Leonard took the overstuffed chair. Fitz looked at Leonard, "Have you given much thought about what I spoke to you about today?"

Leonard filled the three cups with steaming green liquid from the teapot.

"It's been on my mind since we talked. After looking at the facts, I've got one question. What kind of a video game would drive an extremist to try to kill someone?" He looked over at David. "Namely you."

Leonard held out a cup first to Fitz then to David. "Green tea. Mighty full of anti-oxidants." Leonard sipped from his own cup. "I did some advance research and I looked you up. I haven't seen you dance, but the reviews all say you have a great career in front of you.

David looked over at Fitz. "You told him who I was?"

Fitz nodded. "Every bit of information we can provide is valuable. When Leonard and I spoke earlier, I was convinced they were after the device, but he theorized they might be after you as well or instead of the device." Fitz said to David and winced. "I know Jonathan never knew of Leonard, but he's the only other person on this planet I'd trust with my life."

Leonard set his cup on the table. "Fitz is right. So many things can upset an extremist, it's hard to know where to start. The media feeds us examples of the overly militant religions, but with Judeo-Christian based, there's more subterfuge involved. I like to make sure we cover all the bases."

Leonard pulled a large file folder from the top of a pile near his chair. "I researched all the offshoots and branches of Christianity because your attackers have been white Caucasian men. I cross-referenced any reports of violent activity from the groups. Most are U.S.-based. Of course, Americans tend not to need a good reason to be violent."

David leaned forward this time. "Have you figured out what the game does?"

"Possibly. But the identity of the group is important." Leonard read from a page and then dropped it on the floor beside him. "Christianity has always had a violent past, and the Bible is full of extreme references. Lots of God's wrath. Sodom and Gomorrah. Moses whupping the hell out of the Israelites because of the golden calf." He sipped some more tea and pulled a plate of shortbread cookies from a shelf underneath the table.

"In contrast, you don't ever hear about 'The wrath of Buddha' or atheists burning anything." He looked at the fat statue of Buddha in the hat, "But then again, if you piss off Scientologists, they might never let you work in this town again. Christianity gained dominance during the Roman Empire and the Romans were not filled with the milk of human compassion. In fact, it was a time of extreme intolerance. Non-believers were usually put to death."

"Most of this isn't covered in Sunday school," Fitz said.

"You are correct. The slogan of 'turn the other cheek,' doesn't match the reality. The main reason for the intolerance was the church and state were one. If a citizen complained about the state, it would be blasphemy. A nice self-regulating little system. The same system the Americans are fighting in the Middle East, I might add. Isn't payback a bitch? But I digress, back to Christianity for dummies lecture."

Leonard munched on a shortbread. "The Crusades, the Spanish Inquisition, the witch burnings in America; all singular chapters that gave the church license to kill anyone for any reason whatsoever."

David said, "Two days ago, a team of badly dressed amateurs attacked and called me the devil. They looked like untrained military reservists. They wanted me to wait for the big boss." David tilted his head to the side. "But I declined."

"Belief is a strong drug. However, there's more to it. As I said, are they after the device or you?" Leonard let the question hang in the air for a couple of seconds. "I would argue, since you've been implanted with the memories another man, Jonathan could be considered re-incarnated. Which could drive some groups crazy."

"How so?" Fitz asked

"Do you think I'm going to take Jesus' place in the world?" David said.

"A main tenet of the Christian worldview is that life is one-way street. You are born, you sin, you repent, you die and then, at the moment of death, a giant wheel of fortune spins to determine if you go to heaven or hell. Nice and tidy. The overriding message is 'follow the church to the letter or you will spend eternity watching your entrails roasted on an open fire.' But reincarnation screws with all that. Reincarnation says you can make mistakes in this life and get a do-over the next life. Goodbye guilt and persecution."

"I can understand their anxiety over it," Fitz said.

"Exactly. The church loses control and people become self-responsible." He took another sip of his tea.

"But after much deliberation, I'm not convinced David's unwanted mental hitchhiker is the only reason. Based on what you've told me and the initial research, the device seems to be the key. Maybe the reincarnation thing just pisses them off."

Leonard handed the plate of cookies to both. "Please help yourself." Both men reached and took a cookie from their host.

"Let's look at the possibilities. As I said before, what could someone have invented that drives the true believers to kill? Do you know much about the inventor?"

"He was a professor of sorts in Germany." David winced. One side of his head throbbed.

"Interesting. Is this the pain Asher told me about?"

David gritted his teeth and took a deep breath. "Yes." He fumbled in his pocket for some pills and took a large sip of the tea to wash it down.

"Vogler is a memory, but I haven't really accessed it. I feel pain at each initial retrieval."

"I will try to give you some more warning next time." Leonard drained his teacup and placed it on the silver tray. "There are lots of examples of fundamentalist offshoots killing people because their views don't match. Abortion doctors. David Koresh. Jonestown. Even this popular novel about DaVinci." He looked back at David. "I'm going to tell you some things about Miles I've discovered and ask you some questions. Are you ready?"

"Yes," David said.

"I researched him as much as I could in such a short time. He had a variety of doctorates from universities in Germany and Eastern Europe. He traveled extensively, but then stopped and seemed to isolate himself. I found references to papers he'd written but he stopped about fifteen years ago."

David choked out "Elizabeth..."

Fitz said, "David, let me."

"No. I need to do this." He took a breath. A band tightened around his head. "Elizabeth was his daughter and she was murdered fifteen years ago. His wife died a few years before that. Elizabeth was his only family."

"That would explain the isolation, but what was he working on for the last fifteen years that caused a cult to go haywire? This is a rhetorical question by the way. The USB key from Max described some research. But we still don't know what the machine does." He refreshed his cup. "However, technology in general can get groups like that worked up. Morning-after pills, stem cell research, cloning, RFID chips." He stopped and sipped the tea. "RFID came under scrutiny because people believed the tag was the mark of the devil as foretold in Revelations."

"We are nowhere then," David said.

"Not entirely. We start from the other direction and look at groups that have the most to lose. Remember, I said the Romans endorsed Christianity because it reinforced their control over the population. I think we look instead for a group that has the most to lose and then work backward to find out what could cause them the most grief."

"Grief?" David said.

"What is the root of all evil, my young Jedi?"

"Money."

"You are correct. Like every conflict in the world, ultimately, it's about money and who has the most of it. If we find that out, we will have found the other team."

CHAPTER FORTY-SEVEN

The Reverend coughed, scratched himself, and dug through the large sheets of yellow paper, crisp color pictures, and maps of cities. Thick scrawls of writing covered the paper. Several pens had fallen to the floor. He scratched at his face and sanded the tips of his fingers against his scraggy beard and looked at his smashed laptop on the floor beside his desk. He'd had enough of the demon machine a few days ago and took pleasure in breaking its silicon back.

"Where did I put that?" He sorted more of the paper and scowled. "Holy Mother of God, where is that goddamned sermon!" He poured through more paper piled on a heavy chair beside the desk. Nothing.

"Son of a bitch!" He swept all the paper off the desk in one large movement.

A fingerprint smudged tumbler bounced on the thick carpet. He grabbed the glass and poured in two inches of Glenlivet but winced from the effort. His left hip was on fire again. He shook two pills into his hand from a vial and chased them down with a long pull of the scotch.

Some of the scotch had dribbled on to his white shirt. Deep yellow peeked from his underarms. He scratched himself again. "Something stinks in here," he said aloud. He'd order the place steam cleaned after he was done. And he wasn't done yet. He had to find the God-damned paper first.

His vision doubled. The doctor told him not to mix scotch with the pills, but the combination worked. Cleared his mind. Helped him bear the pain. But his body betrayed him. Just like Judas. Screw the doctors anyway, what do they know?

He swallowed more scotch and his focus returned. Earlier in the day, he'd woken in his chair and remembered that the answers appeared to him. The answers to his problems. The church. His sermons. His mission. The problem in Europe. Everything. He wrote down his epiphany. But now couldn't find it.

Large white slices of paper hung thumbtacked to the wall. Paper lay on the floor, discarded like the jetsam on a paper sea. Dark lettering scrawled in undecipherable words.

He pushed himself to standing and lumbered over to the flip chart. Each page contained scrawls in his handwriting, but nothing brilliant. He needed brilliance.

He needed the light to shine on him again. Is this another test, Lord? Couldn't you ease off the pain and suffering a bit? His right hip flared as he moved. He had the suffering down as both hip joints felt slow-roasted over a blowtorch. More Glenlivet went into the glass and he swallowed it straight up before sitting back in one of his chairs and praying the scotch would kick in.

His eyes closed for a second as exhaustion took over. But thinking of his son botching things up snapped his eyes back open. *I should have gone there myself. I'd have this handled in two minutes. That no-good son of mine can't be trusted to wipe his ass. When you need God's work done, send an expert.*

Standing back up, he scribbled great long lengths of text on a blank sheet of the flip chart. He consulted a Bible on his desk and found the passage from Luke he'd highlighted in thick yellow. The tiny script made reading difficult.

On his desk, more yellow highlighting on a Bible opened to Mark. *When in doubt, ask Jesus. Go back to the source. The gospels. Any apostle. They carry such truth in their words as I carry the truth in mine.* He drew a large circle and a cross on his pad of paper and then ripped the page off and crumbled it into a ball. He re-wrote some other words and stood looking at those words for a few seconds.

Knock. Knock.

KNOCK. KNOCK.

"I'm not hungry. I will call for food later." He grabbed a highlighter and scribbled in big stripes across the page in his hand.

"I have urgent information for you," a man's voice said.

"About what?"

"I have an email from your son."

"Slide it under the door."

A thin single sheet of paper appeared.

The Reverend picked it up and stared at it. He rubbed his eyes with his fat fingers and read it again. He reached for the glass of scotch and finished it with one gulp.

"Praise be the Lord."

He pulled the chairs away from the door and clicked the lock open.

A man in a dark suit and red tie stood in the hallway. A tiny earphone hung on his shoulder. He stepped back a foot and wrinkled his nose.

"Tell William, God be with him. I need to make arrangements. Get someone in here to clean this pigsty. I will be in the rectory. Order me some breakfast. I need to get changed and dressed."

"Yes, sir. The building is empty if you wanted to walk to your apartment."

The Reverend nodded and walked into the main lobby of the executive branch. His feet were bare. The clock said 1:00 a.m. Was it that late? *I need to stop losing track of time. I need to get ready. Make arrangements. The machine will be coming here soon. We need to prepare. Prepare for a test. Once I've done that I can die in peace.*

He exited the building out into the garden leading to the rectory. The California night air smelled sweet and the concrete path felt like ice to his feet. A bath would be good. He could use a bath. He should have ordered one drawn for him. He'd do it himself even. Wasn't he still a humble man? He took a deep breath. The bougainvillea smelled sweet in the night air.

CHAPTER FORTY-EIGHT

The Paris evening held a chill as they made their way to the river. The white panel van kept pace with the other traffic, but Fitz winced with every bump. Leonard drove, and David sat in a seat behind the driver.

"Does the memory give you any indication where he stashed the device? The sewers are over a thousand kilometers long," Leonard said.

"I think so. Vogler hinted just before he died," David said.

"Why would he make Jonathan search for it like a word in a crossword puzzle?" Leonard asked.

"I don't think he got the chance to elaborate." The memory of Vogler's whisper floated around in David's conscious and unconscious but didn't cause the pain it first did. Leonard's eyes glanced towards Fitz as if he was trying to assess the answer.

"But why did he say it was in Berlin?" Fitz asked.

"He didn't. You and Jonathan both thought it was Berlin, but in fact, it was Paris. He said he'd make it easy for Jonathan. He knew Jonathan didn't like Berlin. The code word he gave Jonathan for the device was a passage from Victor Hugo."

The van took the next corner as Fitz held on to handle above the passenger seat.

"Les Misérables. The hiding place makes sense, but it doesn't tell us where. I don't want to know, but I might can provide extra help if you need it." He glanced in the rear-view mirror. "The only thing I ask is that you tell me how everything works out, if you can. And if you get the opportunity, bring me the machine to have a look at it. I'd be once again in your debt."

David turned to Fitz. "Do you think the opposing team have solved this as well?"

"Both groups have shown aggressive tactics. I wouldn't put it past them."

David closed his eyes for a second and felt a sharp pain in his left temple.

"What is it, David?"

"I'm remembering something. Something important. The head of the other group. The man who tried to have me killed in Amsterdam. I assumed he's the same person the nut bars with knives from the alley were waiting for."

"Can you remember a name?"

David thought for a second and rubbed his thumb hard against his temple. "Morgan. I knew of him before by the name of William, but there's a block." David looked at Fitz. "He's nasty. Ego the size of the Eiffel tower."

"Are churches hiring hitmen now?" Leonard asked.

"This one is."

"Can you remember anything else about him?"

"No. Nothing specific, but there was something." David's eyes looked up at the ceiling. "Something about his family. A rumor. No, something about his father."

"There's a service entrance near Musée des égouts at Pont de l'Alma," Leonard said.

David shivered and studied the Paris map with the help of a small light to orient himself. Any scraps of Jonathan's memory of the sewers felt old and tired. Or maybe it was just him. The last seven days since they jammed the memories into his head felt like a lifetime had passed and he'd never felt this tired. Everything ached. He'd missed seven days of ballet class, seven rehearsals, and four performances. But he forced himself to not search for any news on the company. He didn't need the guilt.

But Fitz said the memories have a best before date. Like sour cream in a refrigerator. He'd gone seven days without dying. How many more until his body rejects them?

Out the window of the truck, he saw Point de l'Alama and the wide swath the Seine cut through Paris. He remembered an operation Jonathan executed in the sewers. The transfer had been late at night and he'd handed a taxi driver an address for drop off. The address was close to Pont de l'Alama. Accessing the memories ramped up the pain.

"The meeting took place in a storage room. Just being in the sewers wasn't enough security."

"Based on the map, there are several maintenance rooms built over the last several hundred years."

Fitz pulled out several more sheets of papers. More maps.

"I don't remember walking very far underground. The stench was horrific. If Jonathan had to walk very far down below, I don't think he would have made it, the smell would have driven him out," David said.

"We start at the closest to the insertion point. There are four potentials nearby. We search until we find it," Fitz said.

"Are you sure you will be all right?" David asked.

"No. But I'm going anyway," Fitz said.

The white panel van pulled off the street and stopped. Leonard got out and hailed a cab. "This is the end of the line for me, boys. Let me know how this works out."

183

After they watched him drive away, both men pulled on dirty blue coveralls and black boots. Fitz stuck a tiny plastic earpiece in David's hand.

"Two-way communication. In case we get separated."

Fitz wiped his hands on the floor of the van and then rubbed his face. Dirt and grime transformed him from an upper-crust English security consultant to a Paris sewer man. David followed his lead. Leonard stuck orange cones on at the front and the back of the truck as David carried two darkened canvas bags to the sidewalk.

Leonard parked the van in front near the access stairway to the sewer systems. Fitz opened the lock and swung the metal door open. All the landmarks outside felt familiar. By all reckoning, David thought they were close. The lights from the city bounced off the overcast sky looking like a ghastly shroud. He took one last breath.

He entered first with the bags over each shoulder and Fitz pulled the door closed behind them. The stench hit him as soon as the door opened. But he knew it would get worse.

As they descended, wire and glass-encased lights lit their way. The sound of their shoes echoed off the concrete stairs until they reached brick and stone. The air temperature had dropped a few degrees, and the stench increased. They weren't even at the sewers yet.

They both heard the low-level sound of rushing water. At the first door, Fitz raised an electronic map courtesy of Leonard. "We are here," Fitz said. He pointed to a set of lines crisscrossing on the screen. "We need to go through this door and turn left. The first room should be near the corridor." Fitz's voice came through David's earpiece loud and clear.

Fitz pulled a spray can of oil from a bag and squirted on the hinges. David pulled, and the door swung open in relative silence. Dank humidity hit their faces. Tangy acidic humidity.

Night vision goggles lit up the tunnels, but the smell grew worse, if that was possible. Both men pulled on filter masks and continued. How could people work down here? Their footfalls echoed off the hard brick and concrete walls, but it didn't matter. The tunnels came alive with sounds of water rushing some distance away, faded traffic noise high above and a hum of machinery keeping the effluent moving.

Fitz consulted the map again leading them several hundred yards to a final door. After oiling the hinges, David yanked it open to the sound of rushing water. Bright lights were up ahead, but they heard voices in the distance.

Both men backed against a wall and pulled off their night vision gear. David removed his helmet and sneaked a look. He saw two men. Dressed in black. One man had a pistol in his hand, the other an Uzi. Fitz saw them, too.

"Bollocks," Fitz whispered.

David leaned in close and whispered, "Which side?"

Fitz shook his head. "Not sure." The two men disappeared, and the hard footfalls of their boots became fainter. "We only have a few minutes." Fitz looked at the map and found the first room. He pointed to the opposite direction of where the men were. "This way."

David took slow breaths through the mask. The stench alone was reason enough not to breathe fast. Fitz reached into his bag and pulled out a handful of flat black rubber balls the size of large cherries. Each ball was spiked with tiny fingers on them. No sharp edges. "Leonard's contribution. Drop one every few feet."

David whispered. "Are we going to invite these guys to a game of jacks?"

Fitz said, "No. Just do as I say. Take the right side." Fitz walked across some grating to a tiny walkway on the other side of the running water. David stayed on the original side and tossed the rubberized jacks every few feet behind him. The balls didn't roll or bounce. Curious. What kind of magic trick did Leonard provide?

They walked on opposite sides of the effluent expressway, but the others had gone ninja. But whatever the reason, Fitz and David's invisibility wouldn't last long. They arrived at another steel door illuminated by a yellow bulb casting a thin light. Inside was a large storeroom with a bank of lockers on one wall. David pushed the key from his pocket into Locker 57 and turned the key. However, another padlock kept it closed. A sticky note on the metal said in French, "Call x 3456 to have the lock removed. This is a day locker."

David used black bolt cutters from the canvas bag to slice the padlock open. Stuffed inside was a large aluminum case.

"Merry Christmas," David said.

Opening it up, he found an over-sized laptop encased in dense foam and some connectors. "This is it? The video game? It looks like a laptop."

Fitz touched the top of the box. "Jonathan died because of it." David closed the lid, locked it, and slipped the silver box into his backpack.

"Let's get the hell out of here." David slipped the straps of the bag on his shoulder and snapped a belt around his waist.

Fitz pushed the door open and said. "Wait." Fitz pulled out a tiny screen "The spiky balls we dropped detect movement, among other things," Fitz said. "Two bogeys at six o'clock."

"Shit," David said. Their escape route was blocked.

Fitz pulled up the sewer map and pointed out another way. "Left," Fitz said. The men eased through the steel door and walked left. Fitz studied the map as they walked.

"Hurry. The two are now four," Fitz said. He reached into his bag and pulled more jacks, throwing them in clumps behind him. He wasn't as careful as before. Some bounced up, and a few fell into the water, floating instead of sinking.

A hundred yards later, there was a red light with a series of metal bars embedded into the stone. A ladder.

Fitz looked up. "My shoulder. I can't climb up with one hand."

The tiny screen showed the four shapes were getting close. The faint sound of footsteps reverberated down the long tunnels.

"They will find the locker room. We need another way out or we won't make it."

"No," David said. "I have an idea." David dug into his bag and pulled out a long piece of nylon strapping. "Tie this through your belt."

Fitz wrapped it around his waist and through his belt and David tied it to his waist.

"Okay. Follow me. Push up with your legs," David said.

David climbed up and felt the metal case digging into his back. More sounds echoed down the sewer. Raised voices. Must have found the locker and the bolt cutters. David climbed ten feet and felt the drag of Fitz's body. After a few minutes, they got a rhythm of sorts. Pull, pull, then relax as Fitz pushed with his legs and pulled up with one hand. The voices grew louder. Any sound bouncing below rang up through the tunnel as well.

"Stop," Fitz whispered.

David stopped and took a breath. He looked down and saw the tiny screen light up the shaft.

"Fire in the hole," Fitz said. Firecrackers exploded. Then another, then another.

The black rubber balls.

"Micro charges. Keep going," Fitz said. "The men below will be off-balance." David returned to climbing. The rungs of the ladder were slick with condensation and rust. He guessed they hadn't been used in fifty years. But he hoped the hatch outside hadn't been welded shut otherwise they would be in bigger trouble than before.

He climbed with both hands and Fitz's weight tugged at his waist. Back to the rhythm. Climb. Climb. Pull up as Fitz stood and ascended with one hand. Climb, climb, and pull up. More voices. More firecrackers exploding. Then a larger blast. David felt a pressure wave smack his body as he kept going. "What the hell was that?"

"Explosive methane," Fitz said. "Courtesy of the citizens of Paris." Still more voices. Someone screamed.

Below him, light flashed. The men below were getting close. David stopped. A pistol could still wreck their day. "Hold on," Fitz whispered. All the rest of the balls exploded in unison. More yelling, another blast. More methane.

Sweat dripped off David's head and condensation ran down his armpits. His hands slipped on the metal. His legs were on fire from pulling a full-grown man straight up a shaft to the surface. A bit further. The air temperature dropped and smelled cleaner. He climbed until his hard hat bumped against a metal object. A manhole. He held on with one hand and pushed the cover up and peaked out. No cars. With one hand, he pushed up and slid the cover over. The clean air of the Paris night never tasted so sweet. He pulled the rope until Fitz's arms reached the top of the hole. With one last heave, David pulled Fitz up to the street.

"Let's get out of here. They will be busy for a while."

David slid the manhole back in place. As he got his bearings, he realized the white van sat only three blocks away. Behind it, the lights of Paris still shined, and David felt a hint of relaxation. They'd made it; they'd recovered the device and the only thing they needed to do was deliver the damn thing and removed the memories.

After hobbling to their getaway van, David said, "Get in the back and I'll drive."

He pulled open the back door and swung the backpack off his shoulders. He heard a noise that shouldn't be there. A hiss. High pressure.

He turned his head. White spray engulfed his head and body. His arms and legs relaxed, and he slipped into nothingness.

CHAPTER FORTY-NINE

Wyatt opened the door to the Mercedes and made a quick call to Reynolds as his men loaded the boy and the Limey into the waiting van. He thought about taking just the kid and throwing the old man back down into the sewers but came to his senses.

Leverage was everything. He learned that from the military. But Reynolds took leverage to a higher level. He'd seen him use leverage to negotiate multi-million-dollar deals and use leverage to get a free coffee at a local Starbucks. Reynolds always got what he wanted and didn't care who got in the way.

The dancer, however, proved to be more difficult than Wyatt or Reynolds would have predicted. But nothing is impossible when you set your mind to it.

The van pulled out to the main road, and he followed behind. Thirty seconds from start to finish. Thirty seconds he could live with. Twenty would have been ideal. He'd built three different scenarios with three different teams, all costing Reynolds a lot of money. Finding the van and rigging it with knockout gas worked. A sharpshooter with a tranquilizer gun stood by, but he wasn't needed.

Wyatt's phone beeped, and the text message said, "Jet fueled and standing by."

Finally, some good news, Wyatt thought. In about twelve hours, they'd be back in the US of A and get down to the original business, now with the device and the two worst pains in the ass he'd had for over twenty years.

Wyatt fired up the Mercedes and pulled out into the road and kept the white van in his sights all the way to the airport.

CHAPTER FIFTY

Violins. Just out of reach. Some woodwinds, but he heard the strings first. He took a cautionary breath, but nothing moved. He commanded his arms to rise. He commanded his toes to flex. Nothing. He couldn't even open his eyelids. But he still heard the music.

A few moments later, air pressure in the room changed and brought the smell of bleach. Iodine. Ammonia. Lemon. He recognized the music finally. Vivaldi. The Four Seasons. Winter, he thought.

The room brightened in a slow arc, but he still couldn't open his eyes. The heat from the light warmed his skin. Everything else felt thick.

Where was he? He pulled at a memory, but a fog blocked all directional thought. He detected a woman's perfume.

Other noises came into focus. The sharp clink of glass on metal. He seemed like an insect on display. The kind they skewered with a pin.

"Start dictation," a female voice said.

"Subject: Male, twenty-one years old. Muscular. 175 pounds. Healed scar, top left deltoid. Purple bruising at wrists and ankles. I'm administering the Taimavan to facilitate the other tests."

Tests? What tests? What drug? Something sharp pricked him in the inside of his elbow, then warmth. The heat radiated up and across his chest and down his other arm. His fingers moved. The warmth traveled down his torso and down both legs. He wiggled his toes and tested his arm muscles, but they wouldn't move.

Something wrapped around his bicep and vibrated, squeezing tight. A few seconds and the tightness backed off. Another twenty seconds elapsed. The woman's voice said, "Blood pressure normal."

At least he wasn't dead. No one gave dead people physicals. Something jammed into his right ear. "Temperature normal."

"Subject regaining consciousness."

David opened his eyes and blinked away chunks of mucus. A large mirrored light hung over him like a miniature sun. He couldn't see her face. "Where am I?" he croaked.

"Subject shows signs of confusion."

"I'm not confused." His voice was full of gravel. "I want to know where I am."

"Dictation off. Would you like water?"

"Yes."

He sucked some iced water through a straw placed in his mouth.

"You are in a room."

"Thanks for clearing that up. Where is the room?"

"I can't tell you. Please be quiet." She giggled and then whispered. "But I'm very excited. You are the only one."

"Only one what?"

"The only one that lived."

Everything came back. The procedure. Fitz. The ballet. Paris. Sophie. Max. Nikko. Another sharp prick in his other arm made him wince. The needle felt a lot larger. He tried making a fist but could only squeeze as hard as a baby.

"See, you can move."

"I can't lift my arms or head."

"You are restrained for protection," the woman said.

"Mine or yours?" David said. The door opened, and he smelled the doctor from the clinic in Amsterdam. Body odor mixed with curry and tobacco hit him. Deodorant wouldn't touch it.

"We have strapped down the subject because in his current state, he is a threat. Don't underestimate him," the doctor said. He walked in front smiling with big, white teeth. His hair, black and slick. A row of stitches crossed his cheek, the edges of the black threads against his brown skin. "You've given us quite a chase, but I'm glad we have you back. And look at you." He squeezed David's biceps and touched the scar on his shoulder. "Did you have this scar before? I don't remember it."

David said nothing.

"No comment? I'd expect more of a comeback, based on the reports I've read."

David looked at him and wrinkled his nose. "Showering and brushing your teeth every day would be a great habit to get into."

The doctor stopped and said, "You will be a big help to this project and the other one." He emphasized the word "other." "I will be in my office."

The woman smiled but didn't look at him. David heard the door close. "You don't like him, do you?"

"He takes credit for other people's work. That's why I'm doing this and not him. You are an important part of my experiment and I must make sure I document everything."

"Your experiment? You mean the memory implantation?"

"Surprised?" she said.

"I thought Doctor body-odor-with-bad-breath was the lead monster maker here."

"He thinks he is." She looked over towards the door. "I don't like being around him."

"I can't imagine why," David said.

She felt his forehead and said, "How does it feel?" she asked.

"It feels like I'm pissed off."

She leaned over him. Dark skin. Black hair. Fine, thin features. Beautiful. Indian. But no trace of an accent except for a slight California drawl.

"No. I mean how does it feel to use the memories?"

"Untie me and I will let you know."

She laughed. "I've heard what happens when you're untied."

He tried to lift his head but laid it back on the table. He felt stronger with each passing minute. However, he wasn't Superman. He wouldn't be able to break the straps on his own.

"What are you going to do with me?"

"Take more blood. Discover why the experiment worked on you and not the others. In the meantime, you will be asked to dredge up a final memory." Her voice changed. A sad tone." It will be easier if you cooperate."

"I'm sure the police will say the same thing to you."

She smirked. "I will start with the blood test and learn what I can derive from that. Hopefully, that will be only test necessary."

"Can I ask you a question?" She grabbed his arm and pulled a tube of blood from the needle and replaced it with an empty one.

"Maybe."

"Can you remove the memories?"

She paused for a second as if she was weighing her options. "Theoretically, yes. But any tests in removal we've done resulted in complications."

"What kind?"

"Death mostly. But that was on mice." She took a breath and then smiled. "They might also just fade with time."

"How confident are you they will just disappear?" David asked.

"You have to understand this procedure is very new."

"No shit," David said. He saw her looking at him like she was searching for the right words. But he continued to speak. "Just so we are clear. If you try and remove the memories, I could die. If you leave them intact, I could die. And if they just evaporate on their own, there's a possibility one of the goons kills me out of spite."

She didn't respond as she pulled the last tubes, pulled out the IV needle, and placed a piece of gauze on his arm. The adhesive tape pulled on his skin as she secured it to his arm. "Sorry, this needs to be tight or you will start bleeding."

David looked back at the light. Several embedded halogens bounced the light in unison from the mirror to the test subject. He was the test subject.

"They hurt."

"Excuse me?"

"The memories. You asked what it felt like to use the memories. They hurt."

"I'd expect them to."

"How do you know?"

"I designed them that way. If they hurt, they aren't yours."

David gulped. The glass tubes clinked on a tray and the door opened. Vivaldi was still playing. Sad overtones now. Must be at Fall.

"I will be back. Please rest," she said.

The door closed, and a lock snapped shut. He squeezed his fingers into fists. Tighter this time. His strength was returning.

His thoughts were clearer. Where was Fitz? Did they leave him in Paris?

CHAPTER FIFTY-ONE

Handcuffs have a particular sound. The good ones snap each tooth like a tiny hammer hitting an anvil. All business. Unlike in the movies, they can't be undone without a key.

The key that handcuffed David's feet and hands to the metal wheelchair belonged to a red-haired man with a thick goatee and some tape across his nose. He looked familiar, but David couldn't place him.

"G'day. I'm Charlie. Last time we met, you broke my nose."

David didn't respond. But a memory flashed of smashing his head into Charlie's nose at the clinic in Amsterdam.

"Don't move or it will be very unpleasant." Charlie squatted down and snapped the metal cuffs around David's ankle until they pinched the skin.

"It's already unpleasant," David said.

Two men on either side held stun guns against his neck. He decided to say nothing more. If he complained, he knew Charlie would squeeze the clasp tighter. Or order one of the guys to shock him. Charlie stood up and said, "We have two minutes."

The wheelchair used cheap aluminum tubing as if they'd bought it at an estate sale. Some steel bolts and screws, but the main construction was aluminum. The bald man snapped one end of the handcuff to where two tubes bolted together with a steel nut. If left alone, he could snap the metal tube with enough time. He doubted he'd have the chance. But he definitely wasn't in a hospital.

His ankles held tight to the footrests via more steel tubing and chains. David moved his legs, but the chain only allowed two inches of play. Adjusting his heels back and forth, he found a place of the least pain. They were right to hogtie him like this. He'd take any opening they gave him.

Charlie leaned in close, forcing David to get a better look. His eyes were black and blue and thick gauze covered his nose. Just like the Indian doctor. He reached over and squeezed the ratchet two more teeth tighter until they marked David's wrists. Charlie whispered into David's ear. "I owe you something after today's event."

Great, David thought, take a number. David looked straight ahead and engaged no further. No point in pissing him off. He could wait until the right opportunity. But he needed a plan. However, he was all out. For the last seven days, he'd been hunted, shot at, attacked, and pushed. Each time, he survived and did better than he thought possible. But here, trussed up like a pig going to slaughter, he burned in silence. At his first opportunity, he planned to rip Charlie's arms from the sockets and make the broken nose look like a mosquito bite. But still he had no plan.

A plan will emerge, the voice said. *Nice of you to return*, he thought. But restrained like a mental patient, Jonathan's guidance wasn't helpful.

Charlie wheeled him out of the room, into a whiter hallway. No windows and air-conditioned. No other smells either; the air was flat like distilled water. Was he still in Paris or somewhere else? And what day was it? The hallway finishing was standard painted drywall. Stainless steel panels along both walls. It didn't look like a European hallway. More North American. Wider and larger, just like the US.

The guards walked beside the wheelchair holding Tasers in their right hands. No southpaws here. Charlie pushed him past several doors bearing the names of birds. Woodpecker. Sparrow, Raven.

An elevator opened at the end of the hallway and David was pushed straight in, facing the back. The guards entered, and the elevator door slid shut.

He noticed the air pressure change but after only a few seconds, the door opened into another hallway. High-end office finishings. Black slate floor, oak paneling, wide crown molding. Like stepping into the executive suite of a big law firm. He'd been in one once after his Dad died. No windows, but natural light trickled in from large circular portals in the ceiling.

He wasn't in a hospital, but some kind of private facility. Fitz said Reynolds was Silicon Valley royalty, so his best guess put him somewhere south of San Francisco.

More humidity and the faint musty scent of pine trees and sweetness of flowers filled the air. After two minutes, he and his wheelchair turned into a large room. The plaque over the entrance said "Eagle."

Twin screens filled the front wall. A few laptops and some tablets lay scattered on a large table. Whiteboards covered in red and blue diagrams hung on the walls. Boxes and lines. Some equations. Some other symbols David didn't understand.

"Welcome. I'm glad you could join us." David didn't see where the voice came from. After a few seconds, another wheelchair appeared beside him.

Fitz.

The woman doctor pushed him. No extra guards. Too old or hurt to be a threat. Thin wrists wrapped in handcuffs, poked out from underneath his sleeves. He looked like hell. Messy hair, deep circles under his eyes, and a level of exhaustion he hadn't seen before.

"David. I apologize for your treatment, but you and your colleague didn't leave us a lot of choice." The voice paused for a second. "...and please excuse the melodrama, but wheelchairs work well in this application, don't they, Wyatt?"

"Yes sir, they do." A buzz cut appeared at the door. David had seen him before. Stocky. Thick shoulders. Military type. *Special Forces*, the voice said. Except he wore a tailored olive-green suit. We are in California, David thought. That is the only place he'd get away dressed like that. Wyatt's face showed no emotion. Fitz said Wyatt controlled security, but the other voice must be Reynolds.

Wyatt leaned over and said. "Welcome back, we missed you. Both of you."

Fitz said, "We intended to deliver the device."

"We just needed some extra insurance you weren't planning to deliver it to the opposing team." On the table in front of them under the plasma screens sat a thick graphite laptop that mirrored the one they recovered in the sewers. Unpacked and open. The aluminum case had disappeared. A thick stream of wires connected the laptop to a see-through helmet.

A voice boomed from everywhere. "We've brought you both together for a special purpose. Allow me to introduce myself. I'm Richard and I'm the one that insisted you be here for the demonstration."

A tall man, tanned with a sparse salt and pepper beard appeared. Athletic but not muscular. Khaki slacks. White Oxford shirt. The man pressed a button on his belt and his voice disappeared from all the speakers.

"Sorry for the theatrics. I'm trying out this new sound processor," Reynolds said. He showed off a small black tube on his belt. "Very ingenious. A new line we're considering. A computer processes my voice and inflection and broadcasts it to a series of speakers around the room. I can talk anywhere from any direction and my audience hears me with utmost clarity, with no echo or feedback. But I know you aren't here to see that." He bowed and said, "We need your help to demonstrate the result of years of intense research and development."

Reynolds lifted the helmet and looked at it from the side. "The industrial design needs work but I've already engaged the team that designed the iPad to help craft the right look."

David said, "The right look for what?"

Reynolds smiled with bright white teeth and carried himself like someone that had played tennis all his life, with not an extra ounce of fat on him.

"I'd forgotten. We never disclosed the end game. My bad." He sat the helmet beside the computer. "It's about control. Market control and domination." Reynolds laughed to himself. "Not world domination in the literal, James Bond sense. I don't want to run the world. Too much paperwork. I'm talking about domination in technology." He gestured to the device. "This little box, if marketed well, will be the cornerstone of a new renaissance in computer learning, programming, and entertainment."

"People died because of a new video game?" David asked. "What kind of an asshole are you?"

Reynolds raised his eyebrows but didn't respond to David's insult. "It's much, much more than a video game."

"People tried to kill me. Several times. Someone killed Vogler, Jonathan, Max, and Samuel because of your stupid device."

"Believe me; I'm sorry this has all happened. Getting ahead in business can be a cutthroat affair. I engaged this man"—he pointed at Fitz—"after the unfortunate death of his friend and the inventor, to help pick up the pieces. We didn't realize the extent of the competitive threat. We should have predicted that." He turned his back on them and touched the side of the computer.

"Please accept my personal apology for the trouble we've caused the both of you." He turned and stood beside the device. "But it will be worth it. However, I need your help for one last thing." Reynolds ran his finger down the side of the device like he was caressing a fine piece of sculpture.

Fitz spoke, "You still haven't said what the damn thing does."

Reynolds turned and smiled. "Correct." Reynolds touched the switch on the device on his belt. His voice once again boomed from everywhere. The two plasma screens in the front of the room lit up. A man on one and a woman on the other.

"The device represents the future. Not just the future of this company. The future of everything," Reynolds said.

The screens showed the man and woman each working, eating, reading, watching television, attending a class, feeding a baby. Another screen came alive and showed a baby crawling on the floor.

"Life is busy. Jam packed with the mundane and the necessary. Necessary for life to move forward. Today, any extra time left, a person just surfs the Internet."

The screen changed again. People in chairs. Overweight men and old women pushing shopping carts full of junk.

"But there's a danger to this lifestyle. People grow fat and sedentary. Our children are learning less each year. The best universities are filled with foreign students because they know the value of hard work. To summarize, because of our fascination with sitting in front of a screen, Western culture is on a path to destruction."

The screens changed to all white.

"But what if there was a way to prevent all that? What if there was a way to accelerate learning? Or increase the fitness of all its citizens overnight, or provide entertainment that was stimulating and enjoyable and not just one way?"

The screens changed again to a close-up view of climbing a mountain. Each crack and nub from the rock face was crystal clear. The screen panned, and the climber looked down between his legs, a thousand feet below.

The other screen showed a skier's view turning in deep powder and hitting moguls until he reached a cliff and jumped high. After a couple of seconds in the air, the skier landed with a thump and skidded to a stop.

The scene switched to a blackboard filled with mathematical symbols and a floating hand solving a series of equations.

"Do you remember the movie, *The Matrix*, when the real world was a shattered shell of a computer-generated utopia? Our world isn't shattered, but sedate. We can deliver a computer-generated world to augment the real one. The benefits to each of us are incalculable."

David rolled his eyes. "Let me get this straight. You're suggesting that the solution to our society's ills is to create an artificial world instead? How did that work out for Neo?"

Reynolds laughed but didn't answer. "Let me explain what happens. Everything you experience while hooked up to the machine is real for you. Your brain can't tell the difference. If you lift weights while immersed in the computer program, your physical muscles will grow. If you take a class in advanced mathematics, your brain will grow in understanding, but in a sped-up fashion. For example, you could learn a new language in just a few hours, instead of a few years."

David's head hurt. He felt Jonathan's memories were listening to Reynolds' speech as well. Accessing and extrapolating in an almost conscious manner.

"The device will revolutionize everything we do today, and we will be at the center." He pointed to David's head, "and we owe it all to the memories stored in your head."

"Just like in *The Matrix*, except the machines want to kill everyone. Can we leave now?"

Reynolds laughed again. "Nice try. But your work with this company isn't yet done. There's still the small matter of unlocking the prototype to start the demonstration."

David said nothing. Fitz sat quiet and stone-faced.

"Let me first assure you that both of you both will be handsomely compensated for your trouble. Once we finished, you will have enough money to do whatever you want to do. Continue with your dance if you so choose. But before we talk about outcomes, I'd like the code phrase, please."

"I have no idea what you are talking about," David said.

Reynolds' eyes went wide and looked at Fitz. "You told Wyatt here, that your boy remembered everything Vogler told him before their untimely deaths."

"I do. He told Jonathan the location and we found it," David said.

"We still need the phrase to unlock the device and remove any encryption or passwords on it."

"I don't remember Vogler saying anything more. And your Doctor there"—he tilted his head towards the female doctor—"thinks the memories might just evaporate."

Reynolds' eyes twitched, and David could see he was struggling to keep it together.

"But, let's say I do remember this little code, how do I know you won't just kill Fitz and me?"

Reynolds sucked through his teeth then chuckled. "We aren't all Neanderthals around here." He glanced at the bald man and the other guards, "but I can understand your apprehension. You have my word that no harm will come to you."

"I'm still unclear on one thing," David said.

"What is that?"

"What does religion have to do with it?"

Reynolds glanced up at Wyatt. A dark wave had crossed his face.

"Another group wanted me dead and killed Vogler and Jonathan because of the device. They were fanatics. Religious fanatics. What does the device do that would cause them to kill for it?"

Reynolds said, "Don't you know religion is the root of all evil?"

"I thought money was."

Reynolds said nothing.

Fitz spoke, "Regardless of your personal beliefs, why would some religious zealots rise against an overpowered video game?"

Reynolds looked up at the corner of the room but didn't answer the question. "Gentlemen, we are wasting time. I need to prepare for a very important board meeting that's happening in the next few hours. But I need to unlock and test the machine first."

"To your financiers, I believe." David glanced up at Reynolds. "Max discovered your company is in a difficult situation. Your last acquisition failed and drained your company of all its available money."

Reynolds' face grew red in an instant but then relaxed. He walked over to David and hit him in the face with an open palm.

"I'm a patient man, but my generosity has run out. I want the code now."

David spat on the floor. "So much for your promise."

Reynolds balled his fist up and then relaxed. "Well, if the reports of those extra memories are correct, then physical force wouldn't work." He turned towards Fitz. "Maybe your colleague can convince you it's in your best interest to help us out with the device." Reynolds grabbed Fitz's shoulder by the bandage.

"Wyatt told me you were hurt at that nasty business underneath the bridge," Reynolds said and squeezed hard into Fitz's wounded shoulder. Fitz winced but said nothing. "It's unfortunate that a man of your age has to suffer the violence of a gunshot. Your time to heal is compromised." He squeezed and twisted the shoulder. Fitz groaned. Reynolds turned back and looked at David. "But I hear that's not a problem for you, is it?"

Fitz looked in agony and pulled at the handcuffs until he screamed out.

"Enough," David said. "You want the device and the code? It's yours."

Reynolds released his grip on Fitz's shoulder and wiped his hand on Fitz's hospital gown. The cloth underneath his shoulder bloomed a deep red. Reynolds turned to the doctor and said, "Get someone in here to attend to this, will you? I don't want our guest bleeding to death. The code phrase is…" He looked at David.

"One second." David looked up to the ceiling and took a breath. He squinted and brought up the door to the memory. He'd remembered a phrase, but without any context, he dismissed it. Now he couldn't.

Amsterdam came to his mind. Cold, snowing, and damp. Miles appearing before him, disheveled and scraggy, long greasy hair pulled back, his odor coming through the falling snow. Miles leaning into Jonathan whispering, "The code phrase is…"

David said, "The code phrase is 'The great prodigality of Paris is.'"

Reynolds said, "Ah…Victor Hugo. The sewer now makes much more sense." He typed in the code and pressed the enter button.

Wrong phrase. Two tries left.

"Two tries left?" Wyatt handed Reynolds a black pistol. Reynolds pulled the slide back, chambered a bullet, and pointed the gun at David's head.

"Just to be clear. Three strikes and you're out."

"That is the code phrase, asshole. I remember it as clear as day."

Reynolds pulled the gun back and laid it beside the computer on the table.

"Perhaps I mistyped. I'll try again."

Everyone's attention was back on screen.

Reynolds repeated the phrase. "The great prodigality of Paris is." He typed the words letter by letter and pressed enter once again.

The screen showed "Wrong phrase. One try left."

Reynolds yelled before grabbing the gun and pushing it into David's temple. "Don't fuck with me. If you don't provide the right phrase, I will shoot you and Fitz in the gut and let you both die over several days. What's it going to be?"

"Just give me a second," David said.

David closed his eyes again and took another breath. He replayed the memory again and again. Each time there was a little pinprick in his brain. Something wasn't right. The whole thing wasn't right. A Silicon Valley madman had a pistol to his temple.

A buzzer went off in the room and a clear blue light flashed in the corner of the room. Reynolds pulled the pistol back from David's temple.

"What the hell?"

The room's double doors burst open. Soldiers in riot gear entered with machine guns at waist height. An extra-large man was in the middle. Six feet four, three hundred pounds. Black skin showed around his eyes through the balaclavas. The large man said, "Drop your weapons. You won't receive a second warning. Drop your weapons!"

Reynolds dropped the pistol on the floor and raised his hands.

"All of you. Hands above your head."

Wyatt stuck his hand in his jacket. Another masked man said, "Freeze, asshole. Don't even think about it." Wyatt raised his hands in the air. The masked man reached into Wyatt's jacket and pulled out a Glock.

Reynolds' face went red. Twin veins on his forehead pulsed forming the letter "V." After a deep breath, he stepped forward. Palms open. "How can we help you, gentlemen?"

The large black man raised towards Reynolds. "All of you. Place your hands on your head. Kneel on the ground. Now!" Reynolds and Wyatt complied and dropped to their knees. The bald man and the two other guards did the same after dropping their Tasers to the floor.

One of the masked men spoke, "Area secured."

David and Fitz sat in silence. The men held their guns at the group but didn't move. It looked like they were waiting for something or someone.

Wyatt looked up and said, "This is all a giant misunderstanding."

The black man stepped forward and decked him with the back of his fist, "No talk'n." Wyatt's head absorbed the hit but snapped back. A drop of blood formed on the side of his mouth. Wyatt wiped it with his hand and then moved his hands back to the top of his head.

The soldiers didn't move. The blue light kept flashing, but the buzzer stopped. Then David heard the tapping. Like a rod. No. A cane. The rhythmic tap tap tap. He heard the footsteps next. Hard leather shoes on the slate floor. A second set of footsteps echoed off the slate. Two men. One with a cane. The tapping grew closer until it was right at the door.

"Good morning, everyone. I'm so glad we could make your demonstration."

A fat older man leaned on a sleek polished black cane with a silver tip. He wore an expensive suit. Dark, rich fabric. A crucifix on a heavy gold chain around his neck. The man's fat hand engulfed the top of the cane.

Behind the grinning fat man stood a younger man wearing sunglasses. For some reason, David thought the second man was the son. Not really a resemblance.

Different skin color. Different hairline. The younger man was twenty years younger. But not young. Middle-aged. Strong features. Taut body. But father and son, that's for sure. David knew the man. He was the man who ordered his death in Amsterdam.

Morgan.

The masked men parted, and the fat man walked into the center, stopped, and leaned on the cane. He looked around the room until he saw the device under the twin plasma screens. Then his face grew black.

"Is this the device?"

"Yes, we believe this is it," Morgan said.

Reynolds spoke up. "Who do you think you are breaking in here and threatening us with guns? We do a lot of work for the U.S. military and you have just bought yourself a lot of trouble."

The Reverend squinted and nodded to the younger man. "William?"

Morgan stepped forward and punched Reynolds with a solid right hook knocking him to the floor. "Do not speak until spoken to."

The fat man chuckled. "I've almost forgotten. My manners are atrocious. Allow me to introduce myself and my companions here." He stepped forward and bowed. "Oh, before I continue. You needn't worry about the government." He angled his cane from side to side "These men ARE from the U.S. government, under special order from my close friend, the Vice President himself."

Reynolds' eyes went wide.

"The man beside me is my son, William. I am the Reverend Vincent Morgan."

CHAPTER FIFTY-TWO

Another man joined the Reverend and Morgan. Dark blue suit. Older. Thin and lanky. Buzzcut. Wonky left eye that didn't track with his right.

He was the guy that helped David escape from the Amsterdam hospital.

"Good morning," the man said. "My name is Westlake, and I'm sorry we've had to change the agenda of your meeting, but we are here to protect the best interest of the country overall." He glanced at David but didn't speak to him.

Westlake said, "Reverend, thank you for alerting us to this threat of national security. Your country thanks you."

"National security? What bullshit is this? We are in the middle of a product evaluation," Reynolds said.

"…that can once again enslave our youth and pollute the word of God," the Reverend said.

"That's ludicrous, we don't…" Morgan punched Reynolds again, and he collapsed on to the floor. Wyatt jerked as if he would move, but one of the soldiers jammed the gun barrel against his back.

Westlake winced. "Enough. Do not engage in any more force than necessary."

The soldiers stood so close that David smelled the oil from their weapons. Metallic and fresh and ready for action. They weren't from the same gene pool as the knife boys from Paris. The group stood quiet, professional, and calm. Highly trained.

A sharp tack hit his temples, and a memory surfaced.

A mile from Checkpoint Charlie in Berlin and the wall was still up dividing capitalists and communists. Jonathan and his team entered a back room on the main floor of a warehouse.

Fitz was with him.

Inside, a man with his face covered with a balaclava spoke in an American accent. "I'm CIA. It's my interrogation." One of Jonathan's team verified his credentials. In the center of the room was a man tied to a chair.

"You can watch. I'm almost done" The room stunk of blood, urine, and shit. CIA smashed his fist into the man's nose and face.

"What was that?" CIA said. The man muttered something, but his lips just dripped blood.

"I think we have everything we need." Before Jonathan could do anything, CIA pulled a Glock and fired into the man's forehead.

"You son of a bitch!" Jonathan pulled out a pistol and aimed it at CIA.

"Stand down, Brooks," a younger Fitz said. "He's got authority to do whatever he wants."

Jonathan turned, snapping epithets at Fitz, but CIA pushed his pistol back in his holster and laughed. Red with white and blue flecked with yellow-tinged the man's eyes. Jonathan wanted to shoot and puncture enough holes in him to see light behind him.

The memory of a wish played back. Wishing Jonathan's finger on the trigger of the gun. Wishing he pulled it tight and drove a slug into the man's head. Easy. Clean. No judges or tribunals. Fitz walked up beside him, touched his arm, and pushed the barrel down towards the floor. "Stand down. There's nothing to do here."

The memory ended. The cuffs and straps still held David tight to the wheelchair. He didn't know what had triggered the vision. Jonathan's regret was as palpable as a heartache and sat like a hot lump of lead in his right temple.

The Reverend smiled at Reynolds. The prisoners kneeled on the ground with their hands over their head. Morgan walked to the device and touched the keyboard.

"Don't touch that," Reynolds said.

"Why not?" Morgan asked.

Reynolds said nothing. Morgan pulled a pistol from inside his coat and pushed it up into Reynolds' jaw. "I asked you why not."

From the back, Charlie spoke up. "They were about to test it. It needs a password to unlock it. They've tried twice and failed. They have only one chance left before the machine locks up."

"God be praised we were here in time," the Reverend said.

"Thank you, Charlie. Your information is valuable as usual. Please let him up," Morgan said.

Charlie rose and stood behind the Reverend as a knight might stand by the king in a game of chess.

"Son of a bitch," Wyatt muttered under his breath. "He was the fucking mole."

A guard moved close to Wyatt and pushed a pistol into his temple.

"Good help is so hard to find, isn't it?" Morgan laughed.

Westlake said, "Stand down. No one else needs to die in this operation." The guard waited two beats before holstering his pistol.

Morgan moved the gun to David's head. "You. You're the cause of all of this, you little dance fuck."

"That's enough profanity, William," the Reverend said.

"If you knew what evil this man brought to our church." Morgan pulled off his sunglasses and jammed the pistol up into David's jaw.

"No," the Reverend said. "There will be no killing unless God decrees it."

As Morgan dropped the gun, David got a good look at his eyes. He hadn't noticed them before. Red tinged with sharp colored disks. Blue flecked with yellow.

Morgan was the man in the vision. CIA.

David's face flushed as he filled up with Jonathan's hate. Morgan's eyes looked rabid and full of rage. But not for David. Hate for someone else.

His father. The Reverend.

"We need to test him," Morgan said.

"Test?" The Reverend asked.

"Yes. We need to test him for demonic possession. You read my reports and the ones from the others. He's possessed and knows things he shouldn't. He speaks in languages he doesn't know. The body in front of you is a ballet dancer. From Canada. Speaks English. Little French. Never been outside Canada before last week."

David remained silent. No use giving him an easy target. Morgan bowed his head to his father. He's being submissive, but it's an act. Why does he hate him so much?

"We did not agree to this," Westlake said. "You are here as guests of the U.S. government. This boy is under my protection. We won't be doing any exorcisms today."

Morgan nodded his head and two of the assault team flanked Westlake and grabbed his arms. "Stand down. That is a direct order." Westlake said. The two ignored him.

Morgan said, "The government has no authority in this matter. Only the church does. I was happy to find that some of your staff were also members of our church." Morgan motioned to the door and turned to Westlake. "However, if you disagree, you can take it up with the Lord directly. We will give you a free pass to meet him." He pointed to the soldiers on either side. "Please remove our guest to another office and don't hurt him. He has been instrumental to get us this far."

The two men waltzed Westlake through the double doors.

Dividing the assault force. That's not smart, David thought. The voice uttered an agreement. Three left plus Morgan and the fat bastard.

The Reverend spoke. "Now on to the next piece of business. The device. Now that I've seen it, I'm not sure how to proceed."

David glanced at Fitz. He'd been quiet up to now. But what danger did an old man handcuffed to a wheelchair pose?

"What does the device do that frightens you so much?" Fitz asked.

Morgan and the Reverend turned towards Fitz. "And who might you be?" the Reverend asked.

"Another blasphemer. The demon's accomplice. You should stay quiet." Morgan pointed his finger at Fitz, "You might live a little longer."

"You aren't here because of David. He's eluded your traps, but the device drove your agenda. Starting with the murder of my colleague," Fitz said.

The Reverend stood stone-faced. His nose and cheeks burned bright red. *Alcoholic?* the voice questioned.

"You need to hold your tongue, blasphemer," Morgan said.

"But it's just a computer, isn't it? Don't you think you should first review the function?" Fitz smiled, for the first time David could remember. "Or are you just scared you won't find anything?"

What was Fitz doing? He scrambled to figure out what Fitz's plan was. He was provoking Morgan and daring the fat man to do something. If I could get free from shackles and I could grab the fat man and hold him hostage.

Terrible plan, the voice said.

Morgan pulled his hand back to hit Fitz when the Reverend stopped him.

"Wait," the Reverend said. "Moses saw the golden calf with his own eyes. He didn't have to worship it to determine it was a false idol."

"A false idol? I don't see a calf or people offering gifts. I see a laptop. Not a God," Fitz said.

"Could someone please tell me what this damned thing is supposed to do?" David asked.

Morgan backhanded David and cut his lip. "Do not take the Lord's name in vain."

"That's enough, William," the Reverend addressed David. "The specifics are not important, but this device represents all that is wrong with the world and it's our solemn duty to destroy it." He winced and said, "Get me something to sit on." Charlie pulled a chair over to him and the Reverend lowered his bulk to the seat, grunting all the way down.

"It's the Creator program, isn't it?" A man at the back of the room with curly red hair and a white button-down shirt spoke up.

"Shut up!" Reynolds yelled.

"Who are you?" the Reverend asked.

"Becker. Larry Becker. I'm the head of R&D. The device simulates reality through a variety of self-contained experiences. There's one simulation that allows the user to experience what it's like to go inside a virtual church."

"And pray to an imaginary God. Isn't that right?" the Reverend said.

"A user has that option. But the inventor sent us a spec of all the simulations and we believe it's accurate."

"All this is over a computer game that lets you play hunchback of Notre Dame?" David said.

"No. it's more than that. Through the headgear, the device stimulates areas in the brain mapped to a variety of experiences," Becker said. "In the case of the Creator module, the device simulates a spiritual experience for the user."

"Like they would if they were talking to God," the Reverend said.

"It could be any deity. There are options for different places of worship. A cathedral, a mosque, a temple. The user chooses," Becker said.

"It's a false idol," Fitz said.

"No, it's just a simulation," Becker said.

"Thou shall have no other Gods before me," Fitz said.

The Reverend smiled at Fitz's outburst.

Reynolds said, "The device doesn't allow you to talk to God, it stimulates areas in the brain that are active when a person has a spiritual experience."

David saw Reynolds using logic to reach the Reverend and his son, but he knew it wasn't going to work.

"We planned to test the effectiveness for curing things like depression or anxiety."

"That's what the church is for," the Reverend said. The fat man seemed calm and composed like he did this once a week. David wondered why the man wasn't more nervous. He and his group broke into a private company under false pretenses and threatened a CIA agent with death.

Morgan said. "I see no point in continuing this debate. The devil is upon us, this machine is a false god, and the Bible dictates idols are to be destroyed."

David realized what Fitz had been planning. "Test it then," David said.

Both Reynolds and the Reverend turned towards him.

"Even during the inquisition, the accused was tested. You are accusing the device of breaking the Second Commandment," David said.

The Reverend's face brightened. "A boy that reads the Bible. Will wonders never cease? And my learned young man, how do you suppose we test it? We can't solicit a confession out of it, can we?"

"Try it out. See if the function matches the brochure. Talk to a false God using the machine."

The Reverend's face went white as a sheet. He took a swig from a small flask from his jacket.

"That's preposterous. I can't let the future of this machine be decided by a right-winged lunatic!" Reynolds called out.

Morgan jumped towards Reynolds and snapped a punch at his face, breaking his nose and spurting blood. "Your next word will be your last," Morgan said.

The Reverend rubbed the silver head of his cane with his fat hand. The silver looked tarnished and oily. "Try the machine. Talk to a false God." The Reverend grunted and lifted his bulk off the chair to standing. "Yes. That's an excellent idea.

Who else in this room is better qualified than me to determine if the machine is a true tool of the devil?"

"Reverend, I can't allow this. The device is a danger to humanity and the church. We must destroy it at once." Morgan swung his pistol over to the machine and pulled the slide back and chambered a bullet."

"William! Put the gun down. I've already decided."

Morgan kept the gun pointed at the screen. David watched his tendons contract and his fingers tighten around the hand-grip.

"William. Put the gun away," the Reverend called out.

Morgan held the gun for a few more seconds before dropping it against his side.

"Thank you, my boy. Now if someone would help me test it."

Morgan pursed his lips but didn't argue. He called out, "Who can operate it?" The group remained silent. He pointed his gun at Reynolds' head. "I will give you five seconds to find a volunteer."

"Five, four, three." He cocked his gun. "Two."

"I can," Becker said.

Morgan motioned to one of his men to bring him over to the device and sat him down at the keyboard. The screen was cycling "Last try." "What does this mean?" the Reverend asked.

"The boy provided a code phrase, but it was incorrect. We have one last try before the machine self-deletes its programming."

Morgan said, "Isn't that preferable to trying this damned device?"

"No. If you would be so gracious and ask the boy for the code?" The Reverend stared at the keyboard and the dual monitors. "What do I need to do?" he asked.

"Please sit down here." Becker gestured to a slick, leather-covered chair beside the machine. The Reverend moved to the seat, sat down, and handed his cane to Morgan.

Morgan pointed his gun at Becker. "If this is a trick, you' will find that hell will be a preferable place to spend your last days, rather than with me."

Becker pressed a button on the console and the chair lowered a few inches, bringing the Reverend into a prone position. "No trick. Just simulation." He fitted the clear helmet on the Reverend's head and attached a wire bundle to a small black box. "Now we need the code to proceed," he said.

"Yes. The code, young man," the Reverend said.

"Unlock me and I will type it in," David said.

Morgan pointed his gun at David's head. "Now or you are dead."

"You will kill me anyway. Fuck you. No unlocking, no code phrasing."

Morgan pulled the slide back and cocked the gun.

"Unlock him," the Reverend said.

Morgan turned towards him. "What?"

"William, please. Large men with guns are watching him. What could one little boy do?"

David watched the breath go out of Morgan. It looked like he didn't like the Reverend's decisions.

"Him first," David pointed at Fitz.

Morgan turned and motioned to Charlie. "Keep the handcuffs on their wrists." Charlie fished the key out of his front pocket and removed the handcuffs from Fitz's hands. Fitz stood up on unsteady feet. Charlie did the same with David's legs and then locked David's hands together. David stood up toe to toe with his jailer. "We still need to have a chat after this is over," Charlie said.

"Why wait?" David drove his forehead down into Charlie's face smashing into his bandaged nose. Blood spurted out as he collapsed on the floor. Four guns at once cocked and pointed at David.

David raised his chained hands in the air. "Don't know what *possessed* me to do that. Maybe the devil or maybe because he was an asshole."

Morgan stared while David walked over to the computer and sat down at the chair. No one rushed to help Charlie bleeding on the floor.

The screen cycled between "Code phrase?" and "Last try."

David closed his eyes and took a breath. He knew what went wrong. Miles spoke Hugo's phrase in French, not English. But he remembered it in English. The pain should have given it away. He didn't speak more than some high school French and some dance terms.

Dance. He was far away from dance at this moment. Standing at the ballet barre in morning class came to mind. Repetitive movements. Tendu devant, tendu à la seconde, tendu derrière, tendu à la seconde. Repeat to a plié. Repeat to a relevé. He stood beside other dancers. His peers. The Principals and Soloists were up in the front of the class. The younger ones stood near the back. The food chain. There was always jockeying for position.

Where was he in this food chain? A man he hated had a gun to his head. A man he respected had forced this issue. But why? Was there a reason?

Always a reason, the voice said. Fitz was pragmatic and planned ahead. This was part of a plan. He just didn't know which one.

He took another breath and let the memory enter again. Pinprick to his temple. Miles leaned over to him in Jonathan's final thought. "*Le grand prodigality de Paris.*" He keyed the letters in and pressed ENTER. The screen blanked for several seconds. Then a sentence appeared in green lettering.

"Welcome, Mr. Reynolds, to the next generation. Prepare for calibration."

CHAPTER FIFTY-THREE

Becker checked the helmet on the Reverend. On the screen, a wire-frame image of a head appeared with points highlighted on the skull.

"We need to position the sensors correctly or it won't work," Becker said.

He re-positioned the helmet on his head to the right. "Lift your head, please."

The Reverend, the savior of the Christian right, looked like an overstuffed football player trying to protect his mind from aliens. Becker adjusted the cap back several millimeters. The flashing points had turned into green circles.

"We are calibrated," Becker said.

A list appeared underneath the wireframe. "Choose Sim 1, Sim 2, Sim 3, or CreatorSim."

"Standby to enter Sim 1," the screen flashed.

"I don't think this is a good idea," Morgan said.

"William, you worry too much."

Becker touched a tablet on the table and the room darkened. On the front screens, an image of a mountain meadow appeared.

"There should be about a five-minute period to adjust to the environment. You won't lose consciousness, but you won't be able to hear or see what's going on in the room. Please close your eyes and take a deep breath."

Morgan waved his hand over the Reverend face. No response. "Reverend?"

"He's entering the simulation. We will see what he sees after the machine constructs the environment."

"This is astounding!" the Reverend's voice boomed through the speakers of the room. "I'm standing in a grass field. I can smell the air and feel the wind on my skin." No sound came out of his mouth.

Becker pressed a button and spoke into a tiny microphone beside the computer. "How do you feel?"

"Free. Wonderful. I have no pain in my legs. I can jump up and down." The video screens mirrored the first-person view of a svelte man jumping in the air.

Becker pressed the microphone again. "Please take it easy, we don't want to overwhelm your nervous system in the first couple of minutes."

"Overwhelm?"

"This is the first time we've tested this, you understand. But based on how it's constructed and how it's tapping into the brain stem, there's a chance the sensations can tax your nervous system."

The Reverend's voice boomed out again. "I feel like a kid again!"

"Can he hear or see us?" Morgan said.

"No. All his inputs and output are through the device."

"Turn the mike off. Now."

Becker complied.

Morgan waved his hand over the Reverend's eyes. "Reverend?"

No response.

"Don't tell him we've left the room." Morgan yanked David out of the chair and pushed the gun into his neck. "This way," he motioned to the guards. "If anyone says anything or moves, shoot them."

Morgan marched David out the door. "Jacks, come with me." The large black man that entered the building first, followed him. "You and I will have a private chat," he said to David.

The guard on the inside of the door closed it shut. As David was being marched down the hall, the Reverend's voice boomed again. "This is astounding. I can understand why you wanted this so badly."

CHAPTER FIFTY-FOUR

Morgan turned to David and said, "This way, asshole," and shoved him hard down the hallway, the slave chains jingling with every step. A long chain ran to his leg shackles and Morgan walked him like a dog. Morgan stunk of aftershave and cigarettes.

Jacks, one of the largest men David had ever seen, followed behind with a machine gun hung over one shoulder. David assumed Jacks was short for Car Jacks as he was sure the guy could lift the average Toyota. He overpowered the hallway like a double-sized guard dog.

The leg chains caused David to shuffle along with tiny steps.

"Screw this," Morgan said. David felt his feet go out from under him and smacked his head and face against the cold tile as Morgan yanked hard on the chain and kicked David in the side.

"Heard of an eye for an eye, you little shit?" Morgan kicked him again. David tried to protect his stomach, but the kick connected anyway with a crack and a sharp intense pain followed.

As David gasped for air, he curled up tighter. Protecting his body from the next kick. He tried to roll forward, but Morgan pulled the chain again. "Where do you think you are going?" Morgan said.

Laughter spilled out the doors of the boardroom. The Reverend's voice laughed through the room's speakers. Through the machine.

David took shallow breaths and pushed himself to distract from the pain. He imagined doing plies until his quads burned in exhaustion. More laughter from the boardroom caused him to wonder what was going on in there.

Morgan turned towards Jacks. "You know I'd rather do this myself, but I can't be out of the room. Find a place and finish what I started." David grunted and took a breath that stabbed with pain.

But he caught a side view of Jacks as he pulled off his balaclava. A wide smile. Gold canine tooth on the left. Flat broken nose. Bad skin and looked like ten miles of bad road. The balaclava was better.

"Hurt him first then kill him," Morgan said. "Use this."

He handed him a card. "This should open any door. Don't take too long. I need you back here with me."

David lay curled up in a ball. Pain and burning racked his body with every breath. He wanted to fight back but couldn't. Couldn't breathe. Couldn't move. He tasted blood. His lips cut from the fall. Everything hurt, but his left side caught fire as he took a breath.

Morgan's kick had cracked his rib. Breathing was hard. Seeing was harder. The taste of metal was everywhere. He wanted to vomit.

Get up, the voice said. *Get up or you will die.* David rolled to one side and almost got himself on his hands and knees, but his body slammed back to the cold floor as somebody yanked his legs straight. The razor knife sliced his side again.

The black man dragged the chain over his shoulder like he was Goliath. David and Goliath. Each yank of the chain sliced into David's side. *Hold on*, the voice said. *Hold on.*

Jacks said, "This won't be take'n too long. Don't you be worrying none." David twisted around, and the pain lessened but the dragging stopped. He watched the big man peer through a door's window.

"Nope. Not this one"

Jacks dragged him farther down the hallway. *Get him talking*, the voice said.

"Why are you doing this?" he choked out.

Jacks stopped and bent down. A red ring tinged his brown eyes. A thick odor of sweat seeped from under his Riot gear. "None of your damn business. Everyone serves the church in their own way. This is how I'm doing it." Jacks stood up and continued to pull.

David struggled to keep his head raised. His vision had cleared and after an eternity, the dragging stopped. Jacks stood in front of a thick mahogany door with a narrow glass pane on one side. White letters on the door said "Fitness."

"This is more like it." Jacks used the access card to open the door. Proximity access. Every door in the hallway had one.

He dragged David into the middle of the room. Sunlight from skylights streamed in from high above. A few treadmills stood on one side, each with a tiny TV screen in front. To the left, a large collection of exercise weight and machines sat shiny and unused.

"Since you asked politely and all, I will tell ya." Jacks wheezed as he spoke. David thought asthma. The big man took a puff from the inhaler and stuffed it back into his pocket.

That confirmed it.

He finally saw the man's face. A needle dove into his temple. Jonathan knew of him, years before. The man's face slick with sweat. Head shaved and polished.

Swollen cheeks and eyes with a crooked scar trailing down the side. A fight he lost. Craters on his face like a moonscape. Flat and broken nose. One-time Special Forces. Special Forces with asthma. He'd have to have one-punch knockdowns. The swelling of his face and the acne meant something. *Steroids*, the voice said.

"To tell you the truth, I don't like killin', but I will be God's tool if I'm asked. I've got a lot of sins I have to atone for." Jacks dropped the chain on to the gym floor. David took another breath. The flame in his side burned hot. He had to keep him talking.

"I haven't done anything to you," David said. He saw the outline of a Kevlar vest with a pistol in a holster. Looked like a Sig Sauer. A sheathed knife on the other side. But David looked at the exercise equipment. All usual, but he doubted he'd get the chance.

"You haven't. That's the God's truth. But if Mr. Morgan says you are the devil and need to die, then I'm the right person to do it." Jacks pulled off his gloves. Two slabs of meat with fingers appeared.

David needed Jonathan back and now. He took a deep breath and searing pain from his rib cage shot through his body. He forced an even bigger breath and his eyes burst with tears. By instinct, he fought against the memories control even though he wanted them. But after a couple of seconds, the ice-cold memories and consciousness wormed through his skin like frozen mercury. A thin finger of cold entered his brain. Smaller tributaries branched out and spread everywhere. The cold turned hot in an instant. The memories burned in place like hot metal on bare skin.

He screamed out, then nothing.

No more pain.

The cracked rib meant nothing. The memories did something. He opened his eyes and felt Jonathan was looking out. His vision was clear and bright. But David wasn't gone or pushed away this time. He sat beside the memories. Sharing control. At least at the surface. He took another breath. The rib hurt a little, but dull and inconsequential. He could do this. Jonathan knew it. David did, too. Jonathan had a plan. In an instant, David saw it.

He had to tell the truth. Jacks' truth.

And Jacks couldn't handle the truth.

The big man grabbed a towel from the shelf and wiped his face and neck. He pulled a bottle of water from a tiny fridge, twisted the top off, and drained it dry. He crushed the plastic bottle and dropped it into the recycle bin beside the fridge.

Great, David thought, a green assassin. I'm sure he shops at Asshole Foods, too.

"But just because God is working through me, doesn't mean I won't give you a sportin' chance." Jacks unhooked his belt and threw it on the reception counter with a thud. He set the Sig on the counter with the knife. All the weapons were there. David just needed to go get them.

"A man needs to know he's fought the good fight before he dies. If you ain't the devil, the way you die will help God sort out the whole thing." His eyes rose to the ceiling.

Jacks slipped off the Kevlar vest and dropped the heavy fabric to the ground with a thud. He stretched and flexed. Massive chest and arm muscles pulsed under the long sleeve shirt. He looked like a Brahma bull in a turtleneck. All that was missing were the horns.

Jacks dragged David by the chain to the corner of the gym and unlocked the handcuffs. Full-length mirrors touched at 90 degrees.

"You can leave anytime you want. But you has to pass by me first."

David pushed up from the ground and said, "You...you were Special Forces. Jacks. Eugene Jacks."

Jacks frowned at him. His eyebrows bent together in one line. He opened his mouth to say something and white teeth gleamed back with a single gold canine. His face was better covered. He squinted and pursed his lips. The gold tooth disappeared.

"Maybe you is the devil. This makes the job easier." Jacks leaned in and backhanded him in the face. David's head snapped back, and he collapsed to the floor. He felt like a flying truck sideswiped him.

David rolled over and pushed up again. "There was an...incident."

"You know nothin'."

"Croatia."

Jacks moved in close and slapped him again. "Now you startin' to piss me off. Here's I've given you a fightin' chance, but now look what you've up and done."

"You took the coward's way out."

"Whatchu talkin' 'bout, boy?"

David got to his hands and knees and spit blood onto the hardwood floor. "You let the Serbs kill those women to save yourself. They wanted help. The U.S. government's help. Your help. You gave them up to save yourself. You were worse than the Serbs."

"Shut up!" Jacks took a step and kicked at David, but David crabbed out of the way.

"You could have helped those women." The information hit the right mark. Jacks lost his cool.

He reached for David and grabbed the middle of his shirt. David's body lifted like it was on a wire. Jacks' right arm pulled back and shot forward. The one-punch knockdown.

David expected it. He snapped his head to one side. The blow glanced off the side of his temple. His ears rang. David pushed back against Jacks. David's shirt slipped from Jacks' hand.

He couldn't just hit from this close. No inertia. No power. It would be like hitting a truck with a feather. Jonathan had to choose the right time.

He'd better hurry.

David backed up to the mirror. Jacks' chest heaved, and he wheezed in and out. He had no staying power. That's why he put David into a box. He wanted close in fighting. The one-punch knockdown. He'd lose in a title match.

David took another deep breath. "I heard you cried like a baby when the company found you in that Serb jail. They messed you up pretty badly." His voice had changed. Deeper, older. More authority.

Jacks got ready to charge. Maybe a matador's cape was better. His legs flexed, and his chest heaved. David looked past Jacks to the reception desk. "Is your gun loaded?" David asked. For a millisecond, Jacks' eyes looked down and to the left. A classic eye movement that signified the retrieval of a memory. Everyone does it. Jacks wasn't the exception.

David leapt on his left foot to the big man's right side. Jacks pushed off his left foot to block David's end run. David wasn't there. David pivoted instead. Leaped. Spun in a reverse pirouette. Elbow smash into Jacks' face and ripping the top of his nose open. Jacks staggered back. Blood spurted like a fountain. The big man shook his head and narrowed his eyes. Sticky red covered his face. He lunged at David, bear-hug style.

David twisted and dropped to the floor, lashing out with a kick to Jacks' kneecap.

Crack. Something snapped. Bone, tendon, ligament. David didn't know what. But he knew it was the sweet spot. A perfect kick on a knee strained with at least a hundred pounds of extra weight. Jacks screamed and grabbed his knee. David jumped up and stood back. Jacks held on to his knee and raised his head. Swollen and red; full of rage. Unbridled rage.

David heard the wheezing. Jacks' chest rose and fell. Labored. Hard to breath. Hard to get any oxygen. The inhaler was in his front pocket, but he wouldn't grab for it. Jacks pulled a knife from a sheath on his calf and snapped the blade open with a click, palm up. Knife fighter's stance. "I'm gonna slice your heart out."

"I heard the Serbs cut your balls off first. What's life like as a girl?"

Jacks roared and launched himself at David. He seemed to ignore his kneecap. He pushed off his good leg. Knife forward. David exploded upwards, his heavy legs launching him high. He cleared Jacks' body and dove into a roll to the open floor behind them. He reached and grabbed the chain from the floor as he landed.

Jacks screamed and turned.

David rose and turned to face his adversary. Jacks charged him like an elephant. Head down. Knife forward. David waited. Jacks' knife hand rose upwards towards David's chest. David pivoted his body to the left, grabbed Jacks' wrist, twisted away from the body and down. The man's bulk followed, and the three hundred pounds of meat smashed into the ground.

David swung around behind him, wrapped two quick turns of chain around the black man's neck, and pulled. Jacks dropped the knife and grabbed the chain. Any direction he pulled made it tighter. David's ribs began to hurt again. He ignored it. Pulled tighter. Jacks yanked at the chain and tried to roll over. David straightened, jammed his foot into his back and pulled. The thin chain dug into David's hands.

Five seconds.

The chain bit into the heavy ropes of muscles on Jacks' massive neck. Tore the flesh. The wheezing continued but got more futile. He got his fingers under the chain, but they got caught in the trap as well.

Fifteen seconds.

The massive body dropped to the ground and shook like a bull. The legs kicked the floor behind him. David steadied himself and pulled tighter. His face and body slick with sweat.

Thirty seconds.

The shaking stopped as the chain pulled tighter.

Sixty seconds.

No movement. No wheezing. No life. David dropped the chain to the floor. His hands were ripped up. Every breath stoked the fire in his side.

Asshole, the voice said. David watched as his hand grabbed Jacks' knife on the floor and pulled the blade under the thick folds of the man's swollen neck in a quick sweep. A bucket of blood gushed onto the hardwood floor with the strips of varnished oak soaked with blood.

Always guarantee the kill, the voice said. David looked down at the body.

Jacks would have.

CHAPTER FIFTY-FIVE

Morgan walked into the boardroom. Everyone stared at the plasma screens, including the soldiers. What was happening? The screen projected a first-person view of a rock wall as if the climber had a video camera attached to the helmet.

A thin yellow rope ran through the center of the screen. The view looked up to the summit and then down to the ground. The ground looked a million miles away. In the distance, a thin river etched a tiny path near the bottom of the screen. If the rock had been a bean stock, he would have called the climber Jack.

"This is so amazing. My hands and arms feel as strong as steel," the Reverend's voice boomed out of the speakers.

Jesus H. Christ. The Reverend was doing this. The device worked as advertised.

"If I let go what would happen?"

Becker leaned into the microphone and said, "I wouldn't advise it. We aren't exactly sure."

"Let's see, shall we?"

The view changed. With one hand, the climber pulled a knife from the belt and flipped it open. The handle was clear and sharp, but the blade was out of focus and discolored.

"How strange. I can't see the blade well. Do you think the program is broken?"

Morgan watched as Becker clicked the mouse and the image sharpened up.

"That's better," the Reverend said. "The blade seems to be dirty. Anything for realism I presume."

Morgan squinted. The image of the blade was dirty. A brown stain was on the blade. His virtual hands tiled the blade towards the sun. The rays bounced of the blade and reflected the image back to him. The tip and the shank were an image of cold polished steel, but the middle looked soiled.

Used as knives are. As a weapon.

The brown changed hue. Morgan saw it first. Tiny bubbles of stickiness. Crimson color. Thick sweetness of a good kill. Blood covered the knife.

CHAPTER FIFTY-SIX

As Jonathan's presence evaporated, the pain from the cracked rib cycled back to his head and body but had diminished. Narrowed even. David spit blood onto the floor before reaching down and pulling a money clip from the dead man's pocket, full of hundreds. Government ID card in an opposite pocket. Eugene Jacks. Jonathan's memory had been clear. Even the Croatia information.

David pulled a black earpiece from the dead man's ear. All-in-one microphone and earphone. Blinking might mean muted. Goliath heard what others were saying, but they didn't hear him. David pushed it into his ear. Every bit helped.

He hefted the Kevlar vest up, but it was four sizes too big. The pistol was the right size. SIG Sauer P226 series, holding 15 rounds of 40 caliber. He wrapped his fingers around it. The knurls of the hand-grip bit into his palm. He slipped the spare clip from Jacks' belt into the back of his pants. At the last pouch, he extracted a silver cell phone and pocketed it.

One last thing. He picked up the access card Morgan had given Jacks. Reynolds' smiling face on one side of the card, his corporate logo. All-access pass.

David thought about what to do.

The plan, the voice said. *The plan is this...* The voice dictated a short and concise blueprint. Escape. Break out. Run away. The plan unfolded in his head as a memory; images flashing like fast video cuts. But he frowned and thought, what kind of plan was that? It missed a bunch of things and missed getting Fitz out alive. The plan needed David to abandon Fitz to succeed.

No way.

David owed his life to the old man, even when the voice said Fitz would say otherwise. He needed to save Fitz. Any other option was a failure. He opened the door to the hallway and locked it with the deadbolt.

He'd start with his plan and go from there. The voice didn't disagree or say anything.

Fine with him.

He clicked "Map" on a computer sitting on the reception counter. The building appeared. Silicon Valley address. Lots of curves and rat-like cubicles. Several kitchens. Pool tables and foosball games spread around. One fitness center. A shining star blinked. His location. He traced his options to the outside. The aerial view showed steep mountains behind. Parking in front. The highway was a quarter-mile away. Trees, before that.

No way he could make it to the highway with a cracked rib and an old man in rougher shape. They'd be screwed. Reynolds' campus security included a perimeter fence.

Options. He needed other options.

Something bugged him about the whole set up. What was it? He thought back to the when twice-broken-nose Charlie wheeled him into the boardroom and Reynolds talked about the device. Something wasn't right. What was it?

He closed his eyes and remembered the room where the Reverend was currently acting as an advanced product tester. Before and after the guys with guns appeared. Mahogany. Carpets so thick you need snowshoes. Long table polished mirror bright. Podium. Media area to one side. The machine hooked up to the plasma duo. The machine. Black, titanium. Thin. Looked like a friend's hipster laptop. It looked just like it.

What had happened? Another picture formed in his head. From the sewers. His memory seemed photographic. Much better than he'd ever had before. The filmstrip ran through his head again and stopped at every image.

A light bulb went off.

He brought up the corporate web page again and typed "Research and Development." The page returned several hits, but slow as death. Weird. He'd expect an internal web page would blind him with the speed.

The browser chunked along until he found the page he was looking for. A map. The map. Map of the Research and Development facility.

Lots less detailed. Big chunks of white space. White space with edges. No walls or corridors. What was there? Several exam rooms. One he'd been in. He pushed his finger against the screen. Research and Development. Same address. Building B.

His wheelchair trip this morning was white concrete walls. No windows. Elevator to the main floor.

"B" meant below. Two floors down embedded deep in the California hills of Palo Alto. Reynolds wanted his pet projects close. In hindsight, too close. David logged onto his National Ballet email account. After a few minutes of fast typing, he pressed Send. He needed help from several angles. But only one needed to work. He didn't have much time.

"Jacks? Report," a voice boomed in his earpiece.

Too late.

"Jacks? Report!"

Time to go.

He glanced at the map once more and then slipped out the door to the gym. Distant sound boomed from down the hallway. The boardroom again. Holding his side, he sprinted the opposite way and rounded the first corner into a soldier dressed in a black Kevlar jacket and fiberglass helmet. Goggles pulled up onto the helmet. Machine gun slung over his shoulder. Heckler and Koch MP5 9mm.

He held his glove in one hand, the pale white skin bright against the black sleeve. He looked up and his eyes went wide. He'd relaxed. The building had been secured. Any civilians were locked down. No worries. He took off his goggles and gloves to hurry up and wait until this thing finished.

But not anymore.

The soldier dropped the glove and jabbed his right hand down and back on the stock of the gun. The barrel pushed up. Chest height.

David's chest.

The solider fumbled his fingers into the trigger guard.

Missed.

Missed the trigger.

David didn't.

Inertia drove David forward. He grabbed the barrel and pushed it away from his chest and towards the wall. The soldier tried to yank the machine gun out of David's grip.

David's right hand fingers pointed straight and squeezed together. Shuto. Knife hand. He chopped the man's throat with a crack. The man gasped as he tried to breathe through a crushed larynx. He let go of the gun as he gasped for air.

David dropped the gun barrel. Left hook to the soldier's chin. The man's head rolled to the right and David's knuckles smacked up and hard on the man's chin again, dropping the man into a gurgling heap. David yanked the machine gun from the body and slung it over his shoulder.

He'd been looking for the door beside the soldier's body. Room 113. Solid steel. No keyhole. Access card only. He pulled Reynolds' card out and waved it in front of the door. Two seconds later, the door clicked.

He pushed the door open.

CHAPTER FIFTY-SEVEN

Reynolds rolled his sore shoulders to get blood flowing. Zip ties held his hands together behind him forcing his arms back like a peacock. His legs were tied to the chair. At least he wasn't kneeling anymore. In front of him, his twin screens buzzed with life. Virtual life.

The overweight religious piece of shit was using the device. His device. The one he'd bought and paid for. The one that would bring his corporation back to life and put him back on top.

Tested by a fat fool who used religion to justify his own greed. How unusual.

Morgan had re-entered the room and stood near the back. He'd removed that little shit of a dancer out to who knows where. Morgan might have done him a favor, but the kid had a habit of staying alive.

All his other employees sat and watched. The soldiers prevented anyone leaving. But Wyatt and he were the only ones tied up. None of these other assholes were worth a damn in a clinch.

The view switched again. Another training scene if you could trust that idiot German inventor Vogler. Which you couldn't. But still, Reynolds caught himself staring at it with his mouth open. The German wrote detailed emails on the experience, but the detail was far more than what Reynolds expected. High definition. Sand dunes. Crystal blue ocean. Seagulls. A pair of feet touching the water. All rendered by the device on the fly and pushed into the fat bastard's brain stem.

It looked real.

The fat man's voice boomed through the speakers. "This is incredible. It's hard to describe unless you try it."

The first-person view changed as he moved his virtual head. Feet in the water. Back to the ocean. More of the dunes. A hand reached down and cupped water and sand. The water dripped from the fingers of the hand back into the water again. No frame drops. No pixelation. The graphics card by itself could turn the industry on its side, even minus the simulation technology. Research tried to hack the hardware, but the German had encased the circuit board in black plastic polycarbonate. None of his engineers could reverse engineer it, without destroying the damn thing. The German promised full detailed specs with manufacturing information, but only after the first test had been completed.

"The water is ice cold and the sand is so hot it's burning my fingers. Everything seems sharper and more defined than in real life."

Can someone turn that idiot off? Better yet, just pull the plug on the device. That should screw him up. A timer counted down at the top of the screen. The scene dissolved from the seascape to a white canvas.

"The device is increasing the intensity of each simulation," Becker said. "But his heart rate and blood pressure has spiked since we started the test. I suggest we move to a disconnect sequence and back him out of the program."

"Nonsense," the Reverend's voice boomed through the speakers of the room. "I feel perfectly fine. Please continue."

Becker said, "You feel fine because your virtual body feels fine. The device short circuits your body's delivery of information and replaces it with the devices. I'm not your doctor, but your heart rate has risen and your blood pressure seems high for a man of your"—Becker looked around—"stature."

"William, I can't see you, but please ask the man at the computer to continue?"

Morgan nodded to a soldier who gestured with his gun at the device. Becker shrugged and said, "As you wish. Stand by for the next phase."

Reynolds watched the counter on the top of the screen fade in before the program switched.

10:00.

9:59.

9:58.

Ten minutes left to the final simulation.

Four possible outcomes.

One. CreatorSim kicks in. It's wildly realistic and soon the Reverend is talking to the deity du jour. Once he's back in the real word, he declares it evil and destroys the device.

Two. CreatorSim kicks in and it's a piece of crap. The Reverend disconnects and orders it destroyed because it didn't deliver the goods.

Three. CreatorSim kicks in. Realistic and frightens the Reverend so much he has a heart attack and dies. The government confiscates the machine and develops it as a weapon, without us.

Not the first time this has happened.

Four. We gain an advantage and hand these goons their hat. However, some were government, but he had the entire place wired for video. In a court of law, he'd be exonerated. Unless Charlie got to the videos first.

9:45.

Reynolds didn't care which scenario played out. He still had the upper hand. Those assholes just didn't know it yet.

The great mahogany door pushed open and a soldier slid inside. His AK-47 machine gun hung off his shoulder and his goggles were up on his helmet. He moved past the other grunts in the room and whispered to Morgan.

Wyatt was right in making contingency plans. I never thought we'd have to use them.

Morgan's eyes went wide, and his lips pulled back over his teeth. He was clearly holding it in. What happened? Morgan whispered something back to the grunt. The grunt nodded and left the room, taking two other soldiers with him. Morgan followed behind. His face was stone and red. He was mad.

"Keep everything status quo," Morgan told the soldiers left. "If anyone moves or tries anything, shoot first and ask later. Start with those two." He pointed at Reynolds and Wyatt. Six soldiers stood in the room. You needed only one to ruin your day.

"He's pissed at something," Wyatt whispered. "I think the dancer is the problem."

"He caused enough problems for us."

Reynolds tilted his head towards Wyatt. The device had switched to a mountain vista. Beautiful blue skies with endless peaks filled both screens. The rendering was unbelievable.

"Do you still have it on you?"

"Yes."

"Get ready. If this turns out the way I think it might, we may need to use it."

Wyatt nodded.

CHAPTER FIFTY-EIGHT

As the door sealed closed, David's ears popped. Negative air pressure again. Why would a tech company's R&D facility have an expensive air system? Negative meant air couldn't get out. Maybe Reynolds also played with viruses or other pathogens in his spare time.

The stairway walls were stark white and smooth as glass. No push bar on the metal door leading out. This wasn't a fire escape. Heavy armored cable, stapled to the ceiling and connecting every six feet to a solid metal and glass light fixture, lighted the next few feet going down.

Top security. But for what?

The stairway was narrow. The stair edges sharp. The wall corners precise. No handrail. Not wheelchair accessible. Reynolds broke a bunch of state laws with just this single stairway. Each step echoed against the concrete. He walked down three full floors. At the bottom was the same type of metal door. Bright red this time. Access panel to the right side. Red LED in the center of the panel.

He waved the card in front of the panel.

Nothing.

He held it in front of the panel and then pushed it against the plastic. Still nothing. The chip was still in the card. These things were next to indestructible.

He waved again. A soft click this time and the LED turned green. He stuffed the card back into his pocket and pulled the AK-47 up and checked the safety. He felt a stickiness to the fingers. He wiped his hand across the wall and drew a broad streak of red on the white.

Someone else's blood.

As he pushed the door, the air pressure from the corridor pushed back. He kept pushing until he felt a rush of air from the stairway into the lower floor. Negative pressure again. Designed to keep things in the air from leaving the building. What didn't they want to leave? He pushed the door open, but the exertion pushed the hot knife again into his side. After some shallow breaths, the pain lessened.

He couldn't continue for much longer without some medical intervention. Nothing in the hallway. No noise. No music. Just a faint vibration from the air system.

The map flashed in his head. Charlie wheeled him to an elevator approximately three hundred yards to the west. The map didn't show the corridors, so he was flying blind. Retracing his steps in the wheelchair, the examination room sat near the end of the forever hallway. The other direction contained more doors and other access panels.

More security meant they were protecting something.

In the dormitory of the National Ballet School, the boys and girls lived on separate floors with a locked alarmed door between them. Any midnight rendezvous would alert the whole building. But here he had the magic key. He wished he had a similar key when he was a student.

The all-white walls changed to half-white, half stainless steel. Like a surgical ward. Embedded fluorescent lights. Sparkling white tile floors. Tall cabinets every fifty feet with thin air ducts hugging the floor at the join to the wall. He reached into his pocket, pulled out a tiny piece of paper, and dropped it to the middle of the floor. The piece skittered along and disappeared in an instant into the vacuum air system. No wonder the floor looked so clean. A speck of dirt wouldn't stand a chance.

Some doors displayed windows with reinforced safety glass. Some opened into small medical examination rooms. Others were workshops. Banks of computer systems. Oscilloscopes. Test benches. Trays of circuit boards. A number adorned each room that counted down as he moved closer to the elevator.

015. The first room contained an exam table covered in sharp-edged coarse paper. A bank of cupboards. A tiny sink. Like a doctor's office. A doctor's office in maximum security. He searched it and found gauze, tape, and a small covered scalpel. He slipped the scalpel in his sock.

014. Another room looked like a cross between an exam room and a mad science experiment. A brain suspended in liquid sat in a large jar. A gaggle of wires poked into it and connected back into some test equipment and flat-screen. A testing electronic board. The board connected to a desktop computer.

The convergence of electronics and medicine. What did Reynolds use this facility for? Creating video games or a nouveau Frankenstein's monster? Based on what he'd seen so far, probably both.

Frost covered another window. He pressed his fingertips to the window. Ice cold. A large freezer with a window. What could be in there? He waved his access card and the security light switched to green. Six white sheets, covering six gurneys that held six things. Six things of varying sizes. Dead bodies. A large hand and arm hung down from one sheet with a black watch circling the wrist and a gold band on the ring finger. These weren't medical cadavers. Jewelry would be removed. How had these people died?

Under the first sheet was an older white male. Closed eyes. Wearing a dirty shirt and pants. The top of his head opened like the top of a soft-boiled egg exposing the pink brain. Hundreds of thin black wires inserted into the spongy material and combed together joined with a custom connector.

The rest were similar. Some women, some men. All had the soft-boiled egg treatment.

The pain from his rib sliced through him once again. He pushed open the door bar and back out to the hallway. He needed to hurry. Find Fitz and get out of here alive. But seeing the device upstairs made him realize there was another room. A bigger room with the real stuff in it. A room that could be of some help. Not just something out of a Frankenstein movie.

Another hallway. More rooms and test labs. More counting down. But then he found it. The room number gave it away; 001.

It was a big one.

No window on the door. The walls leading up to it curved to either side. No fire escape signs anywhere. If there was any kind of problem or disturbance, this facility would be like an Egyptian tomb. This seemed to be the largest room in the whole floor. No other rooms were after it.

The door had a different design than the others. More steel and re-enforced around the edges. Walls painted stark white. The access panel was different, with two red LEDs and a different sized control box. Different box meant different circuit and maybe a different security system.

He pushed the card to the panel. The LEDs changed color to green and a large metal bolt pulled back into the door like a safe. A safe with something more valuable than money.

The door pushed open. A second set of clear glass doors with a heavy rubber seal on both sides stood open. The room looked like it was ready to go underwater.

He stepped across the barrier into the inner room.

CHAPTER FIFTY-NINE

Morgan entered the corporate gym. One soldier was already inside. Reynolds spent a bundle on the space. High-end hardwood floors. High ceilings. Skylights. High tech exercise equipment. Floor to ceiling mirrors. The room also had a dead Eugene Jacks lying in a big pool of blood. His own blood.

"Shit," Morgan said. He walked to the middle of the floor and looked at the body. "Why is there so much blood?"

"His throat's been slit." The soldier said. "His gun and transmitter are gone."

"Did you find the white ID card I gave him?"

"No."

"Hand me your pistol," Morgan said.

The soldier looked at him and said nothing. The other one standing near the dead body pulled his MP5 up.

"Your pistol, please," Morgan held his right hand out.

The soldier unsnapped the leather cover from his holster, pulled out the Glock, and handed it to Morgan, butt first.

Morgan slid the magazine back in a smooth motion, aimed down at an angle and pulled the trigger. Twice. Double TAP. Two bullets smacked into the dead man's forehead, the smooth brown skull jerking each time. TAP TAP TAP. Three more shots into his chest. Like buttons moving down the tunic. No movement this time

No blood. It was already all on the floor.

He handed the pistol back to the solider.

"Find the dancer. You have ten minutes to do it. I have other things to attend to."

* * *

That son of a bitch, Morgan, again entered the boardroom looking like he'd swallowed a bug. *Maybe a jitterbug,* Reynolds thought.

Morgan stopped and ran his hand over his receding hairline. "Where is he in the process?"

Becker wiped his brow, looked up at Morgan and touched the keyboard. "The system says we have about ten more minutes until we hit the final simulation." He concentrated back to the screen. The screen. Reynolds couldn't read the damn screen from his position. He expected a calibration display, but he hadn't seen it yet in operation. No one else had either.

"Can you hurry it up?"

Becker bent forward and touched two keys. A white dialog box appeared.

"No. The program won't let me."

"Is there any way to just shut it down?" Morgan's lips were tight and white like he wanted to scream but just held it in.

Becker thumbed a tablet and flipped through several pages of text. Reynolds knew they were emails; lots of emails. Every page. The actual documentation, if he could call it that, was in the machine and was available once unlocked, but not during the simulation. Other functions locked down. The emails contained a back and forth conversation between Becker and Vogler. But if a question wasn't asked, then the answer wasn't provided. Sweat stains formed under Becker's armpits. But Reynolds wasn't sure if his scientist was more scared of the device or Morgan.

"I don't think so. Vogler said the first simulation needs to run its course."

"What happens if I unplug him?" Morgan asked.

"That wouldn't be advisable," Reynolds said from the floor.

Morgan turned and glared at him. He turned back Becker. "Well?"

"I don't know what would happen." Becker flipped through some pages and peered at the display. Sweat dripped from his temples onto the paper.

Morgan waited for a second then asked. "Make a guess."

Becker said, "The device shunts a person's sensory input system into the computer simulation. That's your sight, sound, taste, and feeling. If it's disconnected prematurely and because of the subject's current health and blood pressure, he might could suffer a heart attack or worse."

Morgan cursed and stood back.

"What's the problem? Do you have a plane to catch?" Reynolds said.

Morgan narrowed his eyes and walked over to him. "You need to be quiet." He raised his hand and closed his fingers tight into a fist.

Reynolds flinched. "Stop. I want to talk. The device is working and based on what we're seeing, it could be the greatest advancement in simulation ever. But I want you to look at the possibilities for your organization."

Morgan's brow narrowed and licked his lips.

Reynolds kept talking, Morgan hadn't rejected him right away. "We could build a virtual church where the Reverend is conducting a sermon in the simulator. A sermon that's chargeable. Better than TV, better than advertising. The revenue possibilities are limitless."

Morgan lowered his hand and his eyes looked down towards the floor.

He was considering the offer.

"Let's dispense with all the theatrics and we can structure a proper deal. No hard feelings."

"I have a deal for you," Morgan said

Reynolds shifted in his seat.

"…and it's the best deal you will get from me. A limited time offer. If you sign over the company to the church as a gift, then the church owns the machine. Owns everything. The copyright. The intellectual property. And this building we are standing in."

Reynolds' blood pressure spiked. That goddamned son of a bitch.

"You will be compensated for your trouble. Maybe ten cents on the dollar, plus a big tax deduction, because you are donating to a registered charity."

Reynolds strained against his bonds. If he could get free, he'd break this greasy church bastard's head.

Morgan tilted his head and said "Well?"

"Go to hell!"

Morgan slapped him across the face. "That's what I thought you would say."

Reynolds winced. The right side of his face burned hot. He touched the side of his mouth with his tongue and tasted blood.

Morgan motioned to one soldier in the room. "How old are you?"

The solider swallowed and looked at him. "Twenty-one, sir."

"Are you committed fully to the church?"

"Yes, sir, I am."

"Good. I need you to take these blasphemers out of here and lock them in the same room as the government agent. Can you do that?

"Yes, sir."

"Watch these two closely. Tricksters, both. Take every precaution and don't be afraid to shoot in the name of the Lord."

The solder swallowed.

"Get them out of my sight," Morgan said.

The soldier snipped the white plastic ties on both men's legs and motioned them to the door with his machine gun.

Reynolds and Wyatt walked out into the hallway with the soldier trailing behind. Reynolds stopped and looked back. Everyone stared at the front screens as the virtual world was somewhere else. Somewhere Reynolds hadn't even imagined before.

* * *

The soldier kept his machine gun raised at the Reynolds and Wyatt and barked an order. "Straight down the hall, then left."

Reynolds looked over at Wyatt and raised his eyebrows. Where was the grunt taking them?

The hallway jutted a sharp left and the boardroom behind disappeared. To the east side, soft tinted windows opened to a view of Palo Alto proper. The Stanford campus cluster to the south and the city north and east.

Reynolds bought the land and built the facility at the height of the dot com boom, when the original owner ran out of money. He'd wanted a sleek modern building built into the side of the Palo Alto hills. He'd gotten that, plus more. Government funding paid for the facility's bio lab three floors down, but on the ground floor, the floor plan was closer to a labyrinth. Oblique hallway angles with hidden kitchens and relax zones where the angles joined.

"Next right," the soldier said.

"I'm not feeling well," Wyatt said.

"No talking."

Wyatt slowed his walk and stumbled. The soldier pulled the machine gun slide back. The stock lodged in his armpit. Ready to fire.

"Keep walking."

Wyatt blinked his eyes and stumbled. With the next step, his legs buckled, and he collapsed on to the carpet. His shoulder hit first then his head smacking on the ruddy nylon. His body shook, and his eyes were squeezed shut.

Reynolds whirled around. "You have to help him. He's having a seizure. He needs medication. In his front pocket. Give it to him." Wyatt twitched and writhed on the floor in front of the two men.

"Back away," the soldier ordered.

"Release my hands. I can help."

The grunt pointed the barrel at Reynolds, but he saw the guy shaking. Nervous. Excited. Maybe his first real operation. He could use that.

"I won't tell you again." the soldier said.

Reynolds backed up to the wall. The grunt knelt and tried to fish the bottle out of Wyatt's pocket, but Wyatt twisted and shook.

"Hold still, damn you."

Reynolds inched along the wall towards the men.

The soldier swung the rifle towards Reynolds and snapped the safety off. "This is your last warning. Next time you move, I shoot." He looked down at Wyatt's body. "And you hold still."

Wyatt's body became still. The grunt leaned in and pulled Wyatt over onto his back.

"Thanks." Wyatt twisted and kicked the grunt's hand holding the gun, snapping several bones. The gun shot bullets rapid fire. Reynolds jumped and landed a kick on the soldier's chin. The machine gun stopped as the man collapsed into a heap on the floor.

Reynolds reached down and grabbed the cutters from the man's belt. He planned to cut Wyatt's bonds first when he saw a red bloom growing around Wyatt's stomach.

"Sorry... I..." Wyatt stopped talking and his head fell back to the floor.

He twisted the cutters around until he snipped the plastic on the zip tie and freed his hands. He knelt to Wyatt and said, "I will get a doctor," but he had already slipped into unconsciousness. A river of blood poured out of his security chief's belly.

Reynolds always knew the odds of winning a deal. He'd done this countless times; he changed the stakes, the game, the players, anything to gain an edge. As the blood seeped on to the floor from his number one, he hesitated. There was no doctor around that could make his wound disappear, and even if he gave himself up, the chances of the maniac giving a shit about Wyatt was slim to none. He counted to three and in those seconds, he looked at all the options.

A river of regret flowed through him. He'd never watched a friend die before, but Wyatt knew the risks and Reynolds always paid him well. His chief of security would have wanted him to finish the operation. Everything was a business decision—including letting someone die. When he hit three, he grabbed the soldier's pistol and machine gun and sprinted down the hallway deeper into the labyrinth.

He knew where he had to go, but like any betting man, he needed some insurance first.

CHAPTER SIXTY

"Come on in. The door's open."

David heard a voice. A kid's voice. High pitched. As he moved into the room, the edges of the glass doors retreated into the walls. Heavy rubber gaskets remained.

The vault door behind him closed and metal rods slid into place. He was safe in a room without any visible means of escape. But unless he got what he needed and escaped the room, he would be screwed.

French fries, onion rings, burnt coffee, and body odor stunk up the room like the kid's play area at a fast-food restaurant.

Inside the vault, long desks lined the sides of the room. At the end, was a large platform and several racks of computer equipment. To one side, a cot with a crumpled sleeping bag and pillow. A stained coffee maker sat with an inch of black liquid in the pot on another table. The red light was on.

"I'm making a fresh pot. Want some?"

A kid, really, even though they were probably the same age, sat in an articulated chair. He pushed a long lock of greasy black hair from the front of his eyes and smiled. A patchwork beard covered his face.

"Who are you?" David asked.

The kid leaned back and put his feet up by a keyboard. A mound of half-eaten fries sat on white paper beside it. "I'm Fred."

"Okay, Fred. Why are you locked down here?"

"I'm a hacker, man and this is the coolest thing I've ever hacked. There's some sweet tech going on here. Reynolds' security guy, Wyatt, caught me trying to hack into their system six months ago and gave me a job instead of sending me to jail. But for the last couple of days, Wyatt's locked me in here."

The room resembled a dorm room and smelled like one.

"I would have expected this room to be sterile, in an *Andromeda Strain* kind of way," David said

"Andromeda strain? Is that a new punk band?"

"No. Killer viruses."

"I guess at one time this room was that," Fred burped. "But it hasn't been for a few days."

"I gathered that." David staggered and grabbed his side. Any movement hurt like blazes. He expected the pain would lessen, like the other times, but instead it was getting worse. Did the doctor do something to him when he was out? He reached down and felt the bandages where the IV was inserted. He took another breath. The pain shot through from front to back. He gasped and bent over.

"Are you okay?"

"I will be in a minute."

Fred got up from his chair and bent over. David swung the pistol up towards him.

"Whoa, cowboy." Fred raised his hands. His stained T-shirt said in black letters, *Stick it to the Man.* "I'm not packing any heat. I have to check on a couple of things."

David stared at him for a minute then dropped the gun to his side. He didn't feel any kind of threat coming off Fred. Just curiosity.

Fred poured the last of the coffee into a cup and walked to the opposite side of the room. Touching a screen, a graph zoomed up. Fred's pants hung six inches below his hips and were cinched up tight with a black leather belt with silver studs. "I have to say"—the boy shook a stream of white powder into the cup—"that you kick ass, man! I watched you from here and saw everything." Fred motioned to David to come over. A set of LCD screens showed a variety of images.

"What am I looking at?"

"The building. I've patched into the building's security feed, so I can see what's happening. Reynolds kept having someone bring me fresh food and water, but I felt so out of touch. It was easy to hack in and get a private view of what the hell is happening."

Fred enlarged a set of smaller images and clicked two of them in series.

"But, there's no sound. I couldn't find the channel. It was like watching a silent movie with no cue cards of what was happening." Fred turned and smiled. "But what you did to that black man mountain, I thought he would smash you into turtle poo."

"So did I."

"But it was like watching a chop-socky flick. Die hard with a vengeance. You're a twenty-year-old version of Bruce Willis man. BAM!" Fred sliced the air with his hands. "But even without sound, I figured out that these assholes"—he pointed to the Reverend and an image of Morgan—"are bad news and have been trying to screw over the boss right royally. But they don't know."

"Know what?"

"That they have their work cut out for them."

David nodded. "That the real device, isn't it?" David pointed to a titanium laptop to the side of the desk. A couple of smaller screens sat connected to it.

"Yes, sir. You are the lucky winner. That's the one you delivered to Mr. Reynolds." David didn't respond. "But I suspect you didn't deliver it, did you?"

"No."

He slapped his hand on the counter. "Man, I KNEW IT. He's building up some serious bad karma." He took a long swig from the coffee cup and made a face. "Reynolds told me he wanted the real machine down here where it's safe and had me build an interface, so I could display it upstairs for all the board of director shitheads."

He pressed two keys on the keyboard. A video display of the boardroom from three angles appeared.

"But I didn't think he was going to lock me up this crappy room for three days. Ever since the device and you showed up."

"The machine upstairs isn't doing anything?"

"It's just a glorified terminal. I hacked the harness to the headpiece and the device carried a standard fiber jack on it. Like hooking up a DV system."

"DV?"

"Digital video."

"Oh… Does anyone else but Reynolds know?"

Fred rolled his eyes at him. "What do you think?"

"Wyatt does."

"Correct. And that Walter White-looking dude, Becker. But only Reynolds and Wyatt have access down here. Frick and Frack."

Flat-panel screens adorned every table. Three high-end video games sat in one corner. One showed a man with a big shotgun, kicking the shit out of some ugly aliens.

David took a breath and grabbed his side. He looked at himself. Blood on his hands. Shirt ripped. Dried blood on his leg. Feet dirty. He rubbed the stubble on his face and came away with more blood.

"You need a hospital."

"Good point. Right after all this is finished." Another wave of pain hit him. "Tell me. Is the device worth all this trouble?"

"Worth it? It's the most awesome device thing I've ever seen. You've watched the displays. You've seen the way it renders the virtual scene? And to jack in like that? It's the most amazing thing I've ever seen."

"Did you try it first?"

"No way. Not without some testing. You see how that fat bastard is jacked in? It's William Gibson all over the place. It might be a *Hotel California* experience."

David raised his eyes.

"You can jack in any time you want, but you can never leave."

David said nothing, but he knew the reference.

"When they try and unhook the fat boy, they might not be able to. Then the shit is going to fly."

"Even with the dangers, what's the potential of the device?" David asked.

The boy looked away and down to his feet.

"Big, the biggest. But…"

"But what?"

"There's just one little problem."

Fred pointed at a green screen to the left that showed a graph like a stock ticker. All the indicators sat at the top of the graph.

"Problem? What kind?

"You see the graph over there?

David looked to where Fred was pointing.

"That's network traffic. There's more coming in here than should be on a Sunday. A lot more."

"And?"

"Well…here's what I think is happening…"

A red light blinked on the counter.

"Shit."

"What is it?"

"We got company."

David raised the Sig as a loud buzzer sounded and twin white strobe lights flashed. The large metal wheels turned, and the metal rods slid back into the door. Two seconds later, the vault door pushed back and slide open. In the doorway, Reynolds stood with a pistol pointed at David and a machine gun pointed at an unconscious body in a wheelchair.

Fitz.

"I suspected you made it this far," Reynolds said. "Give me the device and then you and your friend can go."

A purple bruise hung under Reynolds' one eye. His bottom lip was fat. Gobs of dried blood dribbled down his chin. His white shirt was ripped and splattered in red. Blood. A dark stain on his gabardine pants. He'd won a fight. David wished he hadn't.

"Make your decision. I can shoot both of you or none of you. You decide."

David leveled his pistol at Reynolds.

Reynolds face softened. "Look. We can all part friends. No one must die. I just want the device."

David's eyes narrowed. "Screw you! You ripped my life away. You have to pay for your actions."

"Get real, dance boy. The only one going to pay for my actions is you. If we don't hurry the goons from upstairs will find this room and kill us all."

David heard Fred turning and pressing keys on the computer. A screen up high near the door changed images. Four men in black outfits were walking down a white stairway. Balaclavas. Machine guns. Black combat boots. More Special Forces. Jonathan's voice came through. Quiet. Whispering almost. The stairway looked like the same one David came down.

"They are already coming," Fred said.

"Look, I don't want to kill him. But you don't leave me much choice," Reynolds said.

"You kill him. I kill you."

"Maybe. But can you take the chance with his life?"

David stood for a second. He winced. Pain shot from under his arm to his fingertips. He gripped the handle tight, but it weighed heavy in his hand. It hurt to keep breathing.

"If I let you go, how are we going to get out of here?"

"We need a diversion. A big one. But there's no time left," Reynolds said.

David looked at the rifle. MP5. Black. Polished. Well maintained. A heavy pull on the trigger. Reynolds would have to squeeze hard to start the flow of bullets. However, the bullets would make a mess. Of Fitz. Something he'd hoped to avoid.

David reached around, grunted and in one swift motion pulled the other pistol from the back of his pants. He swiveled his arm until the gun pointed at the device. Right in the middle of the case. Through the keyboard and into the motherboard. Maybe the hard drive too if he got lucky.

"Drop the gun or the device becomes recycling."

Reynolds swallowed and spit a wad of blood on the floor. "You can't aim like that. You'll miss."

"Try me. I'm a dancer. I know where my arms are, and Jonathan was an excellent shot. I won't miss. Drop the gun and you the get device."

Reynolds glanced up at the surveillance camera. The soldiers had made it to the bottom of the stairway. "Damn it! Okay." He holstered the pistol in the back of his pants and swung the machine gun, barrel facing down. "Take the old man and just let me take the machine. Otherwise we all die."

Fred looked over at David. David nodded.

"The disconnection might kill the fat guy," Fred said.

Reynolds yelled. "Look at his vitals, for God sake. His heart is about to explode. This might save his life." Fred looked at another screen. Heart rate, blood pressure. Blood pressure kept rising. Heart rate was close to the top of the scale.

"He's in the final simulation. He's going to meet the deity du jour," Fred said.

"We all are anyway. But I don't want to at this particular time. Turn it off NOW."

Fred looked at Reynolds and back at David.

"I have to do a normal shutdown, or it could hurt the machine."

"Quick, man. We have to leave!" Reynolds said.

Fred typed keys and the screen changed. A fast set of images filled the screen. Flying fast through a mass of clouds. Just like Superman. Fred typed another series of commands after checking the binder again.

"Shutdown started," Fred said.

Sounds of muffled gunfire entered the vault. David looked up at the security video feed. A goon was shooting at the lock on the door at the stairway. "They will be here soon."

"You have to pull the plug."

"I don't know if I can."

"Pull the plug or I pull yours." Reynolds aimed the pistol at Fred's head.

* * *

Westlake was pissed off. Enraged, furious and overall angrier than he'd ever been in his life. Frustration and irritation came with the job, but hot poker level rage never did.

Not until today.

Westlake started the week planning to approach Reynolds and give him the easy way or the hard way speech, to gain the memory technology. But before he could, The Reverend pulled strings in Washington and forced Westlake's hand under the pretense of Homeland Security. An operation was put together to enter Reynolds' R&D facility and confiscate any or all devices that posed a threat. Westlake wasn't interested in an overactive video game. He wanted the memory implant technology. Yes, it's unproven. Yes, it's dangerous. Yes, the other test subjects died. But something about the dancer has made it work and work well, from all accounts. During the operation, he'd scare the shit out of the dancer and have him submit to a battery of tests to find out why the procedure worked on him and no one else

But right now, all he wanted was to kill that son-of-a-bitch Reverend and that asshole son of his.

Westlake shifted back and forth in the big leather briefing chair, with his hands cuffed together in front. An old man like himself didn't require the LA police zip line behind the back trick.

Morgan left one guard with a machine gun to cover him. However, his guard was smaller and thinner than the rest of the mouth breathers he'd brought in with him. The guard's helmet seemed one size too big and the military garb seemed to somewhat just fit. Or would fit, if the guard had spent several hours a day in a gym for years. The guard had a striking resemblance to Rick Astley, a red-haired pop singer from the 80s. Westlake suspected that Morgan used anyone in the department that was loyal to the Reverend. In this case, the guard looked more like a bean counter than ex-Special Forces.

"You should sit down and relax. I'm not going anywhere," Westlake said.

"No small talk," the guard said.

"I understand that. I know how stressful these kinds of situations can be. You storm into a building pumped full of adrenaline and then nothing happens. Fatigue sets in. Makes you dull. You don't want that."

The guard ignored him and instead opened the door a crack and peered down the hallway.

"Can I ask you a question?"

"I said, no small talk." The guard continued to look down the hallway. He reminded Westlake of a kid left behind while all the other kids go to a theme park.

"Are you a God-fearing man?"

That did it. The guard shut the door and stared at Westlake with a snarl in his eye. Westlake couldn't shake the image that Rick Astley held a gun on him.

"I'd expect you to be God-fearing as your allegiance to that fat bastard out there seems to prove it."

"The Reverend is a great man."

"A great man that will spend a lot of time in jail."

The guard snickered, "You know nothing."

"I know that the Reverend will go to prison for a long time and end up being someone's bitch. I suspect a ginger like you will be traded back and forth like a hockey card."

That did it. The guard stormed over and jammed the machine gun into Westlake's chest.

"You will be judged. You will all be judged, and you will go to hell and pay for your sins."

"Well, if that's true, then what's the sin for having the safety on your machine gun engaged?"

The guard's head swiveled down to look at the engaged safety on the side of the gun. Westlake rose in one quick movement, grabbed the barrel, and shoved it fast into the man's head and helmet. The guard wrestled with it, stunned from the hit. Westlake grabbed for the stock and slammed the end into the guard's chin, dropping him into a heap.

As the guard moaned and writhed on the floor, Westlake smashed the butt of the gun into his forehead. The guard stopped moving.

After finding the keys and unlocking himself, Westlake realized there was no value in spending any more time in the building. The religious nuts had control. If he wanted to live for another day, he had to escape and call for reinforcements.

Maybe the technology could be saved. Maybe the kid could be saved. But Westlake couldn't see how just himself and a machine gun would help. He wasn't Rambo or even Bruce Willis.

He opened the door a crack and looked down the long hallway. From the plans he reviewed before the operation, he knew there were other exits at the other end of the building. The gun would help if guards stood by the exits, but he hoped he didn't need to. He'd just gotten his suit back from the cleaners.

CHAPTER SIXTY-ONE

The screens darkened to a jet black then bright streaks of light screamed across the virtual sky. The sound of rushing air with loud thunderclaps every few seconds filled the room.

"Turn that down," Morgan said.

Becker stared at the screen and touched the keyboard, but nothing happened.

"I said, turn that down."

"I can't. The system won't let me, and the audio controls are frozen."

"Unplug the speakers."

"Can't. They're wireless."

The sound kept rising. BOOM. A clap of thunder screamed and reverberated through the room.

Morgan yelled to the soldier nearest to one of the mounted speakers. "Remove that speaker!"

The soldier grabbed the corner and pulled, but nothing happened. He reefed on it, using all his weight, but to no avail. The large speaker seemed cemented to the wall.

"USE YOUR GUN!" Morgan yelled over the blast of noise.

The soldier nodded then stepped back a few feet before raising his machine gun and firing a burst into the center. The bullets cracked the metal grill, but the sound kept playing.

"Kevlar sound cone," Becker yelled over the din.

The sound wound up like the room stood behind a jet ready for takeoff. More bright streaks of light whizzed by the screens, coupled with an almost painful white noise. Then, as if by magic, the sound stopped.

Both screens displayed soft blobs bouncing in slow motion across both screens as if they were playing a game; almost like tiny fairy sprites from a children's tale. A bright spot in the center emerged and the Reverend's voice boomed through the speakers again.

"Where am I?" A large boom followed his voice and then another, almost in answer to his question. The sound came from everywhere, instead of just the room speakers. One of Reynolds' audio tricks, Morgan thought.

"I don't believe it." The Reverend's voice sounded muffled like they only heard one side of the conversation. His voice became stilted and nonsensical as if he was speaking a different language. The booming continued as if answering a question. *Who is he talking to?* Morgan thought.

Crying echoed through the room. On the couch, long tears streamed down his chubby face. His eyes were still closed. Everyone in the room heard the Reverend say, "I had no idea…it's so beautiful."

"Who is he talking to?" Morgan said. No one answered. He stared at the images on the screen. Abstract. White. Pure. No shape. Just hints at outlines.

The booming conversation continued. The Reverend said more words, but they were disjointed. At the bottom of both screens, a question appeared. 'You've lost connection. Reconnect?'

Becker touched the keyboard, "Cannot connect to host" showed on the screen. Becker tried again.

In the chair, the Reverend's body vibrated and then shook like he had severe palsy.

"Do something!" Morgan yelled. "Disconnect the damn machine!"

"I did," Becker said.

"Turn it off!" Morgan said.

Becker pulled the power plug and jabbed his finger on the power button, but nothing happened. The soft white images and amorphous shapes floated between the two screens. Becker jumped to the couch and pulled the headgear off the Reverend's head. The Reverend said in a faint voice, "Goddamn it." The entire room still heard him.

Morgan had to do something. He wanted his father dead, but not like this. He needed the old man alive to take the blame from the government and use his influence to squash whatever repercussions there might be. The raid had been the Reverend's idea in the first place and he called in enough favors to make it happen.

The last thing he wanted was his father to become a martyr. If the old man died now, he'd be held responsible without the ability to control the church or its wealth.

Morgan pulled his gun and fired two shots into the case, causing the screen to blank. The room's sound and the twin screens died. The Reverend's body stopped shaking.

An Indian woman stood up and ran to over to the Reverend. "I'm a doctor." She put two fingers on his carotid artery. The Reverend's eyes remained closed and his chest rose and fell as if he was panting.

"I don't understand what just happened. The receiving unit lost connection to the device," Becker said. He looked around in the room like he was searching for something.

Morgan grabbed him by the front of his jacket. "What did you say?"

"We lost the connection to the simulation machine several minutes ago. It wasn't anything we did."

"You mean this isn't the actual machine?"

"No… No…" Becker stammered out.

"Where is it?" Morgan's eye twitched like a grain of sand got stuck.

"Underground."

"Underground where?"

"Underneath this building."

"Son of a bitch."

The screens snapped on again and an impossible bright light filled both screens. A single musical note filled the room. More notes followed. Like human voices but changed somehow. Modulated. Amplified. Reverberation, as if the sound was coming from the largest concert hall in the world.

"What the hell is happening now?" Morgan turned to the doctor and Becker. Both had shocked looks on their faces. The Reverend's body shook like he was having a seizure.

"Help me hold him down. I don't want him to fall off." The doctor said.

One of the employees grabbed the Reverend's shoulders and another held on to his legs. The Reverend's body shook like he was operating a jackhammer.

"Do something!" Morgan yelled out.

The doctor pulled out a black bag from underneath the table and withdrew a bottle and a syringe. She jabbed the syringe into the bottle and filled the plastic reservoir with the clear fluid.

"Hold his head tight."

The employee held the Reverend's head tight as the doctor jabbed the syringe into his neck and pushed the plunger. The vibrations slowed, but his body jerked and twitched like someone had shot him with a Taser.

Deafening sound filled the room. Thousands of voices sang in unison, but the tone changed. What started calm and restful, now had discord and an edge to it.

"I can't treat him here. I have to move him to the clinic."

The sound changed again. Off-key. Sinister. The screens changed. The bright white light had gone blue and moved to a deep red. Thunder erupted through the speakers.

"Get a gurney. We can't carry him down. The male nurse looked at Morgan and the female doctor. "There's one down the hallway."

"Go," Morgan said.

This whole thing was a cluster fuck.

The Reverend's lips were moving.

"He's trying to say something," someone said.

The doctor leaned into the Reverend's face and put her ear to his lips.

"What's he saying?" Morgan asked.

She squinted and frowned.

"Prepare."

"Prepare?" Morgan said.

"Prepare for judgment."

She pulled back in horror.

Boom Boom Boom. More thunder came through the speakers. The choir turned to discord. The music stopped.

CHAPTER SIXTY-TWO

"Disconnect the power unit. Unplug the fiber and we can shut it down as we go," Reynolds said.

Sweat dripped from Fred's forehead. He reached around to the back of the computer and pulled out a thin cable and the power cord. The image on the screen flashed once but stayed on.

"It's got a big battery. I should be able to execute the shutdown sequence," Fred said.

"Okay, let's go."

Reynolds motioned to Fitz with the pistol. "Here he is. I'm a man of my word."

"What did you give him?"

"A smaller dose of what I gave you. He should come out of this in an hour."

Fred typed on the computer. A set of rapid-fire letters filled the screen.

"Put it in the case. We don't want to damage it. Hurry."

Fred grabbed the aluminum case and slid the device inside. As he closed it, the screen they used for the device flickered. "Look!" A ghost-like apparition in a blinding white screen appeared to fly towards of sea of blinding incandescence. That was the destination.

David looked over and frowned. The screen wasn't connected. How could this be happening?

"What the hell is going on?" Reynolds said. The image overtook the screen raising the brightness until they heard a zap like a short circuit and the image went black. The smell of burnt plastic filled the air. A crack of gunshots echoed down the hallway. "It doesn't matter anyway. They've blown the first door because I killed the access cards. We all have to leave."

David bent over, grabbed Fitz's arms, and lifted. The pain sliced through his side and his eyes teared from the pain.

He squatted and pushed Fitz up like a weightlifter swinging him over his shoulder in a fireman's carry. Taking a breath, he tightened every muscle he could, but still felt he'd been stuck with a knife.

Reynolds motioned to the boy. "Let's go. I need you to come with me."

Fred's eyes widened, and he stuttered. "What for?"

"I'm offering you a way out and a full partnership in this thing. Opportunities like this don't come along often."

Fred looked over at David. "I'm not sure...I..." Reynolds jammed a syringe into Fred's arm. The kid collapsed into Reynolds' arms.

"You bastard! I..." David said. Fitz's weight compressed the broken rib. It took everything he had not to scream out in pain.

More sounds of gunfire raked the hallway.

"I will take good care of him. I suggest you hurry." Reynolds hoisted Fred over his shoulder. "Head left then right to the end elevator. That will take you to the back-loading dock. Once outside, head into the woods."

Fitz stirred as Reynolds slid a panel open on the inside of the vault door, inserted a key, and flipped a switch.

"I'm setting up a diversion. Don't be in the vicinity when they find it."

Reynolds slapped a button on the wall. The vault door slid closed. Reynolds and Fred were still inside. There must be another exit. Shit. He'd have to go out the hard way.

David turned and looked down the hallway. He heard footfalls and more voices. He turned with Fitz on his shoulder and limped left. Goliath had kicked him in the leg. But it hadn't hurt much before carrying Fitz.

The air system seemed off. The acrid smell of cordite filled the air. He heard the hard jackboots clomping down the hallway. Fitz stirred.

"Stay still. I've got you."

David stumbled. The fractured ribs slid against each other and David bit into his tongue to stop from screaming in pain. The pain was molten lava burning through his skin.

Limping as he went farther down; he needed to get them out of there. They passed two more rooms. One like the meat locker he saw on the way in. He kept going. Elevator to the left, two hundred feet. More shots fired. Doors being smashed open. Glass shattering.

One last portal. Two glass doors stood in his way. The black access panel to the side. He looked through narrow glass windows and glimpsed black pants, black boots. One soldier only. Coming in the other direction.

Shit.

He swung Fitz around on his shoulders and hobbled down the hallway, thumped the wall with the access card, and kicked the door open.

Cold. Frosty.

Another meat locker. Cold air blew from an air conditioner high on the wall.

245

Fitz groaned on his shoulder. He walked to the back of the room. More gurneys. More bodies covered in sheets. The sheets rippled as the cold wind blew across them. Hell's halfway house he thought. He didn't want to know what this room contained. The air was sharp with the smell of formaldehyde. At the back, two empty gurneys lay side by side. He lowered Fitz on one and pulled a sheet from a stack on a shelf over top. He struggled but got on the second and pulled a sheet over himself. The door handle snapped, and David heard the door hinge's squeak as the soldier pushed the door open. With the sheet over his face, he couldn't see anything. In his hand, he held the Glock, raised up a little and pointing towards the door. His finger was on the trigger. He heard the clomps of Jackboots walking on the floor. Then nothing. The soldier was standing still.

The soldier's radio squawked. "Hustle to the end of the hallway. We found something."

David heard the sharp squeak of rubber on tile. The soldier must have spun around. Through the thin sheet, David made out a dark shape coming closer. He adjusted his grip and put his finger on the trigger. The sheets on the gurney rustled ahead of him.

"Jesus Christ," the soldier said. "What kind of a hell is this?"

The shape bent over, and David heard retching as the soldier vomited on the floor. More boots against the floor. The sound of the door opening and closing.

David pulled off the sheet and swung his legs over to the floor. Ahead on a stainless gurney was a body. A sheet lay bunched up on the floor covered in vomit. He saw why. The body's face had been removed. Skin stripped to the bone. One eye socket empty with wires threaded through the sinus cavities into the brain. The chest was flayed open. More wires fed into the chest cavity and what looked like into the spinal cord. The wires ended to a small circuit board connected to the gurney. Something out of a horror movie.

David ignored the gore and pulled the sheet off Fitz. "Let's go."

Fitz blinked his eyes "Are we dead yet?"

"Not yet, but it's still early."

Fitz sniffed the air and made a face. "What on earth is that awful smell?"

"You don't want to know."

David hoisted Fitz on to his feet, but Fitz's legs collapsed. David grunted, but caught Fitz by the arm before he fell.

"We have to leave."

"You don't have to convince me, my boy."

David pulled Fitz over to the door. He peered out the frosted glass but saw nothing.

"Hold on, I will open the door."

David pressed the metal bar across the door and the lock clicked open, but just before he pushed the door open, an explosion rocked the floor. The safety glass splintered but held in place. The hallway darkened.

"Shit. Reynolds booby-trapped the room. We need another way out."

David pushed the door open and the hallway sat thick with smoke. The emergency lights blinked on. A shower of water came from the ceiling. Sprinklers. David heard the air system kick back in.

"Come on, let's go."

David put Fitz's arm around his shoulder and limped to the left away from the explosion. A set of doors stood in their way. David swung the door inward. The fire must have disabled the security system.

They went through and the door swung closed. David and Fitz both coughed, but the smoke hadn't come through to this segment of the hallway. They had some breathable air.

David just needed a few more minutes of good luck and they could get out of here.

Half-pulling and half-carrying Fitz down the hall, David stumbled all the way. Every breath hurt as it felt like the fractured rib twisted with every breath. Fitz coughed more, but his legs regained more strength.

One hundred yards then left. Ninety yards then left. Eighty yards then left. David tried to lick his lips. No saliva. He needed water. He needed medical attention. He needed to get out of this damn place.

After some agonizing minutes, they reached the end of the hallway. A lone elevator door sat at the end. David leaned Fitz up against the wall and pulled the access card from his pocket with Reynolds' shining face looking back at him from the card. He pushed it close to the black plastic card reader and the elevator door slid open.

David grabbed Fitz and the two men entered the elevator. The door slid closed and he felt the metal box move upwards towards the surface.

Fitz held onto the steel handrail; his face was gaunt and drawn out. Large black circles were under his eyes. They had stripped him of his Paris clothes and gave him an orderly's pants and shirt.

"We're almost home free." David coughed again and spit on the floor. The saliva was black. Reynold and Fred likely made it, but he wasn't sure if anyone else made it out alive.

The elevator stopped, and the door opened into a large room with no windows. Whitewashed walls. Concrete floor. Painted white. A large set of double metal doors stood in front.

They were ready to leave, except for the large Sig Sauer pistol pointed straight at David's forehead.

Morgan held the gun with his finger on the trigger. Safety off.

"Get out." He waved the gun at Fitz. "You, too."

David looked at Morgan. No fancy Italian jacket. No tie. Sweat stains had formed under his arms. He'd rolled up his sleeves and his forearms were covered with angry red scars. Some circles and some straight lines. They looked like burns. But his eyes were unmistakable. Red. Fiery. Looked like he was the devil. At least a demon.

David grabbed Fitz's arm and limped them both out of the elevator.

"The machine was destroyed in the explosion."

"Shut up." Morgan waved the gun around like it was a toy. "Kneel."

David stared at him and took a breath. His pulse raced, and his chest pumped. He needed help. He needed Jonathan back again. Full force. He waited. Waited for the tendrils of the other memory to push him into the backseat. Take the pain away. Take the fear away.

David frowned. Nothing was happening. He felt and heard his heartbeat in his ears. His mouth was bone dry. His stomach shook in fear.

"Kneel or I will shoot you standing up."

"He's not much of a threat, sir." The soldier behind Morgan spoke.

David looked at the soldier. His helmet was off. Sweat trickled down his shaved skull. His eyes were wide. His face was thin. Pockmarked. Loads of acne in his youth. But youth wasn't a faraway place. He was about the same age as David and looked scared. Maybe more scared then David.

Morgan turned to the soldier. "Hold your tongue or you will receive the same punishment." He turned back to David. "Kneel."

David didn't move. It took all his strength not to pass out. His leg cramped, and his ribs still smoldered in white-hot pain.

Morgan lashed out with a kick to David's leg. David screamed out and his leg collapsed. He dropped to the concrete floor.

Morgan kept his finger on the trigger. "You will die. And I promise to send you to Lucifer himself."

David lifted his head up. "Like your father?"

"He was weak and paid for his sins."

"And right now."

"What did you say?"

"We watched the screen. It sounded like his entrails are being roasted as we speak."

Morgan sneered. "Soldier! Front and center."

The soldier moved over and stood beside Morgan. His machine gun pointed down to the floor.

"Chamber a round into your weapon and take it off automatic."

David closed his eyes and imagined the gun at his temple. His guts churned. Nothing. No Jonathan. No memories. No nothing.

The soldier gulped but followed orders.

"Place the barrel up to his temple."

"This man is no threat to you."

"Place the barrel to his temple."

"He isn't a threat." His voice cracked.

Morgan swung his pistol up and aimed it at the soldier's head.

"I'm ordering you to shoot the prisoner or I will shoot you."

The soldier's eyes opened wide and filled with tears. "Please don't make me do that. Please don't make…"

Morgan pulled the trigger and the lead slug blasted from the barrel. It traveled twenty-four inches and entered the soldier's temple. As it punched through the hair, skin, and bone, its blossoming lead mushroom ripped through the man's brain until it stopped just short of the other side of his skull. The soldier's body collapsed on the floor in a heap.

Morgan leveled the pistol at David and pulled the trigger. *Click.*

Nothing happened. Morgan dropped the gun and reached for the soldier's pistol. David twisted, kicked his left foot, and connected with Morgan's elbow.

Morgan screamed. David rolled over and pushed his body up. David didn't see the punch coming. Morgan's left fist smashed into David's nose and snapped his head back. David felt a sickening crack and blood spurted from his nostrils.

David staggered back, smacking the back of his head into the white wall. He blinked his eyes. His vision was blurry. He made out Morgan coming closer. His left hand cradling his right arm where David had kicked it.

"Screw the gun. I will kill you with my bare hands instead." Morgan lashed out and landed a kick in David's gut, knocking the wind out of him.

He would die. This megalomaniac would beat him to death. David felt Morgan's hands grab the back of his shirt and throw him back into the wall. David put his hands up and protect his face, but blood from his nose smeared across the white-washed wall.

"You aren't so tough. My grandmother could take you."

David turned. His vision cleared but his head hurt. Morgan grabbed a truncheon from the belt of the soldier and hefted it in his left hand.

"This is more like it."

You can do this. David heard a voice. Not Jonathan's

Morgan swung the truncheon like a bat, but David pulled back against the wall.

You can do this. A voice again. Different. Older maybe. Familiar, but David couldn't tell from where.

Morgan swung the wooden club at David's head. David twisted, and the wood bounced hard against the wall.

You can do it, David. I have faith in you.

His father's voice.

From long ago. His own memory. His experiences. Not someone else. He squeezed his hands. Jonathan was gone. But the training remained. Body memory.

"Quit running away like a girl, so I can finish beating the shit out of you, you little faggot!"

David relaxed, took a breath, and steadied himself. He had shooting pains in his side. His leg was on fire. He turned and wiped the blood on his nose with his forearm. Like how he felt when he danced in the middle of a ballet. Minus the blood.

Morgan pulled his arm back to get maximum velocity of the club. David prepared and pushed off with his right leg, leaped, and closed the distance between them. He drove his forehead into the bridge of Morgan's nose. Blood spurted from the broken cartilage. David followed with a right hook into Morgan's chin. Morgan's head snapped back. Morgan shook his head and pulled the truncheon down, but David danced left, grabbed it, and tore it from Morgan's grasp.

David swung the butt hard into Morgan's solar plexus. He found the sweet spot. Morgan buckled over and collapsed to the floor.

David looked at the man lying before him. A swath of blood from his nose painted a wide streak as Morgan struggled to get up again.

"Stay down," David said.

Morgan's body moved, and his hands pushed up from underneath. He heard the gasping of breath.

"I'll kill...you..."

"No, you won't," Fitz said.

Fitz had the soldier's pistol in his hand and pressed to Morgan's temple. "You need to atone for your sins, my boy." Fitz's hand shook, but he kept his finger on the trigger.

Fitz coughed. "David...would you be so kind as to disable this troublemaker? The soldier had handcuffs on his belt."

David reached down and hand-cuffed Morgan's hands behind his back. He grabbed a second set and cuffed one ankle to cuffs already on his wrists.

David reached over and pulled Fitz to a standing position. "Thanks, my boy."

"What do we do with him now?" David said.

"Homeland Security doesn't have a sense of humor. There's so much video surveillance in the building, the authorities won't have any problem untangling the good from the bad."

David draped Fitz's arm over his shoulder. David opened the twin doors. California sunlight and warmth streamed in. Outside. Freedom. Safety.

"What happened to the bloody device?"

"I will tell you later," David said. The two men stepped down the concrete stairs and out to the pine needle path.

From the edge of the trees, David saw someone dressed in light green camo gear with a knapsack. No weapons visible. Her shirt was pulled open, exposing a low-cut white top. Long blonde hair tied up at the back.

Alicia.

Her face was tight, but she ran over to help them.

"I got your email. My jeep is just over the bluff," she said. "Did you end it?"

"Yes," David said.

She put Fitz's other arm over her shoulder and the three of them disappeared down the path.

CHAPTER SIXTY-THREE

The Learjet 60 XR taxied onto the east runway of San Jose's international airport. At the height of the dot com boom, over twenty Learjets sat parked and ready to jet their twenty-something owners anywhere they wanted.

Most of them weren't there anymore.

Inside this one, a fifty-something sat waiting. A billionaire still. At least on paper.

Reynolds felt the weight from the takeoff pushing him back into the beige calfskin seat. He touched the chafed skin around his wrists where he'd been tied up. He'd use the first aid kit once they were in the air. The bastard guard had pulled the plastic bonds tight and cut his circulation off. Wyatt had removed them back…before.

Wyatt.

He looked down at his dirty shirt. Streaks of Wyatt's blood covered one side. He sighed. Wyatt had been loyal right to the end. Too bad.

He'd have a glass of scotch in his memory, once they landed and completed the negotiations.

Reynolds looked down at the dented aluminum case that housed the device and shook his head. That old minister got quite a ride right up to when he died. No wonder the government was so interested in it. He'd bet everything on the device. He was glad he'd made the decision to cut and run.

He touched the ripped pocket on his linen shirt. He looked like he had just escaped from prison. It didn't help that he had carried on an unconscious man as well. However, the pilot had just welcomed him on board. No questions. A handsome retainer with a larger bonus once the flight had been completed always did the trick. Having enough money certainly didn't buy happiness, but it sure made being miserable a lot easier.

Reynolds drained the bottle of Evian. He smelled something rank. Lowering his head, he sniffed. It was him. He'd shower at their first refueling stop. Other than that, this jet had everything he needed. A change of clothes. Double the flying range of a normal Learjet. He'd had the pilot order some take out as well as the chef he used didn't have enough time to prepare anything.

As the jet pulled toward Oakland, Reynolds heard the landing gear pull up into the fuselage. Short of an F16 ordering them to land, he was going to start over.

Anger rushed over him. "Goddamned bastards! I hope they got what was coming to them."

He snapped open his laptop and logged on to his bank via his satellite Internet access. He didn't want to look at what RRT was trading at this morning. Most of his shares were in options anyway. Deep underwater. Not even worth the ink they were printed on. When the news hit the streets, he'd probably owe the printer money.

He checked a couple of more bank accounts. Some Eurobonds in Switzerland. Some cash offshore in the Caribbean. He totaled the assets in his head. He was down to his last million dollars of real money.

A million dollars.

That used to be a lot of money. In the old economy.

Time to reset, recalibrate, and restart.

It would be different this time. Less manufacturing. More annuity revenue. Revenue from licensing. Licensing agreements for the new technology. Agreements done by lawyers. His kind of lawyers.

Sharks. Sharks in suits.

Paid a bonus on the deal's profit. Lawyers could make more money for companies than with any product. Reset maybe in some other base industry. Entertainment perhaps.

The jet tilted, and the engine whine settled down as they cut a wide curve westbound out over the Pacific. The shiny steel towers of downtown San Jose glared back at him. Like long-dead Egyptian obelisks. He wanted never to see this airport or city again. He'd had enough of the valley. He'd had enough of the goddamned country.

Good riddance.

Whatever was about to happen, he was ready for a new life and a new challenge.

He'd seen the power of the damned device. He could go in any direction he wanted to. Complete on delivering a console, but he might approach it like a major corporate acquisition and just break it up into smaller pieces. Graphics, simulation, AI—the parts could be worth more than the sum. His Chinese partners were masters of duplication and manufacturing. They'd be invaluable to assist.

But like always, it was him. He knew how to do it. He'd done it before.

He yawned. The day's activities were weighing on him. He needed some sleep.

He looked over at his charge. The nerd was still out. He'd given him enough to keep him quiet for several hours. He'd probably sleep until they got close to Shanghai. No matter. Getting ready for a new life as a new Shanghai millionaire would be the easy part. Girls, luxury apartments, privileges of the new Chinese elite. It was a hard life, but he'd get used to it. Reynolds looked out over the ocean. The sun had started its decline in the west. Hannah would have liked this view.

Hannah.

She never came back. He'd left New York a few days ago and she was incommunicado. No cell phone messages or anything. The building security checked his penthouse. She wasn't there, and her clothes were gone. Maybe she just decided enough was enough.

Bitch.

It was weird. He missed her. Her laughter and her body and the way she smelled. He never figured out what she perfume she wore. She was as close to a girlfriend as he'd ever had before. He'd miss her for a few days at least. Once he reached China, he'd have his partners set up some interviews for a new girl. It would be a tough job, but he could see his way through it.

He slid the shade down on the window and felt his energy drain out of his body as the adrenalin from the day's events wore off.

In less than thirty seconds, he was asleep.

Several hours later, he stared out the side window and watched a Chinese afternoon sun heading towards Europe. Dark clouds lay underneath the tiny jet as far as he could see. They'd be landing in Shanghai in less than an hour. He pulled apart one of the croissants from the Fiji food tray and dabbed some blackberry jam on the tip. The pilot would have preferred Hawaiian croissants and fuel, but Reynolds didn't want to take the chance of entering the U.S. again. Who knows who would be looking for him? Fiji was fine.

When they landed, Reynolds stretched his legs, grabbed a quick shower in the tiny terminal building, and breathed in as much of the salty humid air as he could. Before climbing back in the plane, he took another look at the blue seas and palm trees. Maybe he'd build the business back up and sell it all off in one big transaction. Then, a little older and wiser, he'd buy an island out here and live the rest of his life swimming, fishing, and screwing.

He'd arranged new identification. New passports. New credit cards. A foreign investor. Born in France. Educated in the best schools. Worked on removing his accent, but he kept a light Germanic lilt. He wasn't Richard Reynolds anymore. Reynolds was dead. Dying in the building. He'd been so deeply leveraged, he hadn't owned anything outright for a while now.

Reynolds knelt and grabbed the wrist of his shanghaied passenger. Pulse strong. Fred's body was warm but unmoving. He didn't have any other drug to wake him out of it. Reynolds thought he probably gave him too much. But not enough to kill him, he hoped.

Reynolds opened a plastic box from under the seat and pulled out a metal bottle. He unwrapped a clear plastic hose and mask, connected it to the tank, and turned the knob on the top. He pressed the mask to Fred's face and heard the hiss of the pure oxygen flowing into the mask. Fred's chest rose and fell. A little faster than before and then his body jerked. The oxygen was doing its job. Like vaporized caffeine.

Reynolds watched his eyelids. The eyeballs were rolling around underneath. Fred's hands jerked up again until finally, Reynolds saw him open his eyes.

"Good afternoon." Reynolds smiled. "Do you remember what happened?"

Fred's eyes grew wide. He pulled the mask from his face.

"Whoa, young fellow. Just relax. Everything is okay."

Fred's breathing doubled, and he looked scared.

"What happened? Where the hell am I?" Fred said.

"You've already started on the next stage of your career. The rich stage."

Fred tried to push up on his elbows but then collapsed back down on the bed.

"Easy, son. The effects of the drug will take a wee bit to wear off." Reynolds handed the oxygen mask back to him. "This is pure oxygen. This should help you get your bearings."

Fred reached up, took the mask, and placed it back on his face and seemed to relax somewhat. He'd have the boy looked at by an English-speaking doctor once they were on the ground.

"A life of luxury awaits. Money. Cars. Jewelry. Women. Whatever you want."

Fred took another breath and frowned. Reynolds wondered if the drug affected his brain. Fred leaned back and took another breath and squinted like he was trying to see something.

"Mr. Reynolds. We've been cleared on the final approach. We will be landing soon. Please buckle yourself and your companion in." The pilot's voice came through the embedded sound system. Sounded like he was right beside him.

Fred said something through the face mask. Reynolds didn't understand him.

"Don't worry. We'll be on the ground soon starting our new life and it's all thanks to you and your work with the device."

Fred took another deep breath and coughed, "Where are we going?"

"China. We're landing in Shanghai. The Chinese wanted the device, even before we tested it. But due to the situation back in the U.S., I've decided to take them up on the offer to head the new company here."

"Mr. Reynolds, we are descending through adverse weather and the landing might be a little rough," the pilot said through the speakers.

Reynolds pushed a button on the side of the bed. The kid rose up to a sitting position.

"I want to go home," Fred said.

The landing gear opened with a crunch. Reynolds looked outside and felt his ears pop. The jet dove into the dark clouds and almost instantly rain pelted the windows and winds shook the jet back and forth and the occupants with it.

"I understand it will seem a little foreign to you, but it's a great opportunity. You will see."

"I want to go home!" Fred yelled. He pounded on the armrests of the seat.

"Let's talk once we've landed."

"You don't understand. The device won't work."

Reynolds shook his head and turned to the kid. The drug must be affecting his thought processes.

"I saw it work in bold, beautiful Technicolor. Of course, it will work. We just need to get the manufacturing right."

The plane was hit by another buffet of air, shaking the plane from side to side like a tiny matchbox. He heard the rain continue to pound on the metal skin.

"It was the virus attack."

The plane jerked back and forth. Reynolds turned, and Fred's face was white as a sheet. "Don't worry, we will be landing real soon."

"The device didn't do anything but..."

A crack of lightning struck the jet and dimmed the lights. Reynolds felt his heart pounding. When was the pilot going to land the damn plane?

The pilot spoke again. "Nothing to worry about. I will have you down in a minute."

The wind noise increased. Reynolds heard the whine of the engine crank up.

"It only displayed the images and fed them into the fat man's brain," Fred said.

"What?"

"It didn't create them. The machine I mean. It's a fancy TV."

Reynolds looked down through the window. He couldn't see the ground yet.

Another crack of lightning struck the jet. But Reynolds still heard the whine of the jet engines. They'd be landing soon, and he was going to kiss the pilot right before he punched him out.

"What are you talking about? Of course it will work. I saw it with my own eyes."

The plane jostled up and down like a 300-mph roller coaster.

"Twenty years!" Fred yelled.

"What did you say?"

"Twenty years!"

"What do you mean?"

"You will have to wait twenty years before you can build a working one."

Reynolds turned back, looked at him, and frowned. He looked down through the window. The jet had descended finally through the clouds. He saw farmland, roads, and the lights from the airport. The buffeting had slowed. It looked like they were landing in one piece, but the jet seemed to be losing altitude very fast. Maybe they were flying on fumes.

"What the hell did we watch then?" Reynolds said.

"The result of millions of virus-infected computers doing the simulations. The inventor designed the world's largest grid computer."

Reynolds shook his head. What was this idiot talking about? Technology geeks were a dime a dozen in this country. He might just send this one back.

"He hooked up a million computers to do the work and send it to your stupid device. You got taken to the cleaners, man!" Fred burst out in laughter.

The third bolt of lightning hit the plane with a loud crack of thunder. Reynolds felt the plane jump and all the lights went out and stayed out. The boy's laughter stopped. The engines continued to whine. His stomach was doing loops. He wanted off this plane as soon as humanly possible, so he could kill the little asshole sitting beside him.

The door to the cockpit slammed opened. The pilot yelled out, "Brace yourself and prepare for a crash landing. We've lost all hydraulics!"

Reynolds felt the plane falling and dug his fingers into the armrest while he braced his feet against the seat in front of him. The plane tipped forward and he glanced out the window.

The ground was coming up fast. There was so much rain and wind, he couldn't tell how far from the ground they were. Then he saw it. Runway lights. The pilot had gotten them to the airport. The wheels were down. He should be able to land with no problem.

The jet hit the runway nose first with a massive crack that jarred him down to his bones. He heard a screeching sound then an explosion. The front tire. The plane jerked again and tossed him around in the seat. Reynolds grabbed for the seatback in front of him and held on. After a few more seconds, the plane dropped another three feet and slammed into the ground. The landing gear collapsed. He saw fireworks through a glance out the side window. Fireworks. Dragging metal on asphalt is the same as fireworks. Sparks and lots of them.

After a few more seconds, the jet skidded to one side and stopped. Reynolds fell back into the seat. His heart pounded in his ears as he looked around. Tiny emergency lights came on. Reynolds turned and looked. The boy was still strapped in holding onto the seat in front of him.

The pilot yelled back from the cockpit, "Everyone okay back there?"

Reynolds sat looking outside. In the distance, he saw the bright lights of the Shanghai international airport and the red emergency lights of the emergency crew. China. His new home.

But he didn't say anything. Fred's words had finally sunk in. The machine was an elaborate sham. A one-shot wonder.

"Mr. Reynolds? Are you okay? We must get out of here. There's a danger of explosion."

His face ran white as all the blood drained from his head. He realized finally what the little nerd was saying. He'd been scammed. The world's biggest scam even. An intense cold coursed through his chest and back. He was going into shock.

White foam covered the window, but he saw the firetruck's red lights glaring through the bubbles. The fire was out, and they were safe, or as safe as he could be until his new benefactors found out the truth.

The game had been lost.

* * *

Antivirus and operating vendors from around the world attended a groundbreaking but hastily set up web conference. Some had used VOIP phones, or HD Video. Others just dialed in with cell phones.

The world had been hit with a devious and devastating computer virus. No operating system was immune. Most computers, corporate, government, or enterprise earlier in the day had started to borrow cycles from their host computer and send massive amounts of data to other supernodes around the planet, which aggregated and resent the data to one single address in Silicon Valley.

The call was quick and to the point. Every operating system was vulnerable. Windows, macOS, Android, or Linux. It didn't matter. The anti-virus vendors came together and reported on what had happened. Zombie, rootkits, interrupt vectors were all discussed, but no one seemed to know why it happened or who caused it. However, all heard where the vulnerabilities were and what they had to do to prevent it.

The conference call lasted many hours, along with a real time logged chat to capture ideas on how to prevent future attacks. Halfway during the call, a government representative told the wide audience that the target computers had been found and removed for further investigation. Results would be delivered back to the group as soon as possible. Within a few weeks, every operating system vendor released patches to the operating system that closed the loopholes. The entire event was carried on the news wires for several weeks, but after the patches had been released, the news became stale and less newsworthy. Just like news of a new vaccine for a deadly disease. Once the vaccine was developed, the disease lost its notoriety. It was still news. But no one cared about it. They went on with their lives.

The results of the government forensic tests were never made public. No one ever knew what had really happened.

CHAPTER SIXTY-FOUR

Rehearsal studios reek no matter how vigilant the maintenance people are. Years of sweat, breath, body odor, pheromones, and hair gel takes its toll. But a spring rehearsal pumps lightness and energy into the dancers.

In the old Toronto studio at the bottom of King Street, the first couple of dancers pushed the old windows open as far as they could. The Lake Ontario breeze refreshed the studio like a fresh coat of white paint.

After the morning class and before lunch, the company rehearsed a new variation of a Midsummer's Night Dream. An appropriate piece for the summer ballet audiences. David stood in the middle, with a new partner. Since his return, his opportunities to advance grew faster than he expected. He took a deep breath and in one giant movement, raised his lithe partner over his head and lightly brought her back to earth.

In the weeks after the incident at Reynold's compound, Fitz met with Westlake on neutral ground and insisted he clear David of any wrong doings both in Europe and on U.S. soil. He also convinced Westlake to fly David back to Toronto from San Francisco first class courtesy of Uncle Sam. Westlake didn't put up a fight although he wanted David to submit to some tests. However, Fitz stood firm; David had been through enough.

Plus the memories, the emotions, and the inner voice of Jonathan Brooks ex-spy had evaporated like a morning fog across San Francisco Bay. In David's mind, and Fitz concurred, his value as a test pilot for a clandestine government memory implant program was limited. Westlake gave in but David thought he hadn't seen the last of him.

Alicia was another story. Grief stricken but stoic about her father's death, she flew back to Paris to pick up the pieces of her father's estate, but David suspected she wasn't going to take over the family business anytime soon.

Back in Canada even without the memories, some things were different. Once he was cleared to start dancing again, David discovered he danced with a confidence of an older dancer. He experienced and displayed a level of maturity on stage that he'd never felt before.

And others could too.

"That's great, just great. Nice movement, David. How's your body feeling?"

David turned to the new artistic director and smiled. "Great."

Robert Lester, the former artistic director left under veiled sexual harassment charges. But many thought his attack on David in Paris was the final straw. The new Artistic Director was a breath of fresh air.

"Okay, people, before we take a lunch break, let's do one final run-through. This afternoon, both casts need to be ready for their parts," the AD said.

David grabbed a towel and a bottle of water and drained it. Dancing was hard work and the lead was his most challenging role to date. But every rehearsal, every step he took was like a gift. Being shot at was hard; dancing in front of a crowd of several thousand people was easy.

A man entered from the side door and stood at the back against the wall. He wore a medium summer weight grey suit. Black loafers.

He watched in silence at the last run-through, as the dancers performed small bits of the dance, like small puzzle pieces. The piece concluded, and he listened as the artistic director thanked the company for the effort and gave them time for lunch.

The other dancers filed out past him, oblivious to his dress and manner. All except one.

"Hello, Fitz," David said. A warm feeling came over him, like meeting a long lost relative.

"Hello, David."

"You are too early. Auditions won't start for another two weeks."

Fitz smiled a little. The small scar across his left eye had healed nicely and would barely show in another few weeks.

"I didn't come for a job," Fitz said.

"No? Why are you here then?"

"I have a proposition for you. Are you willing to hear it?"

END

Acknowledgments

A book is a huge undertaking and almost no one really understands how much effort it takes to bring the damn thing to market!

Thanks to Bob and Jack who started me on the Hero's journey, timed writing, and forced me to use concrete nouns and verbs. And to Jack who taught me about myth bases, subtext, and metaphor.

To all the writing teachers and writing groups I've been in over the years. Many thanks to Eileen Cook for telling me I was "close" in getting this published.

To my beautiful wife Jo-Ann who made sure the dance terms and situations were accurate and reflected what goes on in a dance company.

And finally to Zara and all my friends at Pandamoon Publishing that helped me bring this story to the world.

About the Author

Tony Ollivier has stacked hay bales, picked tobacco, pinstriped cars, and bartended his way through Canada before settling in Vancouver. Moving into technology early on, he's worked for Xerox, Apple, IBM, and Microsoft. He now writes thriller novels while doing most of the cooking for his full-time family. He lives in Vancouver, British Columbia with his wife, son, and daughter.

Thank you for purchasing this copy of *The Amsterdam Deception*, Book 1 in <u>The David Knight Series</u>. If you enjoyed this book, please let the author know by posting a review.

pandamoon
publishing

Growing good ideas into great reads…one book at a time.

Visit http://www.pandamoonpublishing.com to learn about other works by our talented authors.

Mystery/Thriller/Suspense

- *A Rocky Series of Mysteries Book 1: A Rocky Divorce* by Matt Coleman
- *A Flash of Red* by Sarah K. Stephens
- *Ballpark Mysteries Book 1: Murder at First Pitch* by Nicole Asselin
- *Code Gray* by Benny Sims
- *Evening in the Yellow Wood* by Laura Kemp
- *Fate's Past* by Jason Huebinger
- *Graffiti Creek* by Matt Coleman
- *Juggling Kittens* by Matt Coleman
- *Killer Secrets* by Sherrie Orvik
- *Knights of the Shield* by Jeff Messick
- *Kricket* by Penni Jones
- *Looking into the Sun* by Todd Tavolazzi
- *On the Bricks Series Book 1: On the Bricks* by Penni Jones
- *Project 137* by Seth Augenstein
- *Rogue Alliance* by Michelle Bellon
- *Southbound* by Jason Beem
- *The Amsterdam Deception* by Tony Ollivier
- *The Juliet* by Laura Ellen Scott
- *The Last Detective* by Brian Cohn
- *The Moses Winter Mysteries Book 1: Made Safe* by Francis Sparks
- *The New Royal Mysteries Book 1: The Mean Bone in Her Body* by Laura Ellen Scott
- *The New Royal Mysteries Book 2: Crybaby Lane* by Laura Ellen Scott
- *The Ramadan Drummer* by Randolph Splitter
- *The Teratologist Series Book 1: The Teratologist* by Ward Parker
- *The Unraveling of Brendan Meeks* by Brian Cohn
- *The Zeke Adams Series Book 1: Pariah* by Ward Parker
- *This Darkness Got to Give* by Dave Housley

Science Fiction/Fantasy

- *Children of Colonodona Book 1: The Wizard's Apprentice* by Alisse Lee Goldenberg
- *Children of Colonodona Book 2: The Island of Mystics* by Alisse Lee Goldenberg
- *Dybbuk Scrolls Trilogy Book 1: The Song of Hadariah* by Alisse Lee Goldenberg
- *Dybbuk Scrolls Trilogy Book 2: The Song of Vengeance* by Alisse Lee Goldenberg
- *Dybbuk Scrolls Trilogy Book 3: The Song of War* by Alisse Lee Goldenberg
- *Everly Series Book 1: Everly* by Meg Bonney
- *Hello World* by Alexandra Tauber and Tiffany Rose
- *Finder Series Book 1: Chimera Catalyst* by Susan Kuchinskas
- *Fried Windows (In a Light White Sauce)* by Elgon Williams
- *Magehunter Saga Book 1: Magehunter* by Jeff Messick
- *Revengers* by David Valdes Greenwood
- *The Bath Salts Journals: Volume One* by Alisse Lee Goldenberg and An Tran
- *The Crimson Chronicles Book 1: Crimson Forest* by Christine Gabriel
- *The Crimson Chronicles Book 2: Crimson Moon* by Christine Gabriel
- *The Phaethon Series Book 1: Phaethon* by Rachel Sharp
- *The Phaethon Series Book 2: Pharos* by Rachel Sharp
- *The Sitnalta Series Book 1: Sitnalta* by Alisse Lee Goldenberg
- *The Sitnalta Series Book 2: The Kingdom Thief* by Alisse Lee Goldenberg
- *The Sitnalta Series Book 3: The City of Arches* by Alisse Lee Goldenberg
- *The Sitnalta Series Book 4: The Hedgewitch's Charm* by Alisse Lee Goldenberg
- *The Sitnalta Series Book 5: The False Princess* by Alisse Lee Goldenberg
- *The Thuperman Trilogy Book 1: Becoming Thuperman* by Elgon Williams
- *The Thuperman Trilogy Book 2: Homer Underby* by Elgon Williams
- *The Wolfcat Chronicles Book 1: Dammerwald* by Elgon Williams

Women's Fiction

- *Beautiful Secret* by Dana Faletti
- *Find Me in Florence* by Jule Selbo
- *The Long Way Home* by Regina West
- *The Mason Siblings Series Book 1: Love's Misadventure* by Cheri Champagne
- *The Mason Siblings Series Book 2: The Trouble with Love* by Cheri Champagne
- *The Mason Siblings Series Book 3: Love and Deceit* by Cheri Champagne
- *The Mason Siblings Series Book 4: Final Battle for Love* by Cheri Champagne
- *The Seductive Spies Series Book 1: The Thespian Spy* by Cheri Champagne
- *The Seductive Spy Series Book 2: The Seamstress and the Spy* by Cheri Champagne
- *The Shape of the Atmosphere* by Jessica Dainty
- *The To-Hell-And-Back Club Book 1: The To-Hell-And-Back Club* by Jill Hannah Anderson
- *The To-Hell-And-Back Club Book 2: Crazy Little Town Called Love* by Jill Hannah Anderson